Trial By Fire

(Schooled in Magic VII)

Christopher G. Nuttall

Twilight Times Books
Kingsport Tennessee

Trial By Fire

Paladin Timeless Books, an imprint of
Twilight Times Books
P O Box 3340
Kingsport TN 37664
http://twilighttimesbooks.com/

First Edition, December 2015

ISBN: 978-1-60619-310-5

Library of Congress Control Number: 2015949539

Cover art by Brad Fraunfelter

Printed in the United States of America

Prologue

CALEB STOPPED OUTSIDE THE STONE DOOR TO HIS FATHER'S STUDY AND PAUSED, FEELING HIS heart pound inside his chest. He had few good memories of his father's study; he and the other children had never been allowed to enter, save for long lectures and punishments when they'd disappointed their parents. Caleb had never dared to try to break the complex network of spells on the lock, knowing it would displease his mother and father.

And both of his parents were formidable indeed.

"Caleb," his mother called. "Come in."

Caleb bit his lip and pushed at the door. The house was small - living space was at a premium in Beneficence - and his mother had had over twenty-five years to weave protective spells and wards into the stone building. She'd always known what her children were doing while they lived in her house. Her children had rapidly learned to keep their misdeeds well away from home if they didn't want to get caught at once. He shivered when he felt another protective ward shimmering over him as he stepped through the door, then bowed formally to his father. His father looked at him for a long moment, and nodded. Beside him, Caleb's mother kept her face impassive.

They made an odd couple, Caleb had often thought, once he'd grown old enough to meet other soldiers and magicians. General Pollock - his father - was short, stubby and muscular, tough enough to march with the younger men instead of riding a horse to battle, while Mediator Sienna was tall, willowy and one of the most experienced combat sorcerers in the Allied Lands. She might not have been classically beautiful, her stern face edged by long black hair, but she was striking, with a trim athletic build even after giving birth to five children. And there were few people who would dare insult her to her face.

"Caleb," his father grunted. He'd never really seen Caleb as anything other than a disappointment, once it became clear that his second son was more interested in theoretical work than fighting. "You wished to speak with us?"

"Yes, father," Caleb said. His parents weren't stuck-up enough to insist that their children make appointments to speak with them, but certain things had to be done formally. The little rituals of politeness, as always, kept civilization going. "I do."

His father waved a hand, impatiently. "Then speak," he ordered.

Caleb took a long breath. Casper - handsome Casper, confident Casper - would have found it easy to speak to their parents, he was sure. But his elder brother had basked in the approval of their father, while even their stern mother could rarely remain angry at him for long. What Casper wanted, Casper got. Their parents hadn't really spoiled Casper, Caleb had to admit, but he'd had advantages none of the younger children shared. He'd set out to walk in their footsteps, after all.

"I ask your permission to open a Courtship," he said, allowing his voice to slip into cool formality. "I ask for your blessings and your wisdom."

His parents exchanged glances. A simple relationship was one thing, but a Courtship was quite another. It implied that Caleb was willing to spend the rest of his life with the girl, if she proved receptive to his advances. And his parents...they might have to welcome the girl into their family, if the Courtship worked out. Caleb was the first of the family to discuss a Courtship. Even Casper had yet to bring a girl home to meet their parents.

His mother spoke first. "Who is this girl?"

Caleb held himself steady, refusing to be swayed by the bite in her tone. "Emily," he said, simply. "Daughter of Void."

"I see," General Pollack said. His voice revealed nothing. "You overreach yourself, do you not? She is a Baroness of Zangaria."

"I am a sorcerer," Caleb countered. He'd known his father would object on those grounds, if nothing else. General Pollack came from aristocratic stock, but *his* father had been a mere Knight. Grandfather Karuk had been powerful enough to buy his son a commission, yet he'd never been as wealthy and powerful as a baron. "We are social equals."

"And her father is a Lone Power," Mediator Sienna said, slowly. "Do you not fear his thoughts on the matter?"

Caleb hesitated, but pressed on. "That is why I have decided on a formal Courtship," he said. He'd always had the impression that Emily was largely flying free - he didn't think that an experienced sorcerer would have allowed the crisis in Cockatrice to get so badly out of hand - but marriage was quite another issue. "It would allow him a chance to object before matters became serious."

"She may reject you," General Pollack warned. "You are not a wealthy man."

"I know," Caleb said. The family wealth, what little there was of it, would go to Casper, once his parents passed away. General Pollack was a poor man, by the standards of their social equals. But not using his position to enrich himself had made him popular with the troops under his command. "I do, however, have excellent prospects."

His father's face darkened. "But not as a defender of the Allied Lands."

Caleb bit down the response that came to mind. His father had expected his children - his male children, at least - to go into the military, to fight for the Allied Lands. Casper, whatever his flaws, *was* a halfway decent combat sorcerer. But Caleb? He'd always been more interested in fundamental magic research than fighting. The transfer to Whitehall had been the best thing that had ever happened to him.

"His research may prove useful," Mediator Sienna said.

General Pollack gave her a surprised look.

Caleb couldn't help staring at her in astonishment. His mother might be formidable, but it was rare for her to disagree with her husband in public. Caleb knew they'd had some spectacular rows, yet they'd always been held in private. They'd always put forward a united front.

His mother ignored their surprise. "Do you believe she likes you?"

Caleb swallowed. That was the question, wasn't it? He had never been able to read a girl, to tell if she was interested in him or if she was just being polite. The lads in the barracks had bragged endlessly about how many girls they'd slept with - Caleb was privately sure most of them were lying - but *he* had never had a serious relationship with anyone. Stronghold had enrolled only a handful of female students, while he'd been too busy at Whitehall to consider the possibilities. He'd never had the nerve to go into a brothel when he'd been on leave.

"I think so," he said, finally. He went on before his mother could start demanding details. "That's why I decided on a formal Courtship. If she thinks otherwise..."

"You can back off without shame," his mother finished. It would be embarrassing to be rejected, Caleb was sure, but better that than getting into a muddle. Courtship, if nothing else, was a ritual intended to ensure that everything was open, without even the merest hint of impropriety. "I would advise you to be careful, though. It is rare for a Lone Power to have a child."

"And one so grossly irresponsible, at that," General Pollack growled. "Inviting both the Ashworths and Ashfalls to the Faire. What *was* she thinking?"

"She shut them both down," Caleb reminded him.

His mother met his eyes. "Yes, she did," she agreed. "But it was still irresponsible."

"I like her," Caleb said, refusing to look away. "I request your blessing for the Courtship."

General Pollack exchanged a long look with his wife. "We shall discuss it in private," he said, finally. "Wait."

Caleb scowled inwardly as his mother cast a privacy ward, ensuring he couldn't hear a word of what passed between them. It galled him to have to go to his parents, but he knew they would have been furious if he'd approached someone with serious intentions without consulting them first. There were times when he wouldn't have minded being disowned, yet - in truth - he loved his family. Even Casper...

Father has no magic, he reminded himself. *And yet he rules the family with a rod of iron.*

He looked down at the stone floor, then up as the privacy ward dispelled. His father looked irked, while his mother was smiling coldly to herself. Caleb schooled his face into a dispassionate expression, waiting patiently for their answer. There were strong advantages to the match, he was sure, but there were also dangers. His mother was powerful, yet she was no match for a Lone Power.

"We have considered the matter," General Pollack said. "You may proceed with your Courtship."

Caleb let out a sigh of relief. "Thank you, father—"

"Now we will discuss the practicalities," his mother added, cutting him off. "And precisely how you intend to proceed. You will have to present her with flowers within the month. Choosing the right ones will be important."

"Yes, mother," Caleb said.

He cursed under his breath. It wasn't something he wanted to talk about, not to his blunt, plainspoken mother, but it was clear he wasn't being offered a choice. His father's brief lecture on matters sexual had been bad enough, back when he'd started to realize there was something different about girls, yet this was likely to be worse. He cringed mentally, then steadied himself. At least they hadn't said no.

And now all you have to do is go through with the Courtship, he told himself. *And that won't be easy.*

Chapter One

SHADYE LOOMS ABOVE HER, HIS SKULL-LIKE FACE CRUMBLING AS THE POWER WITHIN HIM threatens to spill out. Emily stumbles backwards, clutching desperately for something - anything - she can use as a weapon, but there is nothing. The necromancer grabs her shirt, hauls her to her feet and draws a stone knife from his belt. Emily feels her entire body go limp as he holds the knife in front of her eyes, then stabs it into her chest...

Emily snapped awake, feeling sweat pouring down her back and onto the blanket. For a long moment, she was unsure where and when she was; the nightmare had been so strong that part of her half-wondered if Shadye had killed her and everything she'd experienced had been nothing more than the final flickers of life before she died. And then she forced herself to remember, somehow, that she was in a tent, in the Blighted Lands. She'd had nightmares every night since they'd crossed the Craggy Mountains and started their long walk towards the Dark Fortress.

Just a dream, she told herself, as she wiped her forehead. The prospect of returning to Shadye's fortress, where she'd barely escaped with her life, was terrifying. If there hadn't been a very real possibility she'd inherited Shadye's possessions, she wouldn't have chosen to come within a thousand miles of the place. *It was just a nightmare. It wasn't real.*

She started as something slithered towards her, but smiled as Aurelius butted his head into her thigh. The Death Viper looked up at her beseechingly, his golden eyes somehow managing to convey a sense of hunger even though she'd fed him only the previous night and he should still be digesting his meal. Emily had been told, when she'd brought the snake back to Whitehall, that Death Vipers could live for weeks without eating, while their last meal was digesting in their bellies, but Aurelius seemed to disagree. Perhaps the familiar bond that tied them together demanded more energy...

Or perhaps he's picking up on my hunger, she thought, as she sat upright and picked up the snake. *I could do with something to eat too.*

Aurelius slithered forward. She giggled helplessly as the snake crawled up her arm and settled around her neck. She reached into her pack, pulled out a piece of dried meat and offered it to Aurelius, then pulled her trousers on, followed by her shirt. Sleeping without her clothes hadn't been easy, but it had just been too hot inside the tent. She knew several spells to chill the air, but the Grandmaster had forbidden her to use magic unless it was urgent. Thankfully, he'd insisted on keeping watch half the night rather than sharing a tent with her.

She crawled forward and opened the flap, then poked her head out of the tent. The Grandmaster was sitting in front of a fire, his back to her, cooking something that smelled faintly like bacon, although she had no idea if it was. It smelled good, but the stench of the Blighted Lands - a faint hint of burning that seemed to grow stronger with every breath she took - threatened to overpower it.

"Good morning, Emily," the Grandmaster said. "I trust you slept well."

"Well enough," Emily lied. There was no point in complaining about the night-mares. "And yourself?"

"You know I don't sleep," the Grandmaster said.

I assumed it was a metaphor, Emily thought, ruefully. But it was true; the Grandmaster hadn't slept since the day they'd walked through the mountains and into the Blighted Lands. *It can't be good for his mental health.*

She pushed the thought aside as she stood and looked around. The Blighted Lands were strange, perhaps the strangest place she'd ever seen. Lands that had once been green and verdant were now covered in a thin layer of ash. There wasn't a single living thing in sight, apart from the pair of them. A faint haze shimmered in the air, making it hard to see beyond a few dozen meters. The sky was a dull grey, the sun barely bright enough to burn through the clouds hanging in the sky; the air was unnaturally still, tinted with the faint scent of burning, and wisps of raw magic that danced across her awareness for long seconds before fading away. She could barely force herself to remain calm, even though she knew there was no real threat. The landscape spoke to her on a very primal level.

It looked very much like hell.

"I'm pleased to see your monster is taking things calmly," the Grandmaster said, as she paced around the campsite before looking at him. He was a short, wizened man, with a dirty cloth wrapped around his eyes, but he was surrounded by an aura of power she knew to take seriously. "I was worried, but I would have preferred not to deprive you of your familiar."

Emily nodded. If anyone else had tried to wear a Death Viper as a necklace, she knew all too well, they would have died before they could wrap it around their necks. It was hard to remember, sometimes, that Aurelius was one of the deadliest creatures known to exist, with a venom so poisonous that even a mere touch could prove fatal. Only the familiar bond protected her from the snake, allowing her to keep Aurelius as a secret weapon. He'd already saved her life twice.

"He seems to be happier here than I am," Emily admitted. She squatted down and took the mug he offered her with a nod of thanks. The Kava tasted strong, but she knew from experience that it would jolt her awake. "Is that normal?"

"The Blighted Lands may be where the Death Vipers were spawned," the Grandmaster said, as he ladled food onto two plates. "He may feel like he's home."

Emily looked up, staring at the mountains in the distance. "I hope not," she muttered. "I wouldn't want to live here."

The Grandmaster laughed, and passed her a plate of food. "Eat quickly," he urged, as Emily took it. "I want to get to the Dark Fortress before it gets dark."

Emily swallowed. Years ago - so long ago it seemed almost like another life - Shadye had accidentally brought her to the Nameless World, seeking a Child of Destiny. It had never occurred to him that someone would be *named* Destiny, or that her child would be a *literal* Child of Destiny. Shadye had meant to kill her, to sacrifice her to something called the Harrowing, yet in some ways she was almost grateful to the mad necromancer. If she'd stayed on Earth, trapped between her stepfather and her suicidal urges, she was sure she would be dead by now.

"Yes, sir," she said, as she ate her meal. It tasted better than anything she'd cooked back on Earth, although the ever-present scent of burning had worked its way into the food. "How long will it take us to get there?"

"About an hour," the Grandmaster said. "Unless we run into trouble, that is."

They finished their breakfast. Emily wiped the plates and cooking equipment while the Grandmaster answered a call of nature, and started to pack away the tent. He hadn't wanted a tent for himself, something that made her feel vaguely guilty, but he'd dismissed the matter when she'd offered to sleep in the open too. She couldn't help feeling relieved; quite apart from her concerns about sleeping near a man, she wouldn't have cared to sleep in the open, not in the Blighted Lands. The raw magic seemed to grow stronger at night.

That must be why so few people risk entering the Blighted Lands, she thought, as she packed up the rucksack. *You could go to sleep in the wrong place and wake up in a very different form.*

She shuddered at the thought, then pulled the rucksack on and braced herself against the weight. The Grandmaster nodded to her, checked the campsite for anything they might have left behind, then led the way into the distance. Emily gritted her teeth and forced herself to follow him. The flickers of wild magic in the air were growing stronger the further they moved from the Craggy Mountains that blocked the way to Whitehall. If she'd been alone, she had a feeling she would have turned back a long time before reaching the Dark Fortress.

"There's no need to push yourself too hard," the Grandmaster said, slowing. "If worst comes to worst, we'll set up our tents near the Dark Fortress and wait until sunrise."

Emily glanced up. It was early morning, by her watch, but the sun was already high in the sky. And yet, the light seemed dim, the clouds growing darker as they walked deeper into the Blighted Lands. She'd thought it was night when Shadye had snatched her, but had his lands been buried in permanent darkness? Or was she merely imagining things?

"I thought you said it wasn't safe to lurk too close to the fortress," she said instead.

"It isn't," the Grandmaster confirmed. "But I would prefer not to have to enter the Dark Fortress in darkness."

He said nothing else until they stumbled across the ruins of a village, so hidden within the haze that they practically walked into the ruins before realizing they were there. It was hard to imagine that it had once been a living village, with farmers tending their crops and raising their children; now, it was nothing more than grey stone, all life and light leached away by the Blighted Lands. The eerie *sameness* sent chills down her spine.

"Be careful," the Grandmaster warned as she peered into one of the buildings. "You never know what might be lurking here."

Emily nodded, pausing as she caught sight of a child's doll lying on the ground. It looked...*normal*, surprisingly intact despite the Blighted Lands. But when she reached for the doll and picked it up, it crumbled to dust in her hands. She swallowed hard, trying not to cry for the girl who'd owned the doll, untold centuries ago. Had she died quickly, at the hands of a necromancer, or fled with her family to the untouched lands to the north? There was no way Emily would ever know.

"There has to be something we can do for the Blighted Lands," she said, as she wiped the dust off her fingers. "Can't we...cleanse the lands, or something?"

"The necromancers unleashed wild magic," the Grandmaster said. "Every year, some people try to set up settlements within the edge of the Blighted Lands, in hopes of reclaiming the territory for themselves. And they always come to grief. If the necromancers don't get them, the wild magic does."

He took a long look around the village - Emily was *sure* he had some way to see, despite having lost his eyes years ago - and then led the way out of it, back to the south. She followed him, feeling an odd urge to stay within the village even though she knew it was suicide. It worried her for a long moment - it could be a sign of subtle magic - and then she realized the village had felt safe, despite being within the Blighted Lands. The urge to turn back and flee grew stronger with every step they took.

"The White Council was quite impressed with you," the Grandmaster said. He spoke in a conversational tone of voice, as if he were trying to keep her mind off the growing urge to just turn and run. "They were not too pleased with the management of the Cockatrice Faire, but...they were relieved at the outcome."

Emily nodded. Everyone from Lady Barb to the Grandmaster himself had pointed out that she'd been careless, at the very least, and that her carelessness could easily have resulted in disaster. If the Ashworths and the Ashfalls had gone to war, it would not only have led to the deaths of the leaders of both families, but also to the slaughter of hundreds of other magicians and the devastation of her lands. She knew she'd been lucky, very lucky. If she hadn't managed to get a battery to work...

She touched the ring, hidden within her pocket, and smiled. Lady Barb had urged her to create and charge a second battery while preparing for the trip to the Blighted Lands, and Emily had done as her mentor suggested. Now she had a battery she could use, although without a valve it was useless. And they had a tendency to work once and then burn out. Putting a spare valve together with the help of an enchanter in Dragon's Den had been harder than charging up the battery.

"You showed a staggering amount of power," the Grandmaster added. "They were *very* impressed."

Thank you, Emily thought, sardonically. *Is that actually a good thing?*

She eyed the Grandmaster's back, wondering if he knew just what she'd actually done. He hadn't treated her any differently when Lady Barb had returned her to Whitehall after the Faire, but he wouldn't have. Others...had stared at her in awe. In some ways, she was even dreading the day when the rest of the students returned to

Whitehall. If they'd stared at her after beating Shadye - and they had - they would be paying far more attention to her now.

"Some of them even considered...*insisting*...that you take the oaths now," the Grandmaster told her. "Others thought you should be apprenticed at once to someone who could control your power, if necessary."

But I cheated, Emily thought.

It wasn't a reassuring thought. If she'd tried to channel so much power through her mind, it would have killed her or driven her insane. It had been bad enough, years ago, to have people watching her, suspicious of necromancy. Now...they probably thought she was a staggeringly powerful magician instead, a young girl fully on the same level as Void or another Lone Power. The idea that she could match the Grandmaster for raw power was absurd...

...But, to anyone who didn't know about the batteries, it might not *seem* absurd.

She swallowed. "What are they going to do?"

"Nothing," the Grandmaster said, simply.

Emily blinked. "Nothing?"

"I am Grandmaster of Whitehall School," the Grandmaster said. "I have never had a student forced to take the oaths ahead of time, and I'm not about to start now. If you *want* an apprenticeship with someone...well, that could be arranged, but you have no obligation to find a master. Or mistress. Still..."

He shrugged. "Have you thought about your career?"

"I don't know," Emily admitted. "I'd like to stay at Whitehall for the rest of my life."

"You'd need much more experience before you could *teach*," the Grandmaster said. "I like my tutors to have at least ten years of practical experience before they start touching young and impressionable minds. But you could get a slot as a teaching assistant, I suppose, or a research student. We do have a few of them at Whitehall."

He paused, then turned to look at her. "You do need to decide on a major before you enter Fifth Year," he added. "Going by your marks, I'd recommend majoring in charms and perhaps healing, but it depends on what you actually *want* to do with your life. If you want to be a healer, you'll need alchemy; if you want to be a combat sorceress, you'll need martial magic and history..."

Emily sighed, feeling a little overwhelmed. "Randor expects me to go back to Cockatrice and be the baroness," she said. "I..."

"*King* Randor," the Grandmaster corrected, quietly.

"But I don't know what I want to do," Emily continued. "There are so *many* interesting subjects."

"You could probably study them all, if you spread out your years," the Grandmaster mused. "It isn't unknown for students to repeat their last two years at Whitehall. However, most students tend to discover the subject they want to major in while they're in their Fourth Year and stick with it. Your marks in Healing are not bad."

Emily winced. Healing was an interesting class, but she didn't want to spend the rest of her life working with ill people. She'd seen enough of that life during the walk through the Cairngorms to know she didn't want to do it permanently. There had been too many horrors there, hidden in small shacks or behind high stone walls. She had no idea how Lady Barb did it without cursing everyone in sight.

"I think I just want to study," she said. It was a shame there were no universities in the Nameless World. She could have stepped into one quite happily and never come out. "And go into magical research, perhaps."

"That would suit you," the Grandmaster agreed.

He shrugged, then turned back to resume walking. "You need to remember that you're not just *any* magician," he added, as he walked. "Too many people are already showing an interest in you, not least our friends to the south."

The necromancers, Emily thought.

She'd killed Shadye - and the Allied Lands had declared her the Necromancer's Bane. The other necromancers seemed to believe she could kill them at will, if only because none of them had tried to claim Shadye's lands or attack Whitehall. But that wouldn't last, she was sure. Sooner or later, the necromancers would resume their offensive against the Allied Lands. Their endless need for new victims to sacrifice would ensure it.

And what will happen, she asked herself, *when they do?*

She kept her thoughts to herself as she followed the Grandmaster, feeling the air grow steadily colder as they made their way to the south. Slowly, the twisted shape of the Dark Fortress - and, beside it, the Inverse Shadow - came into view. They didn't look anything like the half-remembered shapes in her nightmares, but there hadn't really been time to take much note of the scenery the last time she'd visited. She'd been half out of her mind with fear when Shadye's animated skeletons had dragged her into the Inverse Shadow, preparing her for death. If Void hadn't been there, she would have died that day.

The Grandmaster stopped, sharply. "Listen," he said. "Can you hear that?"

Emily paused, listening hard. There was a faint sound in the distance, a howling that seemed to come from many throats. It was growing louder, although she didn't *think* the source of the sound was actually coming *closer*. Whatever it was - and there was something about it that touched a memory - it chilled her to the bone.

"I think we'd better go see what that is," the Grandmaster said, after a quick glance at his watch. "Follow me."

Chapter Two

THE HOWLING GREW LOUDER AS THEY WALKED, BUT IT WAS STILL A SURPRISE WHEN THE haze parted long enough to reveal a colossal pit in the ashy ground. Emily started, then stumbled back as the soil started to give way under her feet, threatening to send her falling down the side and into the pit. She steadied herself, then peered down as she saw figures swarming at the bottom, fighting each other with a savage intensity that shocked her to the bone. It had been nearly three years since she'd last seen an orc, outside lessons, but they were unmistakable, even though the distance made them look tiny.

"A breeding frenzy," the Grandmaster said, quietly. "That isn't a good sign."

Emily stroked Aurelius as she took in the sight. The orcs were huge, each one easily two meters tall; shambling parodies of humanity. They carried swords that were taller than the Grandmaster, lashing out at one another with more determination than skill, their blades cutting into stone-hard skin. She knew from grim experience that they were far stronger than the average human, although they weren't very bright and could be outrun if someone was prepared to show them their backs and flee. They needed a strong leader to pose anything more than a minor threat to travelers. Shadye had recruited an army through force and led them against Whitehall. She felt the snake's discontent at the presence of the warped monsters and shuddered, before smiling to herself. The orcs would be equally discomfited to see a Death Viper.

"Only one in ten of them will survive - the strongest or the smartest," the Grandmaster commented. "They will go back down into the tunnels and impregnate the women, then wait for the next generation to be born. There will be hundreds of thousands of new orcs soon enough, just looking for a leader."

Emily looked at him. "Why now?"

"Good question," the Grandmaster said. "Shadye would have pushed them into building a new army, but Shadye is dead."

"They might have another leader," Emily said. She looked back at the orcs and grimaced. It wouldn't be easy to beat one in a fight, without magic. Even the greatest swordsman in the land would have problems. Bows and arrows wouldn't make much of an impression on their solid hides...but would bullets? "Someone else intent on forming an army."

"It's a possibility," the Grandmaster acknowledged.

He took one last look into the pit, then turned and led her back towards the Dark Fortress. Emily followed, gritting her teeth as the howling grew louder and louder until it echoed within her very bones. The orcs might have seen them and given chase...she found herself glancing backwards as the haze closed in again, making it impossible to see if anything was climbing out of the pit. She shaped spells in her mind - the only way to win was to knock the orc down and out as quickly as possible - and waited. Nothing seemed to be following them.

Aurelius would sense it if someone came after us, she told herself, firmly. It had been a disappointment to learn that animals couldn't really talk to their human masters, but she was learning how to interpret the sensations Aurelius pushed towards her. *There's nothing up here but us chickens.*

She pushed the thought aside as the Inverse Shadow came into view. It was a towering building, but it was impossible to actually get a sense of what it looked like. Her eyes kept slipping over the exterior; one moment, it looked like a towering cathedral, the next it looked like something bent and twisted out of shape. She peered into the open doors, seemingly waiting to see who would walk inside, then shuddered as she sensed the magic - and something else - coiling around the outer walls. If Shadye hadn't been mad before he'd walked into the Inverse Shadow, long exposure to the twisted building would have driven him mad.

Her throat was suddenly dry, but she forced herself to speak. "What *is* the Inverse Shadow?"

"No one knows," the Grandmaster said. For once, he looked perturbed. "One school of thought suggests it used to be a nexus point, one that was drained by the necromancers, while others think it's something far older."

Emily frowned. "Maybe someone tried to build another school like Whitehall on a nexus point and something went wrong."

"It's a possibility," the Grandmaster agreed. "If there was a nexus point here, it must be dead. Shadye wouldn't have needed to go to Whitehall if he'd had one right next to his fortress. But there is clearly magic, ancient magic, in this place. Perhaps Shadye was too scared to try to tap it for his own use."

"Maybe," Emily said. It didn't seem likely. Shadye hadn't shown any fear, as far as she could recall; in truth, he'd never had any *reason* to feel fear. What could harm a necromancer with his power? "Why was so much forgotten?"

"They might not have wanted to remember," the Grandmaster said. "Aren't there things in your life you would give a great deal to forget? Or to rewrite?"

Emily nodded, slowly. She'd always had the impression that there was something wrong with the Nameless World's history, at least the version presented to the students, although she'd never been able to put her finger on it. She knew from Earth that history was often a matter of conjecture, of putting together the pieces of a jigsaw puzzle when several of them were missing and then guessing at the final image. And, on the Nameless World, history could be rewritten to suit the people in power. She had a feeling that King Randor's ultimate version of the coup in Zangaria would minimize her role while giving most of the credit to Alassa.

"I suppose," she said, doubtfully. Truth was more important than lies, particularly lies that suited the people in power, but what *was* truth anyway? "I..."

She stopped as she saw a ghostly image in front of her. A young girl - it took her a moment to realize she was looking at her own face, so thin and emaciated it had become - was standing in front of her, staring at her with hopeless eyes. Emily stared back, unable to tear her gaze away, unable even to blink as her doppelganger fell to her knees, bowing her head in fear. Time seemed to slow down...

...And then everything changed. The broken girl vanished, to be replaced by a taller version of Emily, wearing a long dark dress that exposed the tops of her breasts. There was a thin smile on her face Emily didn't like at all, a smug assertion of superiority over the entire world...and, when her doppelganger looked up, bright red eyes bored deep into Emily's. A necromancer...

She stumbled backwards in shock. The images vanished.

"Emily," a voice said, urgently. It took her a moment to realize it was the Grandmaster. "Are you all right?"

Emily hesitated. "Did you see that?"

The Grandmaster caught her arm and swung her around to face him. "See what?"

"I saw...I saw alternate versions of myself," Emily said. She'd seen something similar in the Dark City, she recalled now. "Didn't you see anything?"

"Nothing," the Grandmaster said. He looked uncertain for a long moment, then shrugged thoughtfully. "It could be a sex-specific charm, perhaps, or...or you may simply be more sensitive to certain types of magic than others."

He cleared his throat as he turned back towards the Dark Fortress. "If nothing else, this is an excellent lesson in the importance of understanding where your talents lie," he added, absently. "If you don't have a gift for certain kinds of magic, you'll never be as good with them as those who do."

Emily rolled her eyes at his retreating back - she'd heard the same thing over and over again, from just about every tutor at Whitehall - and then followed him, feeling a dull unease in her breast she wasn't able to suppress. The visions could have been images of her greatest fears, plucked from her mind, but there had been a *reality* about them that chilled her to the bone, as if they *were* real on some level. And yet, she knew they could easily have been enhanced with magic, just to make sure she had the right reaction to them. She pushed the thought aside and clutched the snake tighter, promising herself she wouldn't be either of the doppelgangers. Aurelius shifted around her neck, then relaxed.

The Dark Fortress loomed up in front of them, a brooding mass that dominated the landscape...and yet seemed petty, somehow, compared to the Inverse Shadow. Emily felt the rune on her chest grow warm, warning of the presence of subtle magic, as they walked closer, studying the exterior of the building for a way in. She couldn't help comparing it to a palace, rather than a fortress; it didn't look very secure. Indeed, some of the upper levels were clearly crumbling into ruins. But with a necromancer in residence, very few would dare to enter without permission.

And who in their right mind would want to visit? she asked herself, as the warmth in her chest grew stronger. *Shadye would use anyone who visited as a source of power.*

"There," the Grandmaster said, pointing at a blank stone wall. "Can you see the doorway?"

Emily peered at the wall, gritting her teeth as the rune grew warmer. Her chest hurt as she forced her eyes to look *past* the magic, past the aversion wards designed to keep her from seeing something right in front of her, but she kept going. The world seemed to shimmer, then snap back into place, revealing an open door right in front of them. There was a final burst of heat from the rune before it faded so quickly, it almost felt *cold*.

"I can see it," she said. She rubbed her chest, feeling somewhat frostbitten, then took a step forward. Nothing moved to block her. "Is it safe to enter?"

"Good question," the Grandmaster said. He drew a wand from his belt, and held it in front of him like a divining rod as he walked through the door. "There are a handful of odd wards here, none of them interlocked. I'm surprised they've lasted this long."

Emily nodded as she followed him through the door and into the darkened chamber beyond. Wards could be lodged within stone, but they rarely lasted more than a year without the sorcerer renewing and replenishing them. Shadye had been powerful, staggeringly so, yet he'd lacked the skill and experience of the Grandmaster or Void. His wards might have been crude, rather than subtle. They might well not have lasted long after his death.

She looked at the Grandmaster's back as a thought struck her. "Could someone else have put up the wards?"

"It's possible," the Grandmaster said. "Void might have returned to the Dark Fortress, after Shadye's death. Few others would have dared."

Emily felt a twinge of...*something*. She hadn't seen Void for over a year; she'd written to him, after the events in Cockatrice, but received no reply. Had he been busy searching Shadye's fortress now he knew she would be visiting, or had he been preoccupied with something else? Or...had he decided she was no longer worthy of his attention? He might have saved her life, but everyone she'd met had warned her, in no uncertain terms, that he couldn't really be trusted. It wasn't something she wanted to consider.

"Cast a light globe," the Grandmaster ordered. "Let's see what we find."

Emily obeyed, casting the spell into the air. The globe took shape and form, casting an eerie light into the chamber, but dimmed rapidly, as if something was draining the magic from the spell. Emily blinked in surprise as the globe started to die, then hastily pushed more magic into her spell. The light brightened, but started to dim again. And then it flickered before it went out completely.

"Unfortunate," the Grandmaster observed. He dug into his pockets and produced a Hand of Glory, which he lit with a spell. Emily shuddered; the severed human hand had had the fingertips removed and replaced with charmed candles, which glowed with an eerie - but stable - light. "Take this and hold it in front of you."

The Hand of Glory felt clammy against her bare skin, but whatever had drained the light globe didn't seem able to drain the Hand of Glory. Emily held it high and looked around, frowning in puzzlement as she had a good look at the chamber. It was bare and barren, as if it had been abandoned long ago; pieces of debris lay where they'd fallen from the roof, while dust lay everywhere. Shadye had never bothered to hire housekeepers, the irreverent part of her mind noted; indeed, he'd clearly not been concerned with his personal comfort. It couldn't have been a very pleasant place to live.

"This way," the Grandmaster said, leading her through the door at the end of the chamber. It led to a cold stone corridor, as dark and silent as the grave. "Keep a sharp eye out for traps."

Emily nodded, feeling ice spread through her body as the darkness rose and fell around them. The walls were bare stone, but the floors were covered in skeletons. *Shadye's servants*, she asked herself, *or the remains of his victims?* Some of them looked to have been kneeling, in the last moments before they died, while others had been broken and smashed, pieces of bone lying scattered on the stone ground. How had they decayed so quickly?

She hesitated, then asked the Grandmaster a question. "Why was Shadye expelled from Whitehall?"

"Crimes against his fellow students," the Grandmaster said, shortly. "We caught him torturing First Years and expelled him."

He didn't seem inclined to say anything else, so Emily kept her mouth firmly closed as they walked through another empty chamber, then a third. Shadye hadn't been a packrat, Emily noted, nothing like herself. For all of his power, his life had been consumed by the desperate quest for sustenance. He'd lurked in the Dark Fortress, raided the Allied Lands for people he could drain to keep himself alive and...nothing. If he hadn't been a mass murderer Emily might almost have felt sorry for him.

He made his choices, a voice in her head said. It sounded very much like Lady Barb. *And he had to live with the consequences.*

But if he hadn't, Emily answered, mentally, *I would never have come to the Nameless World.*

She felt a twinge of guilt at the thought, which she pushed aside as they walked into another corridor. This one was long and dark, but at the end there was an eerie green glow. A crystal hung from the ceiling, casting light over the scene. The Grandmaster started to walk towards it, but stopped. Moments later, Emily felt her head swimming and she walked straight into the wall.

"An interesting trick," the Grandmaster observed as she stumbled back. "Not a particularly subtle one, but effective. We can't walk up without having our senses scrambled, which will send us straight into the walls - or worse. And we can't dispel the charm without being a great deal closer."

Emily nodded, and tried to walk up the corridor again. This time, she found herself falling to the ground, so dizzy she could no longer remain upright, before crawling back to the Grandmaster on her hands and knees. She had the feeling she would have been fine, if she'd kept her eyes firmly closed, but she couldn't do that without leaving herself vulnerable. And yet...

"You could destroy the crystal," she said, slowly.

"It would provoke a reaction," the Grandmaster said. "Probably..."

He hesitated, then looked at her. "I could steer you through the charm, if I used your body as a puppet," he said. "I'd be steering you from the outside..."

"No," Emily said, flatly. Shadye had used her as a puppet three years ago, and the experience still gave her nightmares. To have someone moving her arms and legs without her control...she trusted the Grandmaster, but she wasn't about to let him be her puppeteer. "I..."

She stopped as a thought struck her. "I could dispel the charm if I was much closer, right?"

"Standing next to it," the Grandmaster confirmed.

Emily nodded, then - before she could have second thoughts - uncurled Aurelius from her neck and placed the snake on the floor. Aurelius sent a stream of discontented thoughts to her - Death Vipers didn't like dust, it seemed - and then looked at the crystal. The images he sent to Emily were odd, like seeing through warped lenses, but she could see the path to the crystal.

"You need to blind and deafen me," she said, without looking at the Grandmaster. "It's the only way to avoid being overwhelmed."

The Grandmaster gave her a sharp look - such hexes were banned at Whitehall, on pain of severe punishment - but jabbed a finger at her. Emily shuddered as the world went black and silent, then concentrated on the images from the snake. It was hard, so hard, to keep her mind focused with panic yammering at her, screaming that she should cancel his spell, but somehow she held herself together long enough to walk towards the crystal, guided by the snake. As soon as she was standing close to the charm, she cast the dispersal spell. Her eyes snapped back to normal, while the crystal lost its light.

"Well done," the Grandmaster said. "Very well done."

Emily beamed with pride. "I..."

The world went dark. For a moment, she thought the blindness spell had reasserted itself, then she realized she was somewhere else, somewhere both dark and familiar. She opened her mouth to call out to the Grandmaster...

...And then froze as her stepfather walked into the light.

Chapter Three

Y OU WORTHLESS GIRL," HE SNARLED. "CAN'T YOU DO ANYTHING RIGHT?"

Emily could only stare at him, feeling her entire body trembling. Her stepfather looked larger than she recalled, his meaty fists pounding the air in front of him as he advanced towards her; no, *she* was smaller. She looked down at herself and realized she was barely a child of ten, chewing helplessly on her long hair and wearing second-hand clothes she'd bought or begged for herself from the charity shops. But she'd been an adult of nineteen...

Her head swam. She'd been with the Grandmaster, hadn't she? Or had she imagined everything? Her stepfather strode up to her, thrusting his face right into hers and breathing horrendous fumes of alcohol into her mouth. She cringed as he caught her arm, then shoved her to the floor. It felt solid - too solid - under her body.

"Waste of fucking space," he snapped. He loomed over her, glaring down. "Why I adopted you I will never know. You should have been a boy. A boy might have been fun."

Emily swallowed hard to keep from throwing up. He was there. He was always there. There was no point in looking to her mother for protection, not when her mother spent most of her life crashed out on the couch, watching TV and drinking heavily. Her stepfather could do whatever he liked to her and no one would do anything to help. A feeling of pure hopelessness overcame her, forcing her to curl into a ball...

"Get up," her stepfather snarled. He reached out, grabbed the front of her shirt and hauled her to her feet. "Wasting all your time in fantasies when there's real work to do."

He slapped her across the face, hard. "Thinking you're Harry fucking Potter, a magical little princess just waiting for the chance to go to your *real* parents," he snapped. "Your father abandoned you, *princess*, and left you here with your worthless piece of trash drunkard of a mother. You're pathetic! You waste your life in fantasy when you have work to do."

Emily staggered, her mind screaming at her. It was real, wasn't it? She was older, much older, than the child she seemed now...and she had all the memories to prove it. But they felt translucent, as if they were nothing more than childish fantasies. She was suddenly unsure of anything beyond the fact that she was trapped in the room with a monster. Desperately, she looked around and saw her old living room, her mother lying on the couch and stoned out of her mind. Empty bottles of cheap wine lay everywhere...

...She'd gathered them up, when she'd been much younger, and taken them back to the shop for a handful of coins...

The memory was so strong it shocked her. No one had raised an eyebrow at a nine-year-old girl handing back empty booze bottles. No one had really given a damn, yet...

Her stepfather slapped her, again. "Get to cleaning up the mess, you worthless bitch," he ordered. The force of the blow sent her staggering back to the floor, tasting blood in her mouth. "I want this room clean by the time I get back from the bar..."

He knew about my dreams, Emily thought. *How did he know?*

She looked down at her hands. They weren't childish any longer. Her chest was growing - her stepfather leered, but she ignored him - and she felt older. How had he known? She wasn't in the habit of sharing anything with him, certainly not her innermost fantasies. He couldn't have thrown the suggestion that she had magic in her face unless he'd known she had dreams of magic...

"You're not real," she said, as she stood. She looked down at herself again and saw the shirt and trousers she'd worn in the Nameless World. No, the shirt and trousers that she was *still* wearing in the Nameless World. Her memory clicked and she put two and two together. "You're just a Nightmare Hex."

Her stepfather snarled at her, his eyes moving over her chest and leaving trails of slime over her breasts, then lunged forward. Emily snapped into a fighting crouch automatically, silently thanking Sergeant Harkin for his lessons, then caught his arm as he took a swing at her. He seemed smaller, somehow, as she pushed him aside before she knifed her hand into his eye, where he was vulnerable. She felt something squish under her finger; her stepfather jumped backwards, screaming in pain and rubbing his eyes desperately. Emily watched blood spilling from his eye, too much blood to be real, and she *knew*, beyond all doubt, that it was an illusion.

"You're definitely a Nightmare Hex," she said. She'd seen one before, in Blackhall, and it had almost killed her. "You're not real."

"Bitch," her stepfather swore at her. "I *am* real."

Emily smiled. "Then why are you shrinking?"

She forced herself forward as he glared at her. "You're a monster," she said, as coldly and precisely as she could. "You dominated my life ever since you married my mother. You overshadowed my life, you made me scared of everything, you destroyed my hope. You..."

Her stepfather, now the size of a small dog, stumbled backwards. "I'm not scared of you any longer," Emily said. She'd met Shadye, and Mother Holly, and Aurelius's namesake; her stepfather was nothing but a petty bully. Her later enemies had been threats to the entire world. "And I will *not* allow you to dominate my life any longer."

She lunged forward...and her stepfather vanished in a flash of light. Emily blinked - the light had been bright enough to hurt - and looked around. She was standing in the chamber, looking at the dead crystal; the Grandmaster was standing beside her, his face worried. A twitch from below told her that Aurelius was waiting for her. She bent down and picked up the snake, wrapping it around her wrist. It hadn't been real.

"I wouldn't have expected a Nightmare Hex to last so long without constant renewal," the Grandmaster said. "They're fantastically complex pieces of work."

Emily nodded, then blinked as she realized the Grandmaster had to have seen his greatest fear, too. How else would he have known what she'd encountered?

She looked at him. "What did you see?"

"Whitehall coming apart around me," the Grandmaster said, shortly. There was something in his voice, an edge, that warned her not to ask any more questions. "What did you see?"

Emily shuddered. "My stepfather."

The Grandmaster gave her a long look, then turned to lead the way into the next chamber. "I believe the remaining defenses have been dispelled," he said. "The magic running through the building has twisted. It may or may not have accepted you as its new mistress, but it shouldn't pose a danger any longer."

Emily followed him, casting a new light globe as she moved. This time, the globe behaved normally. She puzzled over it for a moment, and looked around. The room was barren, save for a throne perched in the exact center of the chamber. It was made of cold iron, she saw as she walked closer, and decorated with runes that looked scorched and broken. She touched the rune at her chest, in anticipation of pain, but felt nothing. Whatever magic had been stored within the throne had faded long ago.

"Shadye would have used it to help control his powers," the Grandmaster said, studying the throne. "I don't think it would have done much, though. He held too much power within his wards to be easily controlled."

"I thought runes only worked with subtle magic," Emily said. "Can a necromancer use runes?"

"They would have bolstered his ability to resist the madness, I expect," the Grandmaster said. He pointed to a handful of broken runes, then gave her a sharp look. "Those runes enhance feelings of stubbornness and determination. Shadye was literally manipulating his own mind."

Emily shook her head as the Grandmaster stepped into the next chamber. There were spells, countless spells, to help someone change their behavior, but she had been warned - in no uncertain terms - that they tended to have nasty side effects. Shadye might have kept his stolen power under control, yet they might have cost him his reasoning abilities or stolen his free will. And something self-inflicted - she touched the rune between her breasts again - was far harder to remove than something imposed by an outsider.

But it kept him going, she thought, grimly. *He never stopped. Every little mistake was worked into his plan.*

"Emily," the Grandmaster called. "Come and look at these."

Aurelius sniffed uncomfortably as Emily entered the next chamber. It was smaller than the throne room, but almost as bare. A large stone table, covered with books and a handful of items she didn't recognize, dominated the room. Several other books lay on the floor, next to the stone walls. She could practically imagine Shadye tearing his way through the manuscripts, then throwing them aside once he was done. He'd been growing increasingly desperate towards the end of his life...

She pushed the thought to one side and looked at the books. A couple were familiar - she knew them to be textbooks that hadn't changed in over a hundred years - but others were new to her. One of them discussed basic charms, at length; another talked about blood magic and how best to use it. And Shadye had used it against her...he'd been here, she realized suddenly, when he'd laid his plans against her. She glanced down at the book and cringed, inwardly, as she realized the control spell lay in front of her. A little blood, obtained through cunning or simple violence, and she could make someone - anyone - do whatever she wished.

"I would advise you not to touch that book," the Grandmaster said, "but in your case it's probably futile."

Emily blushed. She'd grown into the habit of collecting books, now that she actually had the money to buy them. And she'd even kept a book she *knew* to be dark, just because it was hers. If she had any claim to Shadye's properties at all, and no one was quite sure if she did or didn't, she would assert it over the books. They were *hers*.

"I'm sorry, sir," she said.

"No, you're not," the Grandmaster said. He gave her a humorless smile. "Just remember that actually *using* some of those spells will get you in very real trouble."

He looked down at the small collection of objects and shook his head. "The stone knife will have to be destroyed, of course," he said. He picked up a necklace with a single white crystal, then frowned. "The others...if you wish, they can be brought back to Whitehall for study. A couple of these things are new to me."

Emily peered at the necklace as the Grandmaster put it back down on the table. "What is *that?*"

"A heartstone," the Grandmaster said. He shook his head again. "Shadye must have stolen it from someone, years ago. I can't imagine him ever having one himself."

He smiled, seeing the puzzled expression on her face. "A heartstone always comes with a twin," he said. "If you and your partner are deeply in love, or have strong feelings for one another, you can create a pair of stones and use them to be aware of the other at all times. I believe that your friend used some of the linking spells to create her chat parchments. Unlike those...a heartstone requires *genuine* feeling between the couple, as well as a strong level of trust. Relationships have been destroyed because of them."

Emily frowned. "Why?"

The Grandmaster snorted. "You would know when your partner looked at another girl and felt a flicker of attraction, or vice versa," he said. "There would be no white lies, no selective presentations of the truth; there would be nowhere to hide, if your feelings changed. I don't think I've seen someone use one for years."

"No privacy," Emily mused. She couldn't imagine being willing to share so much of herself with someone else, even if she loved him. "One bad thought could destroy the relationship."

"There's a twisted version used by slavers," the Grandmaster added. He peered at Shadye's necklace for a long moment. "Maybe that was what Shadye had in mind."

Emily swallowed. Had *she* been the intended recipient?

The Grandmaster opened his pouch, carefully inserting the books and objects while Emily picked the books off the floor. One reminded her of the books Aurelius had shown her at Mountaintop, the Book of Pacts between demons and their human masters; another seemed to be a book of stories, although she knew better than to dismiss it out of hand. A third bore Whitehall's crest on the cover, but the pages inside were completely blank, save for a handful of scribbles in the margin. She carried it back to the Grandmaster and held it up for his inspection.

"That would have been his personal spellbook, if he'd stayed at Whitehall," the Grandmaster said. "They changed the design before you arrived. I'm surprised he kept that, Emily."

"Maybe he was sentimental," Emily muttered. It would have surprised her if that were true, but she'd seen stranger things on her travels. "Or wanted something to remind him of his plans."

"Or maybe he intended to use the crest to slip into the school," the Grandmaster said. "It might have been possible, if the wards had been weakened in some way. If the Warden had died in First Year, he might have been able to force his way inside."

Emily shuddered.

They paused for a quick bite to eat, then searched the remainder of the fortress. Emily couldn't help feeling disappointed, both by how little there was to find and how poorly the building had been maintained. It looked like a ruined castle from Europe, not a place for someone to live and work. But Shadye hadn't been in any real danger from falling chunks of stone and he'd never entertained guests. He'd lived in a charnel house and he'd never given a damn.

"I think he must have been doing *something* here," the Grandmaster said, as they stepped into yet another room. "There are traces of magic in the air..."

Emily hesitated, feeling with her mind, then nodded. There *was* something in the air, something oddly familiar. She paused, thinking hard. Could it be...? She saw a doorway, set within the wall, and opened it carefully. A small prison cell lay inside, dark and empty - and familiar. There had been nowhere to sit, let alone sleep.

"That's where I arrived," she said, softly. "I appeared in that cell."

"He must have wanted to make sure you were contained," the Grandmaster said. He glanced into the cell, then back at Emily. "If he thought you were dangerous..."

He broke off as a low rattling echoed through the chamber. Something was coming towards them. Emily jumped back, lifting a hand to cast a spell, glancing around to see what was coming their way. Something *moved* in the darkened corridor beyond, then advanced into the light. A skeleton. She shuddered in remembered horror as the skeleton kept moving forward, followed by three others. Shadye's magic had animated them, but Shadye was dead. How had they survived three years without falling back into dust?

"Don't do anything," the Grandmaster said. "Wait."

Emily nodded, holding her hand at the ready. The skeletons didn't *look* dangerous, but they'd been strong enough to drag her through the halls at Shadye's command. She fought down the urge to step backwards as the leader walked up to her, stopping barely a meter from where she stood, then bowed deeply. Magic danced around them as the other three followed suit, then rose, awaiting orders.

"They recognize you as their mistress," the Grandmaster said. "Command them to show us where Shadye hid his treasures."

Emily swallowed, then looked at the lead skeleton. "Show us where Shadye hid his treasures."

The skeleton did nothing for long seconds, just long enough for her to think she didn't really have *any* right to command them, then turned and led them back through the dark corridors towards a barren room. Emily followed, uneasily aware that the other three were bringing up the rear. They might not have been dangerous, at least to her, but they still gave her the creeps. The leader stopped in the center of the room and pointed to a stone slab.

"Powerful protections here," the Grandmaster observed, opening the slab carefully. "And *look* at this!"

Emily followed his gaze. There were a handful of books and several dozen objects, all stored under the slab. A hammer-like artifact, a set of iron knives, a piece of chalk and a ring made of dull metal. The Grandmaster carefully checked the objects for unpleasant surprises - a handful had lethal curses attached - before placing them in his pouch. Emily took the books, after checking them herself, and examined their covers. None of them looked familiar.

"I'd like to have a look at those, when we get back to the school," the Grandmaster said. "And I suggest you find a safe place to keep them."

"Yes, sir," Emily said.

The Grandmaster nodded, and stood. "Ask them if there is anything else," he ordered. "I want to make as clean a sweep as possible."

Emily looked at the skeletons and repeated the question. The skeletons stood there for long seconds, then collapsed into piles of bones. Emily blinked, feeling the magic running through the building start to fade. Had Shadye's magic finally reached its limit? Or had dispelling the Nightmare Hex started a slow process of collapse?

"Time to take our leave," the Grandmaster said, sharply. Something crashed to the ground, not too far away. "The entire building might be about to fall down around our heads."

He caught Emily's arm. "Brace yourself," he ordered. "Here we go."

Emily gritted her teeth as the teleportation field caught them both. Teleporting *into* the Blighted Lands was dangerous, she'd been told, but getting out...it could be done, if one had the power. She closed her eyes as the world went white...

...And, when she opened them again, she was staring at Whitehall School.

Chapter Four

NOT A BAD HAUL, ALL THINGS CONSIDERED," THE GRANDMASTER SAID, AS HE HELD EMILY steady. She leaned on his arm, reluctantly, until her feet felt able to support her weight. The air felt cool, but blessedly *alive* compared to the tainted deadness of the Blighted Lands. "And much safer in our hands than in others'."

"I suppose," Emily said. She felt sick to her stomach. "What are you going to do with the objects we found?"

"Study them," the Grandmaster said. "Do you *want* them?"

Emily shook her head. "Just the books," she said. "What do we do about the fortress?"

"I'll arrange for someone to take another look, in a week or so," the Grandmaster said, as he gently let go of her arm. "If the Dark Fortress is completely drained of Shadye's magic, someone else may move in...or it may be left abandoned. It takes a strong-minded person to live next to the Inverse Shadow."

He shrugged. "The orcs worry me," he added. "Either they have a new leader or they've found a new chieftain. They might do a little raiding on their own account once the new generation grows to maturity."

"In a couple of years," Emily said. Orcs grew *fast*. A baby might become an adult within a couple of years, ready to go into combat or start competing for mates of his own. "Will you strike first?"

"We might," the Grandmaster said. He turned and started to walk towards Whitehall. "Your friends will be arriving later this evening, Emily. I suggest you pack your bags, and wait in the library until they arrive."

Emily nodded, reluctantly. For some arcane reason, she hadn't been allowed to move straight into the room she would occupy during term, even though she wouldn't have slept there while she'd been in the Blighted Lands. Perhaps other students staked their claims to the best of everything, if they got there first, but *she* wouldn't have done that, would she? Didn't the Grandmaster know her better than that? She shrugged at the thought, wondering just who she'd get as roommates this time, and followed the Grandmaster back to Whitehall. It was funny just how much the school felt like home.

"If you have time, write out a detailed report of everything you saw in the Blighted Lands," the Grandmaster said, as they reached the doors. "And return that little monster to its normal form."

"Yes, sir," Emily said, as Aurelius slithered off her neck and wrapped himself around her arm. She cast the spell and watched as the snake became a seemingly-harmless bangle, surrounded by anti-thief jinxes and runes designed to make it hard to see. "My friends *do* know about him..."

"The last thing I need is someone deciding to save you from a Death Viper," the Grandmaster said, dryly. "Or fainting when they see one wrapped around your neck."

Emily smiled at the thought, bowed to him and hurried up the stairs, back to her temporary room. It was small, with a bed, a desk, a set of bookshelves and not much else, but she was fond of it. In Sixth Year, she'd been told, she would have a room of her own; until then, she had to share with two roommates during term. At least she didn't have to sleep in dorms, she reminded herself as she placed the bag of books on the desk. Mountaintop hadn't been a very pleasant place to sleep, even when people *weren't* hanging hexes on the drapes or practicing nasty spells. She'd been lucky, she suspected. If she'd gone to Mountaintop as a newcomer, she would have been as badly abused as Frieda.

She sat down, glancing at the small pile of letters awaiting her. Caleb had written twice - she felt an unaccustomed warm sensation in her chest as she saw his handwriting - and Alassa had written several more times, probably to discuss her impending wedding. She opened her sealed drawer, picked up the chat parchment from where she'd hidden it and scribbled a brief note to say she was fine. Her friends would reply when they saw the message.

Shaking her head, she opened the letters and read them one by one, making sure there wasn't anything urgent she might have missed while she was in the Blighted Lands. Caleb's letters were friendly, apart from a handful of thoughts on their joint project; she surprised herself by smiling after she'd finished reading them both. Alassa was definitely worried about her wedding; *Emily* hadn't objected, but some of the other barons had grumbled about their future Prince Consort being of such low birth. Emily would have thought they'd be relieved - Jade couldn't rule the country in his own right - yet it seemed snobbery had trumped common sense. Beside it, the notes on other political developments in Zangaria were almost welcome.

"Fools," she muttered, as she read through the latest attempt to block the spread of her innovations. "You can't bottleneck something a person can get from anywhere."

She put the letters aside for later contemplation, rose to her feet, undressed rapidly and stepped into the shower. The memory of her stepfather mocked her as water ran down her body, reminding her of the times she'd showered at school or gone without, just to avoid his gaze. She'd felt so helpless back then. And yet, the fear that had gripped her, holding her firmly in place, was gone. He was just another person to leave in the past, someone so far away it was certain she would never see him again. Unless she *did* find a way to go back to Earth...

No, she told herself firmly, as she stopped the shower and reached for a towel, slowly wiping the water droplets off her body. *I'll never go back.*

Outside, she dressed rapidly, donning her favorite blue dress. It felt soft and unrestricting against her skin, contrasting neatly with her brown hair without showing off too much of her body. She would need to wear shapeless robes again tomorrow, or something lighter when she didn't have class, but for the moment she might as well enjoy the dress. The thought made her smile as she checked her appearance in the mirror, pulled her hair back into a long ponytail and turned to pack her trunk. It wasn't hard to make sure that all of Shadye's books were stored within a specific compartment, accessible only to her. There would be time to study them later.

She jumped as she heard someone rap on the door, and opened it without checking the wards. Only one person rapped like that; she smiled broadly as Lady Barb stepped into the room, wearing the black robes of a combat sorcerer and carrying a small sheaf of papers in one hand. Her long blonde hair shimmered in the light as she passed the papers to Emily, then nodded to her.

"I hear you had a good trip," she said, briskly.

"We did," Emily said. She'd talk about what she'd seen when the Nightmare Hex had gripped her later, when she'd had a chance to think about it properly. "We found quite a few books."

"I expect you to be *very* careful with them," Lady Barb said. Her blue eyes met Emily's and held them. "You could be held responsible if they fall into the wrong hands."

"Yeah," Emily said. "I have them sealed in my trunk."

"I'll be trying to break into it later," Lady Barb warned. "Make sure you have it as secure as possible, or else."

Emily nodded and hastily changed the subject, holding up the papers. "What are these?"

"Background information on potential career choices," Lady Barb said. "At some point within the first month, Emily, you will sit down with someone from the White Council and discuss your future career. You won't be expected to follow it slavishly, but they will give you useful advice and perhaps a few contacts. I suggest" - her tone indicated that it was actually an *order* - "that you go through the papers over the next few days, then make up your mind."

"Oh," Emily said. She wasn't sure she wanted to discuss her future with strangers. "What if I don't want to talk to them?"

"It's mandatory, unless you have a legitimate reason to refuse," Lady Barb said. "Alassa has one, Emily, but you don't."

She shrugged. "Pick a handful of possible careers, and talk to them about the prerequisites for apprenticeships or training programs," she added. "You'll find them quite useful, if you ask the right questions. They won't expect you to be *certain* of what you want to do in life."

"I want to be a researcher," Emily said. "Or a tutor..."

"I wouldn't put you in front of a class," Lady Barb said. "You'd have to maintain control of a whole crowd of louts, brats, snobs, and ignorers without turning them into toads...it isn't easy."

"You make it look easy," Emily said.

"A one-on-one tutoring job would probably suit you better," Lady Barb added, slowly. "You did a good job with Frieda, although you might have done better to curb her more...rebellious instincts."

Emily had to smile. Frieda had invented Freeze Tag, gleefully taught it to the other First Year students and played it through Whitehall's corridors. *It might have worked out fine*, she thought, *if they hadn't accidentally caught a pair of tutors in the game*. Weeks of detention hadn't curbed Frieda's sense of playfulness in the slightest.

"I'll be discussing prerequisites for Healing in class," Lady Barb said. "The other tutors will be doing the same. Take their words to heart, consider them carefully, then choose wisely."

"The Grandmaster said I would have to choose a major," Emily said.

"He was right," Lady Barb said. "I know you're interested in everything, Emily, but you do have to choose a major for your final two years at Whitehall."

She looked at the trunk. "Have you packed everything?"

"Just about," Emily said. "I haven't moved my letters yet."

"Do that now," Lady Barb ordered. "You're in Room 4-01. I'll take your trunk down; you can go down later, at five bells. Your roommates should have arrived by then."

Emily hurried to obey. "I can take my trunk myself," she said, as she hastily stuffed the letters into the trunk and the chat parchment into her pocket. "You don't have to do it..."

"Tradition must be upheld," Lady Barb said, sternly. Her blue eyes twinkled with amusement as she hefted the trunk with one hand. "Go to the library, Emily, or wander around the school. You shouldn't get an edge on your roommates."

She left, closing the door behind her. Emily sighed, made sure her dirty clothes were clearly marked for the maids, then stepped out the door herself. A handful of early arrivals - all boys - were walking down the corridor; they stared at her as she appeared, some with fear in their eyes, others with frank speculation. Not sexual, she knew, but something else, something *hungry*. Using the battery had made her a far more desirable match for anyone who wanted to infuse power into their families.

And it's a trick, she thought, as she walked past them towards the library. *I couldn't muster that sort of power on my own.*

She pushed the thought aside as she entered the library. It was open, but almost completely empty. Lady Aliya was standing behind her desk, looking through a colossal pile of newly-printed books, while a pair of younger students were standing in the stacks, frantically looking for reference material they'd need for their projects. Emily didn't blame them for wanting to get ahead, not when she'd had to work through the holidays to get up to speed. It hadn't been easy.

"Emily," Lady Aliya said. "Have you come to help?"

"I could," Emily said. She hadn't had time to help in the library last year, when she'd been trying desperately to catch up with her friends, but now...she had time. "What would you like me to do?"

"These new textbooks all need to be charmed," Lady Aliya said. "They're going on the shelves for the First Years."

Printed on my printing presses, Emily thought. What would it do to Whitehall when books were no longer scarce? *Each and every one of the First Years could have their own copy, if they wished.*

She worked her way through the pile of books, charming them one by one and then adding them to the trolleys to be put on the shelves. There was still no real order to the library, beyond a basic division by subject; it had always astonished her that someone, anyone, could actually *find* anything amid the chaos. But redesigning the library to use a modified version of the Library of Congress System would be impossible. It would be easier to start with a whole new library and catalogue the books as they came in.

I wonder if I could work as a librarian, she thought. *Would I need experience for that?*

She asked Lady Aliya, who frowned. "You'd have to work for the guild," she said, after a moment. "I think they'd be glad to have you, but they would still insist on you taking the oaths. On the other hand...you *could* work for me, as an apprentice, for a year without sealing anything. That would let you decide if you *wanted* the job."

Emily hesitated. "Is it a good job?"

"It would probably suit you, in some ways," Lady Aliya said. "You like books, you're good with them and you actually *respect* them. On the other hand, you wouldn't have the option of saying no if you worked at a library and someone demanded knowledge. That isn't a problem here, but in the White City...Emily, the librarians there have to share their knowledge with *everyone*."

"So they might wind up giving knowledge to a Dark Wizard," Emily mused.

"Among other things," Lady Aliya said. "There are places where the librarians are sworn not to actually read the books, merely to tend to them. And other places where the librarians are practically chained to the bookshelves. We're not meant to get involved in matters political - and *you* are a very political person."

She picked up a stack of books and carried them over to the shelves. "Think about it, apprentice with me if you wish, then make up your mind," she called back. "If you don't like what you do, you won't have to take the final step. But once you do take that step, you're committed."

Emily nodded, and turned her attention back to the new books. It hadn't been easy, back when she'd been working as a library assistant, to put interesting books on the shelves when her brain had been demanding she sit down and start reading. She'd known it would have cost her the job, if she'd been caught, yet there had been days when she'd opened the books and allowed them to suck her in. At least Lady Aliya had allowed her to put some books aside to read when she wasn't on the desk or shelving books. She doubted she would be allowed to do that if she was a library apprentice.

Or maybe I could, she thought. Had Lady Aliya ever held back a book so she could read it first? She didn't know - but she wouldn't, not if the Head Librarian chose to keep it from her. Lady Aliya knew far more than anyone else about hiding books within the stacks, or in her office. *Maybe I should ask her about that, too...*

She glanced at Lady Aliya, who was telling off a Third Year for some offense, and decided it would be better to ask later. Instead, she kept charming and shelving the books until her watch told her it was five bells, an hour before dinner was served in the Great Hall. Her stomach rumbled, reminding her that she hadn't eaten anything since before Shadye's fortress had started to collapse, but she did her best to ignore it. She needed to see who her roommates were instead of eating dinner...

"That's me," she called. "Should I come back and finish the rest later?"

"Don't worry about it," Lady Aliya said. "Just enjoy yourself."

Emily left the room, feeling a leaden weight in her stomach. The first set of roommates she'd had had been picked at random, but she'd requested her friends for the second set and been denied. And she'd shared a room with Frieda for her Third Year... who would she have *this* time? She walked through the corridors, doing her best to ignore the glances and stares, until she found the entrance to the Third Year dorms. Madame Beauregard was standing outside, looking strict; Emily knew, from bitter experience, that the pinched-face woman made Lady Barb look soft.

"Room 4-01," she snapped at Emily. "Your roommates are already there."

"Thank you," Emily said.

She stepped into the dorm corridor - it looked identical to the ones she'd used earlier, although the common room was larger and there were paintings hanging from the walls - and pressed her hand against the wooden door marked 4-01. It clicked open at her touch, revealing a room with three beds, three desks, three chairs, three wardrobes and a door at the rear leading to the bathroom and shower compartment. Emily hesitated, then stepped inside...

...And smiled as she saw her friends.

"Emily," Alassa called, from where she was unpacking her trunk. "Welcome back!"

She stood and gave Emily a hug. Imaiqah sat up on her bed and waved, then stood to welcome Emily too. Emily felt tears pricking at her eyes as she hugged both of her friends, and glanced at her bed. It looked bare, as always, just waiting for her to make her bed and unpack her trunk.

"So," Alassa said. "How was your trip?"

"Complex," Emily said, finally. She couldn't keep the smile off her face. "But I'll tell you all about it tonight."

Chapter Five

E MILY," FRIEDA CALLED, AS EMILY STEPPED INTO THE DINING HALL. "COME JOIN ME?"
Emily smiled at her younger friend, practically her younger sister, nodded and walked over to her table. Frieda was alone, even though she was entering Second Year; she'd come back early with Alassa and Imaiqah, rather than stay in Zangaria for another couple of days until the other Second Years arrived. Emily couldn't help wondering why *she* was allowed to enter her bedroom early, but dismissed the thought. It was quite likely Frieda had been assigned a singleton for a couple of days, before her future roommates arrived.

"It's good to see you again," Frieda said, as she rose to her feet and gave Emily a quick hug. She wore a long blue dress that reminded Emily of her own, probably yet another gift from Queen Marlena. "I was hoping we'd be sharing a room again."

Emily shook her head. "I think they wanted you to bunk with people your own age," she said. She sat down next to Frieda and smiled as Alassa and Imaiqah sat facing them. "It's supposed to be good for your social development or something."

"Or something," Imaiqah echoed, dryly. The three of them had asked to share a room for Second Year, only to be denied by Master Tor. "But you would be better off with roommates at the same level as yourself."

Frieda looked at Emily. "Is that true?"

"It depends on who you get as roommates," Emily muttered, uncomfortably. *She* hadn't treated Frieda badly, not when they'd been sharing a room, but someone else with two years between her and her roommate might well rule the roost. "And you'd be able to invite more guests to your room."

"I suppose," Frieda said. She'd kept her friends *out* of the room they'd shared, although Emily had never been sure if she'd been trying to keep them from distracting the older girl or merely wanted somewhere peaceful she could retreat to, if necessary. "We're going to be a lot busier this term, aren't we?"

"There will be plenty of time to play Ken," Alassa assured her. She winked at Emily. "I think Frieda will be the latest member of our team. We're having try-outs at the end of the week, once everyone is back to school."

"And for those of us who are actually intent on studying," a new voice said, "we have to get back to work."

Emily looked up and smiled as she saw the Gorgon, wearing her robes rather than a dress. "It's good to see you again, too," she said. "I dare say we can hide in the library while the try-outs are taking place."

The Gorgon sat down, her greenish face tired. She had to travel farther than any of them, Emily knew, and might well have been denied access to some of the portals along the way. The Allied Lands had little classical racism, but it was perfectly legal to discriminate against gorgons, werewolves and others who had been touched by magic. And vampires could be exterminated on sight. She felt a stab of sympathy for her friend, wondering if there was anything she could do to deal with the problem.

But so far she hadn't been able to think of anything, besides making it clear that the Gorgon was her friend.

"I understand you were going to be working on your project," the Gorgon said. "How did that go?"

"She wound up with a boyfriend," Imaiqah said, quickly. "It was very sweet!"

"He isn't my boyfriend," Emily protested, feeling her cheeks heat. Beside her, Frieda giggled. "He isn't..."

Imaiqah smirked. "We shall see," she said. "But you did make it through to Fourth Year."

"That's very well done," the Gorgon said.

"Thank you," Emily said.

"I'm getting married," Alassa said, drawing the conversation away from Emily. "You will be coming to the wedding, won't you?"

The Gorgon looked shocked. "Would I be welcome?"

"By me," Alassa said. "And Jade. And everyone else can go jump off the battlements."

"Or throw *you* off the battlements," the Gorgon predicted, mournfully. "That would be a tragic end to the wedding."

"The last one was quite peaceful," Alassa said. She nodded to Emily. "Of course, it *did* require someone to silence everyone with a spell."

Emily nodded back, slowly. Markus and Melissa's wedding had been small, with only a handful of guests. Melissa had deserved a bigger wedding, given what she'd had to do to get married to Markus, but she'd been disowned by her family. In the end, even her former friends had failed to make it. Emily couldn't help feeling another stab of sympathy for someone who had started out as an enemy, or at least a rival. Melissa hadn't deserved to be disowned, let alone cut off from her entire former life.

But at least she has Markus, Emily thought. *They'll get through it, won't they?*

"So I heard," the Gorgon said, breaking into Emily's thoughts. "I didn't know you had *that* sort of power."

Emily cringed, inwardly. Gorgon magic was strange, different; it wasn't easy to undo their ability to turn someone into a stone statue. *Emily* had been caught in the Gorgon's magic and it had taken nearly a week for Whitehall's staff to free them both from the spell. No wonder so many people were scared of gorgons...and now, she suspected, they would be scared of her too. It wasn't something she'd ever wanted.

"I was desperate," she said, shortly. The Gorgon was brilliant - there was a fine mind in there, combined with two additional years of schooling - and quite perceptive. She might reason out that a trick had been involved, although Emily hoped she would never figure out how it was actually done. "I tried something and it worked."

"Yeah, well everyone is talking about it," the Gorgon said. "You're going to have everyone staring at you this year."

"Again," Alassa put in.

"Try and steal the show," Emily urged. "Talk about your wedding or something, *please!*"

"Wear a glamor," Frieda suggested. "Pretend to be a younger student or something. Hang out with us in Second Year."

Alassa giggled. "I don't think she'd do *that*," she said. "Really."

Emily shook her head, slowly. It was rare for the older students to hang around with the younger students, even if they were related. They were on entirely different levels, or so they believed, and even *talking* to younger students made them look weak in the eyes of their equals. It had never made any sense to her, but then...she rarely tried to talk to *anyone* outside her circle. Frieda was something of an exception to the rule.

"Then you'll just have to endure it," the Gorgon said, briskly. "Good luck."

"Thank you," Emily said.

"I hear Aloha has already returned to school," the Gorgon said. "Have you seen her?"

Emily shook her head. "Not yet," she said. "I thought the upper classes were told to stay out of our way."

"I think she's in 5.07," Imaiqah said. "That's what she said on the chat parchment, anyway."

"Be careful when you go there," Frieda offered. "We were playing games up near the doors and they chased us away."

"I think that had something to do with the racket you were making," Imaiqah pointed out, dryly. "They *were* trying to study, weren't they?"

"We were very quiet," Frieda protested.

Emily smiled. She'd seen Frieda and her friends at play and *quiet* was not the word she would have used to describe them. The shouting and screaming alone was enough to put anyone off their work, while they had a tendency to run into empty classrooms and turn them into impromptu playrooms. For girls who were approaching seventeen, if they weren't already there, they were remarkably childish. But then, at least they were enjoying themselves. It was more than could be said for herself before she'd come to Whitehall.

She looked up as dinner arrived: great steaming plates of goulash, bowls of noodles and boiled potatoes, slices of roast beef and chicken and giant tureens of soup. Frieda tucked in hastily, without anything resembling decorum; Emily shook her head in tired amusement before she started to ladle food onto her own plate. Frieda had never had enough to eat before she'd met Emily; even now, she ate far more than seemed humanly possible at each meal. But she definitely needed the energy. Magic tapped the body's reserves far more than any physical exercise.

And she really was too thin when we first met, Emily reminded herself. *She needed to bulk up before she drained herself too far and died.*

The food tasted heavenly, as always. Emily finished her plate and then pushed it into the center of the table rather than take another helping. It had always struck her as odd that Whitehall served so many *different* kinds of food, but perhaps, with students coming from all over the Allied Lands, it wasn't strange at all. The food in

Zangaria tended towards roast meat, overcooked potatoes and stewed vegetables. It wasn't unpleasant, but it tended to get wearying after a while.

If someone had the money to buy meat, she reminded herself. Poaching wasn't forbidden in Cockatrice - she'd never been inclined to go hunting, let alone reserve wide swathes of the forest for her personal use - but elsewhere it was harshly punished. *The commoners are lucky if they get one helping of meat per week.*

She pushed the thought aside, angrily. Here, in Whitehall, it was easy to forget about Cockatrice and her responsibilities there. But she couldn't look away, not when she knew just how many injustices had been perpetrated on a daily basis. People had been whipped, murdered, or worse, just for offending the old baron in some way. It wasn't something she could allow to continue...

"Hey," Imaiqah said, quickly. "Look behind you."

Emily turned - and smiled as she saw Caleb standing at the door, looking uncertain. She didn't really blame him, not when he was being forced to repeat an entire year. It shouldn't have shamed him, she thought, but she knew it did; it shamed anyone who had to remain in the lower classes when their peers had advanced to Year Five. Caleb was a year older than the students he had to join...

"Better go speak to him," Imaiqah urged. "He won't get any food at all if he doesn't come in."

"We'll save you some dessert," Alassa added. "Unless it's trifle, in which case we'll eat it all."

Emily hesitated, feeling an odd sensation in the pit of her stomach, and then rose and walked towards the door. Caleb looked relieved to see her, yet he seemed to have problems looking her in the eye. Maybe he'd been teased, too - Emily's mother had told her what boys said to one another, when they thought girls weren't listening - or maybe he was just awkward about stepping into a room infested with younger students. A year wasn't *that* much of a gap, Emily thought, but...

The Gorgon stayed back a year, she reminded herself, firmly. *But she was almost friendly anyway.*

"It's good to see you again," she said. She cast a privacy ward as she noted several people pretending not to listen to their conversation. "How was your family?"

Caleb colored, slightly. "My mother and my father are well," he said. "Still disappointed in me, still thinking I should be doing something more *practical* with my time, but accepting that I want to remain at Whitehall."

"That's good," Emily said, feeling a little tongue-tied. "And your siblings?"

"Casper is apparently in training to be a combat sorcerer," Caleb said. His lips twitched into a smile, just for a second. "His master seems to think he isn't *quite* ready to be released, not yet."

Emily nodded. Jade had been Master Grey's student for two years before he'd been released, although he *had* been working with Sergeant Miles rather than setting out on his own. Even so, it suggested that Jade was a truly brilliant student. Alassa was lucky to have him.

"The younger ones are still at school," Caleb added. "Well, Karan just entered Stronghold - she made a fuss about me not going because she wanted an older brother there - while Marian is studying her letters and numbers before she comes into her magic. Croce had a very successful first term, or so he says. He spent half the summer in Melrose with a friend of his."

"You spent half the summer in Zangaria," Emily pointed out.

Caleb smiled. "It was far better than spending it with my family," he said, looking down at his hands. They were still covered with faint scars. "My parents were none too pleased when I managed to injure myself."

"You recovered," Emily said.

"That's not the point," Caleb said. "The point is that I messed up and hurt myself - and almost hurt someone else."

"I know," Emily said, awkwardly.

"They asked a few questions about you too," Caleb added, reluctantly. "Mother wanted to know what you intended to do with yourself. Father talked about enlisting you into his great plan to wage war on the necromancers."

Emily blinked in surprise. Killing a necromancer wasn't easy. *She* was the only person known to have killed two, both through cheating. Sending an army of men armed with swords and spears against a necromancer was dangerously futile; they'd just be providing the necromancer with more fuel for his magic. Caleb's father had to know better, didn't he?

"They'd smash any army we sent," she said, slowly. "Even a hundred combat sorcerers would have problems stopping a necromancer."

"He thinks we need to take the initiative," Caleb said. "They're killing us, right now, with gentle pressure along the borders. We almost lost Whitehall two years ago. He thinks we need to find a way to strike back."

"If we can," Emily said. She had some tricks she knew she could use, but she wasn't sure she dared let them out of the bag. The nuke-spell might be worse than necromancy, once it spread widely. "Maybe we should wait until after I graduate."

By which time he might have thought better of it, she thought, inwardly.

She paused, trying to think of something to say. "Are you going to join us for dinner?"

Caleb hesitated. "I'm not hungry," he said. "I..."

"Come join us," Emily urged. She liked his company, even though she knew her friends were going to tease her. It wasn't as if he was her *real* boyfriend, merely someone she enjoyed spending time with. "There will be trifle, if Alassa hasn't eaten it all."

She caught Caleb's arm and tugged him gently towards the table, dispelling the privacy ward as they moved. Imaiqah smirked at them as they approached, then motioned for Frieda to move to one side, clearing the way for Caleb to sit next to Emily. He didn't seem put out by the Gorgon at all, Emily noted in relief. She wasn't sure she would have liked him so much if he'd been repulsed by one of her friends.

"Welcome back," Imaiqah said, as they sat. The servers were already bringing out pudding, along with jugs of cream and glasses of juice. "Did you have a nice chat?"

"Yes, thank you," Emily said, blushing. Privacy wards made it impossible for anyone to overhear their words - or even lip-read - but they tended to be easy to see. They could have been talking about something far more romantic than Caleb's parents and the looming threat of the necromancers. "We did."

The Gorgon cleared her throat. "As a student who entered Fourth Year," she said, "do you have any words of advice?"

Caleb frowned, running one scarred hand through his brown hair. "Make sure you don't miss the Grandmaster's speech tomorrow," he said. "They sometimes set an essay on the speech and its meaning, when they run out of other horrid things to do."

"Seriously?" Alassa said. "But no one ever pays attention to those things."

"Pay attention to this one," Caleb said. "It's quite important."

He looked down at his hand. "And try not to injure yourself too," he added. "That's *also* quite important."

"I can see why," Frieda said. There was an odd edge in her voice. "You nearly killed yourself."

"A moment of carelessness," Caleb agreed. He looked at Imaiqah. "You have a project plan ready to go?"

"Yes," Imaiqah said. She glanced at Alassa. "How long do we have to make it work?"

"You'll be expected to present a progress report just before the first break, then a completed project after the *second* break," Caleb said. "Didn't you have this explained to you at the start of Third Year?"

"It's always better to hear from someone who's actually gone though the experience," Imaiqah said, blandly.

She's trying to get him to open up, Emily realized, suddenly. Imaiqah might not be as studious as the Gorgon, or Emily herself, but she was perfectly capable of reading notes and following instructions. And yet, by asking Caleb questions, she was encouraging him to talk about a subject he might find comfortable. *Clever.*

"I didn't have *that* much experience before I managed to put myself out of the running for the year," Caleb pointed out. He held up his scarred hand. "All I can tell you is that they will go over everything you do with a chilling precision."

"Joy," Alassa muttered.

"You have to be able to defend it forwards and backwards," Caleb added. "And make sure you understand every last bit of the project."

"We can do that," Alassa said. "But what is the Grandmaster going to tell us?"

Caleb smirked. "Wait and see," he said. "Just you wait and see."

Emily frowned inwardly, but kept her thoughts to herself. Tomorrow, they would have the speech...and then, they would go back to classes. It was going to be hard, she knew all too well, but she couldn't wait. Whitehall was her home now, as far as she was concerned...

...And it was where she belonged.

Chapter Six

Emily didn't expect to get much sleep after they finally finished dinner and were chased out of the Dining Hall, but she fell asleep almost as soon as her head hit the pillow. She jerked awake the following morning when her bed quivered restlessly, preparing to throw her out onto the stone cold floor. She jumped out of bed, hurried into the bathroom and showered, then pulled her shapeless robes over her head.

"You could have woken me," she said to Imaiqah. Alassa was nowhere to be seen. "I don't want to be late for the speech."

"You looked as though you needed a rest," Imaiqah said, unrepentantly. "There's plenty of time, I think. We're not expected to be in the Great Hall until ten bells."

Emily glanced at her watch, then nodded reluctantly. Classes normally started at nine bells, but the first day was always chaotic. She should have time to snag a mug of Kava and a snack – even though she didn't feel like eating - before hurrying down to the Great Hall. Her bed quivered warningly as she sat down on it, pulled her shoes on and nodded to her friend.

"Where's Alassa?"

"She had a very early morning meeting with Madame Beauregard," Imaiqah said. "She's not back yet."

Emily blinked. "Is she in trouble already?"

"I don't *think* so," Imaiqah said. She rose and joined Emily as she walked towards the door. "I think there was just a dispute over what she could and couldn't bring into the dorms."

They walked down the stairs into the Dining Hall and sat down. Servers brought them hot Kava - Emily winced at the bitter taste, but at least it woke her up - and bowls of porridge, crammed with raisins and sultanas. Emily ate quickly, surprised at her own hunger; she'd eaten plenty the previous night and done very little to work it off. But she knew she'd need the energy when classes restarted in earnest. Not eating was akin to self-harm where magic was involved.

"I have my timetable here," Imaiqah said, digging through her pockets. "How close is it to yours?"

Emily pulled out her own - she'd barely had a chance to glance at it - and frowned, comparing the two papers. Most of their classes were identical, but there were blank spots for her where Imaiqah had Defensive Magic and Artwork. She sighed at the list of introductory classes - as if they'd have a chance to change their classes now - and then scowled as she realized she wouldn't have Martial Magic. It was vanishingly rare for a student to take the class early and she'd completed both years offered at Whitehall.

Aloha will have the same problem, she thought. She reached for the chat parchment to ask her older friend a question, then shook her head. *We can talk about it later.*

"They probably won't want to put you in Defensive Magic," Imaiqah said, thoughtfully. "I think you're well ahead of us, at least in some levels. You could probably teach the class."

Emily shook her head. Sergeant Harkin - she said a silent prayer for his soul - and Sergeant Miles were both formidable personalities, able to cow an unruly student with a single disapproving look. No one had dared defy Harkin openly before his death - before Shadye had made her stab him - and no one had realized he didn't even have a single spark of magic to his name. *She* knew, all too well, that she didn't have the presence to keep a class's attention, not when they were experimenting with dangerous magic.

"No, thank you," she said. "Maybe they just mean to give me some more research time."

"I doubt it," Imaiqah said. "They'd want you to build on what you have."

They finished breakfast, and hurried through the corridors to the Great Hall. Several more students cast wary glances at her, as if they expected her to start lashing out in all directions; Emily did her best to ignore it, even though it was worrying. She would have preferred to be ignored, rather than to be treated as a volcano that might explode at any moment. But then, by the time the story had swept from one end of the Allied Lands and back again, it had probably grown in the telling. God alone knew what the students had heard before they'd returned to Whitehall.

She smiled to herself as she stepped into the Great Hall and waved to Caleb, who was leaning against the stone walls and trying not to be seen. Imaiqah caught her arm and tugged her towards Caleb, beckoning to Alassa as she entered the chamber. Emily smiled inwardly as Alassa came to join them, noting how she managed to make even the shapeless robes look good. She didn't even have a single hair out of place.

"Madame Beauregard wanted to offer me a job," she said, as she leaned against the wall next to them. "Dorm Monitor."

"Wow," Imaiqah said. "She must think highly of you."

Alassa shrugged. "It's extra responsibility," she said. "I didn't even know the post *existed*."

"They start from Fourth Year," Caleb put in. "One male, one female; they're meant to keep an eye on their fellow students while Madame Beauregard keeps an eye on the Third Years. I wasn't one."

Imaiqah elbowed Alassa. "Bet Jade was," she said. "Write to him and ask."

"I will," Alassa said. "Who do you think the other Dorm Monitor will be?"

Emily tuned them both out as they started discussing the various boys in their year and contemplating the most likely candidates. It wasn't a post *she* wanted, not when she'd be the same age as the students she was meant to supervise. Jade had been a prefect, she recalled, but he'd never had to boss around his fellow Sixth Year students, only students who had been younger than him. Alassa would need reserves of tact and diplomacy Emily suspected she didn't have to make the position anything more than an empty title.

Caleb cleared his throat. "Did you want the post?"

"No," Emily said. "I didn't know it existed either."

She leaned against the wall and watched as students kept flowing into the Great Hall. There were only eighty Fourth Year students, divided almost evenly between male and female; she knew a handful of them by name, but others were strangers. Imaiqah would be able to talk about anyone in their year in great detail, Emily knew, yet Emily herself had never had the knack for learning about people, let alone making friends. She only knew Melissa and her cronies because they'd tried to make her life miserable.

The doors started to close, a handful of remaining students hastily running to get into the Great Hall before it was too late. Melissa was one of the last, her long red hair spilling out behind her as she ran into the chamber. She looked different, Emily noted, although it was hard to put her finger on *why*. There was a new resilience in the way she moved that surprised Emily. She waved, wondering if Melissa would come over, but Melissa did not approach them. Instead, she merely found a place to stand and waited.

Should have chairs here for us, Emily thought. *Standing here for hours is no fun.*

She pushed the thought aside as the Grandmaster stepped through a door and walked onto the stage. The lights dimmed slightly, drawing everyone's attention to him. Emily stood straighter, clasping her hands behind her back. The Grandmaster was not someone to ignore.

"Greetings," the Grandmaster said. "Welcome back to Whitehall."

There was a long pause. Normally, Emily knew, he would introduce the Year Head and allow him to make the rest of the speech, but this time he merely waited, his hidden eyes sweeping the room. Whitehall was *his*, Emily knew; the wards respected him as their master, even though he would one day stand aside for a new Grandmaster. That day, Emily hoped, would be a very long time in coming.

"This is your Fourth Year at Whitehall," the Grandmaster continued. "As such, it is perhaps your most *important* year at Whitehall. Your Year Head, therefore, stands before you now."

It took Emily a moment to realize he meant *him*, that *he* was the Year Head. She couldn't help smiling as a rustle of understanding ran through the giant chamber. She *liked* the Grandmaster, while Master Tor had been a jerk and Mistress Irene had been sharp-tongued and strict. If the Grandmaster had time to serve as Year Head as well as his Grandmaster duties, there were few indeed who would wish for someone else. The Grandmaster could open doors no one else could, at least at Whitehall.

"First, a handful of minor announcements," the Grandmaster said. "Quite a few of you have obtained chat parchments from their inventor. Anyone caught using one in class, at least not without a very good excuse, will be caned. I strongly suggest you do not bring your parchment into the classroom, as the tutor may simply destroy it. In addition, last year there were an alarming number of blue books smuggled into the school. The school board has banned them from the school and anyone caught with one will regret it."

Oops, Emily thought. If she'd known that the printing presses she'd introduced would be used to print Blue Books, erotic stories, she might have thought twice about introducing them to the Nameless World. She'd glanced at a handful of the stories and they'd been universally awful. *But they won't blame me for that, will they?*

"On a more serious note, I strongly advise you not to miss any classes during this year," the Grandmaster warned. "Fourth Year lays the groundwork for your later career and it is vitally important to pass your exams with good grades. If you feel you are falling behind, go to your advisers and ask for assistance before it is too late. Your advisers are there to help you, so take advantage of them. Should you fail Fourth Year, as some of you already know, you may have to go all the way back to Third Year. I am reliably informed that most students would consider this a fate worse than death."

There were some nervous chuckles. Emily understood; none of them would really be considered adults, whatever their age, until they passed Fourth Year. Being two years older than her fellow students would be bad enough, but to be treated as a child rather than an adult…it was *not* a pleasant thought. She silently resolved to pass Fourth Year on her first try.

"In addition, there will be career sessions with an adviser from the White Council," the Grandmaster stated. "You *will* be expected to attend these sessions; you've been provided with papers detailing procedures, career requirements and your options. Talk to your advisers, sort out a handful of prospective careers and plan how you intend to approach the session."

He paused. Emily couldn't help feeling a stab of guilt. She'd barely glanced at the papers after shoving them into her pockets; hell, she'd left them back in her bedroom, rather than carry them with her. She made a mental note to read them when she got back, then turned her attention back to the Grandmaster. He looked stern.

"There is something that needs to be said, and said clearly," he said. "It is why I am serving as your Year Head, even though you are Fourth Years rather than Sixth Years, and why I am speaking to you now."

This was it, Emily realized. She glanced at Caleb and saw him smile. This was what he'd hinted at, yesterday. But the Grandmaster was still talking.

"Over the years," he continued, "many students – young men and women like yourselves – have questioned the very purpose of Whitehall School. And when we, your tutors and teachers, have answered, we have told you about the advantages of learning in groups, of meeting your fellows before you reach true adulthood, of sharing the experience of discovering magic together. All of those answers are true.

"But there is another answer. Whitehall School exists for your protection and the protection of others.

"Magic is a great gift, but it can also be a curse. Here, you have learned how to use magic safely – and, perhaps, learned what it feels like to be without magic, to be at the mercy of those with greater power. Here, we can cope with problems that would kill you, if you lived outside the school; here, we can discipline you if you act like children, if you use your magic as a weapon. The outside world has fewer options when it comes to children granted the powers of gods. They must kill you, if you remain weak, or bow to you if you become strong."

Emily shuddered. How long had it been since she'd come within a hairsbreadth of killing Alassa?

"Some of you, raised among mundanes, will see magic as a way to boost yourself, to become powerful, to exact revenge for slights real and imagined. Others, raised among magicians, will see yourselves as separate from the mundane world, able to interact with it on terms you choose. Neither feeling is healthy, nor is it good for the future of the Allied Lands. We seek to teach you how to handle your powers responsibly, because in the wider world it is often the case that the only check on your power is *you*.

"For many of you, this will be your final year at Whitehall. You will be released to walk the land, to become everything from alchemists to court wizards, taking with you what we have taught you. You will be released on a world that will bow to you, that will see your robes and your power and grant you respect. You will define yourself by how you handle what you have become, if you tame magic or if you allow the magic to tame *you*."

He paused, looking down at them. Emily felt her breath catch in her throat.

"I do not count our successes as those who learn to handle great power, who can perform vast feats of magic, although those things are important. I count our successes as those who end up calm and confident, reasonable people whom the Allied Lands can depend upon in the endless war. Some of you will feel otherwise, and that is understandable. However, you must learn to shape your own path in the future. Your lives are what you make of them."

He repeated himself, slowly. "Your lives are what you make of them."

There was a long silent pause. He was right, Emily knew; she'd seen too much abuse of mundanes by magicians to believe otherwise. If her life had been different, if she'd had magic on Earth, her stepfather wouldn't have lived a year...and how many others, perhaps, would she have sought to hurt? There were times when she wondered why Frieda hadn't gone back home, one final time, to avenge herself on those who had cast her out. Maybe Frieda was just a better person...

"Dismissed," the Grandmaster said, very quietly.

The doors opened, allowing light to spill into the Great Hall from the corridor outside. Emily looked at Caleb, then at her thoughtful friends, and started towards the door. Outside, Aloha stood leaning against the wall, wearing the red robes of a Fifth Year student. Her dark face was marred by a worried frown.

"Emily," she called. "I have orders to take you to the Grandmaster's office."

Alassa elbowed Emily. "What have you done now?"

"Nothing," Emily said. She hastily recalled her timetable. "I'll see you in Healing?"

"Of course," Alassa said. "We'll take very good care of Caleb, don't you worry."

Emily felt herself flush - Caleb was blushing, too - and followed Aloha up a small staircase to the Grandmaster's office. The room was unlocked, but she felt the wards probing at her magic as she stepped inside; if she hadn't been cleared to enter, she suspected she wouldn't have enjoyed the consequences. Trying to break into offices was an old tradition at Whitehall, but so were a whole series of unpleasant hexes intended to keep out trespassers.

"It's good to see you again," Aloha said, as she closed the door. "I heard interesting things about your summer."

"It was...*eventful*," Emily said. She didn't really want to talk about it. Aloha was the brightest student at Whitehall; given time, she might figure out the truth. "And yours?"

"I studied," Aloha said, flatly. "I..."

She broke off as the door opened and the Grandmaster stepped into the room. "Emily, Aloha," he said, as he closed the door behind him. "Thank you both for coming."

Emily nodded, once.

"The pair of you present us with an odd problem," the Grandmaster said. "You have both completed the levels of Martial Magic provided at Whitehall, at least for students, but you're too young to go straight to an apprenticeship. I have no intention of allowing you to waste what you've learned, however, so I have taken the liberty of arranging for private training sessions with a respected combat sorcerer."

"Thank you, sir," Aloha said.

Emily smiled. Someone she knew? Lady Barb? Sergeant Miles? She could learn from both of them...

"You will study with him when you should have Martial Magic," the Grandmaster continued. "It will not be a full apprenticeship, but you should be well-prepared for one by the time you graduate from Whitehall. I believe you may be able to complete such an apprenticeship within a year. If, of course, you choose to work towards becoming combat sorceresses."

He waved a hand at the door, commanding it to open...

...And Master Grey stepped into the room.

Chapter Seven

EMILY FELT A LEADEN WEIGHT DROP INTO HER CHEST AS MASTER GREY BOWED POLITELY TO the Grandmaster, then stared at Aloha and her. Master Grey didn't like her. Master Grey had *never* liked her. He'd expressed his disapproval time and time again, first to Jade and then to Emily's face. To have him teaching her...

Aloha elbowed her, none too gently. "You're meant to bow," she reminded Emily, very quietly. "Now."

Emily did as she was told, even though she hated the idea of taking her eyes off him for longer than a second. Master Grey merely nodded, his cold blue eyes fixed on her face. He was a tall, powerfully-built man, his black robes carefully tailored to both show off his muscles and allow him to move freely. His head had been shaved, like a monk; a silver stud was placed in each ear, presumably charmed to offer protection. Emily forced herself to keep looking at him, even though she wanted to step backwards. Master Grey scared her in a way she couldn't quite name.

"Master Grey has considerable experience preparing younger students for their apprenticeships," the Grandmaster said. If he was aware of the tension in the room, he didn't show it. "I believe he will make a suitable tutor for both of you, probably for a single year."

"I have no objections to remaining longer," Master Grey said, gravely.

Emily swallowed. Who'd had the bright idea of inviting *him?* Lady Barb would have known it was a bad idea, Sergeant Miles would have had his doubts; hell, surely the Grandmaster would have consulted Lady Barb before inviting Master Grey to the school. Or...had Master Grey *volunteered* for the task? And if so, why? It wouldn't give him any more apprentices to his name, only deprive him of the chance to find another apprentice or whatever else he did when he wasn't attending fairs or patrolling the Allied Lands.

"We will see how things go," the Grandmaster said. Emily wanted to protest, but she knew from bitter experience that it would be unwise to protest with Master Grey in the same room. "I believe their timetables have been arranged to allow you to have Tuesday and Thursday afternoons with them - and perhaps more, if you find it to be necessary."

He can't kill you, Emily's thoughts reassured her. *He really can't kill you.*

Of course not, her own thoughts answered. *But he can make your life miserable.*

The Grandmaster cleared his throat. "I expect you to make the most of this opportunity," he said. His words were addressed to both of them, but Emily had a feeling they were aimed specifically at her. "It was not easy to find someone willing to teach you both."

He rose. "I'd like my office back in an hour," he added. "Until then, I suggest you spend the time to get acquainted. You must have much to discuss."

Emily wanted to ask him to stay, to beg him to stay, but she couldn't speak. She watched numbly as the Grandmaster walked past her, out the door and into the corridor. The door closed with an audible *thud*, sending chills down her spine. They were alone with a powerful magician who hated her.

"Your posture is bad," Master Grey said, looking her up and down. "You need to straighten your back and hold your hands behind your back."

Emily flushed, but did as she was told. Sergeant Harkin had told her how to stand properly, but she'd slipped after going to Mountaintop and then desperately working to complete Third Year with her friends. Mountaintop...another shiver ran down her spine as she recalled that Master Grey had graduated from Mountaintop, the school she'd turned upside down. He had more than one reason to hate her.

"Your posture isn't bad, but it's too tight," Master Grey said, turning his cold gaze to Aloha. "Relax slightly, very slightly."

He watched her for a long moment, then turned his gaze back to Emily. "It has been a month since we last spoke," he said. "Do you recall what I said?"

Emily nodded, looking down at the floor.

"Look me in the eye," Master Gray ordered. "Do you recall what I said?"

"Yes, sir," Emily said. It was easier to look at the Gorgon, snakes and all, than it was to raise her eyes to meet Master Grey's. "I remember what you said."

"Good," Master Grey said.

He clasped his hands behind him, never taking his eyes off her face. "The two of you are in an odd position, as you should be able to understand for yourself," he said. "On one hand, you have passed both years of Martial Magic at Whitehall; on the other, you need more experience - and to graduate - before you can take up an apprenticeship."

"The Grandmaster said that," Emily said.

Master Grey scowled at her. "One demerit for interrupting me," he snapped.

Emily blinked. *A demerit?*

"I will therefore be concentrating on building up the military and self-defense skills you both need," Master Grey continued, resuming his speech. "You will be taught some skills which are rarely taught outside apprenticeships, but you will also be introduced to concepts that are not covered in your selected classes, purely because of their military value. *And* you will be doing a great deal of physical exercise."

He paused, then went on in a decidedly nasty tone of voice. "Each demerit will be paid for, young ladies, with an hour of physical exercise," he informed them. "I expect each demerit to be worked off within the next few days. Should you build up five demerits without paying them off, there will be a harsher punishment in store. I was intending to explain this to you later, but as one of you has already managed to earn a demerit..."

Emily flushed, looking back down at the floor.

"Look me in the eye, Lady Emily," Master Grey repeated, tartly. "You must learn to present yourself as a confident person, no matter what you're feeling inside. Far too many little tragedies might have been avoided if the victim had looked able and willing to defend herself."

He'd read the reports, Emily realized, and probably her school records too. Lady Barb had made the same observation, the day after Hodge had tried to rape her. If she'd looked more confident, she'd told Emily, Hodge might have known better than to try to attack her - or anyone. And maybe the Ashworths and Ashfalls would have thought better of allowing themselves to come to the brink of open war in her territory.

And if he'd read her school records, she wondered, what else did he know about her?

Master Grey peered at her, then stepped backwards. "You will report to the Armory after lunch on Tuesday and Thursday," he added, coldly. "I will not accept any excuses for lateness; if you happen to be in a sickbed, bring that sickbed with you. Do you understand me?"

"Yes, sir," Aloha said.

Emily echoed her a moment later. Her friend seemed almost enchanted...but then, Aloha had always thrived on challenges. Master Grey might come across as a bloody-minded asshole to her, yet he was also someone at the top of his game, someone who could actually teach her how to expand her skills. Emily understood...but she also wished it had been someone - anyone - else. She had the nasty feeling that Master Grey's bite was a *lot* worse than his bark.

"We will be using that time to carry out practical exercises," Master Grey informed them. "I expect you to wear standard uniforms for Martial Magic, not your robes or anything you might wear outside class. You *will* be worked hard.

"In addition, you will be set homework each week, which I will expect you to complete and hand in on schedule. You will need access to the military annexe of the library, for which I have made arrangements with Lady Aliya. Do *not* try to take any of those books out of the library without special permission. Some of them are quite rare and valuable. Failure to hand in your homework on time will not go unpunished."

Of course not, Emily thought, sarcastically. Her teachers on Earth hadn't given a damn if she completed her homework or not, but Whitehall's tutors were quite prepared to issue punishment exercises, to be completed in detention, for anyone who failed to do their work outside class. *He's just looking for an excuse to punish us.*

"This is a rare opportunity for you - for anyone," Master Grey concluded. "I don't think I have to tell you just how few students are given personalized training. The Grandmaster, I believe, will have told you what advantages you can expect from these sessions. A student who does well, here and now, will complete an apprentice-ship far quicker than the average apprentice. Even your former boyfriend" - he eyed Emily darkly - "took two years to complete his apprenticeship."

Emily flushed. Jade might have asked her to marry him, and she thought he'd meant well, but it wouldn't have worked out. He was decent, but he was far too forceful and he wouldn't have given her any time to herself. Alassa and he made a far better couple. It had stung, when she'd heard they'd become engaged, yet she didn't begrudge them their happiness. Alassa deserved someone who not only challenged her, but watched her back.

"Good," Master Grey said. "You kept your eyes on me, this time."

He watched her for a long moment, then smiled. "With that in mind, remember this: I have no obligation to teach you and, if you act badly, I will have no hesitation in evicting you from the lessons. The Grandmaster cannot *force* me to take you on, not like this. If I decide you cannot be taught in this hybrid format, you will not be taught. Do you understand me?"

"Yes, sir," Emily said. It crossed her mind that she could convince him to kick her out, but Aloha would be furious. "I do understand."

"Glad to hear it," Master Grey said, once Aloha had echoed Emily. "You will report to the Armory, after lunch, on Thursday for your first lesson. I suggest" - his voice hardened - "that you recall what you *might* have been taught about eating before intensive physical activity. If you are late, you will regret it."

He reached into a hidden pocket and produced another sheaf of papers. "These papers discuss potential careers in the military, almost all of them relating to combat sorcery in all of its forms," he added. "I do not believe that either of you are suited to non-magical positions in the fighting forces."

Emily felt Aloha stiffen beside her, but - for once - she found herself in agreement with Master Grey.

"I will not, thanks be to all the gods, offer you any career counseling," Master Grey continued, as he passed her the first sheaf of papers. "Should you wish it, speak to Sergeant Miles, who will be happy to advise you. Bear in mind that applications for apprenticeships do not have to be submitted until the end of Fifth Year, so you do have some time to make up your minds."

He paused. "Do you have any questions?"

"Yes, sir," Aloha said. "What will you be doing when you are not teaching us?"

"Paperwork," Master Grey said, bluntly.

So you won't be working with Sergeant Miles and the other Martial Magic students, Emily thought, feeling a flicker of despair. *You'll only have to worry about making our lives miserable.*

Aloha nodded. "And are we allowed to ask you questions?"

"If they're valid questions," Master Grey said. "Waste my time, just once, and you will regret it."

Emily nodded. *That*, at least, wasn't an uncommon attitude at Whitehall. Help might be provided, if a student needed it, but only after the student had become well and truly stuck. A tutor who felt his time had been deliberately wasted wouldn't take it very well.

Master Grey cleared his throat. "Lady Emily? Do you have any questions?"

Emily met his eyes...and fought down the urge to take a step backwards. "No, sir."

"Good," Master Grey said. He looked at Aloha, then back at Emily. "I have been assigned an office next to the Armory. Should you think of any questions - *valid* questions - you may find me there, during the school day. I will be residing in Dragon's Den at night."

He paused, as if he was waiting to see if they were going to ask any questions, then smiled coldly.

"You are dismissed," he said, quietly. "I will see you on Thursday. *Do not* be late."

Emily nodded, then turned and hurried out of the office. Aloha followed her, her dark face glowing with excitement. *She* was happy, but it was hard for Emily not to feel a pang of jealousy, mixed with fear. If she'd been injured a dozen times with Sergeant Miles supervising, a man who liked her, who knew what would happen when Master Grey took the helm? She found herself breathing hard as the door closed behind them, as if she was on the verge of a panic attack. Why hadn't anyone *warned* her?

"Emily?" Aloha said. Her voice sounded tinny, as if it were coming from a far distance. "Emily? Are you all right?"

"No," Emily said. She felt sick...she swallowed hard, cursing the porridge she'd had for breakfast. Maybe she shouldn't have eaten at all. "I..."

Aloha caught her arm. "Do you want me to carry you to the infirmary?"

"*No*," Emily said, shaking her head violently. Hair spilled out of her neat ponytail and over her eyes. "I don't. I..."

"I should," Aloha said. She half-pulled Emily into a sideroom, then closed the door firmly and erected a privacy ward. "Sit down and take several deep breaths."

Emily forced herself to calm down, trying to understand her feelings. Master Grey scared her...but so had Sergeant Harkin, once, and she'd never had such a reaction to *him*! Indeed, she'd almost come to think of the sergeant as a father figure before his untimely death. But Master Grey...she felt her body starting to shake again, no matter how hard she tried to calm herself and focus her thoughts. That damned Nightmare Hex had brought far too much bubbling out of the back of her mind.

But you're not scared of your stepfather any longer, she told herself. *Why are you scared of Master Grey?*

"I need you to tell me what's wrong," Aloha said. The excited light was gone from her eyes, replaced by concern. "Tell me or I call Lady Barb."

"That's not fair," Emily muttered, resentfully.

"All's fair in love, war and magical research," Aloha countered. She knelt down next to Emily and wrapped an arm around her shoulders. "What *happened* in there?"

"He hates me," Emily confessed. It wasn't something she wanted to talk about, but Aloha wasn't giving her a choice. "He...he thinks I'm like...like my father."

"Quite a few people think that," Aloha observed.

"He hates me," Emily repeated.

"You certainly had quite a bad reaction to him," Aloha agreed. "But I don't think he actually *hates* you. Why would he have taken time out of his schedule to teach us if he hated you?"

"Maybe he just wanted to teach *you*," Emily said. She could understand why, too. Aloha was brilliant; she'd make a fine apprentice, then a mistress in her own right. Master Grey could really make something of her, if he wished. "Maybe the Grandmaster just insisted on adding me to the list."

Aloha snorted. "You're the Necromancer's Bane," she said, sarcastically. "Who *wouldn't* want a chance to call you their apprentice?"

"I don't know," Emily said. Surely it could have been Sergeant Miles? Or Lady Barb? Or someone with no history with her at all? Why a man who hated the very ground she walked on, who considered her a national menace? "I..."

She gritted her teeth, then forced herself to calm down. Her robes were drenched in sweat; she'd have to go back to the bedroom and shower before lunchtime, then Healing. There would be a chance to talk to Lady Barb afterwards, she was sure. Lady Barb was her Advisor, after all. She might be able to offer useful advice.

"Emily," Aloha said slowly, "I think you're panicking over nothing. They wouldn't have let him in the school if they thought he was dangerous."

"I know," Emily said. "But I..."

"I didn't like Mistress Irene, either," Aloha admitted. "She was too strict, too ready to resort to punishment if someone didn't listen. But she taught me a great deal about how to do charms. Even now, I still dislike her, but she's someone I can *learn* from."

Emily nodded in silent understanding. Aloha had worked for her genius, for the brilliance the tutors feted; she'd worked so hard, she'd been allowed to enter Martial Magic in her Second Year. Emily still shuddered at the thought of the argument they'd had, back when *she'd* been pushed into Martial Magic in her *First* Year. Aloha had threatened her with a fate worse than death if she let the side down. She hadn't been the only one.

"You can learn from Master Grey too," Aloha added. "Even if he doesn't like you, and he clearly has some doubts about you, you can still learn from him."

And if I don't, Emily thought, *you'll be mad at me.*

She swallowed, then rose to her feet. "I'll do my best," she said, looking at the papers in her hand. She'd clenched her fist so hard that they were crumpled, almost torn, but they were still readable. "Thank you."

"Don't mention it," Aloha said. "*Ever.*"

Chapter Eight

EMILY STEPPED THROUGH THE DOOR INTO THE HEALING CLASSROOM AND STOPPED DEAD AS she took in the scene. Lady Barb had changed everything, again. Instead of the neat rows of chairs and tables, all facing the front of the class, the chairs and tables had been drawn into a circle, surrounding the central table. The walls were covered, once again, with drawings of human anatomy, while two skeletons hung from the ceiling. Emily eyed them nervously, remembering Shadye's servants, but forced herself to relax. Lady Barb was hardly the kind of person to be experimenting with Death Magics.

"Be seated," Lady Barb ordered. She was seated behind a desk, wearing an expression of disapproval as she worked through her notes. She would have had the Second Years earlier, Emily recalled; boys and girls who were just trying her class before deciding if they wanted to commit themselves to a year of study. Half of them probably wouldn't return after the first couple of days. "We have a lot of ground to cover and not much time."

Emily nodded - thankfully, Healing was her first and only class of the day - and took a seat in the middle of the room. Moments later, Alassa and Imaiqah hurried in, followed by the Gorgon and Melissa. Melissa sat at the opposite side of the room, not entirely to Emily's surprise, although there seemed to be a new distance between her and her former cronies. They'd all come from magical families and, now that Melissa had been disowned, probably had orders not to remain her friend. Emily felt a brief stab of pity, then looked away. Melissa wouldn't want anything from her, not when she already owed Emily so much.

"Missed you at dinner," Alassa said, softly. "Where were you?"

"I ate first," Emily said. She'd also showered and changed - and Alassa, who was more perceptive than most people gave her credit for, would probably have noticed her disheveled appearance after visiting the Grandmaster's office. "Talk about it later, all right?"

The classroom filled quickly, but there was plenty of room for everyone. Only a dozen students had stuck around to take Fourth Year Healing, even though Emily definitely recalled having twice that number in Third Year. It was the hardest course in Whitehall, though; it was quite possible that the other students had failed or had been advised to repeat Third Year before moving on to the next level. She opened her desk, retrieved the latest set of textbooks, and glanced at them while Lady Barb counted down the final moments. The books seemed to cover more advanced healing spells than anything she'd seen before, as well as a number of non-magical techniques.

I wonder if I was the only one who went on walkabout after Second Year, Emily thought, looking at the class. Alassa and Imaiqah had gone back to Zangaria, the Gorgon to the desert...but what about the others? She'd been taken to the Cairngorms, so she could see the world and what might be required of a Healer; the others could easily have had the same experience, if in a different place. *They might have tried to show us all what it was like to be a Healer.*

"Well," Lady Barb said. She rose to her feet, a thin smile on her face. "It's the start of class and two people are missing?"

Emily heard the sounds of running footsteps, then turned her head to stare as Tam and Penelope, their faces flushed, practically threw themselves through the door in an attempt to beat the clock. Lady Barb scowled at them, pointed a long finger at their chairs, and nodded at the door. It slammed closed and locked with an audible click.

"For future reference," she said, "the doors will be locked at the precise moment the class starts. Anyone who happens to arrive late, as I am *sure* I have told you before, can report to the Warden and then engage in private study. Repeated lateness will result in the person responsible being dismissed from the class. They will probably not be allowed to retake Healing next year."

She strode back to the table and stood, clasping her hands behind her back in a decidedly military manner. "The only reason I am being merciful now" - she threw Tam and Penelope a sharp glance that made them cringe - "is because I have a great deal of material to cover with you. By the end of this term, you will need to make choices and I, as your tutor, need to ensure you have the knowledge you need to *make* those choices.

"Some of you will not study Healing after this year," she continued. "You will be allowed to add Healing qualifications to your name, should you pass the exams, but you will not be ranked a full-fledged Healer. Those of you who *do* wish to move on to become a Healer will be expected to take the oaths at the start of Fifth Year, then spend two years preparing for an apprenticeship and another year - at least - as an apprentice, before being unleashed upon the world. I should remind you, in case you missed it when you read the briefing notes, that Healing oaths are permanent. You will still be bound by them even if you flunk out of Fifth Year.

"The oaths will be administered by a Quorum of Healers who will visit Whitehall at the start of your Fifth Year. They will also ask you a number of searching questions while you are under the influence of various truth spells and potions. Should they find something that disqualifies you from becoming a Healer, they will refuse to consider you as a potential candidate. I am obliged to point out, for the record, that while confidentiality is included in the oaths, a person denied a chance to study will raise eyebrows."

People will start wondering why, Emily thought.

Lady Barb opened a drawer and removed a handful of packets. "These contain an outline of the oaths, an outline of the questions they will ask you and details concerning your next two years of lessons, should you decide to continue," she said, handing them out one by one. "It is no shame to decide you cannot go any further, but if you are unlikely to be accepted there is no point in going for the oaths. Read these papers now - I am required to certify you actually held them in your hands - and then ask any questions, should you wish to do so."

Because if we don't read them, it's our fault, Emily thought, as she opened the packet. There were only a handful of papers inside. *You don't get blamed for our stupidity, just for not giving us the option to learn.*

She pulled out the first page and skimmed it. It was a brief outline of the Fifth and Sixth Year Healing classes, covering topics from curse removal - she'd already done *some* curse removal - to mundane healing methods and surgery. It looked as though any prospective Healers would spend half of each week in class, or out on field trips. A number of items mentioned on the list were completely unfamiliar, although a couple did jog her memory. She resolved to use a memory charm to dig up the thought later, and moved on to the second paper.

"I can't qualify," Alassa said. "I'm sworn to my father."

Emily nodded, scanning the second paper quickly. A prospective Healer had to separate himself from any formal obligations to his family, ranging from accepting debts and inheritances to carrying on a family feud. She couldn't see many children from magical families accepting the oaths, unless there were plenty of potential replacements. Alassa, an only child, couldn't abandon King Randor and Zangaria.

"You can still complete this year," Emily reminded her. She'd had only one year of training when she'd gone to the Cairngorms, but she'd managed to make herself useful. "It might be helpful in later life."

"I don't think I'll have time to minister to the ill," Alassa said.

"It might make you very popular," Imaiqah said from the other side. "Helping..."

Lady Barb cleared her throat. "Am I interrupting something?"

Imaiqah, wisely, shook her head, and looked back at her packet. Emily smiled to herself and checked the third sheet of parchment. A Healer was sworn to do everything in his power to save lives, to forsake all debts that might otherwise have been incurred, not to take sides in political disputes, to keep the secrets of rich and poor alike...and not, under any circumstances, to use their powers for ill. The explanatory notes below the oath itself warned that a Healer could not kill, save in direct self-defense, and even then the oaths might kill them if there were any other options. Emily frowned, then looked up at Lady Barb. Surely *she'd* killed in the past and she was still alive...

She shook her head, putting the question aside for later, and picked up the fourth sheet. It was crisp and clear, covering the questions that would be asked of any prospective candidate, starting with a warning that anyone who couldn't give the proper answer would summarily be evicted from the class. Emily skimmed it and swore inwardly. The spells Aurelius had taught her, back in Mountaintop, would automatically disqualify her from taking the oaths, even though she'd never used them. Apparently, reading between the lines, she was only meant to learn them *after* taking the oaths.

Because if I spent half my power in saving a life, the person I saved would owe me a considerable debt, she thought, numbly. Lady Barb was going to be disappointed, if she'd thought Emily would go on to be a Healer. She knew a spell that induced a form of cancer that killed within seconds, administered through bodily contact, and another that worked through sexual intercourse and did far worse than kill the victim outright. *Those spells can be perverted far too easily.*

Lady Barb tapped the table, meaningfully. Emily jumped.

"You should all have had a chance to read the important parts," Lady Barb said. "Do you have any questions?"

"Yes," Tam said. "What happens if I decided to leave the course halfway through?"

"You'd still be bound by the oaths," Lady Barb said, curtly.

Emily swallowed. Healers might do good, but they also lived very *restricted* lives. A Healer couldn't do anything, apart from Healing. There could be no involvement in local politics, even something as minor as suggesting the introduction of proper sanitation or not taxing peasant villages so highly their inhabitants had far too little to eat. A Healer could fix the damage, if a wife was beaten into a bloody pulp, but not do anything to the husband, no matter his crimes.

And if you took the oaths and then failed, she thought, *you'd still be stuck.*

Lady Barb's gaze swept the room. "A Healer can do great good - or great evil," she warned, her voice softening slightly. "In order to learn how to *heal*, you have to learn how to *kill*; you have to learn how to inflict pain and suffering on the human body. Those oaths are the only thing preventing you from becoming monsters, should you become detached from the realities of life - and many Healers do. Once you start on this path, you will be committed."

She paused. "I won't say it isn't a rewarding life," she added. "You will save countless people from injuries and curses that would prove fatal. You'll watch as newborn children are brought into the world, children who would have died in the womb were it not for you. You will pass through a community, then leave, knowing that everyone behind you is healthier than they were when you arrived. Healers know the satisfaction of doing nothing but good."

Emily felt almost wistful, just for a moment, before dismissing the thought. It wasn't something she'd want, not really; she'd enjoyed part of her time in the Cairngorms, but there had been too many horrors for her to be comfortable working their permanently. A Healer could *heal*, perhaps, yet he could do nothing about the cause of the problem. *She* could, if she didn't take the oaths.

"You will have your career sessions later in the month, I believe," Lady Barb said. "By then, I expect you to decide if you want to go on to become a Healer or not. If you do, check and double-check the requirements, then take the forms with you to the career adviser. They will go through everything with you, then help you to apply. Regardless..."

She looked from face to face before she continued. "This year, there will be more practical work than ever before," she explained. "There will be field trips to both Dragon's Den and the Halfway House, where some of the worst curse victims are housed while Healers search for a cure or a counter-curse. You will see some of the greatest horrors the human mind, armed with magic, is capable of producing. Some of you, I think, will be unable to tolerate the encounter, even under controlled conditions. I do not advise anyone who feels that way to try to continue to Fifth Year."

Emily nodded. *That* was understandable.

"Those field trips will probably include only three or four of you at a time," Lady Barb added, curtly. "While I'm gone, classes will be supervised by Mistress Kyla, Whitehall's Healer. I suggest, very strongly, that you use the opportunity to question her about her job and the problems she faces here. I also suggest you don't cause problems for her. She takes the post far more seriously than myself.

"And that," she concluded, "leads to a final point.

"In Dragon's Den, you will be assisting people who have *volunteered* to allow you to examine them. Pregnant women, giving birth; men who have injured themselves and require the services of a Healer to regain full use of their bodies; children born with deformities that make it impossible for them to have a normal life...they have all *volunteered* to be examined and worked on by you. We don't charge anyone for the service, nor do we pay them.

"Understand this: if any of you, and I mean *any* of you, mocks them, or treats them as anything other than decent people, you will regret it. Whatever happened to them, be it tragic or funny, I expect you to be professional at all times. You will not mock, you will not judge, you will not dispense unwanted advice. If you break this rule, you will not be allowed to take part in any more field trips and it will be reported to the Quorum of Healers. There is a very strong chance they will deny you the chance to enter Fifth Year."

She scowled. "I may also put you in the stocks for the rest of the day," she added. "A few hours of people throwing rotten vegetables at you would probably teach you a lesson, don't you think?"

Emily winced, inwardly. Lady Barb had a point. She would have hated to be gawked at by a handful of trainees while someone was trying to heal her...and to have those trainees mock her would be more than she could bear. But Lady Barb hadn't issued such a warning while they'd been in the Cairngorms. Had she assumed Emily wouldn't be foolish enough to mock the people they were trying to help, or had she planned to cut Emily off the moment she started?

And it would be worse if I were giving birth, she thought. She'd seen a woman give birth in the Cairngorms, a woman who might have lost the baby without the two magicians. *I'd hate to be stared at by a pair of male magicians.*

"We will go through the procedures for visiting both Dragon's Den and the Halfway House later, once we have a visiting schedule," Lady Barb said. "I will be giving priority to those who plan to take the oaths and go on to Fifth Year. Are there any final questions?"

Melissa raised a hand. "If we're going to the Halfway House," she said, "is there any actual danger?"

"There *may* be some danger," Lady Barb said. "Some of the cursed can behave unpredictably, others are cursed in a manner deliberately designed to harm or kill anyone who tackles the curse. You will be warned before meeting any truly dangerous patients and talked through security precautions. If you do feel yourself to be in any danger, you are authorized to use magic to escape."

Alassa coughed. "If the curses cannot be removed," she asked, "why are they still held at the Halfway House?"

"The Healers in charge have not given up on removing the curses," Lady Barb said. "Bear in mind that the only other option, with some of the patients, is to kill them. Indeed, in some cases it might be a mercy."

But a Healer cannot kill, not even to put someone out of his misery, Emily thought, glancing down at the oath and its ramifications. *The Halfway House is stuck with patients it can't cure, kill or release.*

There was a long pause. "You may come to me at any moment if you wish to discuss the issue further," Lady Barb concluded. She made a show of looking at the clock. "And now, unless there are any more questions, we will make good use of the remaining time by reviewing the material we covered in Third Year."

The class groaned. "Penelope," Lady Barb said. "Why is it dangerous to offer Sleeping Potion to a victim of the Night Terror Hex?"

Penelope gulped. "Because...because it actually enhances the effects of the hex," she said, desperately. "The victim will fall further into its clutches."

"Very good," Lady Barb said, without a trace of irony. "Tam. Why can't you use a simple canceling charm on the victim of a compulsion curse?"

"Because the curse might react badly unless the charm is applied properly," Tam said. "I..."

"Close enough," Lady Barb said, "but do a little additional reading. The curse might only be partly cancelled, causing mental problems for the victim."

Emily sighed and glanced at her watch. There was only half an hour to go before the end of class, but it was going to feel longer. Much longer.

And then she really needed to talk to Lady Barb.

Chapter Nine

E MILY," LADY BARB SAID WHEN THE CLASS CAME TO AN END. "STAY BEHIND A MOMENT."

Emily nodded, relieved. "I'll meet you in the bedroom," she muttered to Alassa. "You can tell me about your day."

"Of course," Alassa said. Her blue eyes glimmered with concern. "Take care of yourself, all right?"

Emily nodded, and waited for the classroom to empty. Lady Barb relocked the door as soon as Melissa had left - she'd hung around long enough for Emily to suspect she wanted to talk to Lady Barb, too - and led Emily through a door into a sideroom. Inside, there was a pair of comfortable chairs, a table, and a pot of steaming liquid. Lady Barb motioned for Emily to sit, then poured a couple of mugs of Kava. Emily took hers and sipped gratefully.

"It's going to be a very busy year for me," Lady Barb said, bluntly. "I may have less time for you than you might have hoped. If the Grandmaster hadn't needed a second tutor at such short notice..."

She shrugged, and sat facing Emily. "As your adviser, it is my duty to discuss your career options with you before you go to your career session," she added. "I should tell you, right now, that you probably wouldn't make a good Healer."

Emily blinked, stung. "Why not?"

"A Healer requires a certain degree of empathy," Lady Barb said, flatly. "You're not very good at noticing when someone else is in pain, or feeling *any* strong emotion. I think you could probably master the healing spells - no one would deny you're good with charms - but you'd have problems actually coping with the job. How long did it take you to notice that Alassa and Jade were in love?"

"I had my nose rubbed in it," Emily said, ruefully. In hindsight, it had been alarmingly obvious. "I didn't notice at all."

"Quite," Lady Barb agreed. "There are times when a Healer has to speak to a patient and gently coax them to talk about their problems, some of which are embarrassing and some of which will reflect badly on others. I don't think you have the empathy required to handle the job."

I helped Frieda, Emily thought, mulishly. But how long had it taken her to notice that Frieda was suffering? *And I...*

She recalled everything she'd seen in the Cairngorms and shuddered. Lady Barb was right; she'd either ignore a problem, missing its very existence, or go overboard in trying to fix it.

And you know you can't take the oaths anyway, her own thoughts mocked her. *Why are you trying to stop someone dissuading you from even trying?*

"I do want to finish the year," she temporised. "But I don't think I could become a Healer permanently."

"It *would* be permanent," Lady Barb said, tartly. "That's the point of the oaths."

Emily *looked* at her. Something *clicked* in her mind. "You're not a Healer, are you?"

"They wanted me to become a Healer," Lady Barb said. "I was told I had a natural talent for Healing. It wasn't true, of course. I merely had my mother teaching me the basics long before my father sent me to Whitehall. By the time I finished my Fourth Year, the pressure to become a Healer was almost overpowering. My tutor even offered to take me on walkabout, just as I took you, to see that the job needed doing."

"I see," Emily said. "What happened?"

Lady Barb met her eyes. "The third village we visited was dominated by an old crone, a witch with a handful of spells and infinite malice. The day after we arrived, she blinded a young girl for an imaginary offense. Can you imagine what it would be like, growing up in a tiny village, unable to see anything?"

Emily shuddered. The villagers in the Cairngorms hadn't been able to provide for cripples, not when there was barely enough to feed the men and women who did the hard work of tending to their tiny farms and growing food. If the girl had been lucky, she would have been bought by someone who needed a wife and didn't care about her blindness; if she had been unlucky...Emily shook her head, cursing silently. There was no such thing as a *happy* ending for a cripple in the mountains.

"The spell was easy to break," Lady Barb said. "I broke it. I freed the girl...and then I hunted down the witch. By the time my tutor caught up with me, I had flayed the skin from her bones, using spells my father had taught me to keep her alive. The moment the spells broke, the witch died in agony. My tutor...quietly understood, I think. She took me straight back to Whitehall, and nothing else was said about me becoming a Healer."

"Because you'd killed someone in cold blood," Emily said.

"It was very hot blood," Lady Barb said. "I wanted the witch to *suffer.*"

She shrugged. "Emily, Healers can only *heal*," she said. "I've known Healers who were forced by their oaths to heal people who had been tortured, so the torturers could start all over again. Or keep quiet about people committing truly ghastly acts. Or...

"I wanted to do more than just heal," she concluded. "And I think that's true of you too."

Emily nodded, slowly. She understood just how the younger Lady Barb had felt, even if she'd grown harder and more cynical between then and their first meeting. Someone preying on the villagers could not be tolerated, not when there was no one who could help her victims.

"It is," she said. "But I am still going to try to pass Fourth Year."

"So you should," Lady Barb said.

Emily took a breath. "Can I ask you about something else?"

"Master Grey," Lady Barb said. It wasn't a question. "I believe he volunteered for the job."

"Oh," Emily said. "Why?"

Lady Barb smiled. "Why did he want the job, or why did the Grandmaster accept his application?"

"Both," Emily said.

"I have no idea why he wanted the job," Lady Barb said. "It isn't a post that will allow him to claim a permanent tie to you - or Aloha. He may expect you to apprentice with him formally, at the end of Sixth Year, but that would be rare. We normally prefer to have someone apprentice with a master they haven't met beforehand, just so they start with a blank slate."

"Master Grey doesn't have a blank slate," Emily muttered. "He hates me. And...and I almost had a panic attack."

Lady Barb eyed her for a long moment. "You *did* face a Nightmare Hex yesterday," she reminded her, dryly. "They do tend to dig up long-buried feelings and memories."

Emily nodded. She would have liked to believe that was true, but...there was a part of her that couldn't help feeling worried, as if Master Grey had darker ambitions than merely supervising two semi-apprentices for a year. The same nagging fear that overshadowed her memories of her stepfather pulsed over Master Grey, the sensation that he might not do something today, but he *would* one day.

"As for why the Grandmaster accepted him," Lady Barb continued, "you *do* realize that he *is* a practiced combat sorcerer with a proven track record of turning out above-average apprentices? Jade is merely the latest in a long line of students who owe him for their training. And he's a champion duelist as well. You could do worse, much worse, for a tutor."

"Dueling is barbaric," Emily muttered. She'd seen Master Grey in action, after the end of Second Year. He'd insisted that anyone who challenged him had to fight to the death, just to keep the number of challenges down. And he'd never even *looked* like losing. "And he hates me..."

"I don't think he actually *hates* you," Lady Barb said, curtly. "His report from the Faire did make interesting reading - he called you grossly irresponsible no less than seven times - but I don't think he hates you. He may feel that *someone* has to take you in hand and teach you some common sense before your luck runs out."

Emily cringed. "Why couldn't it have been you?"

"I like you too much," Lady Barb said.

Emily started. Lady Barb liked her *too much?*

The older woman reached out and patted Emily's shoulder. "You told me you thought of me as a mother," she said. "Will you take some motherly advice?"

"That isn't fair," Emily mumbled.

"All's fair in love and war," Lady Barb said. She smiled, tightly. "Will you take some advice?"

"Yes, please," Emily said.

"The world is full of assholes," Lady Barb said. "You will have to meet and deal with people who will be abrasive, or unpleasant, or outright hate you because of what you've done, the titles you hold, or merely because they just don't like your face. I don't think you have the option of vanishing into your castle and hiding, just because you're afraid of confrontation, not given the position you hold. You need to learn how to cope with people who don't like you."

"And the Grandmaster selected Master Grey," Emily mused, "because he *knew* we disliked each other?"

"It's a possibility," Lady Barb said. "Did you listen to his speech, earlier today?"

Emily nodded, once.

"We try to turn out magicians who can handle anything without losing control," Lady Barb said, softly. "Having a hard time with Master Grey, here and now, will be better than having a hard time outside Whitehall. He may push you to the limit, he may force you to carry on no matter the pain, but he won't kill you."

"But I had a panic attack when I saw him," Emily protested.

"Then you need to work to overcome it," Lady Barb said. "Do you realize that could be a dangerous weakness?"

She sighed, looking down at her hands. "You are growing in power every year - even without the battery," she added. "In three years, you will be let loose upon the world. A person with the perceptiveness to understand your weaknesses could easily use them against you, even if they don't have magic themselves. I've seen people dominated by others who should, on the surface, be far weaker than them. You could wind up the same way."

Emily shuddered. "I wouldn't..."

"It's easy to say that," Lady Barb said. "But is it actually true?" She smiled, but it didn't touch her eyes. "Are you familiar with the Duchy of Bothell?"

"No," Emily said. It was somewhere to the south of Zangaria, if she recalled correctly, but she'd never visited. Alassa's procession through the Allied Lands hadn't bothered to stop at such a minor state. "Why?"

"I was there three years ago, back when I was working for King Randor," Lady Barb said, softly. "The Duke himself died six years ago, leaving his daughter on the throne. She was the undisputed ruler of the duchy, but she was ruled by her husband, someone she'd met and married just after her father died. He was horrible to her, Emily, even though a single word from her could have had him beheaded. Instead, she just... did as she was told.

"You could wind up just like her, if you're not careful. Better to learn how to deal with assholes here and now, where you have friends and advisers, than out in the wider world."

"I know," Emily said, miserably. Her stepfather had held a similar influence over her early life. "Can't I just stay in Whitehall for the rest of my life?"

"It depends," Lady Barb said, tartly. "Do you want to give up Cockatrice and everything you've created?"

"I think I'm just going to put researcher down as my planned career," Emily said. She didn't want to think about the prospect of abandoning Cockatrice. "I could research in my spare time."

"You could always point out that you will probably spend most of your time at Cockatrice," Lady Barb offered. "I doubt Alassa's session will be anything more than a pleasant chat, assuming she goes at all. But they may want you to consider serving the Allied Lands in other ways. You would probably make a good Mediator."

Emily blinked. She hadn't considered the possibility.

"It's a worthwhile job," Lady Barb added. "And you have the power, courage and connections to see it through."

"I'll look it up," Emily said. "Can I pick your brains about it later?"

"Of course," Lady Barb said. "But then, you could also ask Master Grey. He would be happy to talk to you about it."

Emily rather doubted it. "I'd prefer to talk to you," she said. "Really..."

"And I will send you to Master Grey," Lady Barb said, sharply. "You *do* have to learn how to cope with assholes, Emily, and one of my motherly duties involves pushing you to learn how to handle them."

She sighed. "Look at it this way," she added. "Spend the next term learning from him. If it really turns bad, if it really fails, I will raise the issue with the Grandmaster. He will not be pleased, of course, and nor will I, but we may be able to find another option."

"Oh," Emily said.

She swallowed, thinking hard. Cold logic told her Lady Barb was right. She *did* need to learn to handle people like Master Grey, people who would hate and resent her. But emotionally...she didn't even want to *think* about facing him. He reminded her far too much of her stepfather for her to be rational about him...

Which was the point, wasn't it?

"I'll do my best," she promised. She would force herself to remember, time and time again, that Master Grey was *not* her stepfather until she actually believed it. And she would try to go to his lessons with an open mind. Aloha was right. Master Grey could actually teach them something new. "But what if -"

"Look at it this way," Lady Barb said. "Are you actually going to let him win?"

Emily shook her head, slowly. Master Grey disliked her; worse, he thought she was grossly irresponsible. She was damned if she was proving him right.

"Good," Lady Barb said. "That's a much better attitude."

She finished her Kava and leaned forward. "Have you arranged a working meeting with Caleb yet?"

"Not yet," Emily said. In all the excitement, it was something she'd overlooked. She pulled her timetable out of her pocket and glanced at it. "I was thinking tomorrow afternoon."

"You'd better remember to tell *him* that," Lady Barb said, dryly. "I'm not going to be taking messages to him for you."

Emily blushed. "Sorry..."

Lady Barb laughed as Emily looked down at her mug. "I'll give you a piece of advice for free, Emily, because you should know it already," she added. "Get started on your project as soon as possible and do as much as you can before classes really start to get tougher, because they will. You know the milestone deadlines?"

Emily nodded. "End of the first term, start of the third term."

"Good," Lady Barb said. "Missing either of those could cause you to fail."

"Thank you," Emily said. She finished her Kava and stood up. "If I'm not going to become a Healer, will I still have to go on the field trips?"

"I will probably take you to the Halfway House," Lady Barb said. "You've already amassed some experience in the Cairngorms, so there should be no need to take you to Dragon's Den to observe more mundane problems. Still...we will see."

Emily nodded, then turned and walked out of the room and through the classroom back into the corridor. Melissa waited outside, leaning against the stone wall and looking impatient. Emily hesitated, then smiled. Maybe Melissa had been an enemy, once upon a time, but they weren't enemies any longer. And Melissa owed her a considerable debt.

"She should be free now," Emily said. "Are you hoping to become a Healer?"

"It's a possibility," Melissa said. "My family can't object any longer."

She looked awkward, so Emily changed the subject. "How's Markus?"

Melissa smiled. She had always been pretty, but now Emily could see *just* what Markus saw in her. The smile made her face come alive.

"He's fine," she said. "He has a place to stay in Beneficence, but he's going to be coming here every weekend. The Gorgon - you know, my roommate - agreed to let us have the bedroom in exchange for some books I happen to own."

"I'm happy for you," Emily said, and meant it. "Where is she going to sleep?"

"I thought she had an agreement with you," Melissa said. She frowned. "She could sleep on the floor, couldn't she? If she took her blankets?"

"Maybe," Emily said. The Gorgon hadn't asked her - nor, as far as she knew, had she asked Alassa or Imaiqah. Maybe she'd found a boyfriend herself. It wasn't impossible, even if she did look inhuman. "Just don't get in trouble with Madame Beauregard."

"Tell me about it," Melissa said. "She's strict!"

Emily smiled as Melissa stepped into the classroom, then hastily walked back to the dorms, dodging a line of First Year students as she headed up the stairs. They stared at her, awestruck, which made her shake her head in disbelief. If they knew the truth, she was sure, they would be a great deal less impressed.

"Emily," Alassa said, as Emily entered the bedroom. She was wearing trousers and a shirt with a tiny silver button pinned just above her left breast. "You're looking at the new Dorm Monitor for Fourth Year!"

"Well done," Emily said, closing the door behind her. "What sort of powers do you have?"

"Apparently, I'm meant to report any malefactors to Madame Beauregard, if they don't stop misbehaving at once," Alassa said.

"So she can't punish anyone on her own authority," Imaiqah put in. "We're saved."

Emily rolled her eyes and sat down on her bed. "I had a bit of bad news today," she said, "but I'm going to get through it."

"Good," Alassa said. "Now, what *was* it?"

"Master Grey is going to be my tutor for Martial Magic," Emily said.

"Ouch," Alassa said. "Jade says he's tough."

"He is," Emily agreed. "Very tough."

Chapter Ten

I HEAR THAT ALASSA IS DEFINITELY THE DORM MONITOR," CALEB SAID, AS HE ENTERED THE workroom Emily had booked the previous day. "Is that good or bad?"

Emily shrugged. "I don't know yet," she said. "What was the last one like?"

"Chased a couple of us through the corridors, once upon a time," Caleb said. He looked down at his scarred hands. "I didn't stick around long enough to know if they get nastier as the year goes on."

"I suppose they do," Emily said. "They don't have that much power, do they?"

She ran her hand through her hair as she sat down, then looked at the three metal worktables, the wok and the ingredients she'd borrowed from Professor Thande after his introductory class in the morning. He'd insisted on going through safety precautions with her time and time again, pointing out that *Manaskol* was dangerously volatile at the best of times and Caleb, at least, had been seriously injured trying to brew it. Emily had listened carefully, knowing he was right. If Zed hadn't patiently taught her to brew the potion, again and again, she wouldn't be so confident now.

"No, they don't have *that* much power," Caleb said. He placed his bag on the table and started to pull out the mass-produced pieces of spell mosaics. "The worst they can do is report troublemakers to the House Mothers or Fathers."

Emily winced. Alassa would have a choice between doing her duty, which would earn her a reputation as a sneak, or not doing her duty and being punished for failure. It wasn't something Emily would have wanted, not when her natural instinct was to shy away from confrontation. But would she have said no if she'd been asked?

"I'm sure she'll do a good job," she said, instead. "Did you get approval to have the rest of the mosaics produced in Dragon's Den?"

"We'll be responsible for paying for them, but yes," Caleb said. "We have to submit a list of expenses at the end of the year, I think; if they agree we spent the money on items related to the project, they'll give us a refund."

Emily nodded, slowly. "Good," she said. It was almost a shame that Yodel had moved to Cockatrice, but there were other enchanters - and blacksmiths, and wood-carvers - in Dragon's Den. "Have you found any likely candidates?"

"We'll have to go visit the city, probably towards the end of the month," Caleb said. "Unless we can convince the tutors to let us go early..."

"Maybe," Emily said. Fifth and Sixth Year students could visit Dragon's Den at any time, but First to Fourth Years could only go in a set rota. Their first weekend in Dragon's Den, according to the timetable, was two weeks off. "We could *try* to convince them that you really should be in Fifth Year."

"I don't think the Grandmaster would be impressed," Caleb said. "I'm *not* a Fifth Year student."

Emily nodded reluctantly, and started to set up the wok. It had been years since her first lecture, but Professor Thande hadn't hesitated to call out anyone who forgot how to prepare to make a potion, let alone basic safety precautions. She checked the recipe - she doubted she could brew it from memory - and lined up the ingredients in neat little rows. Once she needed to add them, she recalled from painful experience, there would be no time to fetch them from the cupboard.

"I'm not sure how much help I'll be," Caleb said, apologetically. "My hands..."

"Don't worry about it," Emily said. *She* wouldn't have cared to try to brew even a *basic* potion with shaky hands. Adding too much of almost anything would probably lead to an explosion. "Once the *Manaskol* is brewed, I'll need to dab it on the wood very quickly."

"I'll set them up over here," Caleb said. He moved his bag to the second table, starting to pull the pieces of wood and iron out onto the table. Emily couldn't help being reminded of custard creams; a piece of wood on each side, glued together by the *Manaskol*. But the *Manaskol* would hold the spell components, just ready and raring to go. "How long should this take?"

"Not long," Emily said. She pulled her wand from the bag, placed it on the table, and lit the heat under the wok. "I'll get started now."

Alchemy had never been her favorite subject, not when it was sometimes dangerously unpredictable, but she had to admit there was something almost relaxing about putting the ingredients together to create a magical effect. The liquid started to bubble almost at once, then turned a dark golden color as she added more ingredients; moments later, she reached for the wand and used it to stir the brew, watching as magic flowed into the liquid. It started to bubble alarmingly - Emily braced herself, ready to dive beneath the table at the first sign of an impending explosion - and then settled. A sheen of magic shimmered over the wok as she put out the heat and used the wand to part the liquid. It slowly congealed into something resembling glue.

"It's ready," she said.

"You're good at this," Caleb said with open admiration. "I managed to blow myself up."

Emily blushed. "Practice," she said. Whitehall's students were introduced to *Manaskol* in Fourth Year, a year later than Mountaintop's. Caleb had needed to learn to brew the potion very quickly, just so he could use it for himself. Haste, in this case, had led to disaster. "I spent half of Third Year learning to brew it."

"Thank you," Caleb said. "You might have made the difference between success and failure!"

He reached for a brush, picked up a piece of wood and carefully dabbed the *Manaskol* onto the rune carved into it. The *Manaskol* settled quickly; he hastily picked up a second piece of wood and jammed it on top of the first. Emily watched as the glue-like material gummed up, locking the pieces of wood together, smiling as it became clear it had worked.

They now had a working spell mosaic.

"We have one piece," Caleb said. "Can you start putting together the others? Make sure the runes match or...or *something* will happen."

Emily smiled - that *something* was probably *nothing* - and did as she was told. It wasn't easy putting the pieces together, but she kept working on it until she thought she had mastered the skill. Caleb put several more together - his hands shook at one point, causing him to lose his grip on one of the pieces of wood - and turned his attention to the larger pieces of wood, the ones that would have to be carved up once they were stuck together. It wasn't long until they had something that looked like a flattened sandwich.

"We can't use magic to cut them," Caleb said. "I'm going to have to take this one down to the woodcarver and see what he makes of it."

"True," Emily agreed.

She contemplated it for a long moment. *Manaskol* conducted magic. Even something as minor as a charmed blade would react badly when it touched the liquid. How had it been done on Earth? A powered fretsaw would be perfect, but she knew there was no way she could produce one in time to be useful. Unless...she *could* make a very thin blade and try to use it to cut the wood. Or would that count as magic?

"We might be able to make a very thin blade," she said, carefully. Maybe it would be better not to discuss molecules, even though part of her wanted to show off, to impress him. It was only a short step from molecules to atoms and then to something that might split those atoms and release a flash of energy. "But it might just be touched by magic."

"We could probably experiment," Caleb agreed. "Can you bottle the remaining *Manaskol?* I think we'll need more of it in the future."

Emily nodded, carefully pouring the liquid into a charmed bottle. Professor Thande had demonstrated, once, that they were unbreakable by anything short of greater magic. He'd also outlined, in loving detail, just what kind of disasters they could expect by shattering several bottles in close proximity, allowing the contents to mix together. They'd be lucky, he'd concluded, if they survived the experience.

"Done," she said, capping the bottle with the ease of long practice. The golden liquid inside seemed to be shimmering gently, sending waves of light into the room. "It'll be ready when we need it."

"Better make sure no one else takes it," Caleb suggested. "That's worth a small fortune in itself."

"We can always sell it if we end up with too much," Emily agreed. She opened a cupboard, linked it to her magical signature to ensure no one else could open it without permission, and placed the bottle inside. "It's supposed to be good for paying a year's taxes."

"That's true in Beneficence," Caleb said, as she walked back to the table. "Mother brews a big wok every year, then gives it to the Guildsmen. They're always very grateful."

He picked up the first spell mosaic, held it so she could see the rune, and carefully placed it on the table between them. Emily watched as he put together the next five pieces as carefully as if they were part of a simple jigsaw puzzle, without ever quite allowing them to touch. Piece by piece, the runes on the top spelled out a diagram, a flowchart of commands for magic. Emily remembered Mistress Irene's patient lessons, back when she'd first come to Whitehall, and smiled. In some ways, it was like going back to First Year and returning to first principles.

"It's harder to recall how to do this now," Caleb confessed. "Casting spells has become second nature to me."

"Me too," Emily said. Once, she'd had to work her way through the variables before casting the spell; now, casting a spell was largely a matter of instinct. No wonder Basic Charms was such a vital class, she reminded herself. Without a good understanding of the underlying theory of magic, the student would be forever crippled. "But this isn't that different from using a wand."

"It is," Caleb objected. "A wand will only cast the spell embedded in it, unless you overpower the spell and the wand explodes. Here, we can craft the spell and channel magic into the mosaic."

He put the final piece in place and looked up at her. "Does that look suitable?"

Emily walked around to stand beside him, then worked her way through the spell components, one by one. The light spell was one of the simplest spells she'd learned in First Year, yet - with a little bit of work - it could be alarmingly complex. Mistress Irene had taught her that everything from brightness to the light globe's position could be altered, simply by altering the variables within the spell. But she couldn't see anything wrong with Caleb's work.

"I think so," she said. "Nothing should happen if you put them together, not now."

Caleb nodded, carefully assembling the mosaic. It occurred to Emily - too late - that the *Manaskol* might not have dried, that the pieces might remain stuck together. If that had happened, they'd have to make more...she cursed inwardly, and watched to see what would happen. Next time, they'd be more careful.

"There," Caleb said, once the pieces were linked together. "Do you want to do the honors?"

"You can," Emily said. She'd already made the *Manaskol* and besides, the spell mosaics were his idea. "I'll watch from here."

Caleb nodded, and carefully pressed his fingertips against the first piece. Emily closed her eyes for a moment, gathering her senses, opening them again once she felt a flow of magic spilling from Caleb into the wood. There was a long second when nothing happened - she wondered if they'd made a mistake somewhere - and then a light globe shimmered into existence, hanging over the table. Emily took one look and *knew* they'd done something wrong. Instead of the soft light they'd ordered, the light globe was so bright it hurt her eyes and it wobbled erratically on its axis. She covered her eyes hastily as the temperature rose sharply, and yanked Caleb back as the light started to flicker into a color she could only call nasty. And then there was a small explosion on the table as the globe snapped out of existence.

Caleb shoved her to the floor as the table shuddered a second time, blowing pieces of sawdust into the air.

"Drat," Caleb said, as he rolled off her. "I..."

"At least we got something," Emily said, reassuringly. His touch had felt...odd. "We know we're doing *something* right."

She blinked hard - spots danced in front of her eyes - before sitting upright and looking at the mess they'd made. The table seemed intact - it was made of solid iron, after all - but the pieces of wood they'd glued together had been shattered into their component atoms. It was impossible to tell which piece had exploded first, yet it had clearly set off the others. She stood, then frowned. Apart from a small scar to the metal, there was no evidence they'd done *anything* on the table.

"The variables may need to be altered for the mosaic," Caleb said, looking down at his fingertips. "Or maybe I didn't manage to charge them properly."

"Or maybe we used too much *Manaskol*," Emily said. She wasn't sure how they could produce something industry-standard, not with just the two of them, but it should be possible. "Or the power you pumped in was simply too much for the spell."

"That sounds possible," Caleb said, doubtfully.

He sat down at the table and checked his notes. "We spent five years learning how to channel magic through our minds and wards," he said. "How long has it been since we were truly *precise*?"

"Years," Emily agreed. "We should probably rebuild the spell mosaics, then practice with the spell until we only channel the bare minimum of power. Or" - she glanced at the wand, lying next to the wok - "practice with a wand instead."

Caleb shuddered. "Too dangerous, I would have thought," he said. "But it might be workable."

"Maybe we can set up runes to draw excess power away from the spell," Emily offered diffidently. She was fairly sure Professor Thande wouldn't thank them for contaminating one of his workrooms with excess magic. Alchemy was dangerous enough without stray magic disrupting the process. "Even channel it back into the mosaic and keep the spell going..."

"It might work," Caleb said. He scribbled out a spell diagram on a piece of paper, and studied it thoughtfully. "There would probably still be some leakage. Perhaps if we nailed the pieces of wood together?"

"They'd explode under the pressure," Emily said. Pieces of wood flying around would be bad enough, but pieces of metal would be actively dangerous. "Maybe if we piled one set of mosaics on top of another."

"It's something to consider," Caleb agreed. "We'll clean up now, and plot the next stage in the library."

Emily nodded. Together, they cleared up the remains of the wooden tiles and cleaned up the wok before returning it to the alchemy storeroom. Professor Thande was used to losing caldrons and woks, but he wouldn't hesitate to bill them for any damage caused outside the planned lessons. Caleb checked his notes, muttered a duplicating charm, and passed Emily the spare copy. Emily took it gratefully and stuffed it in her pocket, then checked her watch.

"Nearly dinnertime," she said. "Are you coming?"

"I will," Caleb said. He hesitated. "Emily?"

Emily looked up. "Yes?"

Caleb paused, then looked down at the ground. "When do you want to meet again?"

"I've got Martial Magic tomorrow afternoon," Emily said. She had the odd impression that Caleb wanted to say something else. "I normally wind up aching, so shall we say Friday afternoon? That would give us some time to rebuild the spell mosaics and rewrite the spell."

"That would be fine," Caleb said. "What are you doing on the weekend?"

"I don't know," Emily said. The correct answer to that was probably studying, but if she knew Alassa, she would probably be dragged out to the gardens or the playing fields. "What about yourself?"

"I think I may try to get some more wood," Caleb said. "Master Crun said he couldn't get it, but Master Tamer should have a new delivery on Friday. I'll ask him for something harder, something that might stand up better to the abuse we heap on it."

"Good thinking," Emily said.

She finished packing her bag and slung it over her shoulder. "Coming to dinner?"

"I'll see you there," Caleb promised. "I want to take these back to my room before dinner, then look up a few references in the library. I've just had a thought."

Emily nodded, waved goodbye and walked out of the room. It had been fun, putting the experiment together, even if it hadn't worked properly. But once they did manage to get it to work, she was sure, it would be *very* useful. Who knew *what* she could do if she linked a battery to the spell mosaic?

Or those poor students who can figure out how to channel magic, but not to cast spells, she thought. *This could change their lives.*

"Hey, Emily," Frieda called as she walked down to the Dining Hall. "What are you doing this evening?"

"Nothing, yet," Emily said. She knew she should be going through her textbooks - or trying to decipher more of the spellbook Void had given her for a gift - but she didn't feel like doing anything. "You?"

"Come for a walk," Frieda urged. "It's a beautiful day out there."

Emily smiled. "All right," she said. "We'll go for a walk after dinner."

Chapter Eleven

IT HAD BEEN FAR TOO LONG, EMILY DECIDED, SINCE SHE'D SIMPLY WALKED FOR PLEASURE. BUT then, the last person who'd taken her out of Whitehall had been Jade, before he'd gone to study with Master Grey. And it had been snowing when she'd returned to Whitehall for Second Year, a droll reminder that the weather near the castle was always chaotic and completely unpredictable. The hot summer evening might become a raging snowstorm within seconds.

Frieda chatted happily about her classes in Second Year as they walked up the path, keeping a wary eye out for dangerous animals. Emily hadn't seen anything more dangerous than a rabbit when she'd been walking with Jade - and certainly nothing more dangerous than the creature wrapped around her wrist - but she knew to stay alert. If they ran into trouble, it might be hours - or days - before anyone realized they were missing.

"I think it's going to be a harder year," Frieda said. "But those books you insisted I read really helped."

"Glad to hear it," Emily said. She'd listed the textbooks she'd read herself, in Second Year, and advised Frieda to read them over the holidays. "Lady Barb won't be happy if you don't focus your mind and actually work."

Frieda shuddered, theatrically. "You know she told us that the doors would be locked the moment class started? And that anyone who was late would be marked absent for the day?"

"She did that to us too," Emily said. "I don't think she likes being interrupted."

"Yeah," Frieda agreed. She sounded subdued for a long moment. Had she been late on the first day and received a tongue-lashing for it? "But she's a great teacher."

"You'll learn more than you did in First Year," Emily said. "Just remember to put your studies before everything else."

Frieda looked rebellious, her face flushing. "I'm going to be trying out for the Ken team on Saturday," she said, insistently. "Alassa said I could."

"I have no idea how Alassa manages to keep her grades while she spends two days a week drilling the team," Emily said, shaking her head. Alassa's obsession bemused her, but she had to admit it was good for her friend. "Just make sure you don't let your studies suffer while you're having fun."

Frieda snorted and grabbed Emily's arm. "I need to ask you something," she said. "Will you be my adviser?"

"I don't think I can be," Emily said. She hadn't given the subject any consideration. "They'll want a staff member, someone who can speak for you, not an older student."

"You'd be good at advising me," Frieda said. "You already do."

"It's not the same," Emily pointed out. "Lady Barb is old enough to give proper advice, while I'm only two years older than you."

Frieda frowned. "Then who do you suggest?"

"Pick a tutor you respect," Emily advised. She'd selected Lady Barb because the older woman could be abrasive at times, but she'd always given good advice. "Someone who will help you out, if you need it, and also kick you in the ass if necessary."

"Oh," Frieda said. "And how often did Lady Barb kick *you* in the ass?"

"Often enough," Emily said. She looked down at the muddy ground. "I...she was the one urging me to make the best of working with Master Grey."

Frieda cocked her head to one side. "I'm sure you'll do fine," she said. "Zed hated you when you came to Mountaintop, but by the time you left I think he loved you."

"I doubt it," Emily said. She'd made Zed Mountaintop's MageMaster, knowing him to be the best of a bad set of choices. Later, she'd learned that while he'd settled into his role, he wasn't entirely happy about it. "Maybe he respected me, a little, but I don't think he liked me."

"He would have found nastier work for you if he hadn't liked you," Frieda said. "I used to spend hours cleaning cauldrons for him."

Emily winced. Mountaintop had treated Frieda - and the other common-born magicians - as slaves, to all intents and purposes. Frieda had been lucky, very lucky, to be assigned to Emily, who'd helped her and taught her how to use magic properly. The others hadn't been so lucky. She hoped Zed would reform the Shadow system, but in truth she knew the matter was out of her hands.

"I think the Administrator probably told him to behave himself, or else," Emily said, looking down at the bangle on her wrist. Aurelius - the snake's namesake - had been trying to seduce her, to convince her to join his side. He wouldn't have found it any easier if Zed had used his classes as an excuse to humiliate or injure her. "I'm still nervous."

Frieda elbowed her. "You've survived two necromancers," she said. "I'm sure you can survive Master Grey."

"I hope so," Emily said. She was due to meet him tomorrow for the first lesson and, despite her newfound resolve, she still felt an unpleasant sensation in her chest. It felt worse than the first time she'd gone to Martial Magic, with threats from Aloha and a dozen other students ringing in her ears. "It's not going to be easy."

"I suppose," Frieda said. "Have you thought about asking Jade for advice?"

"I wrote to him," Emily said. Jade was in Zangaria, settling into his role as Court Wizard and getting to know his future father-in-law. "I won't hear back for at least a week."

"Use the chat parchment," Frieda suggested. "He'll reply instantly."

"Everyone else will see it too," Emily said. Aloha had been working on ways to make it more secure, but the only way to keep a conversation private between her and Jade was to make two entirely new parchments, bonded to their blood. "I'd prefer to keep it private."

She sighed, inwardly. Even if they had had a private piece of parchment, what could Jade tell her that she didn't already know? Master Grey was tough - and *very* harsh with his apprentices, although they all went on to shining careers. It would be months of torment, even if she emerged stronger at the end. Jade would probably tell her to listen, do what Master Grey said, and *learn*.

"Maybe that would be a bad idea," Frieda teased. "Who knows what Alassa would make of it?"

"I can show her the letter," Emily said, feeling her cheeks heat. What *would* Alassa say if Emily was having private conversations with her fiancé? "That wouldn't be true of a chat parchment."

"You and Jade would have made an awful couple," Frieda said. "I think it would have ended badly."

Emily gave her a sharp look. "And how would you know that?"

Frieda gazed back, mischievous light sparkling in her eyes. "I don't need to jump off a cliff or try to levitate myself in the air to know it would be a bad idea," she said. "You're a studious girl and he's a very physical man. He'd get on better with Alassa."

"He *is* getting on better with Alassa," Emily said. "They're going to get married next year, remember? Imaiqah will be Maid of Honor."

"That should have been you," Frieda said. "You're the most important noble-woman in Zangaria."

Emily shook her head. "I got into one mess by not checking it out carefully before agreeing," she said. It had been careless, as Lady Barb - and Master Grey - had pointed out, several times. "I'm not going to go through that again."

"But it still should be you," Frieda insisted. She ran her hand through her dark hair. "Won't some people see it as Alassa insulting you?"

"Probably," Emily said. "I *was* asked."

She shook her head, again. She'd looked up the duties of a Maid of Honor in a Royal Wedding and discovered they were nightmarish. If she'd taken the job, she would have been expected to chaperone Alassa, organize the bridesmaids, plan the bachelorette party - it had a fancy name, but it was basically a bachelorette party - and try to keep various aristocrats from killing each other before the wedding was over. Imaiqah, at least, was much more diplomatic than either Alassa or Emily herself. And, as a close personal friend of the Princess, she would have more clout than her formal title suggested.

"Seems a little unfair," Frieda observed. "It should be you."

"No, thank you," Emily said. "It would be a white elephant of a reward."

Frieda blinked. "A white elephant?"

Emily explained as they turned and slowly headed back towards Whitehall, the sun starting to set over the distant mountains. "There was a ruler, a very long way away, in a place where white elephants were sacred," she said. "Anyone who owned one had to take care of it, as much care as a magician would take of his familiar, but couldn't get any work out of it. The idea was to cripple the finances of anyone the ruler didn't like, by making them expend time and money caring for a useless creature."

Frieda giggled. "You mean like when King Randor visits his noblemen?"

"Same basic principle," Emily agreed. The poor nobleman would have to spend frantically to keep ahead of the king's demands, no matter how unstated. She would have found it amusing, if she hadn't known the money was extracted from the commoners. "Force someone to waste resources on entertaining the king, rather than plotting."

Frieda considered it. "I don't understand," she said, finally. "Why couldn't they pass the elephant to someone else?"

"It was a gift from the king," Emily pointed out. "How would you feel if I took something you gave me and passed it to Alassa?"

"Hurt," Frieda admitted. "But if it was something you couldn't use, and she could..."

Emily nodded in understanding as Frieda's voice trailed off. Frieda had grown up in the Cairngorms, where families were so poor that having knives and forks would be considered luxurious. The idea of someone being able to keep something for herself was absurd. Private possessions were almost non-existent. Hell, they even buried the dead nude, knowing that clothes were wasted in the ground. If something was useless to Emily, Frieda's family would think nothing of her passing it to Alassa, even if it *had* been a gift.

But Frieda came here, to a place of abundance, Emily thought. *She could give me a gift and expect me to keep it.*

She dismissed the thought as they reached the door, where a prefect was standing on guard and watching the sun sinking in the distance. "Welcome home," he grunted. "You'd better get upstairs before Lights Out. I hear the tutors are on the prowl."

"They probably are," Emily said. The prefect wore a Fifth Year robe; he'd presumably known Caleb, before his accident. She didn't know him at all. "It's the second night back for half the school."

"Yeah," Frieda agreed. "Everyone will be trying to sneak out of bed."

Emily rolled her eyes. Sneaking through the darkened school was an old tradition at Whitehall - and Mountaintop, somewhat to her surprise. She'd always had the impression that it was tacitly encouraged, if only to help the students to stretch their minds and discover some of the school's many secrets. Unfortunately, harsh punishment for anyone caught out of bed was *also* an old tradition. Alassa had managed to get the three of them in trouble, more than once, when they'd gone exploring at night.

And I bet Frieda will get herself into trouble too, she thought, although she had a feeling that catching Frieda would be difficult. The former Shadow had a knack for remaining quiet and still, or lurking in the darkness to avoid detection. *She won't lose the opportunity to explore the school.*

"Come on," she said, as she led the way into the school. "We'd better get into bed before the lights start to dim."

Frieda nodded, following Emily up the stairs towards the Second Year dorms. Emily sighed inwardly as they passed the portrait of her someone had hung in the corridor - it looked rather more like Alassa than her, if Alassa had dyed her hair and worn a somewhat indecent dress - and stopped as she realized there was a second portrait. This one showed her standing in front of a throne, magic crackling around her and a cold expression on her face. If her name hadn't been written at the bottom, along with a signature she couldn't decipher, she would have thought it was meant to be someone else.

"I think the artist never actually saw you," Frieda said, holding one hand in front of her face to hide a smile.

"Clearly not," Emily muttered. The second painting showed her wearing a red dress, with hair shading to red...maybe the painter had read a description of Melissa instead. It didn't look *that* much like Melissa either, but at least the hair and dress color matched. "Why do they keep hanging them up here?"

"You're famous," Frieda said. "There's a whole set of portraits of famous graduates in the North Corridor. Mistress Irene had me cleaning them once for a detention."

"I won't ask what you did to deserve it," Emily said. "They weren't all of *me*, were they?"

"No," Frieda said. "I think one of them was of the Grandmaster, but the others were strangers."

They reached the entrance to the Second Year dorms. Madame Razz was standing outside, a nasty expression on her face, as the remaining stragglers filtered through the doors and into the corridor. Emily waved goodbye to Frieda as she ran towards the entrance, and turned and hurried up the stairs to the next level. The lights started to dim sharply, reminding her that she really should be in bed - or, at least, in her bedroom. She reached the top of the stairs, and stopped. Alassa was standing outside the door, looking grim.

"I'm meant to make a note of everyone who gets back late, after the lights go out," she said, as she saw Emily. "Get inside before I have to write your name."

"Ouch," Emily said. She hurried through the door, then stopped. "What happens if you catch any of us?"

"I have to give the list to the House Mother," Alassa said. "Madame Beauregard is known to be strict. After that, I have to patrol the corridors for twenty minutes, rounding up strays."

Emily winced in sympathy. "Remember to be diplomatic," she said. What could Alassa do if she caught someone from one of the upper years? "And keep your wards up."

"I know," Alassa said. "I got told a whole series of horror stories by Thomas - you know him?"

"No," Emily said. She'd known a handful of Fifth and Sixth Years in her first two years as a student, thanks to Martial Magic, but she didn't know many of the students who'd been in Third or Fourth Year. "I don't think I know him."

"He's one of the prefects for Sixth Year," Alassa explained. "He said that Dorm Monitor was one of the worst jobs in the school, because students would try to turn them into things just so they could get away. By the time he managed to undo the spell, the person who'd cast it was safely out of reach."

"Oh dear," Emily said. Assaulting a tutor would be very bad - it would be easy to identify the culprit - but someone quick enough to cast a spell on the Dorm Monitor and run? It was quite possible the tutors would regard it as a learning experience, rather than something requiring punishment. "How are you feeling?"

"I've felt better," Alassa said. "I..."

The lights went out. Alassa hastily cast a light globe, then smiled, her face illuminated by the soft radiance. "Go to bed," she said. "I'll be back as soon as possible."

Emily nodded, headed down the corridor and stepped through the door into her room. Imaiqah was already there, lying in bed with the covers pulled over her head. Emily hastily undressed, pulled her nightgown on and climbed into bed herself. There would be time for a shower in the morning before she had to get to class. And then she had a free period before lunch...

And then I have Martial Magic, she thought, feeling the butterflies returning to her stomach. Intellectually, she knew Lady Barb was right; this *was* an opportunity to learn from one of the most skilled sorcerers in the world. But emotionally...she caught herself starting to panic again and concentrated on her breathing exercises. *I survived Shadye. I can survive Master Grey.*

She was still breathing, in and out, in and out, when Alassa entered the room and glanced into Emily's bed. "You awake?"

"No," Emily said, dryly. "Are you asleep. too?"

Alassa smiled, then sobered. "I just caught Tam and Penelope trying to sneak back into the dorms," she said. "They could have waited half an hour, if they hadn't wanted to be caught..."

"Idiots," Emily agreed. It might have been possible to wait until Alassa set off on her patrols, then sneak through the door. "Didn't they know you'd be waiting outside?"

"Probably not," Alassa said. "Madame Beauregard didn't usually hang around outside the door in Third Year."

That was true, Emily recalled. She'd stayed in her office, further down the corridor, and waited. If someone had made enough noise to summon her, that someone would not have had a very pleasant time of it. But Alassa had waited at the door.

"Bad for them," she said, dryly. "What did you do?"

"Took their names," Alassa said. "What else *can* I do?"

Emily shuddered, remembering Mountaintop. "Be glad of it," she said, as her friend started to undress. "This might be intended to teach you something about wielding power."

"I already know how to wield power," Alassa muttered. She finished undressing and climbed into bed, without bothering to don a nightgown. "Goodnight."

"Goodnight," Emily echoed.

She closed her eyes and concentrated on her breathing, but it was a very long time before she finally fell asleep.

Chapter Twelve

"THIS SHOULD BE FUN," ALOHA SAID, THE FOLLOWING AFTERNOON. "HOW ARE YOU FEELING?"

"Nervous," Emily grunted, as she pulled the uniform jacket over her head. It seemed to be a rule that uniforms should be ill-fitting, uncomfortable and itchy. "I didn't sleep very well. Then I had Advanced Charms."

"Just wait until you get to Fifth Year," Aloha said, unsympathetically. "You'll have *Very* Advanced Charms."

Emily sighed, checking her uniform. It was a dark green, something that was supposed to make her harder to see in a jungle, although she had her doubts about its effectiveness in actual combat. The three black bands around her upper left arm puzzled her, unless they were meant to indicate that this was her third year of Martial Magic. She'd worn something similar at Mountaintop, but then she'd been an *actual* Third Year student. She tied her hair back into a long ponytail, and glanced at Aloha. Her friend looked...

Pretty, Emily thought, numbly. Aloha practically *glowed. Is she dressing to impress him?*

She gritted her teeth at the thought. Aloha's uniform was a little tighter than it should be, particularly around her chest, and her face was scrubbed clean. Her long dark hair was bound up in a bun, drawing attention to her face and cheekbones. Was she actually *crushing* on Master Grey? Emily honestly couldn't recall seeing Aloha put so much effort into her appearance before. She opened her mouth to ask, then shut it firmly. Whatever the answer, she didn't want to know.

"Let's go," Aloha said, as she checked her watch. "He's waiting for us outside."

At least he isn't changing in front of us, Emily thought. She'd always hated trips outside the school, even though the boys had given her some privacy. Sergeant Miles had warned her, privately, that that wouldn't always be possible. *He's just waiting for us to get changed on our own.*

She pushed the thought to the back of her mind as Aloha led the way out of the changing room and into the Armory. It was a giant room, crammed with all kinds of weapons both mundane and magical, but Emily had no time to look at them. Master Grey stood in the exact center of the room, hands clasped behind his back, watching them through cold blue eyes. Emily shuddered inwardly as his gaze moved over her, but forced herself to straighten up and hold herself steady. Beside her, Aloha snapped to attention, and held herself at parade rest.

"Your uniform needs adjusting," Master Grey said, eyeing Emily sharply. He walked forward and tugged at it, almost pulling Emily over. "And you need to tie your hair back or shorten it considerably."

Emily fought to keep her face calm. Her long hair was her one real vanity, something she'd kept even though she knew it would be easier to handle short hair. Carefully, not taking her eyes off him, she undid her ponytail and bound her hair into a bun, like Aloha. Master Grey nodded once in cold approval, then walked around them both. Emily shivered as she felt his gaze moving over her, then on to Aloha. If Master Grey noticed how pretty she looked, he said nothing.

"Follow me," he said, curtly.

He turned and jogged out of the room, forcing them to follow him. Emily groaned under her breath as he picked up speed, jogging through the doors that led to the training field. Sergeant Miles was lecturing a group of new students just outside; Master Grey ignored them as he led Emily and Aloha towards the lightning-blasted tree at one edge of the fields, then into the path that ran into the forest. Emily forced herself to keep going when her body started to ache as she followed Master Grey and Aloha, cursing mentally. She simply hadn't had time to walk in Cockatrice, let alone run, and her body had weakened. Neither Master Grey nor Aloha seemed to be breathing hard, let alone showing any other signs of tiredness. Aloha must have been keeping up with her physical exercises as well as preparing for her next year at school.

Probably didn't have to worry about anything else, Emily thought, resentfully. She knew nothing about Aloha's family, but surely they'd be proud of such a brilliant girl. There wouldn't be any suggestion that she should find a husband, or do anything other than what she was doing. *She could devote all her time to her studies.*

Master Grey stopped, standing next to a tree trunk. Beyond him, the pathway led down towards a second marker, half a mile away. Emily knew, from running the path before with the sergeants, that there were four markers in all, between them covering two miles. Students like her, graduates of Martial Magic, were expected to run the entire track in less than nine minutes. It wasn't something she'd ever enjoyed.

"I shall be bringing up the rear," Master Grey informed them, removing a baton from his belt. "I expect you to complete the track in ten minutes - and that's being generous."

Very generous, Emily thought, sourly. *It took me months to complete the track in less than fifteen.*

"Go," Master Grey ordered.

Aloha ran, sprinting down the path as though a wild animal were after her. Emily followed, cursing Master Grey under her breath. She'd been told to pace herself, back when she'd been running for the very first time, but it wasn't easy when she heard Master Grey's pounding footsteps behind her. She forced herself onwards, despite the growing stitch in her side, yet no matter how hard she tried she found herself slowing down. He swatted her backside with the baton, pushing her to run faster, yet it was hopeless. By the time she finally reached the final marker, she knew she was running very late.

"Thirteen minutes, with a little encouragement," Master Grey sneered. Emily fought down the urge to rub her behind as he glowered at her, then shot Aloha a droll smile. "You made it in ten, barely."

"Thank you, sir," Aloha said.

"You will both have to do better," Master Grey said. He produced a canteen of water from his belt and passed it to Aloha, who took a long swig and then held it out to Emily. "You may discover your lives depend, one day, on being able to outrun someone."

He smirked, took back the canteen after Emily had taken a drink, and turned to lead them back down the path. "Follow me," he ordered, as he sprang into a jog. "You don't want to fall too far behind."

Because the forest is charmed to make life difficult for unwary students, Emily thought, as she followed him down the path. The pain in her backside was fading, but her body ached due to the sudden exercise. He was right; she'd need to go running more, at least if she wanted to stay in the class. *And you probably added a few nasty surprises for us personally.*

The pathway opened suddenly to reveal Blackhall, a towering mansion that wouldn't have been out of place in a gothic horror novel. Emily caught her breath as Master Grey stopped outside, forcing herself to remain calm. The original defenses of Blackhall might have been removed long ago - although Sergeant Miles had hinted that some remained intact - but hundreds of Martial Magic instructors had charmed the building to test their students to the limit. Emily had been inside too many times to be sanguine about whatever they might have to face.

"Your mission is very simple," Master Grey said. He turned to face them, his cloak swirling around his body to reveal he was wearing a silver breastplate over his chest. "I will be going inside Blackhall. You will follow me in ten minutes" - he jabbed a finger at them; Emily felt her feet suddenly and firmly stuck to the ground - "when that spell wears off, and try to catch me. I will be using no active magic of my own; you two may use whatever you please."

Emily blinked. "You won't be using magic?"

"I won't be using any active magic," Master Grey repeated. "Are you deaf?"

"No, sir," Emily said, biting her lip.

"You are to catch me and take me out of Blackhall within the hour, before the next class arrives," Master Grey continued. "That's all you have to do."

He turned and walked through the door, which closed with an ominous creaking sound. Emily hastily tested the spell binding her feet in place and discovered it was unbreakable, at least with the standard spells. It would probably take longer than the spell would last to break it, unless she found a shortcut. Maybe it would be better to just wait...

"All we have to do is catch him," Aloha said. "And he won't be using any magic. It sounds easy, doesn't it?"

"There's probably a sting in the tail somewhere," Emily muttered. Blackhall was crammed with traps. "Something we're not seeing."

She gritted her teeth. On the face of it, a mundane - or someone pretending to be a mundane - fighting a magician was committing suicide. She knew a hundred spells that could be used to render a powerless mundane harmless. Hell, she'd learned enough to protect herself in her first few weeks at Whitehall. Master Grey might be more experienced than either of them, but could he fight without magic? Unless he planned to cheat...

The spell holding her in place snapped. "We stick together," Aloha said, as they advanced towards the door. "And check everything for traps. The building will probably go after both of us."

Emily nodded as they checked the door, carefully opening it to reveal a long dark corridor, illuminated only by lanterns hanging from the walls. If she hadn't known it was impossible, she would have thought that whoever had designed the building's interior had spent far too much time watching horror movies set in haunted houses. The door creaked, and so did the floorboards; she inched along the side of the corridor, straining her senses for the first hint of Master Grey's position. But there was nothing, save for an ever-present silence that hung around them like a tangible thing.

He could be moving around the house, keeping ahead of us, she thought. Aloha might have been wrong. The traps infesting the house might be charmed not to go after tutors. *Or he could just have hidden himself somewhere to wait.*

Aloha nodded towards a half-opened door, then cast an illusion of herself and sent it forward, through the door. Emily doubted it would fool anyone for more than a few seconds, but those seconds might be vital...nothing happened as the illusion moved through the door, followed carefully by Aloha. Inside, the room was empty, the wooden walls carved with words and pictograms that sent chills down Emily's spine. At the far end, another door led into darkness.

Emily cast the night vision spell - cursing herself for not having thought of it earlier - and peered into the darkness. There was nothing there, save for a long corridor lined with doors, each one leading to an unknown destination. She checked for traps and found nothing, which alarmed her. Blackhall was supposed to be *loaded* with traps. If there was nothing ahead of them...

He could have disarmed them as he walked down the corridor, she thought. She remembered her first visit to Blackhall and shuddered. *Or the traps could be purely mechanical, without magic.*

"Watch my back," Aloha muttered, as she slipped ahead of Emily. "The door at the end of the corridor is open."

"It could be a trap," Emily muttered back. Sergeant Miles had taught them how to lay down a false trail, pointing out that it might be necessary to put someone off the scent. "He could be lying in wait for us."

"I know," Aloha said. "But we don't have the time to search Blackhall inch by inch."

Emily swallowed and nodded as Aloha inched down towards the door and peered through it, before beckoning Emily to come up to her. Inside, there was another set of stairs, leading upwards. Aloha crawled up, deactivating a nasty trap as she moved, then stepped through a door at the top. Emily followed her, feeling magic crawling around them, but stopped as the door snapped closed as soon as Aloha had stepped through. She hastily used a charm to unlock it, but when it opened there was no sign of Aloha.

Shit, she thought, feeling cold fear running through her veins. They'd been separated, quite deliberately. And there was a funny smell in the air, something oddly familiar that her mind refused to recognize. *Where the hell is she?*

Something *moved* at the end of the corridor, half-hidden in shadow. A cloak... she snapped off a freeze spell, then ran forward. Master Grey's cloak was hanging from the ceiling, frozen solid, but there was no sign of its owner. Emily barely had a moment to stare at it before a pair of strong arms grabbed her and shoved a damp cloth into her face. She struggled, but she couldn't keep herself from breathing in some of the liquid. Her head swam as she fell to the ground; she tried to cast a spell, but the magic refused to form.

Durian, her mind yammered at her. *That's a Durian-based potion.*

Master Grey yanked her arms behind her back, tying them so tightly that Emily couldn't flex them at all. She tried to kick out, but it was futile; Master Grey bound her legs together, rolled her over and pushed the cloth into her mouth. No matter what she tried, it was impossible to work magic. She'd been caught as neatly as a rat in a trap.

"Emily," Aloha said. "What..."

Emily twisted her head, just in time to see Aloha hurl a spell at Master Grey. It struck his silver breastplate and dissipated, harmlessly. Master Grey leapt at her, bowled her over and rammed a second cloth into her face. Aloha struggled viciously, fighting desperately to escape, but to no avail. Emily could only watch helplessly as Aloha was tied up, then dragged over next to her. They'd *both* been caught effortlessly.

"Not the greatest of successes," Master Grey observed, sardonically. "Emily, you allowed yourself to be distracted by my diversion, which gave me an opportunity to drug and capture you. Aloha, you saw me attacking Emily; you should have tried to overwhelm the breastplate" - he tapped the runes carved into the silver - "before I could catch you."

He knew this place would separate us, Emily thought. The interior of Blackhall wasn't as mutable as Whitehall, but the sergeants had worked hard to prepare it for their students. *And I even smelled the potion and didn't recognize it.*

"I didn't use any active magic," Master Grey continued. "That didn't stop me using the potion, of course, or the advantages offered by picking my ground. When you arrived, following the trail I left, you walked right into my trap."

Emily wanted to spit. The taste in her mouth was growing stronger; despite herself, she had to swallow more of the potion. She wouldn't be able to work magic for hours, even if Master Grey let them go. Her wrists were starting to ache from the bonds...

"You are helpless because you underestimated me," Master Grey stated, flatly. "Do you understand what I'm trying to tell you?"

He met Emily's eyes. "You should have been *much* more careful," he added. "If you'd acted with more forethought, Lady Emily, neither you nor your friend would have been caught."

Emily's cheeks burned at the injustice of it all. She'd made a mistake, yes, but so had Aloha. Why wasn't *she* being lectured, publicly, on her own failings?

"You have twenty-five minutes before the next class arrives," Master Grey said, turning to leave. "Wriggle free or be found by them. No doubt they will happily release you from your bonds."

And never let us hear the end of it, Emily thought, miserably.

"Your homework assignments are waiting in your lockers," Master Grey concluded. "Goodbye."

Emily watched him stride off, never looking back, and tried to tug at her bonds. They proved impossible to weaken, no matter how desperately she wriggled. Without magic, she didn't see *how* she could free herself. She tried to spit out the cloth, but it was too firmly wedged in her mouth to allow her to get rid of it. Aloha made a sound as she wriggled too, yet even she couldn't free herself...

The knot, Emily realized, as she looked at Aloha's wrists. Sergeant Harkin had taught her a great deal about tying knots; he'd taught her one that was secure, yet easy to release if the ends were tugged. She managed to roll over until her back was pressed against Aloha, then she grabbed hold of the end of the rope and pulled. Aloha's hands came free; she rubbed them hastily, then pulled the cloth out of her mouth and freed Emily. Emily removed her own gag and spat. The taste lingered in her mouth like a very unwelcome guest.

"We could have done better," Aloha said, as she stood. "He was right."

Emily rubbed her wrists, cursing Master Grey under her breath. Maybe he *was* right, but he was still an asshole. It wouldn't be *easy* to learn from him.

"And now we have to get out of the building," Aloha added. "That won't be easy, will it?"

"No," Emily agreed. The charms infesting the building would go after them even if they were leaving...and, without magic, they would be completely defenseless. "But I don't want to be caught by the Second Years."

"No," Aloha agreed. They shared a long look. Being magic-less at Whitehall would invite attack, even from people who would normally never dare to take a shot at them. "That would be the final humiliation."

Chapter Thirteen

MASTER GREY HADN'T LIED ABOUT THEIR HOMEWORK ASSIGNMENTS, EMILY DISCOVERED, when they finally made it back to Whitehall and checked their lockers. In fact, he'd given Aloha two assignments and Emily three; to write an outline of their mistakes in Blackhall, to detail the strengths and weaknesses of combat sorcerers in battle and - for Emily personally - a complete report on everything she'd seen in the Blighted Lands. Emily, still smarting after the humiliation in Blackhall, pocketed the papers and headed up for a shower, praying that the potion would wear off before she started classes on Friday. Thankfully, when she woke up the following morning, her magic worked as normal.

"You did make mistakes," Alassa pointed out, when Emily complained to her. "But I think leaving you defenseless was a nasty stroke."

Emily nodded. "We could have been attacked by anyone," she agreed. "He set us up deliberately."

Friday turned into the first real day of schooling, she discovered; she had three more classes and, by the time they finished, a small pile of assignments she had to complete by the end of the month. She carried them back to her room, sorted them out as best as she could, and started to work on Master Grey's assignments. In hindsight, it was easy to see just how many mistakes they'd made; she'd seen his breastplate, she'd smelled the potion and she'd allowed herself to be distracted. The breastplate should have been a tip-off, she conceded reluctantly; he'd told them he wasn't going to be using magic, so he shouldn't have any problems wearing a charmed set of armor for protection.

And he showed it to us deliberately, she reasoned. Trying to cast spells while wearing protective armor would be dangerous. *He wanted us to have a chance to see it.*

She gritted her teeth as she finished the essay, then sighed. He'd included a note insisting he wanted the first and the third assignments completed by Tuesday, while Lady Barb had noted she wanted *her* assignment complete on Monday. It didn't look as though she was going to have any time to spare for Caleb, even though they had to get a move on with their joint project. By the time they got the wood, they'd need a new plan of action before too much time was wasted. She reached for another sheet of paper, and started on Master Grey's third assignment. He probably wanted to know all about the orcs.

He'll probably want me to go back there and count, she thought, sourly. *How many were down at the bottom of the pit?*

Imaiqah found her that evening, sleeping on a pile of half-completed work. She helped Emily to undress without saying a word, turning out the light as soon as Emily was in bed. Emily slept, dreaming fitfully of orcs and goblins and things that went bump in the night, but snapped awake the following morning feeling as if she hadn't really slept at all, even though she'd missed Alassa's return to the room. She was halfway through preparing for class when she remembered it was Saturday and she could sleep in, if she wanted.

"I think you need to spend the morning with us," Alassa said. "My father says that it's vitally important to take time for yourself."

"Your father has a small army of minions he can fob his work onto," Emily countered, crossly. She eyed the pieces of homework. Master Grey's second assignment had a later due date, but it would probably be the hardest. And then she had essays to write for both Professor Thande and Professor Lombardi. "I can't get anyone to do my work."

"Not unless you don't care about passing," Alassa agreed. It wasn't impossible to cheat at Whitehall, but failing to grasp the basics generally meant a magician couldn't move on to more advanced matters. "But you really do need a break."

She pulled Emily out of the room, down to breakfast and then out onto the playing fields, where a number of students were already running around. Alassa's team gathered around her, and headed into the arena - Alassa had clearly booked it first - where the would-be players, including Frieda, waited. Emily waved cheerfully to the younger girl, and headed over to the mound to sit on the grass and wait. She might not have enjoyed team sports, either as a player or a spectator, but she knew they were important to her friends. And besides, the sun beaming down from overhead was warm. She lay back on the grass and closed her eyes for a long moment, enjoying the sensation. Maybe there was something to be said for sunbathing after all.

"Hi," Caleb said. "Emily?"

Emily opened her eyes, smiling, as Caleb sat down next to her. "Hi," she said. A loud whoop from the arena cut her off before she could say anything else. "What's happening over there?"

"Someone seems to have scored a point or something," Caleb said. "I wasn't paying attention."

He gave Emily a sharp look. "Don't you like Ken?"

"Not really," Emily said. "I played it once and it was a minor disaster. What about you?"

"Stronghold didn't field more than a single team," Caleb said. "I never actually played."

Emily frowned. "How did they manage to compete?"

Caleb laughed. "Let's just say that there's a reason Stronghold is at the bottom of the tables and leave it at that," he said. "There just aren't enough magicians at the school to put together a proper team, let alone two. The school team gets next to no practice because none of the other schools will play friendly matches..."

"Because it would help their competitors win when the games come around," Emily said. It made sense, in an unethical kind of way. But then, if she'd cared who actually won, she might have been inclined to refuse a friendly match too. "What *do* they play?"

"Football, mostly," Caleb said. He rubbed his jaw meaningfully. "You have to be a hulking brute of a man to survive on the football pitch. Casper, of course, fitted in perfectly."

Emily smiled as another whoop echoed out from the arena. "I think I'm falling behind already," she said. "Master Grey is trying to bury me in assignments, the other tutors aren't far behind...I don't know when I'm going to have time to work on the project."

Caleb looked alarmed. "We can work on Wednesday and Friday evenings," he said, after a moment of thought. "You wouldn't have Martial Magic, would you? Not then."

"No," Emily said. Her body had ached throughout Friday, to the point where she'd reluctantly rubbed cream on her sore muscles. She knew from experience that it would hurt less, the more she practiced, but it was still unpleasant. "But I don't know what sort of condition I'll be in."

It wasn't fair to him, she conceded reluctantly. He needed her to produce the *Manaskol*, if nothing else. She couldn't do that if she was aching everywhere, while his hands were still too shaky to trust with explosive ingredients. Maybe she should talk to the Grandmaster...but that would be too much like letting Master Grey, and her fears, win. She could wait for a few weeks, see how everything went and...and see what happened.

"I do have some additional ideas," Caleb said, reaching into his pocket and producing a small notebook. "I thought you'd like to see them."

"I would," Emily said. She frowned as she remembered Nanette stealing her notes, back in Second Year. God alone knew where they'd ended up. "Do you have protections on the notebook?"

Caleb looked surprised - and a little offended. "Of course," he said, stiffly. "I'm the only person who can open the cover."

He held it out to her. "Here," he said. "Try and open it."

Emily took the notebook and held it in her hand, feeling the charms protecting the notebook from unfriendly eyes. Lady Barb had made Emily work hard to protect all of *her* notebooks, testing and retesting the defenses until they were practically unbreakable. It was immodest, but she was fairly sure she knew more about protective charms and anti-theft jinxes than any of the other students at Whitehall. Lady Barb had been *very* encouraging.

The charms hissed and snapped at her, repelling her touch rather than lashing out, then slowly broke as she concentrated her magic and snapped them, one by one. Caleb let out a strangled sound as the notebook fell open, revealing a handful of sketches. Most of them were of unfamiliar people, but one was of Emily herself. It looked far more realistic than the paintings hung throughout the school.

"I like sketching people," Caleb said. His face was bright red. "It...it isn't something my father used to encourage."

"It's nice," Emily said. She glanced at the other faces - a grim-faced man who had to be Caleb's father, a pair of younger girls - and then looked up at him. "Really, you're very good at this."

"Thank you," Caleb said. He was still blushing. "I...really?"

"Yes," Emily said. She flipped through the pages until she reached the notes. "I think you'll have to work on your protections, though. Lady Barb forced me to work hard on mine."

Caleb grinned, rather nervously. "Do I get to try to crack one of yours?"

Emily fished a notebook out of her pocket, passed it to him and lost herself in reviewing Caleb's spell diagrams. There was nothing shaky about the drawings, even though his hands shook as they held her notebook and probed the defenses with magic. She frowned inwardly, remembering something she'd seen on television years ago, and turned her attention back to Caleb. Lady Barb wouldn't be pleased if Caleb broke into the notebook - if nothing else, she would have to teach Emily how to counter whatever specific trick Caleb had used - but better he cracked the defenses than someone unfriendly.

"No luck," Caleb said, finally. "What do you think of the diagrams?"

"Workable," Emily said. She flicked back to the sketch and admired it for a long moment. It really did look like her. "When did you draw this?"

"Just after the...ah...*confrontation* in Cockatrice," Caleb said.

"It would have to have been after your accident," Emily mused, thinking out loud. "We didn't meet before then, did we?"

"Of course not," Caleb said, puzzled. "Why...?"

"You couldn't have drawn this with shaky hands," Emily said. She flipped back to the spell diagram. "And you couldn't have drawn this either, could you?"

Caleb frowned. "What do you mean?"

"I mean you're having problems when you think about working magic or brewing a potion," Emily said. In hindsight, would their first spell mosaic have worked perfectly if *Emily* had supplied the magic? "But if you're not having problems when drawing out diagrams or sketching me, it suggests there isn't a physical problem..."

She broke off. Lady Barb had told her, in no uncertain terms, that the Allied Lands had never attempted any form of mental treatment - and never would. In a world where powerful sorcerers were a little unstable - and necromancers were madder than hatters - anything that might help them to control their powers would make them a far greater threat. If she found a cure, or something that started to help Caleb recover the full use of his hands, where would it end?

"My hands are damaged," Caleb said. He held one up for her to inspect. His hand looked burned, as if something had permanently damaged his skin. "Those scars don't fade. They had to use rituals to drain some of the excess magic from the wounds."

"Yes, but you're still drawing normally," Emily said. "Why do you have problems brewing potions if your hands work fine for sketching?"

Caleb frowned. "I..."

"Emily," a voice called. Emily looked up to see Frieda running towards them, carrying a ball in her hand. "I got in!"

"Well done," Emily said, as Frieda sat down facing them. "How many others got in?"

"Three more, all in my year," Frieda said. She shot Caleb an unreadable look, then smiled at Emily. "We're still the youngest team in the school!"

"*Very* well done," Emily said. The older teams largely consisted of older players, but Alassa had started recruiting younger students. *She* thought it gave them more time to learn. "You will have to work hard, you know."

"I can do it," Frieda insisted. "I've been practicing casting a spell without making it obvious I cast it."

"Be careful you don't get caught," Emily warned.

She smiled. Using magic on other players was officially forbidden, but everyone agreed it was perfectly fine as long as the caster didn't get caught by the referee. Come to think of it, the rules only forbade using magic on the opposing team. Could there be some advantage in casting spells on one's fellows? She couldn't think of one, but Alassa might see a way to take advantage of the loophole.

"I won't," Frieda assured her. "The princess says that anything is legal as long as you don't get caught."

"And in football, anything is legal if you get caught or not," Caleb said, mournfully. "There are four full Healers at Stronghold and they're kept very busy."

Emily nodded, and gave Frieda a hug. "Well done," she said, again. "I'm proud of you."

"Thank you." Frieda beamed. "What are you going to do now?"

"I'm not sure," Emily said. She wanted to rest, but she needed to exercise - she had to work off that damned demerit at some point - and she had assignments to complete. "I may need to go for a run."

"I can come with you," Frieda said. "It might be fun..."

"I'm not sure I'm allowed to take you into the forest," Emily said. It was officially forbidden to everyone who wasn't taking Martial Magic, although there were no warning signs around the outer edge. She'd always had the impression that the sergeants thought that anyone who ventured in without the proper training deserved everything they got. "We'd have to check with Sergeant Miles."

She passed Caleb his notebook, and got to her feet. "Can we catch up on" - she hastily calculated how long it would take to finish the remaining assignments - "Monday evening?"

"It should be possible," Caleb said. He closed the notebook and resealed it, then frowned. "I may also need to work on my protections."

"Definitely," Emily said. It was unlikely that anyone would want to spy on a random student, but she knew *she'd* been spied on...and both Caleb and Aloha were geniuses, smarter than she was. Someone might well steal their concepts, turn them into workable ideas and then swear blind they were all their own work. "Lady Barb will help, if you ask her."

"I should chat with Professor Lombardi first," Caleb said. "He's my mentor."

He bowed to her, but hesitated just for a second before turning to head back towards the school. Emily watched him go, feeling a sensation she couldn't quite identify, but glanced back at the arena when another cheer split the air. Alassa was probably testing some of the shakier recruits before making up her mind about the final candidates.

"Let's go," she said. "Sergeant Miles should be in the Armory, unless he's outside with the students."

There was no sign of Sergeant Miles when they entered the Armory, but Master Grey was sitting at a desk, working on something that looked like a large piece of clockwork. Emily couldn't even guess at its purpose; she started to back out, but Master Grey looked up and saw them before they could make their escape.

"Lady Emily," he said, his voice cold and hard. "To what do I owe the pleasure of your company?"

Emily forced herself to remain calm. "I would like to take Frieda into the forest, so we can both run along the marked track."

Master Grey rose to his feet. "You plan to take a *Second Year* student into a dangerous forest? A forest infested with wild animals and primed with spells and traps designed to target magicians in their Fifth or Sixth Year?"

"*I* was a Second Year student when I was first taken into the forest," Emily said, refusing to be intimidated. She'd also run through the smaller copse as a First Year. "Sergeant Miles raised no objection to my joining the other students, or running the gauntlet in Blackhall."

"I see," Master Grey said. "Does your friend have the experience of a previous year in Martial Magic?"

"I was at Mountaintop," Frieda piped up.

"So you were," Master Grey agreed. He gave Frieda a sharp look, then returned his gaze to Emily. "You could have put your friend in considerable danger. Detention. Both of you."

Emily felt her heart sink. "I need to finish..."

Master Grey cut her off. "Report to Mistress Irene and inform her that you have both been assigned detention," he said. "I will, of course, be checking to make sure you actually report to her."

Of course, Emily thought, numbly.

"It isn't her fault," she protested. "I..."

Master Grey interrupted her, again. "You have a knack for putting people in danger, Lady Emily," he added, darkly. "I intend to break you of that habit. And the habit other people have, time and again, of listening to you."

He pointed a long finger at the door. "Go."

Emily clenched her teeth to keep from saying something she *knew* would earn her a worse punishment, and turned and walked out of the door, careful to close it tightly behind Frieda and herself. The younger girl seemed surprised, but not shaken. But then, she'd handled worse tutors at Mountaintop.

"I'm sorry," Emily said. A detention on the weekend...they'd be scrubbing floors, if they were lucky. If Mistress Irene was in a bad mood, they'd be sent to the Warden before being dispatched to detention. "I didn't mean to cost you your free time."

"At least it will be with you," Frieda said. She slipped her hand into Emily's, then squeezed lightly. "I don't mind."

Maybe you don't, Emily thought. *But I do.*

Chapter Fourteen

"T HE FOLLOWING PEOPLE ARE TO REMAIN BEHIND," LADY BARB SAID, AS THE FIRST HEALING class of the week came to an end. "Emily, Imaiqah, Pandora, Johan and Robin."

Emily winced, inwardly. Thanks to Master Grey's detention, she hadn't managed to complete her assignment for Lady Barb...the assignment that had to be turned in incomplete. If she'd been held back alone, she would have wondered if Lady Barb had already noted and intended to chew her out for it, but instead...five students had been told to remain. She forced herself to stay calm, knowing that she was in trouble, and waited until the other students had left the room.

Lady Barb closed the door, studying her students carefully. "By a stroke of luck - for whatever definition of luck suits you - the Halfway House has agreed to open its doors for my classes this Friday. This required some careful negotiation as classes from both Mountaintop and Stronghold also need access to the Halfway House. You five will be the first to go, as it offers a chance for any doubters to see the worst of a Healer's job."

But Alassa doesn't want to become a Healer, Emily thought, *and I can't. Why take me and not her? Or the ones who are certain they want to become Healers?*

"You will assemble in the Portal Chamber immediately after lunch on Friday, wearing the outfits I will provide for you," Lady Barb continued. "The Halfway House only opens its portals at the exact moment specified, so anyone left behind will be unable to go and may not be given another chance. These papers" - she picked a pile of packets off her desk and started to hand them round - "give a brief outline of the facility, the details of the patients you will see and the potential dangers. If any of you think better about going, after reading these papers, let me know and I'll drop you from the list."

She paused. "Most of the patients are harmless," she warned, "but some can get violent or nasty. If you feel threatened, get out; if you can't get out, use magic to defend yourself. It is *not* your task to do anything to help the patients; we are only there to observe. Put your safety first and leave the rest to the staff."

Emily swallowed. How many horror movies had started with a bunch of nervous co-eds making a trip to a mental asylum? She'd seen enough such movies to imagine the dangers in far too great detail. What if...she pushed the thought aside, remembering that she had enough magic to defend herself, if she didn't freeze up and forget she had it. She'd frozen once before and it had almost gotten Imaiqah and her killed.

Lady Barb cleared her throat, loudly. "Are there any questions?"

"Yes," Pandora said. Emily didn't know her very well, even though they'd shared three years of schooling together. She'd been nothing more than a face in the background. "Why do we have to wear your outfits?"

"Because they may try to grope you," Lady Barb said, bluntly. "The outfits provided by the facility are charmed to protect you from lecherous patients who have very little to fear, given the nature of their condition. If you're not wearing protective clothing, young lady, the facility staff will not allow you to pass through the entrance hall."

She glanced from face to face, her eyes resting for a long moment on Emily. "Are there any other questions?"

There was a pause. No one said a word. Emily felt nervous, looking down at the packet in her hands and resolving to read it as soon as possible. She'd honestly thought the trip to the Halfway House would be later in the term, if it took place at all. Lady Barb *knew* that she wasn't going to become a Healer.

But she may feel you need to see the place, Emily thought, grimly. *She was showing you other parts of the world on your travels.*

"Dismissed," Lady Barb said. "If there are any further questions, after you read the materials, I will be in my office after classes for the rest of the week."

Emily met Imaiqah's eyes and tried to tell her, silently, to go ahead. Imaiqah nodded slowly, then rose with the other students and left the room. Emily watched the door close, then turned back to look at Lady Barb, who eyed her with a quizzical expression. It wasn't usual for students to remain behind after a long session, not when they needed to shower, eat and rest, preferably in that order. Emily was about the only one who *would*.

"Emily," Lady Barb said. "Do you have a question?"

"Yes," Emily said, slowly. She knew she couldn't delay indefinitely, but maybe if she asked a question first Lady Barb would be in a better mood. "Why am *I* going to the Halfway House?"

"Because you need to see it," Lady Barb said. "You may never serve as a Healer, Emily, but you may wind up condemning someone to the facility."

"Condemning," Emily repeated. It didn't sound pleasant. The Nameless World had magical healing, on one hand, and mundane medical proceedings that made leeches look a safe and sane approach to medicine. Those who couldn't afford to hire a magician tended to take their lives in their hands, every time they approached a doctor. "What's it like?"

Lady Barb gave her a wintry smile. "You'll see," she said. "Unless you choose to back out, you will visit the facility on Friday."

She met Emily's eyes, then sat down facing her. "And what do you actually want to talk to me about? I *do* have another class in an hour and I have to eat something first."

Emily winced. *She* had another class in an hour, Alchemy. And she needed to eat something herself too, before trying to use magic in the class. Professor Thande wouldn't be pleased if she turned up drained of energy, or too tired to think straight.

"I didn't manage to complete my homework," she confessed. There was no point in trying to hide it, not when she knew Lady Barb marked her assignments the evening they were turned in. "I had detention yesterday."

Lady Barb eyed her with cool disapproval. "And how did you manage to get detention on a weekend?"

"I asked Master Grey a question," Emily said, bitterly. "He gave me detention."

"I see," Lady Barb said. "And was it a particularly *stupid* question?"

Emily hesitated. "I'm not sure," she confessed. She'd never been told not to take younger students into the forest, but *she'd* been the youngest student in Martial Magic. Hell, as far as she knew, she still was. "I wanted to take Frieda for a run along the marked track."

Lady Barb frowned. "You *do* realize just how many horrific things could happen to a young girl in a forest deliberately rigged to make life...*interesting* for students?"

Interesting, Emily thought, sarcastically. "I thought the track was safe."

"It should be," Lady Barb confirmed. "Now tell me; would you have stayed on the track?"

"I think so," Emily said. But Frieda would have wanted to explore, wouldn't she? Maybe they would have stepped off the beaten track..."It's just like Master Tor, isn't it?"

Lady Barb quirked her eyebrows. "Is it?"

Emily hesitated, trying to think clearly. Master Tor had taken a dislike to her as soon as they'd met, perhaps earlier, but he'd always had a point, even if she hadn't been in a fit state to appreciate it at the time. He'd been the *only* senior magician, with the possible exception of Lady Barb and Emily herself, to express any concern over the lives of mundanes, men and women who lived on Emily's lands and were at her mercy. She'd seen enough, back during the holidays, to know it wouldn't be hard for her to make their lives miserable.

"I don't know," Emily admitted, finally. "He's always disliked me."

Lady Barb reached out and tapped Emily's hand, forcing her to look up. "How would you feel if someone ran around from place to place, disrupting everything?"

"I'm not like that," Emily protested.

"You could be," Lady Barb said.

She shrugged. "Whatever career you seek, whatever you want to do with your life, you will remain very important to the Allied Lands and the White Council," she added, slowly. "It isn't unsurprising for him to want to test you, to push you hard enough to see where your buttons are. He may well believe that it would be better for you to break here, where there is help on hand if you need it, than out in the field. It's his job."

Emily blinked. "To push me?"

"To find your limits and help you to overcome them," Lady Barb said. "I thought I was pretty good when I left Whitehall, but my Master soon showed me I had a long way to go."

"Oh," Emily said. Jade had told her that Master Grey was a tough tutor, although she hadn't really understood what he'd meant. "And I have a long way to go too, don't I?"

"Yes, you do," Lady Barb said. She leaned back, smiling thinly. "You're a Fourth Year student, at least two years younger than anyone he would have taught person-ally. Jade is...what? Five years older than you?"

"Thereabouts," Emily said.

"You need someone to kick you in the ass from time to time," Lady Barb told her. "Do you want to leave his classes?"

Emily stared down at her hands. She'd thought of Master Grey as a monster, not as a tutor in his own right, or someone who might have had a point. But she'd only asked a simple question...what would he have said, she wondered, if she'd been caught taking Frieda into the forest without bothering to ask permission? She doubted it would have been anything pleasant.

"I need to learn," she said. "Don't I?"

"Yes," Lady Barb said. "And I'll tell you one other thing."

Emily looked up, waiting.

"Combat sorcerers, male or female, are always tested to the limit," Lady Barb said, flatly. "I was tested intensely, first by my master and then by a handful of others. We need to know where the weaknesses lie, which of us is scared of spiders, which of us has problems keeping his wards up when faced by a seductive young woman, which of us..."

She shrugged. "Parsing out your weaknesses, here and now, isn't a bad thing," she added. "It won't cripple you to truly understand your fears."

Emily swallowed. She knew what she feared: *helplessness*. Maybe *that* was why she disliked Master Grey, because he made her feel helpless. There was no shortage of spells that could render her helpless and vulnerable, even though she'd been working on learning how to counter them, but she didn't fear those as much as people with bad intentions. And while she'd feared Master Tor, she knew he'd meant well.

"You can back out, if you like," Lady Barb said, softly. "I can go to the Grandmaster, as your adviser, and tell him that it isn't working out."

Aloha would like that, the treacherous part of Emily's mind muttered. *She's practically in love with Master Grey.*

"No," she said, steeling her resolve as best as she could. "He may be an asshole, but I can and I will learn from him."

Lady Barb's lips twitched. "It isn't generally considered good manners to call one tutor an asshole in front of another."

Emily felt her face heat. "I'm sorry..."

"Don't do it again," Lady Barb said. She cleared her throat. "There is, of course, the matter of your incomplete homework."

"I know," Emily said, feeling her heart sink. "I'm ready."

She forced herself to remain calm, even though it wasn't easy. Lady Barb was utterly merciless. She locked the doors as soon as the bell rang, checked homework with a fine-toothed attention to detail and handed out punishment assignments to anyone who failed to hand it in on time. There was no way she'd allow Emily to get away with not completing her assignment, no matter what she offered as an excuse. Hell, she needed to make it clear she *wasn't* showing favoritism to Emily. She'd be lucky if she wasn't called out and dressed down in front of the entire class.

"For punishment, you can go to Master Grey and ask him about working as a Mediator," Lady Barb said. "He will provide you with some basic information, at least, and point you in the direction of more. I *will* be checking, so make sure you do it before Friday."

Emily gritted her teeth. Resolve or no resolve, she wanted to see as little of Master Grey as possible. Which was the point, she suspected; Lady Barb had taken advantage of her failure to create a situation where she *had* to face her fear.

"Cruel and unusual punishment," she muttered.

"There are crueler punishments," Lady Barb pointed out, dryly. "I do happen to need a living subject for the Third Year classes. They have to study living humans to get much further..."

Emily shook her head, hastily. "I'll speak to him," she said. The idea of undressing in front of a class of students was horrific. Lady Barb normally hired people from Dragon's Den and paid them through the nose. "But what if he just tells me to go away?"

"He's trying to teach you," Lady Barb said. "Ask him a question and he *will* try to answer."

"Very well," Emily said, reluctantly. "I'll ask him after class, tomorrow."

Lady Barb checked her watch. "Go to lunch," she said. "I'll take a look at the assignment this evening, then either give it back to you to redo or add it to the records."

"Thank you," Emily said. Maybe, just maybe, she'd written down enough to earn more than a bare pass. If she hadn't she would have to redo the assignment...and, no matter how well she'd done, she'd only be marked as a pass. It would be reflected in her grades later. "I'll let you know what happens."

"Good," Lady Barb said. She gave Emily another smile, and pointed at the door. "Go."

Emily nodded, hurrying through the door and down to the Dining Hall. It was packed with students trying to eat before going to their afternoon classes. The normal seating order seemed to have broken down; students were sitting wherever they saw a space, or even leaning against the walls to eat from plates. Emily shook her head - it was rare for more than half of the student body to have the same lunch time - then hurried over to the tables and took some curry and rice for herself. She'd never really liked the curries she'd tried to make for herself, back on Earth, but here they tasted far better. Alassa and Imaiqah were leaning against the rear wall, eating dessert. Emily hurried over to join them, picking her way between tables with practiced ease. It helped that many of the older students drew away from her as she approached.

"Everyone decided to have lunch at the same time," Alassa said, as Emily reached her friends and leaned against the wall. "It's sheer chaos in here."

"There must have been a timetable glitch," Emily agreed. She'd never heard of one before, but she supposed it must happen from time to time. Her timetable in Third Year had had to be revised regularly, just to allow her to cram so many classes into her schedule. "Maybe they thought they were opening up the Great Hall for lunch as well as dinner."

Alassa smiled. "Or maybe someone just made a mistake," she said. "Better eat quickly; we'll be tossed out of here soon."

Emily nodded and tucked into her curry. The noise was growing louder as students argued about where they should be sitting, with older students pushing younger students out of chairs they'd already claimed. She saw Aloha and a couple of other prefects trying to maintain order, but there were too many tempers fraying for them to impose calm. It wasn't until the Grandmaster stalked in, surrounded by a wave of power that cowed many of the nearby students, that everything quietened down.

"Sit down and eat your food," he ordered, curtly. It struck Emily, suddenly, that there might not be *enough* food. The cooks wouldn't have expected every student in Whitehall to turn up at once. "Afternoon classes will be delayed by half an hour so that everyone can be fed."

Emily rolled her eyes as a cheer rippled through the room. It wasn't as if the classes were being *shortened*, merely put back half an hour. They would *still* have two straight hours of Alchemy, followed by another two hours of Charms. She doubted that either Professor Thande or Professor Lombardi would allow their classes to end early, just so school could break up at the normal time. The advantage of living in a boarding school was that they could stay longer, if necessary.

But you don't get away from your classmates either, Emily thought. It suited her, she had to admit, but would it suit everyone else? *You spend all your time with them, friends and foes alike.*

She finished her curry and checked her watch. There wasn't time for a shower and a change before Alchemy, so they headed down to the classroom. Professor Thande was standing outside, holding a test tube in one hand as he talked to Master Grey. The look Master Grey shot Emily, when he saw her, was far from friendly.

But I'm going to learn from you, Emily promised herself, meeting his eyes. *And I will not let you break me down.*

Chapter Fifteen

EMILY DARTED BACKWARDS AS MASTER GREY LASHED OUT AT HER WITH A WOODEN SWORD, blocking his blow as best as she could. He gave her a cold smile, jumped forward and slapped the flat of his blade against her hands. Emily yelped in pain and dropped the sword, grunting as he stabbed forward and struck her chest. She was wearing protective padding over her uniform, but it still hurt.

"You need to move quicker," he told her, gruffly. "Show me your hands."

"Yes, sir," Emily muttered through gritted teeth. Her hands *hurt*, but it didn't look as though there was any permanent damage, or anything that couldn't be cured by time and rest. "I don't think there's any damage..."

"I'll be the judge of that," Master Grey said. He took her hands in a surprisingly gentle grip and inspected them, thoroughly. "You shouldn't need any real treatment, but if they're still sore tomorrow go see the Healer."

"Yes, sir," Emily said.

"You need to keep moving," Master Grey added. "If I'd been using a real sword, Lady Emily, you would be bleeding out by now."

Emily nodded, feeling the pain in her chest. She was going to have more aches and pains tomorrow, she was sure, but he was right. If he'd struck her with a real sword, she would probably be dead. She'd learned more than she'd ever expected to learn about swordfighting, but she honestly couldn't say she was any good at it. Magic was so much easier to use.

"Sit down on the bench," Master Grey said. "Aloha and I will spar while you watch."

"Yes, sir," Emily said, relieved.

She sat down gratefully as Aloha stepped up, wooden sword in hand. The older girl looked excited, although - for once - there was a hint of trepidation about her movements. She'd had a chance to see Master Grey in action *before* sparring with him herself and she *knew* he was both faster and stronger than her. The real question, Emily thought as she rubbed her aching fingers, was if she could turn the tables on him before he overwhelmed her? It didn't seem very likely...

Master Grey lunged forward, again. Aloha dodged to one side, rather than trying to block - in hindsight, Emily noted, that might have been her mistake - and then slashed out at his chest in a single smooth motion. Master Grey moved with blinding speed, blocking her blow and trying to stab her with his blade. Aloha jumped backwards, tripped, fell on her rear and brought her feet up to kick Master Grey in the chest. Emily cheered inwardly as Master Grey grunted, but groaned as he brought his sword down on Aloha's chest.

"You're dead," he said. He sounded rather more than a little amused. "I should add that trying to be clever in a swordfight is asking for trouble."

"Yes, sir," Aloha said. She'd wanted to impress him, Emily realized. At least she'd managed to make him smile. "I didn't mean to fall backwards."

"You might well have lost your legs, if I'd had a real blade," Master Grey said, holding out a hand to help her to her feet. "And you would have had bruised ones, if I'd hit you with the wooden sword."

He turned to look at Emily. "Comments?"

Emily swallowed. "She didn't have a choice," she said. "Once she fell over, she was vulnerable."

Master Grey eyed her for a long moment, but finally nodded. "Stay on your feet, if possible," he said, turning back to Aloha. "I expect a paper from both of you, next week, on how you could have done better in your duels. You'll also find the marked papers you handed in yesterday in your lockers. We will discuss any questions you might have on Thursday."

"Yes, sir," Aloha said.

"And it is just about time for us to end the session," Master Grey added. "Go shower, then collect your papers and finish your homework."

Emily watched Aloha walk off, back to the school, then cleared her throat nervously.

"Emily," Master Grey said. "Do you have a question?"

"I would like to discuss my future career with you," Emily said, keeping her voice steady. "Can we talk now?"

"Go shower," Master Grey said. "I'll be in my office in" - he glanced at his watch - "twenty minutes, after I've showered myself. You can speak to me then."

Emily nodded, turned, and hurried back to the barracks. Aloha was there, washing herself thoroughly under the shower, her dark skin already showing a handful of nasty bruises. Emily winced and undressed herself, cursing as she saw the mark on her chest where his sword had struck her. It was going to be sore tomorrow, she was sure; her fingers, at least, felt a little better. She eyed the painkilling potions stored on the wall, seriously considering downing one before the meeting, then dismissed the thought. Master Grey wouldn't be pleased if she turned up under the influence.

"That was fun," Aloha said, as she stepped out of the shower. "I enjoyed myself."

"You fell over backwards," Emily said. She paused as a thought struck her. "Or did you do it deliberately to show him you could recover from a misstep?"

Aloha grinned, showing her teeth. "Whichever one sounds better," she said. "We'd better get more practice in, though. You need to be better at dodging."

Emily sighed, showered rapidly and then pulled her robes back over her head. The uniforms would be dumped in the basket for washing - luckily, they weren't expected to wash their uniforms themselves - and returned to them for Thursday. She pulled her hair into a ponytail, checked her appearance in the mirror and walked out of the barracks. Master Grey's office - the door warded with more hexes and charms than any other tutor at Whitehall - was just down the corridor. She tapped on the door and waited.

"Enter," Master Grey called.

Emily opened the door and stepped inside, looking around with interest. The office was a bare stone chamber with a desk, a pair of chairs and a single large wooden trunk, covered in nasty-looking runes. Master Grey was seated behind his desk, reviewing several papers with a gimlet eye. He looked up at her as she closed the door, his cold gaze flickering over her, then silently pointed to the chair. Emily sat and forced herself to wait as Master Grey finished reading his papers. She could be patient, if necessary.

"You wanted to talk about your career," Master Grey said, suddenly. He looked up at her, his eyes meeting hers. "How may I be of service?"

"You were a Mediator," Emily said. She wasn't entirely sure what to say. "It is a career I have been urged to consider."

"I see," Master Grey said. "And what has your father said about it?"

"Nothing," Emily said. Void hadn't said a word about her future career, at least not to her. "I believe I am expected to choose my own career."

"Odd," Master Grey said. His voice was strictly neutral. "Most patriarchs - or matriarchs - take a hand in determining what careers their children will follow."

Like Fulvia wanted to do with Melissa, Emily thought. If Void had been her *real* father, he would probably have made a few suggestions. *But he isn't and he didn't.*

"My father has said nothing on the matter," Emily said, which happened to be the literal truth. "I would like to know what the requirements are to be a Mediator."

"I'm surprised you didn't look them up before coming here," Master Grey observed. "They *are* a matter of public record."

Emily flushed. *That* was true. She'd been so worried about approaching him in person that she hadn't checked the library.

"To be considered, you would need to earn high marks in everything from Martial Magic to Charms," Master Grey said. For once, he didn't seem inclined to berate her for her oversight. "Alchemy and Healing are considered lesser requirements, but you are expected to have alpha or beta certificates by the time you graduate from Whitehall or private tutoring afterwards. You would also need to take the oaths as a citizen of the Allied Lands, rather than a citizen of any single state."

He gave her a tight smile. "You would have to give up Cockatrice," he added.

Emily looked down at the floor, cursing King Randor under her breath. If she'd known what she was getting into, she would have refused the Barony, even though it would have been in public. Defying the king so openly would probably have landed her in hot water, but it would be better than being caught between her dreams and her obligations. And the longer she kept it, the harder it would be to give it up.

She frowned, not looking up. "I couldn't leave it in someone else's hands?"

"Look at me when you talk to me," Master Grey said, sternly. Emily lifted her gaze to meet his. "You could not be a great noblewoman, with obligations to a single country, and be expected to serve the Allied Lands. It would be a major conflict of interest."

He smiled, rather coldly. "Prospective Mediators apprentice themselves to two or more Mediators, rather than just a single master," he continued. "You would be expected to serve as a combat sorcerer, but also as a diplomat and judge, sorting out problems that bedevil the Allied Lands and make it impossible for us to focus on our true enemy. One day, you might be tracking down a rogue sorcerer, one who needs to be stopped; the next, you might be standing between two armies and convincing them to stand down. People will learn they can rely on you to serve as an impartial representative of the Allied Lands, with the power to bind and loose as you see fit.

"Should the necromancers invade, you will find yourself helping to command a multinational army, smoothing out the problems caused by too many egos in too small a space. You will be expected to be the first in any charge and the last in any retreat, placing yourself and your powers completely at the army's disposal. It may well be that you find yourself trying to prevent soldiers from fleeing, if the battle goes against us, or captured, held by one of the necromancers."

Emily shivered. She'd been Shadye's prisoner, back when he'd plucked her from her own world with the intention of sacrificing her for power. What would another necromancer, one who knew who she was, do to her? The safest course of action would be to kill her at once, she thought, but necromancers weren't known for being rational. Maybe they'd see her as a prospective sacrifice...or maybe they'd see her as something far worse.

"Life is hard," Master Grey admitted. "There will be nights when you sleep in the open air, shivering from the cold and rain and the thought of what tomorrow will bring. There will be days when you look upon the handiwork of rogue sorcerers and curse the very human race. And there will be days when you will find yourself trying to broker peace between two warring factions, when all you want them to do is hurry up and kill each other so you can sit down and rest. You..."

He paused for a long moment. "I was required to pass judgement in a dispute between the King of Alluvia, King Jorlem, and the nearby city-state of Tarzana. You may have heard of them."

"I've met King Jorlem," Emily said. "His son was one of the possible candidates for marrying Alassa."

"Not a pleasant fate," Master Gray stated. Emily wasn't sure which of them was being insulted, Alassa or Prince Hedrick. "King Jorlem pushed his claim quite forcibly, threatening to cut off the city-state's water supply if they refused to uphold his rights. The men and women of Tarzana were running out of water when I arrived, having been tasked to hear the dispute. I reviewed the documents, checked everything I could...and wound up having to rule in the king's favor."

Emily blinked. "Why did you do *that?*"

"Because he was in the right," Master Grey said, simply. "Unpleasant, cruel, calculating, sadistic...but also in the right. I couldn't have done anything else, Lady Emily, once the facts were at my disposal. The king was in the right and the city-state was in the wrong."

He tapped the table, impatiently. "The river started in the king's lands," he said. "By long-standing agreement, the city-state was supposed to render the king due honors and a certain amount of support in exchange for water. For various reasons, the city-state was never called upon to honor its side of the agreement. They had grown used to considering themselves totally independent by the time King Jorlem came to the throne."

"And most of them might not have known the agreement existed," Emily mused.

"Quite," Master Grey said. He gave her a pinched smile. "The king was not interfering within the city, not directly. He was merely threatening to dam a river on his lands."

"Which would have had an effect on the city," Emily pointed out.

"But not *quite* the same as sending an army to burn the city to the ground," Master Grey countered, dryly. "King Jorlem was not breaking the agreement, merely...ensuring the city-state had an incentive to keep *its* side of the agreement."

Emily scowled. "That's what you meant, isn't it? I might find myself helping someone I personally dislike."

"Well, *quite*," Master Grey said.

He rested his elbows on the table and leaned forward. "It's a hard life," he said, "and harder still for a woman. Your mentor" - his face flickered, briefly - "was one of the few to endure the long marches, the intensive training and being forced to share cramped quarters with male trainees. There is no privacy in such quarters. You can expect to be pushed to the limits and beyond. And...if you get captured, you can expect worse than simple death. There are thousands of people out there who hate us and everything we stand for."

"I see," Emily said. She forced herself to look him in the eye. "Is it a rewarding job?"

Master Grey smiled. She thought it was the first time he'd given her a genuinely open smile.

"It's the best position in the Allied Lands," he said. His face fell, slightly. "If, of course, you make it through all the hurdles. Seven out of ten trainees quit within the first year. You'll see sights that will sap your faith in human decency, but you will also have a chance to make a real difference...if you don't wind up dead, or in the Halfway House. I think you'll see some of the failures on Friday. Take note of what happened to them."

He paused. "Do you have any questions?"

Emily frowned. "Why are the requirements so high?"

"We need to know that a prospective recruit has all the skills we need," Master Grey said, simply. "And then we need to know if he - or she - can use them while under pressure."

He rose to his feet. "After hearing all that, Lady Emily, are you still interested in the job?"

"I think so," Emily said.

"Then you will have to work very hard," he said, flatly. "For starters, you can hand in an essay this time next week on the requirements for becoming a Mediator and why they exist, giving examples of what might happen if they are ignored. You'll find all the information you need in the library, within the careers section. I suggest you consider the possible consequences for yourself, rather than simply mirroring the examples given in the books."

"Yes, sir," Emily said. *Another* essay...at least it sounded easier than the essay Professor Thande had assigned them, on *Manaskol.* "I'll get it back to you next week."

"See that you do," Master Grey said. He reached out and caught her hands before she could draw them back, stroking the knuckles with a delicate touch before letting go of them. "You don't seem to be in pain any longer."

"There's just a dull ache," Emily said. It was true; her fingers tingled, but they weren't in real pain. "My chest hurts more."

"Go to the Healer if you're still sore tomorrow morning," Master Grey ordered. "It shouldn't be hard for you to get a potion, if necessary."

Emily nodded, curtly.

"You may also wish to talk to some trainees who didn't make it through," he added. "I can give you contact details, if you like."

"Thank you," Emily said. She hesitated, then plunged on. "Would they talk to me?"

"Some would," Master Grey said. He met her eyes. "Understanding your strengths and weaknesses is a core part of being a sorcerer. Even I have areas where I bow to other masters. To believe that you don't have weaknesses is to court insanity - or death."

And that's what you're trying to teach me, Emily thought.

"Dismissed," Master Grey said. He rose to his feet, slowly. "I'll see you on Thursday."

Emily nodded and left the room, feeling oddly respectful for the first time. He *was* trying to teach her something, even if it was clear he had his doubts about her career prospects. She'd look up the requirements in the library, complete her essay and then...

She shook her head, bitterly. Was there nothing she could do without abandoning Cockatrice? She should have asked when she would have to make that choice. The end of Sixth Year, she assumed, but...

Later, she told herself. She needed to eat dinner, meet Caleb and then make a start on the next set of essays. *I'll worry about it when the time comes.*

Chapter Sixteen

IT WAS, EMILY DISCOVERED, HARD TO KEEP HER RESOLVE TO LISTEN TO MASTER GREY WITH an open mind longer than a couple of days. Thursday afternoon was spent running through Blackhall again, this time without using magic themselves. It ended badly, as Emily had privately expected, and by the time Master Grey had finished detailing their mistakes she was tired, headachy and drained. She crawled into bed as soon as she'd finished eating dinner, and sleepwalked through her classes on Friday morning. By the time Alassa dragged her to lunch and poured Kava down her throat, it was almost too late to reach the Portal Chamber before Lady Barb took her group to the Halfway House.

"You're all dressed properly," Lady Barb said, as they assembled in front of the inactive portal. "I expect you to *remember* what I told you about defending yourselves, understand?"

Emily nodded. The outfit she wore made Whitehall's robes look immodest. It was loose, concealing the shape of her body, while a headscarf hid her hair from prying eyes. The charms woven into the dress, she'd discovered, made it hard for anyone to focus on anything, apart from her face. She checked herself one final time, and hastily prepared for the jump through the portal. Based on past experience, it was going to hurt.

"Be careful," Imaiqah said, catching her hand. The portal flickered into existence, a single white square of light in front of them. "Come on."

Lady Barb gave them all one final look before leading the way into the light. Emily braced herself, feeling a stab of pain and disorientation as she walked through the magic, and staggered as she came out of the far end. Imaiqah held her long enough for her to regain her footing, but she couldn't help feeling sick. It took her several swallows to be sure she wasn't going to vomit, then she gathered herself and looked up. She'd seen the interior of an emergency treatment clinic on Earth, years ago, but this was nothing like it. It looked more like the entrance to a jail cell.

They used to lock up madmen, she recalled. Drugs that could help people with mental problems live a normal life were a relatively new invention on Earth - and completely unknown on the Nameless World. *Here, when those madmen have magic, keeping them anywhere else might be actively dangerous.*

"Follow me," Lady Barb ordered. She led them through a large door, practically crawling with defensive wards. Emily hadn't sensed anything so complex since Mountaintop, where the school had guarded its innermost secrets thoroughly. "Do *not* try to probe the wards."

"They're keyed to specific people," Imaiqah muttered. "I think they must be designed to keep the patients in, rather than others out."

"Correct," Lady Barb said. "Once a patient is keyed into the wards, they cannot leave without approval from the senior staff. One of those staff members is off-site at all times, making it harder for someone to escape."

Emily nodded. The next room looked much nicer, although it still maintained the jailhouse ambience. There were no windows; illumination was provided by a handful of light globes floating near the ceiling, drawing power from the wards. The walls were decorated with small pictures, some clearly drawn by children. She caught her breath as she realized that one of them was from a young boy, practically begging his father to come home. Judging by the date, it was over ten years old.

"Greetings," a voice said. Emily looked up to see a tall thin man wearing white robes. His face was angular - she couldn't help thinking of Mr. Spock - while his head had been shaved bald, then tattooed with runes. "Welcome to the Halfway House. I am Healer Crane."

He paused, eyeing them all darkly. "Should any of you cause any trouble," he continued, "you will be returned to the waiting room" - he waved a hand around the chamber - "and held here until the rest of your class is ready to go. You will also be denied further access to the complex, unless you happen to become a patient. We have enough problems with the patients here without you adding to it."

"You will also be severely punished when you return to Whitehall," Lady Barb reminded them, sharply. "Your classmates will not thank you for making life difficult for them."

Emily nodded, listening as Healer Crane launched into a detailed safety briefing. They wouldn't be meeting any of the truly dangerous patients, he reassured them, but some of the ones they would meet could become violent. His advice was basically the same as Lady Barb's, just more complex. He didn't seem inclined to use one word where three would do.

"Follow me," he concluded, leading them towards a stone wall. There was a shimmer and a solid metal door flickered into view, concealed by a cloak of magic. "Do *not* allow yourself to be separated from the group."

He led them down a long corridor, then stopped in front of a pane of glass. Emily touched it lightly, marvelling at the cost; glass, true glass, was staggeringly expensive in the Nameless World. Someone had charmed it to be both unbreakable and one-way; they could look in, but the patient couldn't look out. She peered into the room and frowned as she saw the patient, a middle-aged woman sitting on a comfortable chair. There didn't seem to be anything wrong with her.

"Patient Current-37," Healer Crane said. "The daughter of a famous alchemist; Current-37 was seven and wanted to be older, so she produced an aging potion and swallowed it, aging twenty years in three. She has the mind of an eleven-year-old trapped in the body of a grown woman. Her aging has slowed, but it is quite likely she will die within five years anyway, no matter what we do."

Emily shuddered. "Why can't she be helped?"

"We don't know precisely what recipe she used," Healer Crane admitted. "Even if we did, it would be impossible to undo the effects without risking further damage. Physically, she is a grown woman; mentally, she's too young to cope with anything more elaborate than playing games. The only thing we can do is keep her here and study the problem."

Imaiqah had a different question. "Don't you even know her *name?*"

"We do, yes," Healer Crane said. "But we are forbidden to share it with you. All medical files are strictly confidential without permission from the patient or their guardians."

He turned and led the way down to the next window. Emily took one last look at the girl-woman and shuddered, again. She hadn't enjoyed the experience of growing from a child into a young woman and *she'd* had it spread out over several years. To grow up so rapidly...no wonder the poor girl had to be kept in the Halfway House. She would be totally incapable of controlling the hormones unleashed by her aging body.

The next scene was far more disturbing. A young man - he couldn't have been any older than Jade - was sitting on the floor, doodling with a set of crayons. The entire room was covered in drawings, all child-like stick figures with oddly disturbing proportions. Emily looked at them, then back at the drawer. There was a love-struck expression on his face that sent chills down her spine.

"Patient Current-45," Healer Crane said. "There was a young woman who wanted him, so she dosed him with a love potion. Again, it was brewed inexpertly; the effects, unfortunately, became permanent. We altered his fixation to drawing, because it was the only way to keep him from killing himself after his lover was executed, but strands of the original fixation still bleed through. It isn't a pleasant sight."

No, Emily agreed. Love potions were akin to rape, banned on pain of immediate expulsion from Whitehall, but they were easy to find in back-alley brewshops. Lady Barb had told her that while most of them could be easily countered, some of them were so strong as to do permanent damage. *It certainly isn't a pleasant anything.*

"He has issues in common with Current-17 and Current-47," Healer Crane continued. "In the case of the former, the love potion - more accurately, a lust potion - spurs the poor girl to attack any man she sees within the right age group. The latter, as far we can determine, made the mistake of using an aged potion for his wedding night. His bride died - the brew had turned poisonous - while he became warped and twisted. He was sent here as an alternative to execution."

"Sickening," Emily said.

"Indeed," Healer Crane said. Emily swallowed. She hadn't realized she'd spoken out loud until he answered her. "Love potions, even when used under strict supervision and with full consent, can have unpleasant effects. We advise people, time and time again, to allow love to develop naturally, rather than seeking the quick fix."

He sniffed before leading them down the corridor to another window. This one had a large sign hanging over the door, banning men from entering. Inside, Emily saw a young woman lying on the bed, her hands and feet chained to the railings. Her eyes were open, but she seemed utterly unaware of her surroundings.

"She would try to jump me, if I went inside," Healer Crane said. "Only female Healers can tend to her and we're nowhere near finding a cure."

"Poor girl," Imaiqah muttered. She raised her voice. "Do you have to keep her chained to the bed?"

"She tries to escape if she isn't obviously restrained," Healer Crane said. "Healer Sami got a broken nose after she made the mistake of undoing one of her hands. Magic is better, but she doesn't seem to realize she's under restraint and keeps struggling against it."

"Some people have no sense for magic," Lady Barb interjected.

Healer Crane nodded, and showed them the next room. A young man lay on the bed, his eyes closed and his chest rising and falling. Emily frowned - there didn't seem to be anything obviously wrong with him - and looked at Lady Barb. The older woman tapped her lips and motioned to the glass. There was still nothing obviously wrong with him.

"Current-51," Healer Crane said. "He was cursed as a young child, cursed by a sorcerer we were never able to identify. All we really know is that he went to sleep when he was five and never woke up. A traveling sorcerer tried to crack the curse, failed, and brought him here for study. He's been here eleven years, sleeping all that time. Nothing we do seems to be able to break the curse."

Pandora snickered. "Have you tried true love's kiss?"

"*That* is just a fairy tale," Healer Crane said, reprovingly. "If the curse had been bound to a specific person, a lover, perhaps it would work. But at the age he was cursed, it would be impossible to determine who, if anyone, he would love. Stories in which someone's true love just happens to come wandering by are nothing more than badly-written fantasy."

Or romantic movies, Emily thought. She'd researched Sleeping Beauty once and discovered that the original version featured Sleeping Beauty being awakened by the birth of twins, after Prince Charming had come and gone. *But magic doesn't work like that, not here.*

Healer Crane scowled at them, then led them to the next window. It looked far more comfortable, as if it was designed for a child. Even so, Emily had to look around carefully before she spotted the occupant, curled up in a corner. Healer Crane tapped the glass and the occupant rolled over, revealing a young girl in shorts and a shirt. She sprang to life and gambolled - Emily could think of no better word - over to the window on all fours, leaping up like a dog. It was impossible to hear anything, but it was clear she was barking like a dog too. The desperation in her eyes chilled Emily to the bone.

"My God," Emily muttered.

"We don't know who cursed her, or why," Healer Crane said. "She cannot talk, nor can she write. The curse has embedded so deeply into her mind that she can do nothing but act like a dog. She knows she's human, she knows she's bespelled, yet... there's nothing we can do to break the spell."

Emily looked at Lady Barb, understanding just why her mentor had turned down the chance to become a Healer. There were too many problems that couldn't be fixed, no matter what the Healers did, and too many people who would get away with it if someone didn't do whatever it took to hunt them down. She toyed with the snake-bracelet, recalling the horrors she'd seen in the Cairngorms. It wouldn't be easy to take an oath that forced her to do nothing more than heal...

Healer Crane led them through a pair of doors and into a small common room. A dozen patients sat at tables, eating food from charmed plates; there was so much magic crawling through the room that Emily thought her hair would stand on end. They wouldn't be able to hurt themselves or anyone else, she realized, as she studied the charms. Knife-blades would blunt, if used against human skin; plates would shatter into harmless dust rather than hit someone and cause injury. It was the most elaborately charmed room she'd seen.

"Talk to some of the patients, if you wish," Healer Crane said. "Or sit back and wait to go home."

Emily nodded, and looked around. One man sat in a wheelchair, without any apparent sensation below the waist. He gave her a wink before turning back to his meal without paying any more attention to her. A woman sitting opposite him had to work to eat her food, as if every morsel tasted too disgusting to chew, let alone swallow. Emily felt a stab of sympathy at the way she washed each tiny morsel down with a big swig of water. And then she looked at the third patient. He just sat in his chair, dead to the world.

"Come with me," Lady Barb ordered. She led Emily over to a dark-skinned man sitting at a table, reading a book. He was the first man Emily had seen wearing silk, let alone something that resembled a ladies nightgown. Somehow, he still managed to look dignified. "Pablo, this is Emily."

"I've heard a great deal about you," Pablo said. "I would shake your hand, but it would hurt me more than you."

Emily looked enquiringly at Lady Barb, who shrugged.

"I was cursed in the Battle of Wanderer's Light," Pablo said. He muttered a number of words under his breath, just loudly enough for Emily to know he was saying *something*. "I deflected the first curse, but the second one bedded in before I could find help. These days, the mere act of touching something brings pain."

"Pablo was a Mediator," Lady Barb said. "He was caught up in a local skirmish..."

"Local skirmish my foot," Pablo said. He shifted slightly, allowing Emily to see that he was practically surrounded with charms designed to insulate him from the rest of the world. "Sir Griffin the Unconquerable took exception to the ruling we made in the case and launched an invasion, hoping to seize and hold enough territory to force his neighbors to let him keep it."

"And one of his pet sorcerers came up with something nasty," Lady Barb added. "Even a Mediator can be brought low."

Pablo eyed Emily sharply. "Are you thinking of taking up the job?"

"It's a possibility," Emily said. She looked back at Lady Barb. "Did you bring me here to meet him?"

"Yes," Lady Barb said, flatly. Her blue eyes, just for a second, reminded Emily of Master Grey. "If you start training in earnest, you may wind up dead - or you may wish you were."

"Never to feel the touch of a lover's hand," Pablo said. His voice became an exaggerated dirge. "Never to hold a weapon without dropping it moments later. Never..."

Emily winced, then covered her ears as she heard the sound of frantic barking from the doorway. The girl she'd seen earlier ran into the room on all-fours, followed by a tired-looking Healer. Emily felt another stab of pity, remembering the curses Mistress Sun and Lady Barb had taught her how to break. If the girl was incurable, the curse that had been cast on her must have been very strong indeed.

A thought struck her. "Was she forced to drink Dogbreath Potion?"

"They would have checked," Lady Barb said. "It would have shown up in her bloodstream, when they ran charms to determine what she might have ingested. And it wouldn't have lasted more than a few hours or so."

She patted Emily on the back. "It was a good thought, though."

"Thank you," Emily said.

"A very good thought," Pablo agreed. He gave her a droll smile. "But you also need to be able to do much more than come up with theories and test them out."

"I know," Emily said. She looked around the room, noting just how many of the other students looked sick at what they'd seen. "I definitely don't want to be a Healer."

"Not everyone does," Lady Barb agreed. "There's far more reward to be had in protecting the innocent from the guilty."

She shook her head. "We'll be going back to Whitehall in an hour," she said. "You can work on your research. I believe your career interview will be on Monday afternoon."

Emily blinked. "That soon?"

"There's no time to waste," Lady Barb said. "It isn't just Whitehall holding these interviews, you know."

"And so they have to visit all the schools," Emily said. She nodded, slowly. "I'll be ready."

Chapter Seventeen

Emily had half-hoped that Lady Barb had been wrong about her careers interview, but when she returned to Whitehall she found a note in her bedroom, inviting her to an interview on Monday and excusing her from Alchemy. Professor Thande wouldn't be happy, Emily suspected, but she was privately relieved. If she didn't have to go back to class after the interview, she could use the rest of the time to catch up on her reading and essay writing.

Maybe they expect my interview to be short, she thought, as she walked through the corridor on Monday to the designated chamber. *Alassa's interview was nothing more than a formality.*

She pushed the thought to the back of her mind as she tapped on the door and waited. The wards buzzed around her, confirming her identity, then the door opened of its own accord, revealing a comfortable office with a pair of chairs, a drinks table and a light globe glowing high overhead. A tall man she vaguely recognized was sitting in the chair, reading a set of parchment notes. It took Emily several seconds to place him as Master Gordian, a man she'd met briefly - very briefly - at the Cockatrice Faire.

"Lady Emily," Master Gordian said, rising to his feet. "Thank you for coming."

Emily shook his hand gravely and took the indicated seat, studying him thoughtfully. He was odd; there was something ageless about his face, as if he were young and old at the same time. It reminded her of Void's ever-changing appearance, although there was none of the sense of power that surrounded the Lone Power. His hair was tied back in a ponytail that somehow added dignity to his face, drawing attention to the shape of his cheekbones. The Nameless World had different standards of beauty, Emily had come to learn, and she had a feeling Master Gordian would be considered handsome. Indeed, he was dressing to show off his character rather than his looks.

Which may mean nothing, she reminded herself, firmly. *A nasty person could hide inside a handsome body.*

"This may be a short interview, depending upon you," Master Gordian said, as he poured them both a mug of Kava and placed them on the table. He seemed very determined to put her at her ease. "I assume you read the briefing papers?"

"Yes, sir," Emily said. They hadn't been *that* detailed; they merely stated that her careers adviser would offer neutral advice, depending on what career she wanted. "I prepared as ordered."

"Good," Master Gordian said. He sat, facing her, and crossed his legs. "You do realize you're in something of an odd position? Your role as Baroness of Cockatrice both offers you guaranteed employment" - he smiled, as if at a joke only he knew - "and restricts your ability to work in any major role. You may feel that you merely want to go back to Cockatrice after completing your schooling and not seek outside employment. If so, please let me know now."

"I don't, sir," Emily said.

She saw a flash of approval in his eyes, which vanished quickly. "Then I need to know your career objectives," Master Gordian said. "What careers do you have in mind?"

"Mediator, Librarian and Teacher," Emily said. It had been easy enough to decide on the first two, but she'd hesitated a long time over the third. If she hadn't needed a third potential career, she would have left the final space blank. "Or a private tutor, if possible."

"Private tutors are very much a mixed bag, these days," Master Gordian muttered. He didn't sound approving. "Some have excellent qualifications; others, unfortunately, have nothing beyond their own wits."

He cleared his throat. "Why do you want to be a Mediator?"

Emily hesitated. She'd come up with several possible answers over the weekend, but now that she was facing Master Gordian, her mind had gone blank. It took her a moment to gather herself before she spoke.

"Because the job needs to be done," she said, finally.

"It doesn't have to be done by you," Master Gordian pointed out. "Why do you feel *you* should do it?"

"Because...I saw the results of rogue magicians," Emily said, after an internal debate. "I saw Shadye, but I also saw the results of petty evil, evil that left its victims marked for life. I can't just sit there and do nothing."

"The Halfway House, I presume," Master Gordian said. He looked down at the parchments for a brief moment. "You might also work as a researcher, solving the problem of breaking the unbreakable curses."

"I could," Emily agreed. "But I'd want to be doing *something.*"

"The glory may go to those on the front lines," Master Gordian said. "But those at the rear, those who solve previously unsolvable problems, are often just as important. You might save more lives as a researcher than you would as a Mediator."

He had a point, Emily had to admit. But there were more reasons than just fighting evil, reasons she didn't really want to discuss. The Allied Lands *needed* to work together to stave off the necromancers, perhaps eventually defeat them. If she could do something to keep them together, she had to do it.

Master Gordian sat back and cleared his throat. "Very well," he said. "I've looked at your grades. Based on your current progress, I believe you will qualify to proceed into Fifth Year without needing to retake your exams. If you are serious about being a Mediator, you will need to stick with several of your current courses and add a couple of new ones. You will also need additional training in Martial Magic *before* you take up an apprenticeship."

He paused. "You may, at the time, be able to trade training for serving as an assistant," he added. "However, I believe Sergeant Miles would be reluctant to take you on."

Emily nodded, unsurprised. Lady Barb had told her, more than once, that it was rare for a woman to serve as a tutor in Martial Magic. The male students required a father figure, someone who could serve as the alpha male; the female students needed to learn, if they wanted to become combat sorcerers, or soldiers, that they would have to forsake both modesty and feminine pursuits. It hadn't struck her as fair, at the time, but she could see the logic.

"Otherwise, you would probably need to make arrangements with someone separate," Master Gordian said. "You would be able to do that through the school administration, although you'd have to pay for it yourself."

"Yes, sir," Emily said.

"The *real* stumbling block would be Cockatrice," Master Gordian warned. "As a Mediator, you would be expected to be neutral at all times. You would *not* be permitted to own lands in a kingdom."

"I know, sir," Emily said. "When would I have to make my choice?"

"Before you started your apprenticeship," Master Gordian told her. "However, you should properly make the choice before then, so you *know* where you're going. And there are other implications..."

He paused. "You wouldn't just be renouncing your title, *permanently*," he added. "You'd be renouncing any future claim your children might have, too. I don't think you could pass the Barony to any child you happened to have now, before starting your apprenticeship."

"I don't *have* a child," Emily said. It wasn't uncommon for girls in the Nameless World to marry young, but even if she'd had a child the year it had become physically possible the baby would be only five or six. "But couldn't I pass the lands to someone I chose?"

"It would depend on your liege lord," Master Gordian said. "I imagine King Randor would want a say in the disposition of your territories. But...the White Council would not want a Mediator who could be influenced by family, friends or former masters. Whatever happened to your lands would have to be something that satisfied them. You couldn't be allowed to put the lands aside, while you work for the Allied Lands, and then return to them once you retire."

Because Randor could hold them over my head, Emily thought. It made sense, in a way; no one would want a Mediator who had good reason *not* to be neutral. *Would he try to manipulate me if I did complete an apprenticeship?*

She shuddered. She had a feeling that the answer to that was *yes*.

"It's a worthwhile job," Master Gordian said. "However, you will need to work very hard to achieve the grades necessary to undertake an apprenticeship. On the other hand" - he shrugged, expressively - "you *will* have two more years to work on Martial Magic. You may have started from a very low position, thanks to your father's influence, but you should be well above average by the time you reach Sixth Year."

"I hope so," Emily said.

Master Gordian met her eyes. "Did your father express any opinion?"

"No," Emily said. She imagined it would have stung, if Void had been her *real* father. "Why does everyone keep asking that question?"

"Because the opinions of parents and guardians cannot be dismissed," Master Gordian said, dryly. "What about your other tutors?"

"They told me I'd need to work hard," Emily said.

"And they were right," Master Gordian said. He sighed. "I'll have a copy of the formal set of requirements sent to you. Now, are you serious about becoming a librarian?"

Emily hesitated. "I'm not sure," she admitted. "It is something I would like to do, but..."

"But you're wealthy enough to set up your own library, if you wished," Master Gordian said. "I don't think you'd need any formal qualifications, let alone guild membership."

I have set up my own library, Emily thought. Or at least she'd started her own legal deposit system. It wasn't a far cry from that to setting up a national library. *But that was part of working in Cockatrice.*

"You would be well-advised to have *some* kind of backup plan," Master Gordian added, softly. "If you take on an apprenticeship and then flunk out, you will be left landless if not penniless. A librarian is one option, true. But there are others."

He paused. "Have you thought about working for the White Council?"

Emily took a moment to think. "In what capacity?"

"You killed two necromancers," Master Gordian said. "I dare say we could find a post for you. Your father worked for the council for a while."

"He never talked to me about it," Emily said. "What would you have me do?"

"You're a magician of great power," Master Gordian said. "You have to realize that there are people out there who consider you a potential threat, and others who think of you as a pawn in their games. The White Council could keep you out of the political wars, if you wished, and help you face the necromancers. *They're* not going to forget you."

Emily nodded, sourly. The necromancers weren't a united force - if they had been, they would have overrun the Allied Lands by now - but a single necromancer and his army of monsters would be a very real threat. They'd been quiet for the last three years, after Shadye's death, yet she knew better than to think that would last indefinitely. Sooner or later, they'd need more victims to feed their magic. And she knew, on that day, she'd be one of their first targets.

"I didn't want to be famous," she muttered. It was true; she'd have been quite happy making a new life for herself at Whitehall, perhaps eventually becoming a tutor in her own right. "Why...?"

"Stories grow in the telling, particularly when someone wants to believe them," Master Gordian said, dryly. "You can try to assume command of your own destiny, like your father, or you can find a way to work with others to shape a life for yourself. The sheer level of power you demonstrated two months ago won't let you do anything else."

Another trick, Emily thought. The weight of the battery, in her pocket, was suddenly much heavier. What would they think of her if they knew the truth? Hell, what would they *do* if they knew the truth? It wouldn't be long before someone started duplicating batteries and using them for themselves. *I can't let that secret get out.*

Master Gordian cleared his throat, loudly. "I'll send you the paperwork for becoming both a librarian and a teacher," he said. "In the case of the latter, you should know that most schools demand a considerable amount of practical experience, after graduation, as well as paper qualifications. Professor Thande, for example, spent years risking his life in alchemical research before transferring to Whitehall to teach."

"I know, sir," Emily said, still feeling down. "Is it wrong of me to want to become a generalist?"

"You have the money, if you wish, to be anything you want," Master Gordian said. "You don't really need to find a job, Lady Emily. I requested to speak with you so soon *precisely* because you are not an urgent case. If you want to spend the rest of your life hiring tutors and just *learning*, you can. However..."

He held up a hand before Emily could say a word. "*However*, your power, reputation and position all make you the object of fear, hatred and envy," he added. "You can either choose to take control of your life, if you wish, or allow others to try to control you."

Emily swallowed. Aurelius of Mountaintop had offered her power and knowledge in exchange for assisting him with his plans to become MageMaster and reshape the Allied Lands. If things had been different, if she hadn't learned just how Mountaintop treated those it considered to be inferior, she would have been tempted. No, she *had* been tempted. He'd understood her very well. Indeed, if Frieda hadn't been there, Emily had to admit she might well have been seduced.

And you went into Mountaintop with your eyes wide open, she thought, numbly. *What might happen if you allowed yourself to be unwary?*

She smiled, tightly. "Is there a career path towards becoming a Lone Power?"

Master Gordian barked a laugh. "You need power, control, and a complete lack of willingness to allow others to dictate your path," he said. "I should point out that, for every magician who achieves that honored status, there are hundreds who fall by the wayside."

Emily nodded, slowly. She knew Void was powerful, but was he more powerful than the combined forces of House Ashworth or House Ashfall? And yet, did it matter? If Void could inflict a horrendous price for any attempt to take him down, the Houses might choose to leave him alone rather than pick a fight. She recalled Shadye tearing through Whitehall and shuddered, inwardly. Void might not have that level of raw power, but he had the control to make his magic far more dangerous.

"You will have the opportunity to change your mind as you go along," Master Gordian informed her. "You may discover that another job suits you better, or you may find yourself called to pure research rather than active service. However, once you start your apprenticeship, you will be committed. Even if you fail your apprenticeship, you will still have abandoned your titles."

"Yes, sir," Emily said. "Do *you* think I can do it?"

"I think that if you don't have faith in yourself, it doesn't matter who else has faith in you," Master Gordian said, sarcastically. "I've reviewed your grades. You have the raw intelligence to cope with the theoretical part of the job, while you have accumulated a great deal of practical experience. On the other hand, you seem to lack in self-confidence, which is odd given your record. I would have expected you to be more confident after flattening a pair of necromancers."

Emily frowned. "Is that a bad thing?"

"You're not arrogant," Master Gordian said. "But confidence and arrogance are not always the same thing."

He tapped Emily's mug. "You didn't drink?"

"I was distracted," Emily said. She'd never liked cold Kava, but she drank it anyway. "It's strong."

"It's meant to be," Master Gordian said. "Students have been known to survive on naught but Kava."

He rose to his feet and held out a hand. "I will be here for another month," he told her. "If you change your mind, or you want to discuss other options, you may make an appointment with me, once I have seen the rest of the students. I should add that any *second* appointment won't come with an automatic excuse note."

Emily had to smile. "Thank you, sir," she said. She rose and walked to the door. "I'll make an appointment if I need anything."

Caleb was waiting outside, looking nervous. "Emily," he said, as she entered the corridor and closed the door behind her. "Do you have time to work on our project?"

Emily glanced at her watch. It was probably too late to sneak into Alchemy, not when the door would be locked and the lesson already in progress. She'd definitely have to borrow notes from Alassa and Imaiqah and try to catch up.

"I think so," she said. "How did you know I'd be here?"

"Lady Barb said you'd probably need a distraction," Caleb said. He smiled at her. "Am I distracting enough?"

"The project is *very* distracting," Emily said. She gave Caleb a sidelong glance. "But you're distracting too."

Caleb beamed at her as they walked down to the workroom. "I would like to get a working model finished by the end of the month," he said. "We need to show it off to the Grandmaster."

"I know," Emily said. She sighed, inwardly. It felt like she'd been back at Whitehall for years, rather than three weeks. If Fourth Year was so hard, what would Fifth Year be like? "We should have one ready in time."

Chapter Eighteen

NONE OF THE TUTORS SEEMED INCLINED TO LET UP, EMILY DISCOVERED, AS SHE WORKED HER way through the first term. Professor Thande, Professor Lombardi and Lady Barb kept piling practical exercises on her in class, accompanied by massive piles of home-work, while Master Grey put Aloha and Emily through their paces time and time again. Each session, she left feeling tired, sore and increasingly determined to grit her teeth and work her way through it, rather than complaining to Lady Barb or anyone else. By the time the end of term rolled around, she was both looking forward to the chance to relax, if only for a few days, and fearing what the next term would bring.

She wasn't the only one to be stressed, she discovered, as the last few days of term slowly came to an end. There was a fight in the corridor between two students that sent several more to the infirmary, a screaming fit between Pandora and Alassa about using the library after hours, and *someone* hexed Alassa while she was trying to catch them out of bounds. She returned to the bedroom furious, practically spitting with rage, but had to admit that she didn't know just who'd turned her into a statue with a spell so powerful she'd been unable to escape without assistance. Madame Beauregard had been *very* sarcastic about the whole affair.

"When I get my hands on the bitch, I'll strangle her," she vowed, as Emily did her best to calm her friend down. "It could have cost me my job!"

"Set a trap next time," Emily advised. Some of Master Grey's training exercises could only be beaten, she'd discovered the hard way, by teamwork. "Have someone guard your back while you patrol the corridors."

"I couldn't bring you with me," Alassa muttered, as she undressed and climbed into bed. Her body moved stiffly, unsurprisingly. She'd been trapped in stone for nearly an hour before she'd been released. "Or anyone else, unless I convinced a pre-fect to join me."

And that wouldn't work, Emily thought, darkly. Alassa had to stand up for herself, not go running to an older student when she encountered something she couldn't handle. It definitely wasn't a job she wanted, no matter how good it looked on her record. She closed her eyes and forced herself to sleep, knowing that the morning would bring a difficult new task. Caleb and she would be presenting their project to the Grandmaster.

"Good luck," Imaiqah said, once they'd eaten breakfast. Emily felt so nervous that she'd had to force herself to eat more than a couple of pieces of dry toast. "You'll be fine, really."

"I hope so," Emily said. She'd arranged to meet Caleb in the workroom and carry their project to the office. "What about yours?"

"That's this afternoon," Alassa put in. There weren't any classes on Friday, allow-ing the students who would be making presentations to do their final preparations. "I'm not looking forward to it."

Emily nodded. Alassa and Imaiqah had been tight-lipped about what they were actually trying to do, but reading between the lines, Emily had the idea it had something to do with negotiations. She'd spent hours trying to figure it out - they'd been warned in Third Year that they weren't allowed to *ask* what someone was doing for their joint project - before giving up and waiting for them to tell her. So far, they'd kept it firmly to themselves.

"You'll be fine," Alassa said, patting her arm. "I don't think they'd fail you unless you accidentally blew up the South Wing."

"We came *close* to blowing up the room," Emily muttered. The second experiment with spell mosaics had worked perfectly, but the third had started well and then exploded with staggering force. Neither she nor Caleb had been able to figure out where the energy had come from. "If we blow up the Grandmaster..."

"You'll probably be expelled," Alassa said, mischievously. "Once they put enough of the pair of you back together so you *can* be expelled, that is."

Emily groaned, waved goodbye and walked through the maze of corridors towards the workroom. Caleb was already there, inspecting the pieces they'd painstakingly put together over the last couple of months. Uniformity was a joke, unsurprisingly, but with the help of a pair of woodcarvers and a blacksmith they'd managed to reduce the unwanted variables to a minimal level.

Or so Emily hoped. A single mistake at the wrong time might cause another explosion, right in front of the Grandmaster. They'd probably be failed on the spot.

"It's ready," Caleb said. He sounded as nervous as Emily felt. "Are you all right?"

"My mouth is dry," Emily admitted. She swallowed hard - she hadn't felt so nervous when she'd gone into the exams at the end of First Year - and picked up one of the boxes. "Coming?"

They walked back through the corridors until they reached the testing chamber and tapped the door. The door opened, revealing the Grandmaster, Mistress Irene, a man Emily didn't recognize and - her heart sank - Master Grey. He gave her a cruel smile as she placed the box on the table, and turned to look at the Grandmaster. Beside her, Caleb did the same.

"You are to assume," the Grandmaster said, "that we know nothing about your project. I want you to explain to us, in simple terms, just what you intend to do before you demonstrate your work. You will be marked for clarity of explanation as well as your practical work. Do you understand me?"

"Yes, sir," Emily said.

The Grandmaster smiled. "Begin."

Emily and Caleb exchanged glances. "In its basic form," Caleb said, his voice stumbling slightly, "a spell is a combination of commands and settings covering the various variables that may be involved. A perfect spell is one where those commands have been precisely worked out to produce an effect, a single effect, as laid down in the structure. Ironically, as magicians get more powerful, casting perfect spells becomes harder."

He paused, then carried on. "One way around this problem is to use a wand," he continued. "I..."

"Stop," the Grandmaster ordered. "Emily?"

Emily winced, unpleasantly aware of Master Grey's eyes boring into her skull. They'd been warned not to talk about what happened on the day their projects were tested, and now she knew why. In hindsight, she should have guessed they'd be forced to outline what they'd done as well as demonstrate it.

"A wand holds a piece of spellwork which, when power is channeled through the wand, casts a spell," she said, forcing herself to think clearly. "This allows the spell to be cast without forethought or practice, but - at the same time - the spell can never be modified by the caster. It can only be cast as specified. For example, you can use a wand-spell to turn someone into a toad, but you cannot alter the spell to turn the victim into a cat instead."

Emily hoped that Caleb would be ordered to take over, but the Grandmaster said nothing. She had to continue.

"By contrast, a spell mosaic allows someone to build up the spell and alter it as necessary," she continued. "A magician using the system can cast a spell by channeling power through the mosaic, having first put the spell together on the table, as we were taught to do in First Year Charms. There is little room for mistakes caused by distraction, or limitations caused by having the spell embedded in a wand. Anyone can change the variables to fit their requirements."

"Very well," the Grandmaster said. He looked past Emily, towards the people standing at the rear of the room. "Any questions?"

"It strikes me that *anyone* could plot out a spell," Master Grey said. "Emily? Would you care to comment?"

Emily turned to face him. "Anyone *can* plot out a spell," she said. She couldn't help a flicker of resentment. He'd singled her out, *again*, when Caleb could have offered a better explanation. "There's no call for magic to design a piece of spellwork. Actually making it work, however, requires magic."

"A good answer," the Grandmaster said.

He waved a hand at the table. "We will watch," he said. "Demonstrate the project, talking us through it as you go."

Emily nodded and opened the boxes, keeping her movements as slow and deliberate as possible. Caleb produced a set of notes, glanced at them and then placed the tiles on the table.

"The diagram here," Caleb said, "shows a basic piece of spellwork. We set up the tiles to match the spellwork, checking and rechecking that the tiles fit the diagram perfectly. Each tile, as you can see, represents a particular spell variable. If we replaced this tile" - he tapped it - "with another tile, the results would be different."

"I see," the Grandmaster said.

Mistress Irene took a step forward. "Do you believe you can control the variables?"

"As long as everything is perfectly determined, it works fine," Caleb said. "It is not, however, as adaptable as a spell cast by a magician."

Emily placed a small ball at the end of the table, then stepped backwards as Caleb rested his fingers on the first tile. "The spell, as you can see, is really designed to do nothing more than lift the ball into the air and hold it there," Caleb added. "As you can see..."

He allowed a flow of magic to enter the tile. There was a pause, just long enough to worry Emily, before the ball rose into the air. Mistress Irene smiled, just slightly; Master Grey and the stranger showed no reaction at all. The Grandmaster, standing behind her, chuckled in delight.

Caleb removed his fingers. The ball dropped to the table and bounced, falling off the table and landing on the floor. Emily picked it up and held it, feeling a moment of pride mixed with fear. What they'd started, added to her other work, would change the world.

"Very clever," Master Grey said, into the silence. "But what would happen if the variables were to be changed? Emily?"

Emily picked up one of the tiles and replaced it with a different tile, and returned the ball to the table. Caleb stepped to one side, allowing her to touch the tiles herself. They felt warm beneath her fingers, but the runes they'd used to drain excess magic had done their job. There didn't seem to be any danger of an explosion.

"Tell us what you're doing," the Grandmaster reminded her, gently.

Emily flushed. "The tile I removed determined that the ball would float thirty centimeters above the table," she said. "This one" - she pointed to the one she'd put in place - "is designed to determine that the ball will actually float one meter in the air. As you can see..."

She braced herself, then allowed magic to flow through her fingers and into the first tile. It grew warmer, but the magic flowed normally. The ball shot upwards and hovered in the air, a meter over the table. Emily took a breath and removed her fingers. The ball dropped down and was caught by Master Grey, who snatched it out of the air.

"It seems to me," Master Grey observed, "that your project is inherently limited. You'd be very dependent on having the right tiles at the right time."

"The tiles are largely interchangeable," Caleb said. "It is our intention to build up a supply covering every known piece of spellwork. Assuming they don't burn out, sir, they can be used and reused indefinitely."

"An interesting piece of work," Mistress Irene said. "I assume you brought your written notes?"

"We did," Caleb confirmed. He removed the notes from his bag and passed them to her. "I think we covered all the possible variables."

"We will see," the Grandmaster said. His face betrayed none of his feelings. "Go outside and wait. We will call you when we have reached our verdict."

Emily swallowed before leading the way outside, feeling her heart starting to race. She was too nervous to talk, so she simply leaned against the wall and waited; beside her, Caleb seemed to feel much the same way. They endured nearly thirty minutes of uncomfortable silence before the door opened, inviting them to step back inside. Two of the tiles on the table were smouldering, while a third seemed to have been reduced to dust. Master Grey was poking at a fourth with magic, testing its carrying capacity.

"You seem to have problems when overpowering the tiles," the Grandmaster observed.

"We detailed the issue in our notes," Caleb said. "There are limits to the levels of excess magic that can be drained off and recycled."

"But you may be able to reuse the magic after the spell is cast," the Grandmaster mused. "Or limit it to the point of dampening excess reactions."

He cleared his throat. "You will receive a formal written response within the week," he informed them, "but we have provisionally agreed that you can go ahead. We suggest you consider ways to handle the limitations, as well as how your concepts may best be used in the real world. You will need to make a presentation on them at the end of the school year, as part of your exams."

"You will be interrogated harshly," Master Grey put in. "Expect to be quizzed on everything."

Emily cursed under her breath. *You don't do that already?*

"It was an interesting and quite innovative project," the Grandmaster concluded. "Your tiles will be returned to you along with the formal response. I look forward to seeing your next presentation."

Mistress Irene accompanied them both outside. "I must remind you," she said as the door slammed closed, "that you are *not* to discuss anything that took place in this room with *anyone*. The consequences for doing so will be dire."

She gave them both a sharp look, then turned and swept down the corridor. Emily understood; they weren't the only team being quizzed and telling someone what they'd gone through, even in vague terms, might give their competition an unfair advantage. And it might force them to completely redo their presentation.

"We made it," Caleb said. "We *did* it!"

He caught Emily up in a hug and swept her around. "We *did* it!"

"We did," Emily agreed, as he put her down. Caleb was stronger than he looked - he'd been at Stronghold for two years, where all students had to undergo physical exercise on a daily basis - but for once she didn't feel threatened. "Now what?"

"Now we go back to work," Caleb said. He hesitated before looking her in the eye. "Would you like to come to Dragon's Den tomorrow to celebrate?"

"Sure," Emily said, without thinking. "I need to go wash now, but I'll see you tomorrow?"

Caleb nodded - his smile had grown wider - and sauntered off down the corridor. Emily watched him go, feeling an odd wave of affection, then turned and hurried back towards the stairwell. It wouldn't be long before the junior students were released from classes and she'd prefer to be in her bedroom before then, if only because they kept staring at her with a strange combination of awe and fear. There had been times when she'd seriously considered wearing a glamor rather than allowing them to recognize her.

"Emily," Imaiqah said, as she entered. She was sitting at her desk, working her way through her papers, while Alassa was standing behind her. Emily couldn't help noticing that she was chewing her fingernails. "How did it go?"

"Very well," Emily said. She thought she could tell them that much without getting into trouble. "But we have to do another presentation at the end of the year."

"I thought you'd do fine," Alassa said. "How did Caleb handle it?"

"He was pleased," Emily said. "We're going to Dragon's Den tomorrow to celebrate."

Imaiqah turned to look at her. "He finally asked you out, then?"

Emily gaped, astonished. "It's a *date?*"

"Well...*yes*," Imaiqah said. "He's clearly liked you from the moment he set eyes on you."

She fluttered her eyelashes. "It's *very* romantic."

"It's a date," Emily repeated. No one had ever asked her out before, with the possible exception of Jade, but she hadn't thought he might be interested in her until he'd asked her to marry him. He certainly hadn't tried to kiss her or anything. "It's a *date?*"

"It certainly *sounds* like a date," Imaiqah said. "Are you *nervous?*"

"*Yes*," Emily snapped. A quiet drink was fine, but a date? "I...I'm..."

"Go with me and William," Imaiqah said. "Call it a double-date."

"Oh," Alassa said. "*That's* his name."

Imaiqah gave her a dirty look. "Take Jade, too," she said. "You could call him through the portals, couldn't you?"

"Madame Beauregard has me on duty tomorrow," Alassa said. "Punishment for being hexed, she said."

"Then you'll hear all about it when we get back," Imaiqah said. She grinned at Emily. "I don't think you really need to worry about a thing, but just in case..."

She stood, walked over to her bed and opened her trunk. "There are some potions here that can be useful, if you get intimate," she said. "This one" - she held up a vial - "ensures you don't end up with a bun in the oven, if you get my drift."

Emily turned bright red. "I'm not going to sleep with him," she said. "I..."

Imaiqah laughed. "Just make sure you take precautions when you do," she said. Her voice dropped, becoming serious. "Do you like him?"

"I...I don't know," Emily said. Her feelings were conflicted. Why hadn't she realized it was a date before Imaiqah had pointed it out? She liked him, but did she *like* him? "I like him, but I'm scared..."

"Then take it calmly, day by day," Imaiqah advised. "And, above all, try to have fun."

Chapter Nineteen

Emily hadn't had a good night's sleep.

She knew, even if she disliked having to admit it, that her mother and stepfather had left scars on her soul. Her stepfather's wandering eyes had been bad enough, but her mother - in her more coherent moments - had told her never to trust young men. They smiled, she had said, to lure innocent young women into sin. It hadn't been until Emily had been much older - and in the Nameless World - that she'd realized her mother was talking about herself. Emily's father had left her, her mother's second husband was a drunken abuser; Emily honestly didn't want to know what her mother had done as a teenager. Emily herself had known girls who'd lost their virginities at fourteen and become mothers at fifteen, so what might her mother have gone through as a child?

The thought had kept her awake half the night. She'd enjoyed spending time with Jade, but it had honestly never crossed her mind that he might be interested in her. She hadn't really grasped that, while she'd been a social outcast on Earth, she was a person of some importance on the Nameless World. Jade had had good reasons to court her - Alassa had matter-of-factly listed them, back when Jade had proposed - but Emily hadn't been able to handle the thought of being courted. Or, for that matter, being more than friends with him. It was lucky, she thought, that they *had* remained friends. If he hadn't started courting Alassa, would they have stayed in touch?

She must have drifted off at some point, because the next thing she knew, Imaiqah was shaking her gently. Emily jerked awake and glanced at her watch. It was early morning, just about time for breakfast to be served. Alassa coughed loudly, and held up a dress Queen Marlena had sent to her. Emily took one look and shook her head firmly. Even if she'd had the body for it, she wouldn't have wanted to wear something that exposed half her chest and had a slit that showed her legs.

"You should wear something different, this time," Alassa said, firmly. She glanced into Emily's wardrobe and frowned. "What happened to the green dress?"

"I left it in Cockatrice," Emily said. Queen Marlena had sent her more dresses than she cared to think about, each one worth at least a hundred gold coins. "If I have to wear something else, I'll wear the dark blue or black dress."

"Black would make you look far too sombre," Alassa said. She plucked another blue dress out of the wardrobe and peered at it. "Maybe this one, if you don't mind."

Emily sighed and gave in. "Do you two *have* to dress me?"

"You need to look good," Imaiqah said, mischievously. She started to chew her fingernails again before she deliberately stopped herself. "You'll be right next to us, remember?"

"No," Emily said, burying her head under the blanket. Maybe she could tell Caleb she was sick, or...part of her just wanted to run and hide. "I should have said no."

Imaiqah pulled back the blanket. "You may discover that you're better off as friends," she said, "or you may find that he holds the key to your heart. Or you may just have fun. But you really *won't* get anywhere if you don't try."

"You sound like Lady Barb," Emily said. She sat up, swung her legs over the side of the bed and stood. Her body felt tired, too tired. If she hadn't agreed to meet Caleb, she would have stayed in bed much longer. "I'll shower, then I can dress."

"Let us help," Imaiqah said. She took the dress from Alassa and held it against Emily's body. "It shouldn't need more than a handful of minor adjustments."

Emily and Alassa shared a look. Emily had never learned to sew on Earth - her mother had never taught her - while Alassa, whose mother loved dressmaking, had never bothered to learn. It hadn't occurred to Emily, until Alassa had admitted it, that not being able to sew was unusual for an aristocratic girl. Their lives were normally so restricted, sewing was one of the few pastimes they were allowed to indulge in without limit. Imaiqah might come from commoner stock, but she knew more about sewing and mending clothes than both Emily and Alassa put together.

"I'll have a shower," Emily grumbled. "And then I can dress myself, thank you."

But her friends proved relentless. As soon as she was washed and dried, Imaiqah made her don the dress, inspecting it closely before Emily took it off, then started alterations with her needle and thread. Emily sighed, pulled her undergarments on, and waited for Imaiqah to finish her work. She had to admit, once she'd pulled on the dress and inspected herself in the mirror, that it flattered her figure. But it was really too tight around her chest for comfort, even if everything was decently covered.

"You look good," Alassa said. "All that exercise must be building up your muscles."

Emily groaned. Master Grey might have been working on building up her strength, but it came with a price. She worked her way through one set of exercises, then a slightly longer set...by the time she was done with each session, her body was aching even when they hadn't sparred physically. And then there was the constant humiliation as he pointed out her mistakes, time and time again. If she hadn't been so resolved to continue...

"I suppose," she said. She would never be as muscular as Aloha, let alone Lady Barb. It was a weakness, Master Grey had insisted, which needed to be understood. "Did Jade work on building up *your* muscles?"

"That may be the Royal Bloodline." Alassa flexed her arms thoughtfully. "I was always physically strong for my age." She sighed, before adding, "Good luck. Next time, you can go on a double-date with Jade and I."

Emily had a feeling that would be awkward as hell, but she kept that thought to herself. On Earth, dating a boy who'd dated one of her friends - if she'd had friends - would have been very difficult. Alassa, on the other hand, seemed to accept it as normal. Being on the marriage market from a very early age, as soon as her father had been sure she'd survive her childhood, was probably far stranger. Alassa had been engaged to a dozen separate princes and then had the engagements broken before she'd been old enough to grasp what she might have to do.

Imaiqah kept a hand on Emily's arm, as if she was afraid Emily would bolt, as they walked down to the courtyard. Caleb waited by one of the coaches, looking as nervous as Emily felt. He stared at Emily, as if he wasn't quite sure where to look, his face flushing with embarrassment. Oddly, that made Emily feel better. Imaiqah had pointed out that he might feel as nervous as she, perhaps more so.

"It's a guy thing," she'd said, and followed up with an example so crude she'd made Emily blush. "They're as nervous as us girls, Emily; they just show it differently."

"I'm glad you made it," he stammered. "You look great."

Emily flushed. "Thank you," she said. "So do you."

Caleb blushed, too.

"You can both get in the coach," Imaiqah said. She waved to a young man, a year or so older than her, wearing dark robes. "Emily, Caleb; this is William."

"Pleased to meet you," Emily said. William wasn't the first of Imaiqah's boyfriends she'd actually met, but he was the first who'd actually been *named*. They came and went so quickly that Emily had given up trying to keep track of them. "Shall we go?"

The ride down to Dragon's Den felt shorter than Emily remembered, but that was something of a relief. William wasn't a bad person, she was sure, yet there was something about him that put her teeth on edge, even though she wasn't sure why. She forced herself to remember that Imaiqah could look after herself, and watched through the window as the coach pulled through the gates and into the city. Imaiqah led the way out onto the streets - they smelled as bad as Emily remembered - and down towards a small eatery.

"This place serves the best food in the city," Imaiqah said, as they walked through the door. "And it is one of the nicest places to visit, if you happen to be a couple."

Emily frowned as the door closed behind them, feeling oddly trapped. It was warm inside, with a small band playing in the corner and a couple of pretty wait-resses on duty. They'd probably be the owner's daughters, Emily figured; they would have been working for their father since the day they were old enough to hold a mop or wipe dishes. One of the waitresses spoke briefly to Imaiqah, then escorted the small party through a side door and into a garden. The rear of the building was surprisingly nice - and deserted.

"You can order what you like," Imaiqah said, "but I'd recommend you share a couple of dishes. That would let you have a taste of two different meals."

She pointed Emily and Caleb to one table, and sat down with William at another. Emily felt a spark of panic - she'd assumed they'd all be sharing a table - but did as she was told. The wooden chair felt hard beneath her; she opened the menu and skimmed down the short list of selections. They probably cooked the food from scratch, she reasoned. She doubted they could afford an enchanted cabinet primed with preservation spells.

"I'm not sure what to eat," Caleb confessed. "What do you recommend?"

Emily shrugged. Dragon's Den was the most cosmopolitan city in the Nameless World - or, at least, the most cosmopolitan city she'd seen - but she'd never been to this particular eatery before and she had no idea what half the items on the menu actually were. She wound up picking something made out of chicken, while Caleb picked the beef. The waitress took their orders and money, placed a large jug of water on the table, then retreated, leaving them alone. Emily glanced at Imaiqah and realized, to her irritation, that her friend had already cast a privacy ward. Whatever she was discussing with William, Emily couldn't hear it. She couldn't even lip-read.

She looked back at Caleb, finding herself at a loss for words. What did one *say* on a date? None of the books she'd read offered her a clue, and there was no way she could say the hackneyed lines she'd heard in a dozen romantic movies. Maybe that was why people talked about the weather, she realized. It gave them something to talk about, something guaranteed to serve as a conversational opener. But what could she say? The only thing they had in common was the project and she didn't want to talk about *that*, not now. And Caleb seemed to be equally tongue-tied...

"I never really asked," she said, frantically. "How did your career interview go?"

"Well enough," Caleb said. "I explained I wanted to go into independent research and Master Gordian suggested I take a short apprenticeship with a research magician. We had quite an interesting chat about some of the limitations inherent in the career training system."

Emily smiled. "What sort of limitations?"

Caleb smiled back, as if he was relieved that the ice had finally broken. "Our project is a mixture of Charms and Alchemy," he said, "as well as some practical work. It wouldn't have been possible if we hadn't worked out how to combine the two fields. But they're considered separate; I could apprentice with an Alchemist, or a Charms Master, but I couldn't combine the two apprenticeships. And it would be very hard to apprentice with first one and then the other."

"I don't see why not," Emily said. "Wouldn't you learn good habits from the first apprenticeship?"

"You'd also be three or so years older than a normal apprentice and have the right to add *Master* to your name," Caleb pointed out. "Would you want an apprentice like that?"

"I don't think I would have cared," Emily said, but she knew it might be different if she was the one tutoring an apprentice. Someone who had already proved himself by winning a coveted title might not be willing to go back to the hard life of an apprentice, being tutored like a child. "Do you have a solution?"

"There are stories of covens, back in the old days, which gathered several masters and apprentices together," Caleb said. "I was thinking we could restart it, perhaps as a form of research institute..."

A university, Emily thought. *It wouldn't be a bad idea.*

"It would have to be small," she said, slowly. "And funding would be a problem."

"Not for Alchemy," Caleb said. "Anyone at that level could brew *Manaskol*. The apprentices could produce it, once a week, and use it to build their finances. I'm pretty sure there would be other ways to make money too..."

Patents, perhaps, Emily thought. There was no such thing in the Nameless World, which was partly why her ideas had spread so far in such a short space of time. *But they wouldn't be very enforceable.*

The waitress returned with two bowls of steaming meat, a pair of plates and a large pot of rice. Emily sniffed the chicken, decided it smelled strong but edible, and took a small helping. Caleb helped himself to both the beef and the chicken, talking all the while. Emily had to admit the idea seemed workable, but if it had been tried once and then fallen out of fashion...why? She made a mental note to look it up.

"It would be easy to combine the two fields in group study," Caleb said. "And it might make it easier to handle other apprenticeships too."

"It would also make it harder for the master to judge the apprentice's progress," Emily said, after a moment. Lady Barb had discussed Healing apprenticeships in some detail, as if she'd been trying to drive away anyone who wasn't actually committed to the role. "There wouldn't be a single person giving one-to-one teaching."

"But they might not be aiming for mastery," Caleb pointed out. "Merely...raw research."

"You'd need somewhere very secure," Emily said. Professor Thande had told them that magicians who pushed the limits too far were told to take themselves off to deserted mountains and carry out their research there. "Hell, you'd need a nexus point."

"There are some we could probably buy," Caleb said. He sighed. "But I'd need to be a Master in my own field first."

Emily nodded. A Master could speak and be heeded, whereas a mere apprentice or journeyman could not. Once he was a Master, Caleb could make proposals and even carry them out, if he had enough backing. Hell, he could even take apprentices of his own, men and women who might be willing to help test his theories. But it would be at least five years before Caleb achieved mastery and set out to change the world.

She glanced down at the plates and was shocked to discover that, between them, they'd eaten everything. Where had the food gone?

"Hey," Imaiqah said. "William and I are going off now. We'll see you back at the school?"

Emily wanted to object, but she couldn't. "I'll see you back there," she said. "Have fun."

"They're happy," Caleb said, as Imaiqah and William walked out the door.

"She'll break up with him within the week," Emily predicted, shortly. Part of her would have liked to be so...carefree, but the rest of her knew it was too dangerous. "And she'll have another boyfriend by the start of next week."

Caleb shrugged. "Do you want to go back to the coaches now?"

Emily hesitated. The first time she'd come to Dragon's Den, they'd had a set number of hours within the city, but after that there had been coaches running backwards and forwards all day. She was tempted to remain in the city with him, yet...she was scared of what might happen if she did.

"If you don't mind," she said. In truth, there was little in Dragon's Den for her right now. "I can go back on my own, if you like."

Caleb shook his head. They left a tip for the waitress - Emily hoped she'd have the wit to keep it from her family - and walked back to the coaches. The trip back up the mountains was slower than the trip down to the city, but it gave Emily a chance to focus her mind. Maybe, just maybe, it hadn't been a complete disaster.

"It's deserted," Caleb said, as they climbed out of the coach. There was no one in sight, not even a student cleaning the cobblestones as a form of detention. "They're all gone."

"Probably round the back of the school," Emily said. Alassa had grumbled about it, when she hadn't been grumbling about detention with Madame Beauregard. She should be there, she'd said, spying on the opposing players. "Everyone who isn't at Dragon's Den will be watching the Ken match."

"Oh," Caleb said. "Emily...?"

Emily turned to face him, feeling her heartbeat suddenly starting to race.

"I had a good time today," Caleb said. He seemed to be looking anywhere, but at her. "Did you?"

"I did," Emily said. She blinked in surprise. He was suddenly very close. "I..."

Caleb took her in his arms and kissed her. For a long moment, Emily was too stunned to move. Jade had kissed her, but it had been different. *Caleb* was different. His lips felt warm, yet demanding; his arms felt strong and firm.

It felt good. She felt as if she trusted him, maybe that she wanted to go further...

And then she panicked. Shoving his arms away, she turned and ran.

Chapter Twenty

CALEB CALLED HER NAME, BUT SHE IGNORED HIM AS SHE TORE THROUGH DESERTED COR-ridors, unsure if she was running from him or her own treacherous feelings. She had *liked* the kiss; she had *wanted* the kiss...and yet, the mere thought of kissing Caleb frightened her. She wanted to go back, to apologize, to have him kiss her again, but she also wanted to flee to her room and hide. Her mother had warned her, time and time again, never to trust her feelings. Emily hadn't understood what she'd meant until now.

It wasn't normal. She *knew* it wasn't normal. But she was torn between wanting to embrace her feelings and throwing them out of her body and soul. She *liked* Caleb; he was smart, funny and caring, not aggressive or unpleasant. And yet, men could change in the wink of an eye. No doubt her mother had loved her new husband until he'd shown his true colors...

She came to a halt and stumbled against the wall, clinging to the dark stone for strength. The school seemed to be humming, a dull throbbing running through the wards that seemed...*off*, somehow, but it was hard to focus when her mind was so confused. She wanted Caleb, yet she didn't trust herself to maintain control...and part of her just wanted to surrender to the wellspring of feeling within her. It was a nightmare...

But Imaiqah has had dozens of boyfriends, her own thoughts mocked her. *How does she do it?*

"Emily?"

She looked up to see Frieda staring at her, alarm written over the younger girl's face. It took everything Emily had to straighten up, to draw on reserves of strength she didn't know she possessed, just so she could let go of the wall. The corridor seemed to spin around her - for a moment, she was convinced she'd been hexed in the back - and then straightened out. Frieda ran forward, caught her arm and stared into her eyes.

"Emily," she asked. "What happened?"

"Caleb kissed me," Emily said, numbly.

Frieda stared at her. "Caleb kissed you and...what did he do?"

It slowly dawned on Emily that Frieda thought Caleb had done something utterly unforgivable. She'd grown up in the mountains; she'd have known, from a very early age, both the facts of life and how unpleasant life could become if the wrong person took a fancy to you. Without magic, the youngest daughter of a family that was already too large would be lucky if she wasn't sold to the highest bidder, who might well be a pimp at the nearest brothel. Or the lord's youngest son, seeking a mistress...

"He kissed me," Emily repeated. Frieda looked doubtful. "He kissed me and I liked it."

Frieda looked at her as if she'd started speaking in tongues. "He kissed you and you *liked* it?"

There was something in her voice, something wrong. But Emily barely noticed.

"Yes," Emily said. She twisted until she was leaning against the wall. "I *liked* it."

"Emily," Frieda said. She sounded...*upset*. "You liked it?"

Emily stared at her. Were they talking about different things?

"Yes, I did," she said. "I just...feel strange."

Frieda let out a strangled sound, then turned and ran. Emily stared after her, completely confused. She knew why she'd run from Caleb, but why had Frieda run from *her*? Had the thought of Emily kissing someone - anyone - shocked her? Or...

"It isn't nice for a Fourth Year to bully a Second Year," an all-too-familiar voice said. Emily slowly turned to look as Master Grey emerged from the shadows. She'd been so upset that she hadn't even known she'd run past his office. "Detention, Lady Emily. Go get that tacky ballroom gown off, and report to Lady Barb. I'm sure she will have something unpleasant for you to do."

Emily clenched her fists, feeling a wave of cold fury that threatened to break through what was left of her control. Master Grey was smirking slightly, his eyes flickering over her; she had to grit her teeth to keep from saying something she knew would get her into even worse trouble. Caleb had kissed her, Frieda had run from her...and she still had to remain calm, to put her stress on the back burner. The charitable part of her mind noted that it was a lesson she needed to learn, but the rest of her found it hard to care. She'd never had to cope with her own body betraying her...

But that's not true, her own thoughts countered. *Your body changed without your consent.*

"Go," Master Grey ordered. "Unless, of course, you want to serve your detention with me, personally?"

"No, thank you," Emily ground out. Lady Barb would probably have some mind-numbing task for her to do, something that would keep her from having to think. "I'll go to Lady Barb."

She forced herself to walk away slowly, despite the growing urge to run. Master Grey's gaze bored into her as she walked, sending chills down her spine. By the time she had walked around the corner and up a flight of stairs, sweat was running down her back. The sensation that someone was preparing to stick a knife in her back was almost overpowering. She walked past a young boy who was tapping his ear with his finger, probably as the result of a curse, then towards the entrance to the dorms. Thankfully, it was unguarded; everyone was either at Dragon's Den or watching the match. She opened the door to her room and stepped inside, feeling her control start to snap as the door closed behind her. And then she saw Alassa, working at her desk.

"You're back early," Alassa said. She looked up. "What happened?"

Emily glanced in the mirror. Her eyes were wide and staring, her dress was disheveled and her hair had fallen out of its ponytail. No *wonder* Frieda had thought the worst, part of her mind noted. She looked far too much like someone who had been through hell.

"Caleb kissed me, I liked it so I ran and then Frieda ran from me," Emily said. She sat down on the bed, feeling her body start to shake. "And then Master Grey gave me detention."

Alassa rose to her feet and paced over to sit beside her. "Start from the beginning," she said, "and go on to the end."

"You sound like Lady Barb," Emily said. "I..."

"I should *call* Lady Barb," Alassa said. "What happened?"

Emily stumbled through the whole story, careful to explain that it had been *she* - not Caleb - who'd messed up her dress. Alassa listened, shaking her head in dismay, as Emily explained what Frieda had done and her own complete lack of comprehension. Master Grey seemed to be very much a secondary concern.

"That could have gone better," Alassa said. She met Emily's eyes. "You *do* realize that Frieda has a monumental crush on you?"

"Pardon?"

"Frieda has a crush on you," Alassa repeated, patiently. "You're her heroine. I think she's probably had a crush on you since Mountaintop."

Emily stared at her. "But why...?"

"You saved her from having to slave at Mountaintop, without learning any proper magic," Alassa pointed out, dryly. "You took her to Cockatrice and gave her a home. You treat her as a friend and an equal rather than an inferior or a servant. Why *shouldn't* she nurse a crush on you?"

Emily closed her eyes in pain. Frieda had wanted to spend time with her, lots of time with her. They'd gone walking, practiced magic, played games...she'd even shown hints of jealousy when Emily had spent time with Caleb. In hindsight, it was all too clear. She'd toyed with Frieda's feelings without ever realizing what she'd done. And...

"I should go see her," Emily said, rising. "I..."

"Sit down," Alassa said. She tugged Emily back onto the bed. "Right now, neither of you are in any fit state for a chat. Give her time to come to terms with you not thinking of her in that manner, *then* you can talk."

"She could have told me," Emily muttered.

Alassa snorted. "And are *you* good at talking about your feelings?"

Emily flushed. "Point taken," she said. "When did *you* become the mature one?"

"I'm sure you asked me that before," Alassa teased lightly, although her smile didn't touch her eyes. "When I have a fight with Jade, I'm sure I can rely on you to calm me down and tell me I'm being an idiot."

"Maybe," Emily said. "What if *he's* being the idiot?"

"Then you can tell me that and we'll both feel better," Alassa said, briskly. "Now; what are you going to do about Caleb?"

"I don't know," Emily said. A thought struck her. "What do you think he's doing?"

"Probably wondering if someone pranked him by sticking girl-repellent on his lips," Alassa said, unkindly. Emily glowered at her. "Or if he forgot to brush his teeth and his breath was so smelly you fled in terror. Or if he accidentally cast a revulsion charm and you now can't bear the sight of him. Or..."

"I left him down in the courtyard," Emily said. "I should go see..."

"If he's still there?" Alassa finished. She shook her head. "He's probably talking to one of his male friends about how unpredictable girls are."

Emily sighed. "I messed this up, didn't I?"

"Now you know why the aristocracy prefers to arrange marriages for its children," Alassa said. "There's less room for emotions to get in the way of cold calculation."

"You chose Jade," Emily said. She looked at her friend. "How did you feel when he kissed you for the first time?"

"Excited and scared," Alassa admitted. "How did *you* feel when Caleb kissed you?"

"Excited and scared," Emily said. The memory taunted her. "But you didn't run."

"No," Alassa agreed. "I didn't."

She patted Emily's back, awkwardly. "Why did you run?"

"I liked it," Emily said. "I wanted to go further. Much further. And the thought was unbearable, so I ran."

"I'm not sure that makes any kind of sense," Alassa said.

Emily rested her head in her hands. "I'm an idiot," she said. "Now I have two people mad at me."

"I don't think Caleb's the sort of person to get mad just because you ran after he kissed you," Alassa said. "If I'd thought he wasn't a nice person, I would have said something *before* you became involved with him. So would Imaiqah. On the other hand, you probably owe him an explanation."

"I don't know what to tell him," Emily confessed. "What do I say?"

"The truth is probably the best option," Alassa said. She stood, then knelt in front of Emily, forcing her to look down. "Do you want to kiss him again?"

"Yes...no...I don't know," Emily said. "I..."

"I spent ages working up the courage to kiss Jade," Alassa said. "It wasn't easy."

"It wouldn't have been," Emily mused. Alassa had to remain a virgin until her wedding night, even though there was no logical reason for it in a world where contraceptive potions and fatherhood spells were common. If her reputation was tarnished, she would - at the very least - have to face a humiliating physical exam to prove she was still a virgin. "Did you want to go further?"

Alassa colored. "Oh yes," she said. "*Much* further."

Emily shook her head. "I'm sorry," she said, although she wasn't sure what she was apologizing for. "I need to go find him and apologize."

"I thought you said you had detention," Alassa said. "Master Grey is pushing you hard, isn't he?"

"Yeah," Emily muttered. She stood, then unhooked the dress and allowed it to fall to the floor. There were a handful of bruises on her body from her last session with Master Grey, all fading slowly into her pale skin. "Let me wash, then I'll go find Lady Barb."

"Leave the dress," Alassa advised. "It can be washed and then you can wear it again, if you like."

Emily shrugged as she stepped into the bathroom. She wanted to spend longer in the shower, but she knew that Master Grey would have made a point of logging her detention as soon as he returned to his office. Lady Barb wouldn't be too pleased if she was late, even though she hadn't been given a specific time. At the very least, she should have gone to the office and requested a time to return to carry out the detention. Her cheeks burned at the injustice of it all as she washed herself down, then used a spell to dry herself. Pulling on a gown, she returned to her bed and found a new set of robes. There was probably no point in donning another dress.

"Good luck," Alassa said, once Emily was dressed. "And if you *do* see Caleb, or Frieda, be honest with them."

"I will," Emily said. She'd be passing the Second Year bedrooms on her way to Lady Barb's office. If Frieda was there, she could have a little chat with the younger girl, even though Alassa had advised against it. "Or at least I'll do my best."

Alassa eyed her doubtfully, then shrugged. "I know what will cheer you up," she added. "We'll have a midnight feast on the battlements again."

Emily blinked. "Aren't you supposed to be the Dorm Monitor?"

"I'll speak to myself very severely afterwards," Alassa said. She grinned. "Don't you remember the last time we sneaked out and had a feast?"

Emily rolled her eyes. Whoever had written stories about the joys of midnight feasts in boarding schools had clearly never been to a boarding school, let alone enjoyed a midnight feast. It had been fun, she had to admit, but it had also left her far too tired the following morning. And there was the ever-present risk of being caught and punished for being out of bounds after Lights Out. Maybe it *was* a tradition, but it wasn't one she really intended to uphold.

"It'll be fun," Alassa wheedled. "And it will do you a power of good."

"If you like," Emily said. "I'll leave you with the task of sorting out the food."

She stepped out of her room and walked down the corridor, passing through the wards that marked the edge of Fourth Year territory. Whitehall still seemed deserted, although she could hear the sound of someone singing in the distance, a sweet but sad song about a witch who'd fallen in love with a dying man and sacrificed her magic to save his life. Given what she'd learned about some of the forbidden medical spells, Emily had a good idea what she'd done to save her lover. The song ended with them settling down together as man and wife, although Emily doubted it would have worked out so well. She'd only had magic for four years and she wasn't sure she could live without it any longer.

Madame Razz was standing outside the entrance to the Second Year rooms, berating a young boy Emily didn't know. His head kept twisting from side to side, as if he was trying to physically avoid the House Mother's lecture. Emily cleared her throat as Madame Razz dispatched him to see the Warden, then waited until the House Mother deigned to notice her presence. She was known for being alternatively motherly and incredibly strict.

"Emily," Madame Razz said. "Speak."

"I would like to see Frieda," Emily said. It wasn't common for older students to visit younger ones in their dorms. She'd need the House Mother's permission to enter if Frieda wasn't there. "Is that possible?"

Madame Razz closed her eyes, reaching out with her mind to touch the wards. "Frieda is not currently in her room," she said. "I suggest you look for her elsewhere."

Emily sighed, inwardly. The wards should be able to locate Frieda within a split-second, but she knew Madame Razz wouldn't help her to find the younger girl unless it was a real emergency. Whitehall's unspoken rules baffled her at times, although she thought she understood. The wards monitored the school too closely for any abuse to pass unnoticed or unreported.

"I will," she said. "If you happen to see her, please will you let her know I was looking for her?"

"I suppose," Madame Razz grumbled. "But I am not your messenger girl."

Emily nodded in thanks, then hurried down the corridor, past a small group of students who appeared to be staring at the floor. She wondered if someone had managed to shrink themselves into near-invisibility or something, then dismissed the thought. Anything really dangerous would have been caught by the wards. She kept a sharp eye out for Caleb as she walked, but saw no sign of him. For all she knew, he and Frieda were both walking outside the school...

She stopped outside Lady Barb's office and knocked on the open door. Lady Barb was tending to a handful of girls, all of whom had bloody noses. Emily stared at them in disbelief. How could nine girls all have the same identical injury? Had they *all* walked into a wall at the same time? Or been pushed?

Lady Barb turned and looked at her. "Emily. Why are you here?"

"I have detention," Emily confessed. At least she'd have a chance to talk to Lady Barb afterwards. "Master Grey sent me here."

"Again," Lady Barb said, disapprovingly.

"Yes," Emily said.

"Well, you can help me heal these people," Lady Barb said, after a long moment. She waved a hand towards a pale-skinned girl who couldn't be any older than Frieda. "Consider it a practical test of your abilities."

Emily swallowed, and went to work.

Chapter Twenty-One

"TELL ME SOMETHING," LADY BARB SAID, ONCE THE LAST OF THE GIRLS HAD BEEN HEALED and dispatched to her bedroom. "How many girls are there in Second Year?"

Emily thought about it. Whitehall normally had around fifty girls and seventy boys per year, but there had been a recruiting shortfall after Shadye's attack, when *she'd* been in her First Year. She had the impression, from Frieda, that there weren't actually that many girls in her year...

"Around thirty," she guessed.

"Thirty-nine," Lady Barb said. "And thirty-seven of them have the same injury."

Emily blinked. "All, but two? How?"

"A very good question," Lady Barb said. "They all say they ran into a wall."

That couldn't be right, Emily was sure. The younger students did go running through the building, and it was at least reasonably possible that one or two might accidentally run into a wall, but how could all of them, save two, make the same stupid mistake? Even if the school had been reconfiguring itself at the time, it wouldn't have produced the same injury...

"They're lying," she said. "They *must* be lying. Someone beat them up or cursed them or..."

"They're all telling the truth," Lady Barb said. "I checked. They all swear they ran into walls and they're all telling the truth."

"I don't believe it," Emily said. "Did someone tamper with their memories?"

"Not according to the wards," Lady Barb said. "No one has used anything more dangerous than a mild compulsion charm over the past couple of weeks, at least outside class. I don't think there was anything strong enough to cause such a lasting effect in one person, let alone thirty-seven. It makes no sense."

Emily considered it. "Who was spared and why?"

"Frieda and Tomas," Lady Barb said. "And there doesn't seem to be any *reason* why they were spared."

She gave Emily a sharp look. "Have you noticed any odd behavior recently?"

"Imaiqah was chewing her fingernails," Emily said, after a moment's thought. "I don't recall anything else."

"Might be nothing," Lady Barb said. She shook her head, then sat down at the desk. "And now we've healed the wounded, perhaps you could explain to me how you managed to earn another detention on a weekend?"

Emily swallowed, and started to explain.

"I shall be having words with Caleb," Lady Barb said, when she'd finished. "Or, rather, I shall be having words with the Grandmaster, who will have words with Caleb."

"But..." Emily caught herself, then pressed on. "He didn't..."

"You are *meant* to be doing a joint project with him," Lady Barb said, coldly. "I don't believe you will find it any easier with this hanging over you."

Emily winced. She'd honestly never considered the possibility of having to work with a former boyfriend. It had never happened before; even Jade, when he'd asked her to marry him, had been on the verge of leaving Whitehall. Caleb...she wasn't sure what he was, here and now, but it wouldn't be easy to work with him if matters remained unresolved between them. God alone knew what he thought of her.

"It wasn't fair of him to spring this on you," Lady Barb continued. "I believe the Grandmaster will be unhappy."

"Please will you let me talk to him first?" Emily pleaded. It wasn't right for Caleb to be punished because of *her* problems. "I don't think it will get in our way."

Lady Barb arched her eyebrows. "And just how many relationships have you had?"

Emily flushed. "You're dating Sergeant Miles..."

"We're not actually in the same job," Lady Barb said, cutting her off. "More to the point" - she started to tick points off on her fingers - "we are both older than you, more mature than you, and considerably more honest with one another. How easy do you think it would be to work together if you happened to be lovers?"

"We could do it," Emily said.

"I'm *sure* you could," Lady Barb said, sarcastically. "Why did you run?"

"I liked the kiss," Emily confessed. "And the feelings were so strong I ran from them."

"Because they made you feel vulnerable," Lady Barb said. She smiled, rather tiredly. "I think you need to learn to cope with your feelings, rather than suppress them or run from them."

"It isn't easy," Emily muttered.

"Very little worth doing is easy," Lady Barb countered. She rested her elbows on the table and leaned forward, placing her fingertips together. "I will delay speaking to the Grandmaster if - *if* - you speak to Caleb today and sort yourself out. If you don't, I will have no option but to report the new problem and let him handle it."

Emily swallowed. "You want me to face up to the problem," she said. "But..."

Lady Barb met her eyes. "But what?"

"Nothing," Emily said, rubbing her forehead. It felt as if she'd been awake for days, rather than hours. "I'll speak to him."

"Good," Lady Barb said. She closed her eyes for a long moment, reaching out and querying the wards. "You'll find him in the workroom, thankfully. He's alone."

She held up a hand before Emily could rise. "I think we'll count your work here as your detention," she said. "However..."

There was a long pause. "There's something that needs to be said," she warned, "and said clearly. You *cannot* keep running from your problems."

"I know," Emily said.

"The Grandmaster - and I - are very concerned about just what will happen when you come of age," Lady Barb continued. "We and--" - her lips thinned in silent disapproval "--Void have spent a great deal of time running interference for you. We have done this, at least in part, because you are both a stranger to our world and underage, at least by magical standards. It cannot last indefinitely. Once you pass Fourth Year, you will be considered fully adult. It will no longer be possible to protect you from some of the less savory elements of our world."

Emily opened her mouth, although she was unsure what to say. "I..."

"You are, quite probably, the most sought-after person in the Allied Lands," Lady Barb warned. "If Whitehall wasn't so strongly defended, if the Grandmaster didn't have so many magicians who owed him a favor, if...if your supposed father wasn't so powerful, if...it's quite possible you would have been assassinated by now. Or kidnapped by someone less inclined to worry about retaliation if they kill you, accidentally or otherwise."

"I know," Emily said.

"Then *learn*," Lady Barb snapped. "You are good, *brilliant* even, at sticking up for others. I dare say the *reason* Frieda is crushing on you is because you are the *first* person ever to give a damn for her. You stuck up for Alassa, you stuck up for Imaiqah, you even stuck up for Melissa when I'd bet good money you were tempted to hurl her into the dragon's mouth. But you're very bad at sticking up for yourself."

Emily felt her breath catch in her throat. "I..."

"You have to learn to toughen up," Lady Barb said. "Because, next year, everything will be different."

"That's why Master Grey is here," Emily said. It wasn't a question. "He was hired to put me through the wringer."

"Yes," Lady Barb said, flatly.

Emily stared down at her hands. She wanted to deny it, she wanted to throw Lady Barb's words back at her, but she knew she could not. The courage that had propelled her into an early confrontation with Alassa, and the Iron Duchess, and so many others had been driven by a concern for others, not herself. Why would anyone show concern for *her*?

"You need to be pushed into deep waters," Lady Barb said. She sounded sympathetic, but there was no give in her tone at all. "Sink or swim. Player or pawn."

"I'm sorry," Emily said.

"Don't be sorry," Lady Barb said. "*Fix it.*"

Lady Barb cleared her throat. "I expect you to report back to me tomorrow with *full* details of what passes between you and Caleb," she added. "If you don't visit me by midmorning, I will have to speak to the Grandmaster. That will not end well for either of you."

"I understand," Emily said. Lady Barb was forcing her to act or risk losing the joint project and having to redo Third Year as well as Fourth. "And thank you."

"You're not the first girl to have problems with boys," Lady Barb said, as Emily rose. "And Caleb isn't the first boy to have problems with girls. Bear that in mind, perhaps, while you're talking to him."

Emily nodded, walked out of the room and down the stairs towards the alchemy workrooms. A couple were open, occupied by other students conducting *their* joint projects; others were locked and sealed, heavily warded to keep out intruders. Emily wished, for a moment, that she could have done the project on her own, but pushed the thought aside. Teamwork wasn't one of her strengths, yet she'd *enjoyed* working with Caleb. Lady Barb was right. It hadn't been fair of him to ask her out before the project was finished, not when it *would* overshadow their work.

She paused outside the door, uncertain if she wanted to take that final step. It would be easy, so easy, just to leave matters alone. Lady Barb would go to the Grandmaster and then...and then what? The project would have to be restarted from scratch, at best; Caleb would have to put up with a third co-worker. Or maybe it would be split between them...

This is what Lady Barb meant, you fool, she told herself. *Do you want her standing behind you with a whip?*

Bracing herself, she opened the door and stepped inside.

Caleb sat on a stool, his head bowed over a piece of wood. His fingers seemed to work perfectly, she noted, as he carved out the rune for later use. He looked up as she entered, his eyes seemingly torn between wariness and relief that she'd finally come to him. It had to have looked worse to him, Emily realized, as she sat down on the other side of the table. God alone knew what had run through his mind after she'd fled.

"Hi," she said, nervously.

"Hi," Caleb said. He put the knife down, but held the piece of wood in his hand. "Emily..."

Emily gathered her courage as best as she could and leaned forward. "It wasn't your fault," she said, softly. What did one *say* to a boy when you'd fled from him? "It was mine."

"I kissed you," Caleb said. It struck her, suddenly, that he must have wondered what *Void* would have had to say about the whole affair. Kissing the daughter of a Lone Power had to rank beside taunting a necromancer as a fancy way to commit suicide. "It was *my* fault. My presumption."

"I had a bad experience when I was younger," Emily said. Greatly daring, she reached over the table and grasped his hand in hers. His skin felt soft, yet somehow leathery when she ran her fingers over the scars. "It left me...untrusting of my own feelings. When you kissed me, I was so overwhelmed that I fled."

Caleb frowned. "My kiss did that to you?"

"The memories did," Emily said. "It wasn't *your* fault."

"I feel guilty," Caleb admitted.

"I feel guilty for leaving you behind," Emily countered. She also felt guilty over Frieda's reaction, but that was something she would have to handle later. No doubt it would be an even more awkward conversation. "And for scaring you so badly."

"It wasn't your fault either," Caleb said. "I assure you, Casper would never have apologized for scaring me."

"I never had siblings," Emily said. She knew from Imaiqah that having siblings could be good and bad in equal measure, but it wasn't something she'd experienced for herself. Her life would not have been any easier, she thought, if she'd had half-sisters or brothers. "I shouldn't have scared you so badly."

"I forgive you," Caleb said. He sounded awkward. "Do you want to work on producing some more tiles?"

Emily shook her head. "I'm not a very confident person," she admitted. "I..."

"You killed two necromancers," Caleb said. "I don't believe that anyone else has managed to kill more than one - and never in single combat."

"Everyone here knows I'm human," Emily said. Jade, Cat and Travis had seen her in Martial Magic. They'd *known* she was grossly unprepared. Travis had even mocked her to her face after the first disastrous attempt to produce a battery. But that had been the Mimic...no matter; it had done what the *real* Travis would have done. "I hate it when people say I'm famous."

"You are," Caleb pointed out, stiffly.

Emily took the wood from his hand and placed it on the table. "It's nearly dinnertime," she said. "Do you want to go for a walk?"

"I do need to make more tiles," Caleb said. "And..."

"You're coming with me," Emily said, firmly. She stood, then took Caleb's hand and pulled him gently towards the door. He could have resisted, if he'd wanted to resist, but instead he just followed her outside, locking and warding the door behind them. "I don't think I've shown you the mountains."

"I thought I'd seen enough of mountains after the first route march I did at Stronghold," Caleb said. "It rained, and then it snowed, and then it rained again, and then..."

Emily smiled. "It snowed?"

"How did you guess?" Caleb asked. "Yes, it snowed. And snowed. And snowed... by the time we finally got back to the school, we looked like ice barbarians from the very far north."

"I've read about them," Emily said. "Ice barbarians and Frost Giants; they're real, aren't they?"

"Of course they're real," Caleb said, as they walked through the door and out into the sunlight. It wouldn't be long before the sun started to set, but they could walk for some distance first. "One of them came to Stronghold once. He was easily three or four times the size of the tallest lout at Stronghold. I saw him pick up an entire table with one hand and hold it in the air."

Emily smiled, remembering the skeleton she'd seen in the Cairngorms. "What was he doing there?"

"We were being taught how to fight them," Caleb said. "They're strong, but they're not very fast."

"I see," Emily said.

She was surprised at her own daring as she led him up a path she knew, from her explorations with Jade, to be rarely used. She'd never had the sense that Jade was interested in her as more than a friend, which was probably why she hadn't minded being alone with him. Now, with a boy she *knew* was interested, she found herself torn between a strange kind of anticipation and an even stranger fear.

"I used to come up here just to be alone for a while," Emily said. "I like having friends, but..."

"They can be a pain at times," Caleb agreed, gravely.

Emily nodded as they reached the overhang and peered down at Whitehall. The school's towers were glittering in the sunlight, a faint haze shimmering around the building. There was something about it that seemed *odd*, as if it wasn't quite right. Emily stared at it, puzzled, and looked at Caleb. He didn't seem aware that anything was different.

"They might have been altering the wards," Caleb said, when she raised the matter. "It isn't uncommon for new discoveries to force them to change everything."

"Maybe," Emily said. There was something about the sensation that made her uneasy, but she knew he was probably right. She put it out of her mind as she took one last look at the school, then turned to face him. "I...can I ask a favor?"

"Of course," Caleb said. "What would you like?"

"Just stay still," Emily said. She braced herself, fighting the same urge to avoid committing herself, to run for her life, and stepped up to him. He was taller than her, but not tall enough to make it impossible to kiss him. His lips felt warm and soft against hers. Her entire body quivered as he kissed her back.

She wrapped her arms around him, and kissed him again. Her body tensed as his arms came up and gently enfolded her; she forced herself to relax as it became clear he wasn't going to try to crush the life out of her, or draw her to him. She was suddenly very - *very* - aware of her body's heartbeat as she kissed him one final time, then drew back.

"We have to take things slowly," she said. The urge to run was fading, but she knew it was still lurking at the back of her mind. "Is that all right?"

"Yes," Caleb said. "You're worth waiting for."

They held hands as they walked back to Whitehall, then parted when they reached the entrance, Caleb heading to the dining hall while Emily went to her room. Her lips felt strange after kissing Caleb - how many times had they kissed? She could almost feel his lips against hers still as she stepped into the bedroom, where Imaiqah and Alassa were talking together in low voices. Imaiqah was *still* chewing her fingernails...

"I see you had fun, eventually," Imaiqah said. Alassa had obviously told her what had happened, at least in some detail. "How are you feeling now?"

"Strange," Emily said. She glanced into the mirror and froze. Her lips looked swollen, while her face was flushed. Anyone who'd seen her would *know* what she'd been doing. "I..."

"It does fade," Imaiqah said. She shared a look with Alassa. "What happened?"

Emily blushed. "I'll tell you later," she promised. "Why are you chewing your fingernails?"

Imaiqah looked down at her hands. "I...I just am," she said. "Does it matter?"

"I don't know," Emily said. It was odd for the normally neat and tidy Imaiqah to do anything as childish as sucking her fingers. "Does it?"

Chapter Twenty-Two

IMAIQAH WASN'T THE ONLY PERSON ACTING ODDLY, EMILY DISCOVERED OVER THE NEXT couple of days. Frieda seemed to be hiding from her, to the point of sneaking into the kitchens rather than eat at regular hours, while a handful of other younger students were showing signs of behaving weirdly in the corridors. Indeed, in the middle of Professor Thande's practical class, Melissa threw an ingredient right across the room into Alassa's wok, causing an explosion that burned through five of the six wards Professor Thande used to protect his students from their mistakes. Professor Thande lost his smile for the first time Emily could remember, at least since the attack on Whitehall; Melissa was sent to the Warden and a shaken class was dismissed early. By the time Tuesday afternoon rolled around, Emily almost welcomed Martial Magic. At least she *knew* it was going to be unpleasant.

"Aloha, you are dismissed," Master Grey said, once they entered the Armory. "Return here in an hour."

"Yes, sir," Aloha said.

You could have told her before she got dressed, Emily thought, darkly. They weren't meant to wear their uniforms on the upper levels, for no reason that made sense to her. *Or do you expect her to sit in the workroom and wait for you there?*

"Come with me," Master Grey ordered. He turned on his heel and marched off without looking back. "Sergeant Miles tells me you know how to use a staff."

"Yes, sir," Emily said. It had been several months since she'd last used one - it was dangerously easy to become dependent on wands or staffs - but she knew what she was doing. "My staff should be in the locker."

"No, it's in the spellchamber," Master Grey said. "I took the liberty of moving it for you."

Emily pursed her lips, but said nothing. It was quite obvious he was trying to get a rise out of her, or - perhaps - to provoke her into saying something that would get her yet another detention. If that was what he had in mind, he showed no sign of disappointment as he opened a stone door, revealing a spellchamber easily five or six times the size of the ones on the upper levels. A simple red circle was marked on the floor, reminding her of demon-summoning rituals she'd seen at Mountaintop; the walls were bare stone, without even a handful of runes to draw away excess magic. Her staff was resting on the table, a long wooden stave almost as tall as herself. She wrapped her hands around the staff and held it in the air.

"If nothing else," Sergeant Miles had said, years ago, "you can hit your opponent with it."

"You will stand in the circle," Master Grey said. Emily looked at the red circle, then back at him. "Should you leave the circle without permission, you will be punished."

Emily gave him a sharp look. "Why don't you stick my feet to the ground again?"

"Because it would be pointless," Master Grey said. He pointed to the circle, then smiled coldly. "And one demerit for cheek. You can work it off while Aloha does *her* time in the circle."

"Yes, sir," Emily said. She walked across the red line, expecting to feel wards snapping into place around her, but nothing happened. It was just paint dabbed on the floor. "What do you want me to do now?"

Master Grey peered at her. "I understand you had some basic dueling training in Mountaintop?"

"Yes, sir," Emily said.

"Wait," Master Grey ordered. He walked over to a second door and opened it, then ushered in a group of Third Years. Emily recognized a couple of them - they'd volunteered to assist in Lady Barb's class - but the others were strangers to her. "This is the current line up for Defensive Magic, Third Year."

Emily swallowed. She had a nasty feeling she knew what was coming.

"These youngsters are going to be hurling hexes at you," Master Grey informed her. He swept his gaze over the younger students, who looked depressingly enthusiastic. "All you have to do is block their hexes. You are not, of course, allowed to hex them back. That would be bullying."

And nine on one isn't? Emily thought. She knew more defensive spells - and probably had more raw power - than any of the Third Years, but nine on one was appallingly poor odds no matter how she looked at it. *This is going to end badly. Very badly.*

Master Grey held up a silver whistle, and eyed the younger students icily. "I will blow this whistle," he said. "When I do, you may start hexing; when I blow it a second time, you will stop. Anyone who fires off a hex after I blow the whistle to stop will feel the lash of both my tongue and belt. If any of you have a problem following these instructions, get out now and save time."

There was a long pause. Emily frantically hefted her staff, and started inputting defensive spells into the wood. If she'd had more time...the wards and hexes she'd placed around herself were strong, but they could be weakened by a sustained barrage of even minor hexes or curses...had he told them not to use curses? The thought sent chills down her spine. A hex might be embarrassing if it struck her unprotected body, but a curse might well be lethal.

"Take aim," Master Grey said, with a disturbing amount of enthusiasm. "And..."

He blew the whistle. Emily ducked instinctively - a handful of hexes flashed over her head and spent themselves on the stone walls - and then lifted her staff to cast a handful of additional protective wards as the younger students lowered their aims. There were so many hexes darting towards her that dodging was probably futile. She might jump *into* the path of one hex while getting *out* of the way of another.

The first handful of more accurate hexes spluttered against her wards; she swept them out of existence and cast a second set of defenses, relying on the staff more than she should. A wave of heat struck her as two hexes intermingled, then exploded in a flash of blinding light; she rubbed her eyes frantically as several more hexes scored hits against her personal protective wards. So far, it didn't seem to have occurred to them to spread out and take her from all sides, but she had a feeling *someone* would think of it before Master Grey blew the whistle a second time. She altered her wards, reflecting a couple of greenish hexes back at the younger students and smiled in relief as they struck their targets. Both students turned into frogs.

Should have thought to ward yourselves too, she thought, vindictively.

"I thought you said she wasn't allowed to hit back," one of the Third Years protested.

Master Grey gave him a clip round the ear. "She reflected your hexes back at you," he said, nastily. The boy rubbed his ear, but had the wit not to argue further. "I didn't tell her she couldn't do *that*."

He kicked one of the frogs, sending it jumping right across the room. "Next time, only use a spell you know how to counter," he added. The second frog got out of the way before he too was hit. "Your enemy may use it against you."

Emily felt an odd burst of...*something* at his words. Master Grey could have jumped on her for deflecting the spells back at their casters, but instead he'd berated the student who'd complained. Maybe he'd left that loophole in there deliberately, to see if she'd make use of it; maybe he'd close it next time...she ducked a much stronger hex, almost a curse, then swore under her breath as the Third Years finally realized they should be spreading out. No matter how she twisted her wards, they were slowly being battered down by the sheer weight of hexes hitting them.

She sucked in her breath, sharply, as she felt a stabbing pain in her chest. Someone had tried a compulsion hex, she realized, and only the rune she'd carved into her bare flesh had saved her. What had they tried to make her do? Another hex slammed home; she barely managed to counter it before it forced her to freeze in place. She deflected two more - she heard a scream as one of the Third Years was picked up and thrown against the wall - and then a final hex slammed into her staff. It blew out of her hands, leaving her momentarily defenseless. Three more hexes struck her and locked her solidly in place. Eerie flickers of magic pulsed around her, as if several different spells were trying to go to work...

Master Grey blew the whistle. "Very well done," he said, eyeing the Third Years. He was, Emily noted, careful to stay within her restricted field of vision. "I did notice, however, that several of you were struck by your own spells."

He pointed his fingers at a spot behind Emily, then clicked them. "You, in particular, were hit with a spell that went right through the circle, instead of being deflected," he added. "If you're going to be in a place where being hexed by your own side is a very real possibility, you should keep your own protective wards up. And, I should add, you should also consider releasing those on your side who have been hexed. Emily could have stopped most of you without ever firing off a hex of her own."

Emily would have gritted her teeth, if she had been able to move. She knew how to counter the regular freeze spell, but this was a whole different animal. Normally, she could tell if someone had turned her into a statue, rather than simply freezing her in place; this spell, whichever one had struck her, was different. Her body felt numb rather than just petrified.

Then concentrate on breaking free, she thought. The spell might fade on its own - or it might hold her until she freed herself or someone else released her. *You've done it before...*

Or had she? She still had nightmares about the day she'd almost killed Alassa, way back in First Year, when she'd accidentally mingled two spells together. How many hexes had struck her unprotected body before Master Grey had blown the whistle? The looks some of the Third Years were shooting her were far from pleasant...was she merely frozen or had parts of her body been transfigured? Cold ice ran down the back of her neck as she remembered Alassa, in the weeks after her lucky escape. It had been a long time before Alassa had recovered fully from the experience.

"Emily, you have thirty minutes to free yourself," Master Grey said. He nodded to her curtly, then turned and motioned the younger students out of the chamber. "If you are not free by then, you will regret it."

I already do, Emily thought, as the door closed behind the laughing and joking Third Years. Master Grey had a talent - no, a *gift* - for triggering her insecurities, for making her feel worthless...Lady Barb was right, she realized numbly. The more she failed to learn how to stand up for herself, the worse it would be when she left Whitehall. *But how do I get out of this?*

Panic welled up in her mind as she recalled Alassa, then she forced it down and tried to break the spell conventionally. It didn't work. Either the freeze spell wasn't the only thing affecting her or it was something very different from the standard spell. Mentally gnashing her teeth, she focused her mind and reached out, feeling for the hexes surrounding her. There seemed to be at least twelve hexes, meshed together into one whole. She could easily have been killed, she realized, if things had been a little different. Master Grey had brought her to the edge of death.

And if I start fiddling with the spells, I may make things worse, she thought. It wasn't a pleasant thought. She was tempted just to wait, even though she knew he was right; she would regret it. Not because of any punishment, but because she would have let him win their silent struggle. *I need to get out of this for myself.*

Bracing herself, she plunged her mind into the maelstrom surrounding her. The entire edifice of spellwork was strange, unsurprisingly; it hadn't been intended as a single unit at all. She probed it mentally, testing the links, then threw her magic at the weak points. The edifice came apart, spell components shattering around her... and then one hex came right at her, slamming into her body. She swore mentally as she shrank, her uniform falling around her as she became a mouse...whoever had cast that spell, she knew, would have been in real trouble if he'd done it elsewhere. Turning someone into an animal or an object was fine, according to Whitehall, but stripping them naked was not.

She scuttled out from under her uniform, marvelling at how strange the room seemed when seen through the eyes of a mouse, and then cast the counterspell. As soon as she was human, she yanked on her clothes and headed to the door. It was locked. She tested it quickly, unsure if Master Grey had meant for her to escape the room as well as the hexes; it didn't seem likely, if only because the lock was easy to undo. Opening the door, she stepped outside...and walked right into Master Grey. He'd been waiting for her.

"That could have killed me," she protested.

"Indeed," Master Grey said. He didn't seem amused or annoyed at her protestations, merely unconcerned. "How many things do you think there are, out there, that can kill a Mediator?"

"I have no idea," Emily said.

"Then you had better find out," Master Grey said. "Follow me."

He didn't say a word until they were both in his office, with the door locked. "You'll find bread, cheese and water in the side room," he added. "Make yourself something to eat, then come back here."

Emily nodded and did as she was told. She was hungry, more hungry than she cared to admit, but somehow she managed to prepare the food and pour herself a glass of water. It crossed her mind that she should ask if *he* wanted something, yet the stubborn part of her mind refused to let her check. If he wanted something, he could damn well ask for it.

"Tell me," Master Grey said, once she'd finished eating her sandwich. "What did you do wrong?"

Stayed in your class, Emily thought. It was hard to maintain her resolve when she was pushed to the limits every time she entered his domain. *If I didn't need the class...*

"I could have reflected more spells at them," she said, slowly. "But those wards drain more energy than normal wards."

"You could also have altered the environment to suit yourself," Master Grey pointed out. "It wouldn't have been hard to create a wall to add extra shielding, or even craft a warding circle..."

Emily swore. She hadn't thought of that, not really. Master Grey had told her she couldn't hit back, not that she couldn't mess with the spellchamber. Hell, there had been nothing stopping her from fiddling with the oxygen in the air, or creating a vapor-based sleeping potion, or...

Maybe that would have broken the rules, she thought. *But it would have given me a chance.*

"Other than those oversights, you could have done a great deal worse," Master Grey said. "I will expect you to do better, next time. Of course, *they* will know your weaknesses too."

"Yes, sir," Emily said. If she'd cared more for her reputation, she might have been alarmed at the prospect of being listed as the Fourth Year who'd been beaten by a pack of Third Years. As it was, she *still* knew that nine on one wasn't exactly fair odds. "Are we going to do this again?"

Master Grey gave her an evil look. "What do you think?"

Emily shivered.

"You will write an essay over the next week on other options for tackling the problem," Master Grey said. "In particular, I want you to think outside the circle..."

"You said I couldn't leave the circle," Emily protested.

"Your next statement had better be very insightful," Master Grey said, "or you will have another demerit for parroting back what I told you."

Emily groaned, inwardly. Working off a single demerit would take more time than she cared to think about, not when she had another pile of work to do. And kissing with Caleb...

It struck her the moment she thought about him. "I could have moved the circle," she said, shaking her head. *Caleb* seemed to like thinking outside the box. "It wouldn't have been hard to move it into a corner and dig in there."

"No, it wouldn't have been," Master Grey agreed. He checked his watch. "But if that had been a real battle, Lady Emily, we would be burying your ashes now."

"If that had been a real battle," Emily countered, "I could have hexed them back."

"True," Master Grey agreed. He looked her in the eye. "Go to the kitchens and tell them I ordered you to eat," he said. "You can work off your demerit tomorrow."

When I have even less time to spare, Emily thought. She had three two-hour classes, then she was meant to spend another hour with Caleb. *That's not merciful at all.*

Biting back the response she wanted to make, she rose.

"And Emily," Master Grey added.

Emily looked at him. "Yes, sir?"

"Well done," Master Grey said. He gave her a humorless smile. "I'm afraid the next test will be harder."

Chapter Twenty-Three

I'M AFRAID FRIEDA IS NOT IN HER ROOM," MADAME RAZZ SAID. "AND IF YOU BOTHER ME with this again, you will regret it."

Emily groaned. She'd looked for Frieda everywhere - at lunch, at dinner; she'd done everything short of breaking into a class she knew the younger girl would be taking - and found nothing. She had known Frieda was hurt, but a whole *week* of hiding somewhere when she wasn't in class? Emily couldn't help wondering if she'd hurt Frieda far worse than she'd feared.

Maybe she's ashamed of me as well as hurt, she thought, grimly. It was astonishing just how badly that thought stung. *It didn't take long for everyone to hear I was overpowered by a bunch of Third Year kids.*

She sighed as she turned her back and started the walk down to the Armory. If Master Grey had told the Third Years to keep their mouths shut - and she wasn't sure if she wanted to extend him that much credit - it hadn't lasted. The entire school knew and, after what she'd done in Cockatrice, they didn't seem to know what to make of it. Some students were laughing at her, which she'd ignored; others thought she'd deliberately allowed the Third Years to win, despite the risks. She'd done her best to ignore the comments, but some of them still hurt. It would have been so much easier if she'd been a nobody, the kind of student who blended into the background and no one ever really saw. The kind of student, she reflected, that she'd been on Earth.

But you're not, she told herself, as she stepped into the Armory. *Everyone knows your name...*

She pushed the thought to the back of her mind as she saw Master Grey doing one-handed push-ups on a mat. Whatever else could be said about him, she had to admit, he was quite capable of doing more than just keeping up with them. He turned his head and saw her, and stood up in one smooth motion. Behind her, she heard a clatter as someone else entered the Armory.

"Emily, Aloha," Master Grey said. He pointed to the mat, and smiled at them. "Fifty press-ups, if you please."

Aloha hurried forward and dropped down to the mat. Emily followed, more reluctantly. It had hurt, the first time she'd gone through her exercises; even now, she still ached after working her way through a demerit. Master Grey watched them both, his cold eyes missing nothing. Emily forced herself to think about something - anything - else as she pushed herself to her limits. She'd survived Shadye and Mother Holly. Who knew? Maybe Master Grey's training would help her to survive a worse threat.

"Emily," Master Grey snapped, as she went through the seventeenth press-up. "You have just found an object that may be cursed. What do you do?"

Emily would have smiled, remembering one of the few happy days of her childhood, if she hadn't been so tired. "You cast at least five separate detection spells," she said. "If one of them shows a curse, you run through the remaining spells anyway; you maybe add a couple more, just to be sure. If the curses can be removed safely, you do so; if not, you destroy the object."

"Seems a bit of a waste of time," Master Grey observed archly. "Why so many detection spells?"

I'm not going to be tripped up so easily, Emily thought. *Sergeant Miles taught us how to handle curse detection and removal back in Second Year.*

"Some curses are designed to be invisible to one or two detection spells," Emily said. It had caught her out, several times, in Blackhall. "You use multiple detection spells to ensure you miss nothing."

Master Grey snorted, but didn't try to correct her. Emily smiled inwardly, knowing she'd gotten the answer right. He wouldn't have hesitated to point out, in great detail, just where she'd gone wrong if she *had* made a mistake. Instead, he turned to Aloha and asked her a more complex question relating to the detection of poisons and battlefield medicine. Emily listened, thinking hard. She knew the next question might be harder.

"You have a badly-wounded comrade and no magic," Master Grey said, turning back to her. "What do you do?"

Emily hesitated. "If you have the equipment to treat the wound, you do so," she said, vaguely. "If not..."

Pray for his soul, her thought finished. Medical science on the Nameless World, at least when magic wasn't involved, was terrifyingly bad. She'd seen too many long-term problems caused by surgeons who acted more like butchers to be sanguine about placing her life in their hands. Magic could cure most anything that wasn't immediately fatal, but without magic...she wouldn't have cared to live in the Nameless World. *There would be nothing you could do for him.*

Master Grey went on. "And if you have a choice between saving the life of one badly-wounded man and tending to two mildly-wounded men, what do you do?"

"You treat the two men," Emily said. It wasn't a thought she liked, but Lady Barb had taught the class a great deal about battlefield medicine. Someone so badly wounded would be a drain on very limited resources. Emily hated the thought, yet - no matter what she did - she couldn't deny the logic. "You can save two men instead of one."

"If the first man is not beyond all hope anyway," Master Grey agreed. "Aloha..."

Emily watched him through narrowed eyes. It was impossible to be sure - and she knew she didn't dare speak to anyone about it - but she was starting to wonder if Master Grey was bipolar. On one hand, he was a good if unpleasant tutor; on the other hand, he seemed determined to make her life as miserable as possible, dropping demerits and detentions at the slightest provocation. Did he really dislike her, she wondered, or was he trying to show her that life outside the school wasn't fair? Or was he treating her more as an apprentice, someone who could spend all her time with him, rather than a student? She hadn't exactly *volunteered* to study with him.

She shook her head as the session finally came to an end, Master Grey dismissing them both with some cutting comments about their homework. Maybe he was tired too, Emily considered, as they made their escape. He didn't seem inclined to spend so much time telling them - or at least her - off as usual. She said goodnight to Aloha, slipped back up the stairs and through the door into the dormitories.

"Tonight's the night," Alassa said, as she entered the room. "Are you ready?"

Emily yawned. She wanted - needed - rest; a hot bath wouldn't have been amiss either. But Alassa had been planning their feast for over a week, silently gathering the food and drink they'd need to have a good time. She really didn't want to disappoint her friend, even though she wanted to sleep. At least tomorrow was a Saturday. She could sleep in if necessary.

"Just let me have a shower first," she said. They'd need to wait an hour or two after Lights Out, just to be sure the tutors were asleep too. "Master Grey is still being a pain."

"Tell the Grandmaster you don't want to take his class any longer," Imaiqah advised. "He'd listen to you."

"Then I'd fail," Emily pointed out. She had wondered why Lady Barb had told her there was a way out, if she wanted to quit...but that would be giving up. The last thing she wanted was to let Master Grey *win*. "I don't want to give the asshole the satisfaction of watching me go."

She removed her clothes, stepped into the shower and inspected herself in the mirror. This time, at least, there were no new bruises, although there were some marks around her shoulders and elbows. The skin must have been stretched further, she reasoned, as she turned on the water and washed away the dirt and grime from her body. The more she exercised, the easier it became...or it would have, if Master Grey wasn't so good at adding more exercises, just to keep pushing her limits. He was *very* good at his job.

"Jade's watching his parchment," Alassa said, as Emily stepped back out of the shower. "I was telling him about your problems."

"Thank you," Emily said, rather sourly. She picked up her parchment and discovered, not entirely to her surprise, that whatever else they'd said to one another had been scrolled off the page. "I'll ask him about his former master."

It felt odd, writing her messages and seeing Jade's words appear below them, but she was growing used to it. Jade had apparently had a hard time too, although *he* had volunteered for the apprenticeship. He wondered, gently, if Master Grey hadn't realized that *Emily* was effectively a conscript. It made a certain kind of sense, Emily reasoned, as Jade outlined some of the more soul-crushing exercises he'd been made to do. If the Mediators needed the best of the best, driving away anyone who couldn't live up to their standards might not be a bad idea. But she hadn't volunteered for the training from hell...

"Time to go," Alassa said, softly. Emily glanced at her watch and realized it was nearly midnight. "Say your goodbyes and then follow me."

Emily yawned again, but nodded. Placing the parchment back in the drawer, she wrapped a cloak around her shoulder - Whitehall could be very cold at night - and then followed Alassa and Imaiqah out the door. The Gorgon, Song, and Pandora were waiting outside, their faces glowing with nervous anticipation. Emily felt a flicker of anticipation too; she'd been loath to admit it, but she'd always enjoyed sneaking through Whitehall at the dead of night.

"Cast a night-vision spell," Alassa ordered. "We don't dare show a light at night."

The door opened, allowing them to slip into the main corridor towards the stairs leading up to the battlements. Emily shivered - the school felt so different at night, as if it was a whole new world - and glanced around, seeing the shadows crawling around them like living things. The wards shimmered at the back of her mind: strong, powerful and somehow not quite right. And yet, the sensation faded the moment she tried to work out *why* the wards felt strange. Maybe she was just tired and imagining it.

Should have brought Caleb, she thought. The idea of sneaking off to a classroom and kissing him was surprisingly attractive. There was no rule against bringing a boy to the bedroom, provided her roommates agreed, but she was too embarrassed to ask them. *Maybe if Alassa had brought Jade, I could have worked up the nerve.*

The thought faded as they slowly climbed up the stairs to the very highest level. Alassa went to work on the door at the top, poking and prodding at it with her magic until it finally unlocked, allowing them to step onto the battlements. It didn't seem very secure, Emily thought, but anyone who tried to climb up the walls would be thrown off, while the wards would prevent anyone from flying into the school. Shadye's army of monsters had made it up, yes, yet he'd had inside help. The nexus point ensured that Whitehall was impossible to take without it.

"We made it," Alassa said, very quietly. "Make sure you jam the door open. We don't want to get locked out here."

"That would be embarrassing," the Gorgon agreed, dryly.

Emily had to smile as Alassa opened her bags and laid the blankets on the stone floor. They wouldn't be in any *danger*, she was sure, but they'd be caught in the morning and laughed at by the entire school. She sat down on the blankets and started to unpack the box of sandwiches, shaking her head in disbelief. Cheese sandwiches, cold chicken and ham, potato salad, lettuce and tomato, lashings of ginger beer...if she hadn't known better, she would have thought that Alassa had been reading stories about the Famous Five. Her friend must have bribed one of the cooks to get so much food on short notice.

The Gorgon had the same idea. "How did you ask them for the food?"

"Told them we were planning a picnic after the games tomorrow," Alassa said. "They were quite happy to provide what I asked."

Emily frowned. She hadn't planned to attend the games - she had far too much work to do - but Frieda would be there...wouldn't she? Alassa would be furious if Frieda didn't show up, particularly after working so hard to earn a place on the team. Emily wouldn't have cared to be a Second Year with a Fourth Year mad at her. But then, *she'd* been a First Year who'd had students from both Fifth and Sixth Year mad at her.

Maybe I should go, she thought. She could take an hour away from her work with Caleb, if he didn't mind. She *needed* to talk to Frieda. *I could wait until the game had finished, then catch up with her.*

"Here," Alassa said, passing her a piece of chicken. "You should try eating instead of thinking."

Emily smiled, took the piece of chicken and began to nibble. It tasted heavenly: pure chicken, without any of the flavorings the cooks used for regular meals. She rose to her feet and strolled over to the battlements, peering out over the darkened countryside. The flow of magic around the school seemed stronger in the open air, but there were no lights beyond the wards. She looked towards Dragon's Den, then up at the stars. Were they the same stars as shone on Earth? There was no way to know.

"I'm going to miss this place," Alassa said, as she stepped up behind Emily. "I can be myself here."

"You should stay," Emily said. "You could do another couple of years, couldn't you?"

"Father wouldn't let me take any of the oaths," Alassa said. "I am the Princess of Zangaria, Heir to the Throne. If I'd had a brother..."

She shook her head. "I have to go back after the end of term and learn how to rule," she added. "Father says he intends to pass more of his duties to me, once I'm out of school. I'm not looking forward to it."

Emily understood. Alassa would have power - *real* power - but she would also live in a gilded cage, even if she *did* have Jade as a husband and magic of her own. She would be forever imprisoned by her name and title. Jade might be able to leave - as a Court Wizard, he would be expected to deal with any magical threats to the kingdom - but Alassa would be trapped. How could *anyone* endure such an existence?

"I'm sorry, you know," Alassa added. "You will come see me, won't you?"

"Of course I will," Emily said. She'd be busy at Whitehall for the next two years, but she *would* have holidays. It wouldn't be hard to travel to Zangaria. "And you will have the parchments."

"I need to get a private one to share with Jade," Alassa said. "He was promising he'd visit, at the end of the second term. We can make one then."

"Good thinking," Emily said.

Alassa nudged her. "And how are you and Caleb getting along?"

Emily blushed. "Very well," she said. "It's...different."

"I suppose it would be," Alassa said, wistfully. "At least you weren't threatened with a chastity spell."

"Your father actually threatened to cast a spell on you?" Emily asked, shocked. "A *chastity* spell?

"I told him I'd leave if he tried," Alassa said. "How could I learn self-discipline with a spell keeping me in line?"

She stared into the darkness, shaking her head. "It isn't easy," she admitted. "But if father hadn't been able to ask questions..."

Someone cleared her throat, loudly. Emily jumped, then spun around. Mistress Irene was standing by the door, scowling at them. Her pinched face didn't look remotely pleased.

"Lights Out was nearly three hours ago," she said, into the aghast silence. "Why are you up here in the middle of the night?"

Emily winced as she was beckoned forward to stand next to the other girls. They'd been caught...the unspoken rules prevented the staff from using the wards to track them, but they *had* left the door open. Maybe Mistress Irene had walked down the corridor and felt the draft. Whatever the cause, it hardly mattered. They were in deep trouble.

"I'm waiting for an explanation," Mistress Irene said, patiently. "Why are you up here?"

Alassa stepped forward. "It was my idea," she said. "I brought them up here."

"I see," Mistress Irene said. Emily didn't dare to even *breathe*. "And you, a Dorm Monitor, decided to break the rules you are charged with enforcing?"

"Yes, Mistress," Alassa said. "It was my fault. I should be punished, not them."

Mistress Irene eyed them all for a long moment. "And so you shall be," she said. "You will come with me, now. The rest of you" - Emily cowered under her cold gaze - "will return to your bedrooms and report to your advisers in the morning. Go."

Emily caught sight of Alassa's pale face before hurrying down the stairs and back to their bedroom. Alassa was in deep trouble, but she wasn't the only one. Emily knew...

She caught herself as a thought occurred to her. Alassa had taken her duties seriously, even though she'd had little power. And now she'd thrown them away...or had she? Had she *meant* to be caught?

By the time Emily woke up to discover that Alassa hadn't returned to the room, suspicion had hardened into certainty.

Chapter Twenty-Four

"THAT WAS DELIBERATE, WASN'T IT?"

Lady Barb lifted her eyebrows. "There are more polite ways to enter a room and start a conversation, you know."

Emily winced, but refused to be deflected. "That was set up deliberately," she said. "I don't think Alassa would have thrown away her position *accidentally*."

"People do make stupid mistakes," Lady Barb observed. "You've been known to do quite a few stupid things yourself."

"This isn't about me," Emily said. Her stomach rumbled, reminding her that she hadn't even had breakfast. "Why did she...just throw it away?"

Lady Barb met her eyes. "Why do *you* think she threw it away?"

"We were caught out of bounds in Second Year," Emily said, sharply. "We were sent to the Warden, caned and then dispatched back to bed. I was not asked whose idea it was..."

"You wouldn't have been," Lady Barb said.

"And no one tried to confess," Emily continued, ignoring the interruption. "I don't think it would have mattered if someone *had* confessed."

Lady Barb shrugged. "You do know that Alassa won't be returning after her Fourth Year?"

Emily nodded. "Alassa said as much," she said. "Is it wrong of me to wish otherwise?"

"Not really," Lady Barb told her. She hadn't taken her eyes off Emily. "Alassa...has good reason to conceal the true scope of her abilities. Being caught luring six students into mischief - and she a Dorm Monitor, no less - will be enough to get her placed into indefinite suspension. To all intents and purposes, she will have been expelled."

Emily felt as if she'd been punched in the chest. "You *can't* expel her!"

"She will complete the rest of the year, along with the exams, but her grades will not be made public," Lady Barb said, as if Emily hadn't spoken. "It will be agreed, after some *secret* negotiations that will *unaccountably* become public, that she will be spared the humiliation of actually being expelled, as long as she doesn't return to the school after Fourth Year. King Randor will, of course, accept this punishment without making a fuss."

"Because it was what he wanted," Emily said. "She could have *told* me."

"Her father would have given her strict orders to tell no one," Lady Barb said. "And you know she can't lie to her father."

"So she had to lead us all into temptation," Emily said. She shook her head, bitterly. "Is it wrong of me to hate this...this whole game of thrones?"

"It's the only one we've got," Lady Barb said. Her voice hardened. "Learn how to play the game, or be nothing more than a pawn for the rest of your life."

Emily sighed. She felt too tired to be mad at Alassa, who might well not have had much choice. If her father asked her, specifically, how many others had known about the plan ahead of time...she would have no choice but to answer. Alassa might not be a pawn any longer, not now she was the Confirmed Heir to the Throne, yet she wasn't a Queen. Not yet.

"I know," she said, in bitter resignation.

"You're doing better than I expected," Lady Barb said. "But you still have a very long way to go and time is short."

She cleared her throat. "We will now discuss your detention."

Emily felt her mouth drop open. "But...but it wasn't real!"

Lady Barb smiled. "Did Alassa cast a spell on you to *make* you take part in her midnight feast?"

"No, she didn't," Emily admitted.

"You made a choice," Lady Barb said. "It would have been easy, I think, for you to have refused when she offered. Instead, you chose to let her lure you out of bounds. I can't let that pass, even though it was always doomed to end badly."

"I'm sorry," Emily said. Something else clicked in her mind. "That's why Alassa wasn't allowed to return, wasn't it? She wasn't actually punished."

"No, she wasn't," Lady Barb agreed. "It would be the height of unfairness to penalize someone for something they didn't actually do."

Master Grey would probably disagree, Emily thought. *He hands out detentions like candy.*

"Let me see," Lady Barb said. She struck a deliberately thoughtful pose. "It has to be something that will make you reflect, but not something too harsh. Do you have any suggestions?"

"You could tell me very loudly I've been very naughty and I'm not to do it again," Emily suggested. It was worth a try. "Or you could put me to work on my homework."

Lady Barb snorted. "I don't think either of those are actually *punishments*," she said. "I think you can spend an hour helping me in the infirmary. The rate of accidents has skyrocketed over the last couple of weeks."

Emily shuddered, remembering the Second Years. "Why?"

"Good question," Lady Barb said. "The Grandmaster thought, at first, that it was merely a run of bad luck. You know how many stupid accidents we get each year. Now, however, he's starting to think there's something badly wrong."

Emily looked at the stone walls. "There's something not quite right with the wards," she said. "I can feel it."

"They've been retuned," Lady Barb said. "Since the start of term, we've discovered a number of attempts to insert various spying and probing spells into the school. One First Year even had his eyes charmed to allow someone else to peer through them. His father, it seems, was interested in something - or someone - at Whitehall."

"Me," Emily said.

"Probably," Lady Barb agreed. "The changes in the wards are probably what you sensed."

She shrugged, then got up. "There's something else you can do, afterwards," she added, as she picked up a couple of bottles and inserted them into her belt. "Go talk to Alassa and reassure her that you're not angry."

"I think she was trying to apologize to me," Emily said, slowly. "But..."

"Go talk to her, once I dismiss you," Lady Barb said. "You need your friends more than ever, I think, and so does she."

Emily nodded, and followed Lady Barb to the infirmary. It was clean and bright, but she'd never liked it, not least because she'd spent too much time there. Normally, only a handful of beds were filled, but today several of the students had to share beds or lie on the floor, with only a thin blanket between them and the cold stone. Lady Barb spoke briefly to the Healer, and turned back to Emily.

"You'll be healing those with minor injuries," she said, flatly. "I expect each and every one of them to be healthy when you have finished, but if you run into any problems you are to call me at once. Do *not* attempt to fix someone when you're not sure what you're doing."

Emily nodded - it beat changing and washing bedpans, at least - and got to work. The students were mostly younger than her, all with minor injuries that seemed to suggest they'd been deliberately hurt - or that they'd deliberately hurt themselves. She fixed a nasty bruise one girl sported, then asked her how she'd hurt herself. The girl said she'd merely run into a ball while playing Ken.

"They all have stupid excuses," she complained to Lady Barb, when the older woman came to check on her. She'd started writing them down after the third such excuse; they *all* claimed to have hurt themselves accidentally. "It *can't* be right."

"The verification spells say they're telling the truth," Lady Barb said. She sounded perplexed. "It isn't uncommon for people who have lost fights to claim something - anything - other than the truth, but the spells insist they're not lying."

Emily felt tired and drained by the time the detention finally came to an end. It was practice, she had to admit, and it was more practical than some of the other detentions she'd had to endure, but it was depressing. Lady Barb eyed her for a long moment, and passed her a potion without comment. Emily drank it, trying hard not to gag at the taste; there was a surge of warmth through her body, leaving her feeling a little better. But she knew it wouldn't last.

"Go talk to Alassa, then get some lunch," Lady Barb advised. "I believe there's food in her room."

"Thanks," Emily said. "Where is she?"

"In your old room," Lady Barb said. "I believe you know it."

Emily nodded, refusing to rise to the bait, and then hurried towards the room. Whitehall seemed oddly quieter now - Alassa's team wasn't the only one playing games, she recalled - and she passed almost no one until she reached the door and knocked. It opened with a click, revealing a tired-looking Alassa lying on the bed, staring up at nothing. Her face was so pale that Emily couldn't help wondering if she'd eaten anything at all.

"I didn't mean to get you in trouble," Alassa said. "It was just..."

"It's alright," Emily said. She sat next to her friend - it didn't seem fair how Alassa managed to look beautiful even when she was clearly tired, upset, and depressed - and wrapped an arm around her. "I do understand."

Alassa's blue eyes moved to her. "Lady Barb told you?"

"I figured it out," Emily said. "If you'd told me in advance...your father would have known."

"I'll have to make it clear *you* figured it out," Alassa said. "Is Imaiqah mad at me too?"

"I don't think she's *pleased*," Emily said. Unlike Alassa - or Emily herself - Imaiqah had fewer options if she had to leave Whitehall early. Maybe she was an aristocrat now, but her siblings would inherit most of the real power. "I'll tell her and she will understand."

"They're all going to hate me," Alassa said. She sat upright and glared down at her hands. "I think that was the lesson father wanted me to learn. That I could do the right thing, the *necessary* thing, and still wind up being hated."

"A king must have a different view than his subjects," Emily agreed, neutrally. How many quarrels had there been between kings and subjects, just because they'd had different views of the world? Or of what needed to be done? "When are you going to come back to the room?"

"Mistress Irene said I'd have to stay here for a day," Alassa said. She waved a hand towards the pile of books someone had left on the desk. "And that I should take advantage of my time to work on my studies."

"Not a bad idea," Emily agreed. Alassa would have to remain out of sight long enough for everyone to believe she'd been punished. Her friends would be angry if she hadn't been, after the detentions they'd been given. "I can stay with you, if you like."

"Please," Alassa said. She shook her head. "Have you managed to corner Frieda?"

Emily shook her head. "I planned to catch her at the games," she said, reluctantly. "But I'll stay with you instead."

"It takes some people time to get over their feelings," Alassa said. "I wasn't in the best frame of mind after...after we first met."

"I remember," Emily said. She sighed, resting her head in her hands. "Why is life so bloody complicated? Wouldn't it be easy to go through life not feeling anything?"

"I'm sure there are wizards who brewed potions to take away their emotions," Alassa said, dryly. "I think they end up in the Halfway House."

She gave Emily a tight hug. "You might not feel bad when you get in trouble, but you wouldn't feel good when someone praised you," she said. "You might not feel grief when someone died, yet you wouldn't feel happiness when a new child was born. You might not wallow in misery when you have a fight with your boyfriend, but you wouldn't have the happiness of making up afterwards."

"And you wouldn't have anything to spur you to better yourself," Emily said. "Or to rise to the top in any field you chose."

"I don't get to choose," Alassa said. "I am the Princess and the Heir and...there isn't anyone else."

Emily nodded. King Randor's brother, the Duke of Iron, was kept in comfortable custody in a castle hundreds of miles from his former lands. His attempt to seize the throne, prompted by his wife, had resulted in absolute disaster. No one would accept him as a ruler even if both Randor and Alassa were dead. It was far more likely that the barons would divide the kingdom up between them, or start a civil war for the throne. Alassa couldn't abandon her country without leaving it in ruins.

"At least you won't be unprepared," Emily said.

"I suppose," Alassa said. She tapped her chest. "My father and I had a long talk about my responsibilities, once I get married. I'm expected to produce an heir very quickly."

Emily shuddered. Alassa was nineteen - she'd be twenty by the time she married - and certainly old enough to have children safely, but it still felt odd to think of one of her friends giving birth. Emily didn't want to think about the pressure King Randor would exert on Alassa and Jade to have children as soon as possible...if, of course, they *could* have children. Jade wasn't related to Alassa on any level, as far as they knew, but it was quite possible that Alassa was barren. No one knew for sure.

"And then you'll have a guaranteed succession," she said, pushing her doubts aside. "And plenty of time to learn how to be queen."

"I hope so," Alassa said. "Father...was very blunt when he talked to me about men and pregnancy and...and having children. It wasn't a pleasant chat."

Emily could imagine. Talking to Lady Barb would be embarrassing; talking to a man, even one she trusted, would be worse. But King Randor needed grandchildren, if he couldn't have more children of his own; he might insist that Alassa remained virginal until her wedding night, but he'd happily have the talk - *The Talk*, her mind insisted - with her. It could only have led to cringing embarrassment on all sides.

Or perhaps not, she thought, inwardly. *Aristocrats are more interested in producing children than anything else.*

"Then I ended up having another chat with Lady Latina," Alassa added. "Do you know what *she* said?"

"I don't want to know," Emily said. She'd probably seen Lady Latina during one of her visits to Zangaria, but she couldn't put a face to the name. "It probably wasn't anything decent..."

"It wasn't," Alassa agreed. Her grin became evil. "She said that marrying a sorcerer was better than marrying an aristocrat because..."

"*I don't want to know*," Emily said, covering her ears. "I really don't want to think about it."

"You may have to," Alassa said. She sobered, meeting Emily's eyes. "What happens when Caleb wants to do something more than just kissing?"

Emily scowled at her, trying hard not to blush. "What happens when *Jade* wants to do something more than just kissing?"

"We've done a bit," Alassa said, blithely. "Imaiqah was happy to tell me a few things we could do that didn't risk a pregnancy. I'm sure she'd be happy to tell you."

I had the Internet, Emily thought. If the Grandmaster had banned Blue Books from the school, she dreaded to think what would have happened if someone had invented the Internet and started using it for porn. It was only a matter of time, she was sure.

The introduction of the scientific method had made it inevitable. *And I saw too much online.*

"I think we'd better go back to our studies," she said, instead. "Or do you want me to make your apologies to Imaiqah and the others?"

"Later, if you wouldn't mind," Alassa said. "I was hoping to talk about other matters with you."

Emily nodded and picked up one of the books. "Right now, we both probably look like idiots," she said. "You for being caught out of bounds; me for being knocked down by a bunch of Third Years."

Alassa snorted. "I think if you'd been able to hex them back things would have been a little different," she said, tartly. "And you really should know it."

"I do," Emily said. Just cutting down the number of students aiming hexes at her had been quite helpful...and she could have stopped more of them if she'd been allowed to fire off her own spells. "But everyone else thinks otherwise."

"Then everyone else is an idiot," Alassa said. She reached out and gripped Emily's hand. "I sometimes wonder what my life would have been like if Lady Barb had kicked me in the ass years ago, back when she was my bodyguard. But..."

She sighed. "Master Grey may be doing you a favor," she added. She didn't sound as if she really believed her words. "You do realize that?"

"It doesn't feel that way," Emily said.

"Of course it doesn't," Alassa said. "I didn't feel like you were doing me a favor, back in First Year. But I think you did."

Emily felt her face heat. "Thank you," she said. "Shall we go back to work?"

Alassa nodded and picked up the book. "I just can't get this spell in Healing," she admitted. "I should be able to make it work, but it keeps failing..."

"You're not allowing the magic to shape itself," Emily said. It reminded her of one of the forbidden spells, one that warped rather than healed. Alassa was closer to reproducing it than she knew. "Lady Barb was saying you needed to help the body, not overpower it."

"I see," Alassa said. She shook her head. "If this wasn't so useful..."

"At least you can rely on yourself," Emily said. She thought, for a moment, that she understood Master Grey perfectly. "Who else can you count on when you're alone?"

Chapter Twenty-Five

IT WASN'T EASY TO TALK TO THE OTHERS, EMILY DISCOVERED, AFTER SHE FINALLY LEFT Alassa and returned to the dorms. Imaiqah had already guessed the truth, but Pandora was furious and the Gorgon disappointed. By the time Emily managed to escape and make her way to the workroom where Caleb awaited her, she was nursing a headache and feeling tired, depressed and cranky. And, when she walked in, she saw that Caleb had a nasty bruise covering his cheek.

"What happened to you?" she asked, concerned. "Someone hit you?"

"Johan did," Caleb said, crossly. He sounded oddly reluctant to talk to her, but pushed ahead anyway. "I think we have a problem."

Emily stared at him. "Johan *hit* you?"

"I hit him back," Caleb said. Emily was surprised at first, but remembered that Caleb came from Stronghold. Basic combat training had been hammered into his head from Day One, while it was optional at Whitehall. "Someone told him that... that I was taking advantage of you."

"*What?*"

"Someone told him that I was taking advantage of you," Caleb repeated. "And that all of this" - he waved a hand at the tiles on the worktable - "was your idea, not mine."

"That's absurd," Emily protested. Johan? She barely *knew* him! God knew he hadn't spent any time with her outside class. "You're the one who came up with the idea in *your* Third Year."

It made no sense. She hadn't prepared a project in *her* Third Year because she'd had no partner. If the Grandmaster hadn't put Caleb and her together, she would probably have had to redo Third Year. Everyone *knew* Caleb had had a good idea, he'd just managed to injure himself and scare off his last partner. He certainly wouldn't have been allowed to copy something from Emily and pass it off as his own work.

But someone might believe it, Emily thought. Most of her inventions remained secret, but she was credited with inventing everything from a new system of writing letters and numbers to stirrups and steam engines. *If all they know is that I'm a genius, they might think Caleb had stolen the idea from me...*

She swore, using a word she'd learned from Lady Barb. "Who told him that...that *lie?*"

Her thoughts flashed to Master Grey, but lying about her...her boyfriend seemed a little petty for him. He could have just piled more detentions on her if he'd wanted to split them up, or suggested she do something else with her time. But then, she *was* meant to do a joint project with Caleb. Preventing them from meeting completely would have been impossible.

She let out a long breath as the answer snapped into place. "Frieda," she said. "Frieda must have told him."

Caleb blinked. "Your friend?"

"She's mad at me," Emily said. It made sense; Frieda resented Caleb, so she'd manipulated Johan into attacking him. "And..."

She shook her head. "I can't explain it. But I need to find her."

"The Grandmaster will know better," Caleb said. "But if she keeps spreading these lies, Emily, it could be bad."

Emily nodded. A rumor could flash through Whitehall quicker than a spell - and, no matter how thoroughly one was debunked, it would still stick. Caleb was an outsider even more than she was, a transfer student who'd stayed...he didn't have the deep bonds of friendship others had formed over the years. If the rumors stuck, and they would, he might find himself in deep trouble. The Grandmaster would definitely know better, but how many others would feel the same way?

"I'm sorry," she said, running her hand through her hair. They didn't need this problem, not on top of everything else. "Can we meet again later? I need to find her."

She gave Caleb a quick kiss and hurried out of the room. There was no point in asking Madame Razz to find Frieda, but Professor Thande was usually just down the corridor, supervising a handful of experiments. As Emily had expected, he didn't bother to ask *why* she wanted to find Frieda; he just checked the wards and told Emily that Frieda was wandering through the gardens outside the school, near the zoo. Emily nodded, thanked him, and hurried down to the gardens. Surprisingly, they were almost deserted.

Frieda stood in front of a pond, staring into it. Emily cleared her throat; the younger girl spun around and stared at her, then turned and started to run as fast as she could. Silently thanking Master Grey for his lessons, Emily threw a tangle spell after her and sent Frieda falling to the grass. Emily was on top of her before she could break the spell and escape.

"We need to talk," she said, as Frieda sat up sullenly. "You've been avoiding me for *days*."

"Weeks," Frieda muttered, looking down at the ground. Emily felt a flicker of guilt as she realized that Frieda had skinned her knee. "I..."

"I didn't mean to upset you," Emily said, softly. "I'm sorry."

Frieda glanced up at her, resentfully. "I thought you liked me."

"I did," Emily said. She corrected herself hastily. "I do."

"You saved me," Frieda said. Her face was bright red, tears glimmering in her eyes. "You saved me and you spent time with me and I thought..."

She shook her head. "I'm sorry, too."

"You should be," Emily said. "Why did you tell lies to Johan?"

Frieda didn't bother to deny it. "Because he admires you," she said. "I knew he'd defend you if he thought you were in trouble."

"I'm not in trouble," Emily said. She thought of Master Grey - and the reception Alassa was likely to get from her roommates - and wondered if that was entirely true. "Well...not more trouble than usual, at least."

Frieda smiled, then sobered. "I don't like Caleb," she said. "You shouldn't be kissing him."

"He's a decent man," Emily said. "I didn't realize you felt that way about me."

"I thought you did," Frieda said. "You never hurt me. You treated me as a friend."

And taking you out to places in Cockatrice must have seemed like a date, Emily thought, morbidly. *I never saw it.*

"I'm appallingly bad at seeing what other people are feeling," Emily admitted. "It took me months to realize you were in trouble."

"At least you noticed," Frieda said, sullenly. She looked up. "If you're bad at reading emotions, Emily, could you be wrong about what *Caleb* feels for you?"

Ouch, Emily thought. It was a nasty thought, all the more so for being quite possible. She might have misread Caleb badly...and if she had, she was likely to leave herself open to something far worse than Nanette's betrayal and theft of her notes. *But I don't think I'm wrong.*

"I think that's different," Emily said.

Frieda crossed her arms under her knees, as if she expected to be hit. "I'm sorry," she said, in a flat tone that almost broke Emily's heart. "I had presumptions above my station, My Lady, and I will not trouble you with them again."

"Frieda," Emily began. "I..."

"I humbly offer my submission to you," Frieda continued. She rose, then fell forward into full prostration. "This unworthy one begs your pardon and accepts whatever punishment you choose to give."

"Get up," Emily snapped. It would have been overdone, if she hadn't been all too aware that Frieda meant every word. Growing up in the Cairngorms, where she had had almost no power, would have taught her to grovel when necessary. But it was disgusting and futile and...it wasn't *right*. "Get up now!"

Frieda sat back on her haunches, staring down at the ground. "Emily..."

Emily suddenly understood just how Lady Barb must have felt, when Emily had acted younger than her age. The impulse to just smack some sense into the younger girl was almost overpowering. Frieda's crush had turned into a nightmare, so she'd crawled back into herself...

She knelt down, facing Frieda. "Listen to me, please," she said. "Look at me."

Frieda looked up, slowly. "Emily..."

"Listen," Emily said. "You're my friend; you're my sister, in all the ways that matter. I do like you, I do care for you and I *do* want to spend time with you..."

"You spent time with *him* at Cockatrice," Frieda said.

"I do have to work on the joint project," Emily pointed out. "Frieda, I like you a great deal..."

"But you don't want me as a partner," Frieda said. Her voice hardened again. "I had ideas above my station."

"I'm not interested in girls," Emily said. She thought that was true; she'd shied away from both boys and girls on Earth. She'd seen Alassa naked plenty of times and felt nothing beyond abstract admiration. "And are you sure you're interested in me?"

"I..." Frieda looked down for a long moment, then looked up. "You're *wonderful*. You saved countless lives."

And how many people will die in the future, Emily asked herself, *because of the weapons and concepts I have introduced to the Allied Lands?*

She looked towards the Craggy Mountains and shuddered. Shadye's lands were there, unprotected; it might not be long, now she'd visited the Dark Fortress, before another necromancer moved into his territory. And then there had been the orcs... Master Grey had been very interested in them, going over everything Emily had seen time and time again, until she felt as though her brain was starting to come apart. He'd pointed out, at the end, that a full-fledged breeding frenzy spelled bad news for the Allied Lands.

We need better weapons and defenses, she reminded herself, bitterly. The battery felt heavy in her pocket, a mocking reminder of how badly she'd almost messed up over the summer. *I might not be able to kill the third necromancer I meet.*

"I don't think I'm wonderful," she said. "I can make mistakes."

"So can I," Frieda said. She took Emily's hand. "Sergeant Miles said that Whitehall is a cork in a bottle. If Shadye had broken through, he would have been able to ravage the lands surrounding Whitehall for hundreds of miles. You stopped him."

"I still don't *feel* wonderful," Emily protested.

"You need a bard singing those ballads about you," Frieda said, sounding much more like her old self. "There was that guy with the really awful voice at the Faire..."

"No," Emily said, flatly. She'd heard seven or eight songs written about her - before the broadsheets, bards had been the quickest way to spread news through the Allied Lands - and they were all appallingly bad. Most of them got the facts wrong, in one way or another; the two that were stunningly explicit were horribly embarrassing. "That will *not* boost my confidence."

Frieda looked doubtful. "Not even the one about..."

"*No*," Emily insisted. She had no idea which one Frieda meant, but they were *all* embarrassing. "I just need to learn from my mistakes."

She got up and helped Frieda to stand. "I'm sorry I don't feel the way you do, but I do like you and I hope we can still be friends."

Frieda sighed. "I'm sorry."

"You don't have to be sorry for feeling anything," Emily said. It was hard to wrap her head around the idea of *anyone* finding her attractive. "But I think you do owe Caleb an apology. How many others did you try to get to attack him?"

"No one else," Frieda said. "Just Johan."

Thank God, Emily thought.

"You probably owe him an apology, too," Emily said. She had no idea which of the two boys was stronger, but Caleb probably had better training. "I'm not sure what happened, but it wasn't anything good."

Frieda gave her a sharp look. "How did you know it was me?"

"You were mad at me and Caleb," Emily said. "I couldn't think of anyone else."

"He'll want to kill me," Frieda said. "They'll *both* want to kill me."

"I don't think they'll be very happy, no," Emily agreed. "Why don't you spend the next hour thinking of ways you can make it up to them?"

"I'll try," Frieda said. "Did...did you ever have a crush on anyone?"

Emily hesitated before shaking her head in negation. She'd been isolated as a child, then her mother's warnings had echoed in her head when she'd grown into a teenager...romantic feelings were dangerous. Romantic feelings led to being trapped in loveless marriages, with a child from a previous partner. Hell, Emily honestly didn't know if her biological father and her mother had been married. The one time she'd asked, her mother had subjected her to a screaming fit that left her ears ringing for days.

"No," she said. "Aurelius" - she played with the bracelet instinctively - "was trying to seduce me, but I wasn't tempted."

Frieda shuddered. "But he was *old*!"

"I don't think that would have mattered," Emily said. The hell of it was that Aurelius had tried to seduce her with knowledge, rather than anything more physical. It might have worked if she hadn't understood what he was trying to do. The idea of disappearing into Mountaintop and forgetting about the rest of the world was very attractive. "He wanted me for my mind."

Frieda looked at her. "No one else?"

"Not until recently," Emily said. And her feelings for Caleb had surprised her, more than she cared to admit. She'd liked him without truly recognizing she liked him. "My life was very different."

She gave Frieda a tight hug. "I'm sorry," she said. "But I will always be your friend."

"And sister," Frieda agreed.

They walked slowly back to Whitehall. The sound of people playing games echoed in the distance; Emily glanced at Frieda, wondering if she should ask what had happened when - if - Frieda had gone to play, then decided to leave it until later. Alassa would be furious if Frieda had skipped the practice, even if she wasn't there. But then, Imaiqah and Song had also missed the practice; they'd had detention, thanks to the midnight feast. It was unlikely the remaining Upstarts had been able to do more than bounce around the playing fields a little.

"Caleb should probably still be in the workroom," Emily said, as they walked into the school and headed up the stairs. "I have no idea where to find Johan."

Frieda hesitated. "Do I *have* to talk to them?"

"Yes," Emily said, flatly. "You need to say *something* before the tutors hear about it."

They stopped outside the workroom door. "I'll go in," Frieda promised. "Please, can you wait outside?"

Emily nodded. Frieda threw a nervous look at her, then opened the door and stepped into the workroom, closing it behind her. Emily glanced at her watch, mentally noting the time, and waited. It was nearly twenty minutes before Frieda stepped out of the room, looking upset but composed.

"He said I owed him a favor," Frieda said. "And that Johan probably owes me a black eye."

"I think he'd get in trouble for hitting you outside Martial Magic," Emily said, dryly. Seniors picking on juniors was banned at Whitehall, although a junior starting the fights was tacitly permitted. The Nameless World might never have heard of Darwin, but its inhabitants believed that natural selection was an excellent way of weeding out the weak. "This isn't Mountaintop."

"I know," Frieda said. "He said...he said he understood, but I was not to do it again."

"Good advice," Emily said. It would have been a great deal worse, she was sure, if Caleb had lost the fight. If he'd blacked Johan's eye, well...the older student wouldn't be very pleased with the person who'd gotten him into the fight. "Just make sure you take it."

Frieda nodded. "I'm sorry," she said, again. "I won't let it happen a second time."

"Good," Emily said.

She led Frieda along the corridor towards the kitchens. Her stomach was rumbling unpleasantly, reminding her that she hadn't eaten anything apart from a snack with Alassa. Two students were standing at the top of the stairs, staring down the railings as if they were contemplating climbing over the banisters and letting themselves fall. Emily cleared her throat, unsure if she should try to stop them with a spell; they started, and ran down the stairs as if the devil himself were after them.

"They've heard of you," Frieda giggled.

Emily scowled at her. That wasn't funny.

The kitchens seemed half-deserted, but there were a number of sandwiches under a preservation charm for older students. Emily took a handful, passed some to Frieda and they ate quickly at a small table before heading back to the dorms.

"I'm sorry," Frieda said, one final time.

"You'd better say that to Alassa, too," Emily said. Something was twitching at the back of her mind, a suggestion that something was very wrong. She tensed automatically, looking around for the threat. If nothing else, Master Grey's lessons had done wonders for her reflexes. "I..."

Frieda frowned. "Emily?"

Emily tapped her lips. There was nothing...nothing she could see. She cast a revealing spell, then two more, but saw nothing. And yet the sense of unease was growing stronger...

"Go back to your room," Emily ordered. The wrongness seemed to grow even stronger as she approached the door that led into the Fourth Year dorms. "Now!"

Frieda nodded and hurried off. Emily held up one hand in a casting stance, and stepped through the door. The sense of wrongness snapped out of existence, as if someone had flicked a switch. Puzzled, Emily looked around and saw...nothing. It was almost as if she'd imagined the whole thing. She lowered her hand and stepped into her bedroom...

...And froze in horror at the sight that greeted her.

Chapter Twenty-Six

A LASSA STOOD IN FRONT OF THE MIRROR, HER BODY SO STILL SHE WAS EITHER PETRIFIED OR entranced. But it wasn't Alassa who caught Emily's attention. Imaiqah sat on her bed, chewing her fingernails so hard that blood was dripping from her mouth and staining her shirt. Emily felt her mouth fall open - she knew how hard it was to force herself to cut her skin - and ran forward. Up close, Imaiqah's teeth were stained with her own blood, her eyes totally fixed on the mess she of her fingernails.

"Stop!" Emily shouted, trying to pull Imaiqah's hand out of her mouth. There was so much blood lying around that Imaiqah would be in very real danger, if someone took advantage of the opportunity to steal some and use it against her. "You'll hurt yourself."

Imaiqah ignored her. Emily tugged at her hand, but it only made matters worse; Imaiqah didn't even seem to be aware of her presence.

Bracing herself, Emily lifted her hand and slapped Imaiqah across the face.

If she'd been under a spell, a compulsion to hurt herself, the slap should have shocked her out of it. But she didn't even seem aware she'd been hit. A nasty red mark appeared on her skin, but she didn't cry out or break free of the spell.

Emily shook her, then looked deeply into her eyes. There was nothing there, no spark of life. Imaiqah might as well have been a puppet. Emily stumbled backwards, then cast a freeze spell. Mercifully, it worked; Imaiqah's body froze. Her teeth were still digging into her flesh, but she wouldn't lose any more blood before the Healers could see to her.

She turned to Alassa and realized that whatever had affected Imaiqah had targeted her, too. Her friend stared into the mirror as if she were enraptured by her own beauty. Emily jumped in front of her, but there was no change until she actually caught hold of Alassa's arm. The moment she touched her friend's bare skin, her body crumpled like a sack of potatoes and hit the ground. Emily ruthlessly forced down panic - maybe this was another of Master Grey's insane tests - and checked her breathing before trying to use magic to jerk Alassa awake. The spell worked, as far as she could tell, but Alassa remained motionless. Her breathing was so shallow it was almost impossible to detect.

Shit, Emily thought, stunned.

She turned and ran towards the door. Madame Beauregard tended to move between the Third and Fourth Year dorms, but she'd explained to the girls when they first moved in that anyone who rang the bell outside her Fourth Year office would summon her, no matter where she was. Outside, everything was eerily quiet, a strange sense of...*anticipation*...hanging in the air that sent chills down her spine. She closed the door behind her, and ran down towards the office. The bell was hanging from a hook just outside the door. Emily thumped the door - there was no answer - then rang the bell. Magic tingled around the wards, summoning the Dorm Mother...

"The key to the future is finding the way," a voice said. It was so distorted that it took Emily a moment to realize that it was Pandora who spoke as she walked down the corridor. "The future lies open to the one who opens the lock to the future."

"Pandora," Emily called. She didn't know Pandora that well, but she needed help. "What are you..."

Pandora turned to look at her. Emily shivered. Pandora's eyes were as dead and cold as Imaiqah's or Alassa's had been, as if someone had reached inside the girl and drained her of everything that made her what she was. It was like staring into the face of a statue, or worse, a zombie, rather than a warm and breathing body.

"Troubled, I waited; a prisoner, I waited," Pandora said. Emily couldn't help wondering if she was trying to talk like a man, or if something else was speaking through her. "Released, I fed; free, I hunt."

Her hand snapped up. Emily threw herself to one side as a hex sizzled past her and struck the walls, then tossed back a freeze spell of her own. Pandora caught it with a technique Emily didn't recognize - where the hell had she learned *that?* - and fired off two more of her own hexes. The spells twisted in midair as Emily dodged, one slamming into her wards and knocking her off her feet, the other throwing her down the corridor towards the stone wall. Emily hastily recast her protective charms a second before she hit the wall -- and bounced.

Pandora wasn't this powerful. Not on her own. The only student Emily could think of who could do something like this was Aloha - and why would she want to?

She gritted her teeth, and threw back the strongest freeze spell she could. Pandora froze, for a second, but freed herself; there was, again, something strange about the technique she used, something impossible. Her entire body seemed to shimmer through the spell. Emily hastily scrambled for something she could do that wouldn't seriously injure the girl, but any prank spell she might use would be easy to deflect. Pandora, seemingly unconcerned about the danger, kept walking towards her.

"Today, I roam free; tomorrow, I return," she said. "I bring..."

A flash of light struck Pandora from the side and she keeled over, her face snapping back to normal a moment before she struck the floor. Emily let out a sigh of relief as she saw the Gorgon, but felt her skin crawl as the Gorgon turned to look at her. Her friend had always seemed inhuman - she wasn't fully human - but now she seemed creepy, too creepy to even *look* at. And her green eyes were flat and cold.

"No," Emily said. It had to be a nightmare, not a test. Even Master Grey wouldn't deliberately injure other students just to teach her a lesson. "Gorgon..."

The Gorgon advanced, her snakes twisting around her head in a manner that was almost hypnotic. No, it *was* hypnotic; Emily found it impossible, despite her fear, to look away from the snakes and the glowing green eyes. Her entire body felt drained; her hands dropped to her sides, her legs buckled as she was caught by the Gorgon's spell. She'd known Gorgons could turn people to stone, and that their magic was terrifyingly hard to undo, but this was different. She *wanted* to surrender her will to the Gorgon.

I will not, she thought, somehow clenching her fist hard enough to hurt. The pain jarred her awake; she mustered a spell and fired it at the Gorgon before she could be caught up again in her hypnotic gaze. The Gorgon stumbled forward, then fell to the floor, stunned.

Emily caught herself before she fell too, then staggered towards her friend. The Gorgon was stunned, completely out of it. Emily checked her pulse - the Gorgon's heartbeat had always been faster than hers - and sighed in relief. It looked as though the Gorgon would recover, even if no one used magic to wake her ahead of time.

It was impossible to believe the school's wards wouldn't have noticed the spells Pandora had hurled at her, or the Gorgon's attempt to overwhelm her. If she could get into trouble for practicing Martial Magic spells in a dedicated spellchamber, surely the wards would have sounded the alert if the spells were used in a dorm.

Someone should have come by now, she thought, as she checked Pandora's body. *Where are they?*

She pinched herself, then walked slowly to the door and peered into the main corridor. A frog was jumped around on the floor, trying to evade a mean-looking rat. Two students had been casting spells on each other...Emily moved to free them, but thought better of it. God alone knew what had gotten into them. She listened, trying to tune out the pleading sounds from the two animals, and heard faint noises in the distance. They sounded very much like screams, which cut off abruptly. What was happening?

How had everything gone to hell so quickly?

The sound of running footsteps caught her attention and she ducked back into the dorms, ready to cast a spell or slam the doors closed. Madame Beauregard came into view, followed by a middle-aged man Emily didn't know. The Dorm Mother looked tired, her eyes filled with horror, but at least she was alive. Emily stepped into view, holding up her hands to signify that she was harmless. If everyone was jumpy after whatever had happened, it was quite likely someone would be hexed by accident.

"Emily," Madame Beauregard said. She sounded relieved. "Are you all right?"

"Yes, but Alassa, Imaiqah, Pandora and the Gorgon are not," Emily said. "What's happening?"

"A handful of students seem to have gone mad," Madame Beauregard said, as she brushed past Emily and strode along the corridor towards Pandora. "What did you do to her?"

"The Gorgon stunned her," Emily said. Clearly, none of them had been in their right mind...but had whatever controlled Pandora moved to the Gorgon when the former was stunned? Or had the Gorgon retained control long enough to stun Pandora? "She's just down the corridor."

Madame Beauregard nodded, and stepped into Emily's room. "What happened here?"

Emily's eyes narrowed. Why not tend to the Gorgon first?

"I had to freeze Imaiqah; Alassa fainted," Emily said. "What about the Gorgon?"

"I'll deal with her in a moment," Madame Beauregard said. She cast a spell; Alassa and Imaiqah rose into the air, then drifted out of the room into the corridor. Moments later, both Pandora and the Gorgon joined them. "They will all have to be taken to the infirmary."

"I'll take them," the man said.

"I'll go down to check on Frieda," Emily said. If she'd walked into hell, what had the younger girl encountered in the Second Year dorms? "Or do you want me to stay here?"

Madame Beauregard frowned. "Go check on your friend," she said. She waved a hand at the two animals, transforming them back into First Years who immediately started to babble about being attacked by an older girl. Madame Beauregard ignored them and kept speaking to Emily. "Come straight back here once you're done."

Emily watched her start to check the other rooms before she turned and hurried back down the corridor. The sense of overwhelming *wrongness* seemed to grow stronger around her, then fade away before she could do more than realize it was there. She stayed alert, watching for possible threats, but saw nothing. The corridors seemed deserted, yet...

She paused outside the entrance to the Second Year dorms before she pushed open the door. The Second Year girls - all of them, apart from Frieda - stood in front of the wall, just staring at it. Madame Razz lay on the ground, her body frozen solid. Emily stared - she would never have been able to overpower a tutor as a Second Year - then hastily checked her former Dorm Mother. Her body was covered in ice. It was impossible to tell what, if anything, an unfreezing charm would do. Emily had the nasty feeling that freezing a living human would cause cell damage only a Healer could fix.

The girls didn't move, not even once. Emily looked at them, then hastily cast a freeze spell of her own over Madame Razz. Time would stop for her until the Healers could take a look at her and do what they could to save her life. She cursed under her breath, and tapped on the door to Frieda's room. It opened, revealing the younger girl lying on her bed, looking depressed. She stared in surprise as Emily entered the room.

"Emily?" Frieda asked. "What are *you* doing here?"

Emily stared back, equally surprised. "Are you all right?"

"Of course," Frieda said. "What happened to *you*?"

"I'm not sure," Emily said, as Frieda stood. "Come and look at your friends."

Frieda followed her out the door, then stopped and stared in horror. "What happened to them?"

"I don't know," Emily said. The Second Year girls, the same ones who'd had identical injuries, were still standing there, motionless. Even their eyes didn't blink. "I think something is very badly wrong."

She led Frieda past the silent girls, then out into the corridor. Professor Lombardi was coming towards them, carrying a wand in one hand and a device she didn't recognize in the other. It ticked unpleasantly as he stopped in front of them, his stern eyes inspecting their faces in minute detail. Emily hesitated, then started to explain what she'd seen when she entered the Second Year dorms.

"A third of the school seems to have gone mad," Professor Lombardi said. The Charms Master sounded very tired. "I'll take them up to the Healers..."

"Be careful of Madame Razz," Emily said. "She was literally frozen, sir, with ice. There might be cellular damage..."

Her voice trailed off as Professor Lombardi glared at her. Emily realized, too late, that he knew the dangers...and didn't like her pointing out what he already knew. She flushed, then braced herself. She'd done the right thing by telling him, just in case he *didn't* know. And, no matter what he said, he couldn't change the facts.

"Go back to your room, young lady," he said, finally. He looked at Frieda. "Are you the only unaffected student in Second Year?"

"I think so," Frieda said. "I don't know about the boys."

"I'll check on them in a moment," Professor Lombardi said. "Go with Emily, for the moment. You'll be told what to do later."

"Yes, sir," Frieda said.

Emily sighed inwardly - sharing a room with Frieda again was going to be embarrassing - but nodded and led the way back to the Fourth Year dorms. Silence seemed to have fallen over the school, broken only by strange echoes and the weirdest sense of someone - or *something* - laughing at her. She shuddered at the sensation, but forced herself to keep going. It hadn't felt so uncomfortable since the Mimic had been on the loose within the wards.

Maybe they all ate something tainted with a curse, she thought, although she knew the wards wouldn't allow anything genuinely dangerous - at least by the Nameless World's standards - to harm the students. Or...

She tensed as someone moved ahead of them, but relaxed when she saw Aloha. The older student smiled in cold delight, then tossed a spell at them both that froze her in place. Emily broken the spell, tried to jump backwards, just as Aloha hurled herself at her. But Emily was too late; Aloha slammed into her and sent her falling back, her head hitting the stone floor hard enough to make her see stars. Aloha was screaming something as she drew back her fists and pounded them into Emily's chest and arms, but Emily could barely hear her. The pain was so great she could hardly focus her mind. Magic seemed to slip away rather than be called to her fingertips. Aloha cackled, lifted her fists and prepared to punch Emily in the face, then froze as a spell struck her. Emily was too disorientated to feel anything but relief at the sight of a tutor, even if it *was* Master Grey.

"Lie still," he snapped, kneeling beside her. "She was trying to *kill* you. Why?"

He shook his head before Emily could say a word. "No, don't try to talk," he said, as he cast a pair of healing spells. Emily felt a dull warmth spreading through her body, but her thoughts still felt sluggish. "Let me heal you first."

It felt like hours before Emily could stand up. "I...she just attacked us," she said. "Froze Frieda and attacked me."

"Odd," Master Grey said. He waved a hand at Frieda, freeing her from the spell. "I would have expected her to use magic."

"She was screaming about competition," Frieda said. "I think it was deeply personal for her."

Emily blinked. *What* competition?

"Everyone seems to have gone mad," Master Grey observed. He gave Emily a long, considering look, and levitated Aloha into the air. "I'll take her to the Warden..."

"I don't think she was in her right mind," Emily stammered. Her head still hurt, despite his spells. "No one seems to be in their right mind."

"She did attack you with murderous intent," Master Grey pointed out. His face was artfully neutral. "Are you always so forgiving to your enemies?"

"I don't blame people for being *compelled* to do something," Emily said, tartly. "And I'm sure *something* was making them all act badly."

"Is," Master Grey corrected. "It's still going on."

He sighed. "Go back to your room and stay there," he ordered. "I dare say the tutors will be glad that you escaped...whatever it is."

Emily nodded and leaned on Frieda as they walked back into the dorms. Madame Beauregard was nowhere to be seen, but a shaken-looking Penelope was standing outside her door, while Talia stood next to her. Emily met their eyes, just long enough to check they were normal, opened the door to her room and ushered Frieda into the chamber. Imaiqah's blood was still all over her bed, hopefully untouched. Emily wanted to clean it up, to dispose of the blood as she'd been taught, but she didn't have the energy. Instead, she just collapsed onto her own bed.

"I'll take the floor," Frieda said. Emily was almost relieved. They'd shared a bed before, but that would be embarrassing now. And Alassa would probably have hexed her bed to keep out unwanted strangers. "I've slept in worse places."

Emily wanted to argue, but sleep overwhelmed her before she could say a word.

Chapter Twenty-Seven

SHE JERKED AWAKE WHEN SHE HEARD SOMEONE OPENING THE DOOR, BUT SMILED IN RELIEF when she saw Lady Barb. The blonde-haired woman looked tired and worn, her robes stained with blood and something that suggested a student - in a fit of suicidal madness - had thrown a stink-spell at her. Emily felt a moment of pity for the student before forcing herself to sit up and pour a glass of water. Her head felt fragile, as if the slightest word or blow would shatter her for good.

Maybe it was a nightmare, she thought. But one look at Imaiqah's bed told her that it had been all too real. *Whatever happened, happened.*

"Emily," Lady Barb said. "Are you all right?"

"My head feels awful," Emily said. She drank the water, poured herself another glass, and drank it too. "What *happened?*"

"I wish I knew," Lady Barb said. "Several hundred students went mad, it seems; some hurt themselves, some lost themselves in contemplating the meaning of life, and some attacked their fellow students. And now they're all in comas. No one died, but it's just a matter of time."

Emily swallowed. "There's something wrong with the wards," she said. "I could *feel* it."

"The wards aren't attacking students," Lady Barb said. She suddenly sounded very old. "I checked, Emily; I checked for spells, I checked for curses, I checked for potions, I checked for subtle magic. I found nothing."

"What about drugs?" Emily asked. "Something non-magical?"

"That could be right," Frieda said. "There were some boys back home who ate something they found in the forest and spent the next couple of days skipping merrily around like idiots."

"It would have shown up when I tested their blood, surely," Lady Barb said. "At the very least, it would be a foreign element in their bodies."

Emily nodded, and glanced at her watch. Seven bells; they'd slept through the night and into the early morning. She stood and looked at herself. The robes she'd worn would need a wash before she could wear them again, if only to get rid of the bloodstains. Aloha's beating had broken her skin.

She was screaming about competition, Emily thought, dully. *Did she think I was competing with her for Master Grey?*

Her stomach rumbled. "I need to eat," she said. She'd stowed away a handful of ration bars in her trunk, but they weren't very tasty. "Can we leave the dorms?"

"I think so," Lady Barb said. "If you happen to see anyone acting oddly, please let us know."

"They probably think *I* act oddly," Emily muttered. She cleared her throat. "Maybe they're ill."

Lady Barb gave her a murderous look. "Are you joking?"

"No," Emily said. She hadn't been ill many times in her life, but she'd caught *something* when she was seven that had caused hallucinations. Or maybe that had just been the illness combined with the shortage of food. "If they caught something, maybe it made them act crazy."

"It would have shown up on the tests," Lady Barb said, flatly. "Whatever happened to the victims, Emily, was beyond our ability to detect."

She turned and strode towards the door. "Get something to eat," she ordered, without looking back. "Classes have been cancelled. The Grandmaster will address the student body later today."

Emily nodded, remembering the days when the Mimic had stalked the school, killing and replacing its victims one by one. Whatever was loose now, at least it wasn't a Mimic. But they knew how to deal with Mimics now. She gritted her teeth, as she watched the older woman leave the room. Frieda stood up beside her, looking pale. It struck Emily, suddenly, that most of her friends were victims.

"I think I have something you can wear," she said. Imaiqah had insisted she buy the adjustable dress in First Year, even though it was uncomfortable; it was charmed to extend or shrink depending on who wore it. "But I need a shower first."

"So do I," Frieda said. She paused. "Do you want to go first?"

"You go," Emily said, feeling her cheeks heat. "I'll dig up the dress for you and leave it on my desk."

She undressed as soon as Frieda had stepped into the shower, then carefully removed the blood from her clothes using a simple charm. The blood splashed onto the floor, allowing her to break the link between it and her body before turning it into dust. Wrapping a robe around herself, she did the same for Imaiqah's blood, knowing her friend was in no condition to do it for herself. By the time Frieda emerged from the shower, Emily had cleaned up all the blood and was feeling dirty and grimy.

"I can finish cleaning up, if you like," Frieda offered, as she took the adjustable dress and pulled it over her head. "Would you like me to?"

"Leave it," Emily said. "They've probably charmed their beds against intruders."

Frieda nodded - she'd been at Mountaintop, where protective wards were necessary - and waited patiently for Emily to shower. Emily checked herself in the mirror as soon as she stepped into the shower - Aloha had left her covered in bruises that Master Grey had been unwilling or unable to remove - and then washed herself, thoroughly. She pulled a clean robe over her head and walked back into the room. Frieda was reading a book Imaiqah had borrowed from the library, slowly parsing out some of the more complex words.

"I'm thinking of trying to apply for Advanced Alchemy in Third Year," she said, as Emily opened the door and glanced around warily. "Would you support me, if I did?"

"Professor Thande would have to make the final call," Emily said. She doubted her support would matter one whit to the Alchemy Tutor. "Do you think you could handle the coursework?"

"I think so," Frieda said. "Alchemy is great fun if you get everything right."

Emily smiled - alchemy had never been her favorite subject - but tension filled her as they walked into the corridors. A handful of other students, all looking as shell-shocked as Emily felt, walked towards the Dining Hall, watched by a pair of grim-faced tutors. Emily couldn't help noticing that Sergeant Miles was wearing his armor as he paced outside the Dining Hall, as if he expected trouble.

He was probably right.

"Emily," he said, as they reached the door. "Report to Master Grey after the Grandmaster's speech."

"Yes, Sergeant," Emily said, tiredly. Master Grey had saved her life yesterday, but he would probably be extra-nasty just to make up for it. He would have found it easy to delay saving Emily until Aloha had smashed her face to a bloody pulp. "Do you know where he'll be?"

"Probably in the Armory," Sergeant Miles said. "I believe he was up half the night, trying to assist the victims."

Emily nodded - she didn't really want to think well of Master Grey - and stepped into the Dining Hall. It was very quiet. Only forty or so students were eating; the servants had placed large bowls of porridge on the tables and let the students take what they wanted. Emily took a bowl, filling it with porridge and raisins. She'd need the energy if Master Grey was going to be giving her private lessons.

"If classes have been cancelled," Frieda said, "what am I meant to do?"

"Go to the library and study," Emily said. She would have liked company when she was facing Master Grey, but she knew Frieda couldn't accompany her. "That's what we did when classes were cancelled the last time."

"Oh," Frieda said. She tensed, suddenly. "Here's someone I didn't want to meet."

Emily looked up, but smiled in relief as she saw Caleb. "Are you all right?"

"I was going to ask you the same question," Caleb said. "Nothing seemed to be wrong until I walked into a pair of Fifth Years bawling like children."

"They probably just failed their exams," Frieda said, darkly.

Emily elbowed her, sharply.

"Then one of them tried to commit suicide," Caleb said, giving Frieda a dirty look. "I had to freeze him to get him to stop."

Emily winced. Suicide was taboo in the Nameless World; it was, quite literally, considered grounds for the death penalty. She'd never quite understood why. Mainstream religions on Earth had told everyone for years that those who commit suicide went to hell, but other religions had believed that suicide, under the right circumstances, was an honorable act. It made very little sense to her. The poor boy was likely to face scrutiny for the rest of his life.

"You saved him, at least," she said. She wanted to kiss him, but it would have been cruel with Frieda right there. "That's something."

"So I've been told," Caleb agreed. "I've also been told to report to the Alchemy Classroom after breakfast to assist in brewing potions that may help the victims."

"My sympathies," Emily said, dryly.

Caleb looked down at his hands. "You suggested I should keep working my way through alchemy," he said. "But my hands shake badly if the potion is likely to explode."

"I think it's not a physical problem," Emily said. Caleb's hands didn't shake when he was carving wood, or even when he was holding her. "You're psychologically scarred by the explosion that almost killed you and it's made you reluctant to risk a second explosion."

Frieda opened her mouth, as if she were about to say something, then shut it as the remaining students entered the Dining Hall. Emily looked up and winced at the faces, the hopelessness and helplessness that came from watching their friends attacked by something they could neither comprehend nor fight. She thought frantically, trying to think of something that could be a cause, but nothing she considered would have been overlooked by Lady Barb and the Grandmaster. And, although she hated to admit it, by Master Grey. The asshole had earned his reputation the hard way.

She glanced towards the head of the room as the Grandmaster cleared his throat. He looked badly worried, although he still looked formidable. Emily felt a chill run down her spine as she sensed the magic bubbling around him, then another chill as she realized that, for all his knowledge, the Grandmaster was as helpless as she was. His students were at risk, and he could do nothing. At least they'd had a *plan* to deal with the Mimic...

And that plan failed, Emily recalled. Who would have thought the Mimic would have gladly remained in captivity, rather than being held prisoner by the wards? But when it had been challenged, it had snapped the wards as if they were made of taffy. *We don't even know what we're fighting now.*

"I will not mince words," the Grandmaster said. "Three hundred students have sunk into comas. Most of them come from First and Second Year; a relative handful comes from the years above them. Nothing we have done has been able to wake them. All we can really say about the effect, whatever it is, is that it is attacking students through their magic."

He paused. Silence echoed around the hall.

"We are currently talking to experts across the Allied Lands," he continued, after a long moment. "We *will* find out what is happening to them and we *will* manage to deal with it. I have faith that we will solve the puzzle."

Before they die, Emily thought.

"For the moment, regular classes have been cancelled," the Grandmaster said. "Those of you tapped for specific duties have already been informed, so carry them out. The rest of you can go to independent study. I *strongly* advise you to refrain from doing anything that will disturb the school further. Anyone caught fighting in the corridors or playing practical jokes will regret it. I should also warn you" - his hidden eyes seemed to sweep the room - "that leaving Whitehall without special permission is currently forbidden. You may not pass beyond the outer edge of the wards. Do *not* try our patience on this, *please.*"

Emily nodded. If the problem was caused by a disease, an epidemic, allowing Whitehall's students to mingle with the rest of the world would be asking for trouble. Hell, perhaps it *was* an epidemic. If a curse could be designed to conceal itself from detection spells, why not a magic-based epidemic? And someone could easily have altered a harmless disease and turned it into a weapon.

She shivered at the thought. Biological warfare, according to the books, wasn't unknown in the Allied Lands. Dropping dead bodies into wells was a common trick... and Healers knew enough to create a genuinely dangerous disease through magic. It was one of the reasons for the Healer Oaths, but she knew that such expertise hadn't remained hidden behind the oaths for long, if indeed it had stayed there at all. She knew enough forbidden spells to make a start on creating a disease...

And combined with what I know from Earth, I could make a really dangerous one, she thought. *One that no one here would be able to stop.*

"Finish your breakfasts, then go," the Grandmaster concluded. "If you notice anyone else acting strangely, inform a staff member as soon as possible."

He sat down and dug into his porridge with every evidence of enjoyment. Emily blinked in surprise, then realized he was trying to suggest that he felt calm and confident. She didn't think it was actually working, not when he'd admitted that the disease - if it *was* a disease - was attacking people through their magic. He couldn't have alarmed his students more if he'd told them that necromancy had suddenly been declared legal and that they would be expected to draw lots to become the first necromancers.

"Anyone acting strangely," Caleb said. "In *Whitehall?*"

Emily had to smile. "Anything that's out of the ordinary for us would be worrying," she agreed. "I..."

She broke off as Lady Barb strode over to the table. "The Grandmaster would like to see you as soon as you have finished breakfast," she said. "You can meet him in the Great Hall."

"I will," Emily said. She frowned, nervously. "But I have to report to Master Grey."

"The Grandmaster comes first," Lady Barb informed her. "Tell Master Grey, when you get to him, that you were summoned."

Emily nodded, finished her breakfast and encouraged Frieda to go to the library. She might have been more use in the alchemy classrooms, but she had a feeling that Caleb and Frieda weren't going to get on in her absence. As soon as the younger girl had headed off, she walked through the corridors and into the Great Hall. It was crammed with makeshift beds, each one holding a student trapped in a coma. Emily shuddered when she saw one of the bodies twitching, as if it were having a nightmare. It would have been easy to believe that most of the students in the room were dead.

"Lady Emily," the Grandmaster said. "Come into this room."

Emily followed him into a small office and looked around. The walls were lined with bookshelves, each one crammed with dozens of books. A pair of comfortable chairs sat in the middle of the room, illuminated by a light globe hovering near the ceiling. She felt the privacy wards, wards stronger than anything she could cast on her own, snap into place as the Grandmaster closed the door. No one could hope to overhear their words.

She played with the snake-bracelet on her arm as the Grandmaster motioned her to a chair, then sat facing her. "Lady Barb tells me you sensed something earlier," he said. "What did you sense?"

"Something *wrong*," Emily said. She described the sensation as best as she could, although it was terrifyingly hard to put into words. "I had the feeling that there was something wrong with the wards, but Lady Barb said they had been changed."

"They were," the Grandmaster said. He paused. "There doesn't seem to be anything wrong with the Warden. We have been unable to identify the cause of the problem."

The problem, Emily thought. Several hundred students in comas wasn't a *problem*, it was a disaster. *But if you can't find the cause...*

"It may be a disease," she said. "Something that attacks them through their magic... it could be a curse designed to hide itself."

She paused. "Have you tried an anti-magic ward?"

"We have," the Grandmaster said. "It's a desperation measure, because the curse might kill its victim before being dissipated, but we tried. It didn't work."

"Then a disease that's purely non-magical," Emily reasoned.

The Grandmaster seemed to look at her, although it was hard to be sure. "Did you have such diseases in your world?"

Emily hesitated. She'd heard of diseases that caused comas - or worse - but she didn't know any specifics. If she'd been trained as a doctor...

And if I'd been trained as a SCA re-enactor, I would have been in a much better state to face the Nameless World, she thought, sharply. *There's no point in wishing for what one cannot have.*

"I don't know the details," she said. How *did* they help people in comas anyway? Her memory suggested electric shocks, but she had a feeling that had been discredited by researchers years ago. "And we don't have magic, so I don't know..."

She paused. "Was there anything the victims had in common? Some non-human blood?"

"The Gorgon is the only student at the school who isn't fully human," the Grandmaster mused. "Although I suppose Alassa might count, given the Royal Bloodline."

"And both of them were affected," Emily said.

"Quite," the Grandmaster agreed. He shook his head, looking tired and defeated. "Go see Master Grey, Emily. Try and take your mind off the crisis."

"It doesn't help," Emily protested. She would almost have preferred him shouting at her than to see him in a broken-down state. "I can help here instead."

"Go," the Grandmaster ordered.

Emily nodded, rose and left his office.

Chapter Twenty-Eight

MASTER GREY WASN'T IN THE ARMORY WHEN SHE ARRIVED, ALTHOUGH SERGEANT MILES and Lady Barb were both there, talking in very low voices. It must have been something intimate, Emily reasoned, as Lady Barb told her where to find Master Grey at once. She smiled tiredly, and walked to the spellchambers.

Master Grey stood in the heart of a warding circle, tossing spells towards a handful of training dummies. Emily would have admired the display of power, perhaps, if she'd trusted him more.

"You're late," he said, as she entered the room.

"The Grandmaster wanted to speak to me, sir," Emily said, simply.

Master Grey grunted, still firing off spells. "Are you carrying anything magical?"

Emily hesitated, thrown by the unexpected question. "Yes, sir," she said. "A wand, a spelled knife and a couple of little protective charms."

And the bracelet, she added silently. She wasn't going to mention the Death Viper to Master Grey, not if it could be avoided. *It probably counts as magic, too.*

Master Grey turned to face her. "Go to the barracks and change into your walking clothes, then meet me at the doors," he ordered. "Place everything - and I mean *everything* - magical that you happen to be carrying into your locker. I *will* check. You will receive one demerit for each magical item you're carrying."

"Yes, sir," Emily said. She'd have to tighten the spell on the snake before taking the bracelet off. The last thing she wanted was for the Death Viper to return to its natural state and start hunting for prey. "May I ask why?"

"I'll explain on the way," Master Grey said. "Go."

Emily blinked - he sounded almost friendly - and hurried to change into her walking clothes. The heavy trousers and shirt felt uncomfortable against her skin, as always, but she knew she'd get used to them. She took the bracelet from her wrist, checked the spell and placed it into the locker, accompanied by her other magical objects. It left her feeling oddly naked, she decided, as she walked back to the doors.

Master Grey stood there, holding a pair of knapsacks in one hand.

"Here," he said, passing one to her. "Cheese sandwiches, a bottle of water and a handful of medical supplies."

"Thank you," Emily said, automatically. "Where are we going?"

"Somewhere," Master Grey said. "It's a long walk, so it's better to take food."

Emily felt her eyes narrow. "Do we have permission to leave the wards?"

Oddly, Master Grey smiled. "Yes, we do," he said. "It was good of you to check, though."

As opposed to checking if I could take Frieda for a run? Emily thought, as she followed him out into the bright sunlight. *Or asking about safety precautions in Blackhall?*

Master Grey took one look at her once the door was closed, turned, and started to walk towards the mountains. Emily followed him, silently wondering why he'd set such a quick pace. It wouldn't be hard to keep up with him, she thought, but given time it would leave her drained. The forest closed in around them while they walked;

she gritted her teeth as she felt flickers of wild magic dancing through the air. Master Grey ignored them; he kept walking, maintaining a steady pace. Emily silently promised herself that she'd keep up with him as long as possible.

"That plant there," Master Grey said, suddenly. "Name one use for it that *everyone* knows."

Emily blinked. There were *several* uses for it...but most of them involved potions. "It makes people throw up," she said, finally. "If someone has eaten poison, the plant can be used to make them expel the poison from their body. You need to mash it down into mush, then make them drink it with water."

"Correct," Master Grey said. "What would happen if you tripled the dose?"

"They'd have an attack of diarrhoea, too," Emily said, grimacing.

"Correct," Master Grey said. "What precautions should you take if administering the cure?"

"The victim will need plenty of water to drink," Emily said. She took a moment to remember what she'd been taught. "They will also need something soft to eat, but only after they've finished...emptying themselves."

"Correct," Master Grey said. He jabbed a finger at another plant, a bush covered in purple flowers Emily didn't recognize. "Name me two uses for that plant."

"I don't know," Emily said. She knew better than to guess. "I haven't seen it before."

"It can be used to prevent infection, if one is desperate," Master Grey said. He didn't seem inclined to berate her for ignorance, for once. "It can also be used as a poison, if treated correctly. There are people who like dipping their arrowheads in the liquid before letting fly, just to make sure the target is poisoned."

He kept tossing questions at her until they reached a line of bushes, half-hidden by subtle magic. Emily felt her chest burn uncomfortably as Master Grey glanced around, then turned to look at her. His gaze was suddenly very cold.

"This is your one chance," he said. "Did you bring anything magical with you?"

"No, sir," Emily said. She looked down at her chest. "There's a rune here..."

"That won't matter," Master Grey said. He performed a detection spell on her, and looked relieved at the results. "I want you to understand, Lady Emily, that I am bringing you here against my better judgement."

Emily held herself steady, refusing to say anything.

"You are *not* to use any magic beyond this point, unless it is in direct self-defense," Master Grey continued, coldly. "If you do, I will flay the skin from your bare back. Cleaning up the mess will be so expensive that you'll have to pawn your entire Barony to pay back the debt."

"Yes, sir," Emily said.

"I mean it," Master Grey said. "No magic beyond this point."

"I understand," Emily said.

"I'd be surprised if you did," Master Grey said. "And if you bring any of your friends here without permission, you will very likely be expelled."

He gave her one final look that warned her to take him seriously, then stepped up to the bushes and through a path that was barely wide enough for him. "Keep sensing the magic, if you wish, but don't cast any spells. And do *not* step off the path."

Emily bit down the urge to say something nasty as she followed him through the bushes, keeping her hands firmly to herself. The first line of bushes looked normal, but the second line was poisonous - she'd had a nasty rash for a week after touching one back in First Year - and the third line was actively dangerous, ready to snap at anyone who crossed the line. She winced, remembering how one of the plants she'd seen had tried to chase Jade, moving with an implacable determination that was more terrifying than anything else. They'd had to burn the plant to ashes to get it to stop.

She closed her eyes as she sensed the flow of magic. It had been ever-present in the Nameless World, once she'd grown accustomed to the sensation, but now...it seemed to flow *towards* her, as if it were being directed away from whatever was at the end of the path. She couldn't help smiling as it washed over her, but gasped in surprise when it abruptly vanished into nothingness. They had reached a clearing at the end of the path.

"Tell me," Master Grey said, as they walked towards a small wooden hut. "What happens to the magic here?"

Emily considered it for a long moment. "You use runes to guide the magic away from the hut," she said. "Why?"

"Correct," Master Grey said. He produced an iron key from his belt and used it to open the door. "Do *not* cast a light globe within this hut."

Good thing you reminded me, Emily thought, as Master Grey led her inside and started to light a handful of lanterns hanging from the walls. *It's become habit to use magic in my daily life.*

"You may eat your sandwiches now, if you wish," Master Grey said. "You'll need energy for what is to come."

Emily frowned, then sat down on the wooden floor and opened her knapsack. Master Grey pottered around for a long moment, searching for something, then sat down facing her and started to dig out his own food. For a long moment, they ate in companionable silence. Food always tasted so much better in the open air, Emily had discovered; it wasn't something she'd ever learned on Earth. Master Grey ate quickly, then tossed a handful of questions at her, forcing her to think before answering. None of the questions seemed particularly important...

"This isn't something taught to everyone," Master Grey said, when they were finished. "I strongly advise you not to discuss this with *anyone* else. If the Grandmaster hadn't insisted, I would have refused to teach you. You're dangerous enough without giving you more ideas."

He paused, waiting for a reaction. Emily kept her mouth firmly shut. She'd seen him at work, dueling challengers at the first Faire she'd attended...and he thought *she* was dangerous? But then, she *had* turned the Allied Lands upside down. Some of her ideas would completely reshape the world, given time. Steam engines alone would change everything, and as for gunpowder...

"This place is designed to keep the level of ambient magic as low as possible," he continued, when it became clear she wasn't going to say a word. "A great deal of time and effort was spent cleansing this clearing, then establishing defenses to keep other magicians from contaminating our work. If you use any magic here, even something as minor as a detection spell, you will force us to cleanse the place once again."

"Yes, sir," Emily said.

Master Grey rose to his feet and paced over to a locked cupboard. "This is one of the greatest secrets in the Allied Lands," he said. "We call it Wildfire."

He opened the cupboard and produced a handful of unbreakable bottles. "I want you to stand there," he said, pointing to the other side of the table. "You are *not* to touch anything without my express permission. In fact, keep your hands clasped behind your back. A single mistake here could kill both of us."

Emily scowled, but did as she was told. Master Grey gave her a probing glance before he placed the bottles on the table beside a glass cauldron. It must have cost hundreds of gold coins, Emily realized; she'd never seen anything like it in Professor Thande's classroom. But then, she supposed she wouldn't have wanted a fragile and expensive dish anywhere near rampaging students. Perhaps the Fifth and Sixth Years got to play with them.

"There are seven separate potions here," Master Grey told her. "Only a dozen alchemists, all working for the Allied Lands, know how to brew them. Three of them, in particular, are so complex and unstable that they have to be brewed in a magic-less environment. Trying to brew them in Whitehall would lead to complete disaster. You will not" - a thin smile flickered across his face - "be taught how to make them."

Emily kept her voice as calm as she could. "And what if I *need* to make them?"

"Only an experienced alchemist would have any hope of brewing them," Master Grey said, coldly. "*Manaskol* is simplicity itself compared to the easiest of the potions here..."

"I see," Emily said. "*You* can't brew them, then?"

Master Grey's face flickered, just for a second. "No," he said. She half-expected a demerit, but he merely nodded to her. "It is a wise magician who knows his limits."

He picked up one of the bottles and opened it, carefully. "Should you need any of these potions, you would apply to the White Council," he said, as he sniffed the contents. "They would decide if your request had merit and, if they agreed, ensure you were sent a sufficient quantity. If they felt otherwise, no amount of arguing, pleading, begging or outright threats would make them change their minds."

Emily grimaced as he held the bottle out to her. She sniffed...and recoiled, instinctively. It smelled worse than the cheap alcohol her mother used to buy. Master Grey smiled at her reaction, then poured a small amount of the black liquid into the glass cauldron. Emily couldn't help noticing that it was thick, like sludge or heavy oil. He followed it up with five more bottles, each one marginally lighter. It looked as though the order had been carefully devised by the first alchemist to create the potion.

"You will notice that I have not stirred the mixture," Master Grey said. "All that really matters, at this point, is that all of the potions are in the same cauldron."

"Yes, sir," Emily said. The different liquids had separated out, like oil in water. "You don't need to do anything else, either?"

"Not really," Master Grey said. "The genius and danger of this...*particular* brew is that it doesn't require much expertise to make, once you have the ingredients. You can, for instance, make it under battlefield conditions."

A shadow crossed his face for a long moment. "I have," he added. "Once."

He picked up a small basin, placed it on the table and poured one of the remaining bottles into it. Emily watched, fascinated, as he produced a firelighter, scratching it along the table until it caught fire. He pressed the firelighter into the basin, which caught fire at once, eerie blue flames reaching up towards the ceiling. Visibly bracing himself, he pushed the basin under a rack and placed the cauldron on top of the rack. Moments later, the contents started to bubble.

Emily stared. "What...?"

A sheet of white flame exploded out of the cauldron, lashing around as if it were a living thing in search of sustenance. Emily stepped backwards hastily as it flickered towards her, then powered up towards the ceiling. She looked up and saw the wood had become scorched and pitted; it struck her, suddenly, that this could hardly be the first time Wildfire was demonstrated to a student. The flames flickered one final time, fell back into the cauldron, and vanished.

"Do *not* touch it," Master Grey ordered, as an unholy stench filled the air. "What do you make of it?"

"It burns," Emily said. Now she'd had a moment to think, it was clear the tendrils of fire had reached out towards him too. All the precautions suddenly made sense. "It burns magic."

"Yes, it does," Master Grey said. "It prefers the focused magic generated by long-established wards, Lady Emily, but it will eat any kind of *mana*, given a chance. Using it in a combat zone is always a risk because it doesn't discriminate; it will happily go after one side, then the other, rather than being aimed at its target. It has rarely been used against anything other than a heavily-warded fortress."

"It could have been used on Shadye," Emily pointed out. The Grandmaster could have presumably gathered the ingredients from the hut while waiting for Shadye and his army to reach Whitehall. "Why wasn't it?"

Master Grey quirked an eyebrow. "Something that draws on magic for fuel, something that won't stop easily, right next to Whitehall and the nexus point?"

Emily felt her face heat. "Sorry."

"So you should be," Master Grey said. "The true danger of Wildfire lies in the simple fact that it is impossible to control. No one, not even a Lone Power, can steer it towards a target. Using it on a moving necromancer would simply be ineffective."

He paused. "And there are only two ways to stop it," he added. "How would you do it?"

Emily considered, rapidly. "Starve it of power," she said. "It wouldn't have anything to burn."

"Correct," Master Grey said. "And the other?"

Water, Emily thought. But perhaps that was too obvious. *Anyone would think to pour water on a fire.*

"Sand," she guessed, remembering sand buckets from Earth. "You pour sand on it."

"Good thinking," Master Grey said. "You need to *bury* the fire in sand, or earth, or anything, as long as it is cut off from the air. Even after the main blaze has been suppressed, there may be moments when smaller blazes will blow up again. Ideally, you need to get people without magic to handle the task. As far as the fire is concerned, people like you and me are a walking source of fuel."

He gave her a long glance, then sighed. "I'm going to check the outer edge of the defenses," he said. "Wait until everything is cool, then pick up everything I've used and put it into the sack. We'll be taking it back with us."

"Yes, sir," Emily said. She hesitated before asking the question that was nagging at her mind. "Why don't we recycle the cauldron?"

"Because it's badly damaged," Master Grey said, simply. "*Look* at it."

He had a point, Emily had to admit. The glass was not only scorched, it was warped and threatening to shatter. It would be useless for anything else, she suspected, even if it could be cleaned. The blackened remains of the mixture had bonded so firmly to the glass that nothing short of a monofilament knife would be able to cut them free. If anyone had hoped to recycle the remains, she realized, they would be disappointed.

"I'll be back," Master Grey said. He opened two of the windows, allowing cool air to blow through the hut. "And remember, no magic."

"Yes, sir," Emily muttered. "No magic unless in direct self-defense."

He gave her one last look before hurrying out the door.

Chapter Twenty-Nine

Emily had hoped, against all hope, that the Grandmaster would have found a solution by the time they returned to the castle. That perhaps everything would return to normal. But, as the day turned into evening, it became clear that nothing had really changed. Alassa, Imaiqah, and the rest were still in their comas, joined by two more Third Year students who'd started to rant in the library before they collapsed. The epidemic, whatever it was, seemed to be spreading.

"There must be something they have in common," Emily said, as she stared down at Alassa's body. Her friend seemed inhumanly still, the only sign of life her chest rising and falling slowly as she breathed in and out. "Something that separates them from everyone else."

"We've found nothing," Lady Barb said. "Sex? There's five more boys than girls affected, but that may be just random chance. Age? The young seem to be more vulnerable than the older students, while none of the staff have been affected…"

"Frieda seems to be fine," Emily said. She'd seen the younger girl briefly at dinnertime, before making her way to the infirmary. "What about students who went to different schools, if only briefly? Frieda and I were at Mountaintop; Caleb was at Stronghold…"

"There are several students who spent time at other schools lying in comas," Lady Barb said, quietly. "It could be that some students simply don't channel enough magic to save themselves."

Emily frowned. "Pandora was rambling, as if she'd been possessed," she said, slowly. "It could be a form of possession."

"It's a possibility," Lady Barb agreed. "But most demonic possessions require consent from the victim. It's unlikely that so many students would be able to summon a demon, then make the same deal with it, all at the same time."

"I suppose not," Emily said. "Is there nothing else we can do?"

"We can feed them, keep them alive," Lady Barb said, sternly. "While there's life, there's hope."

Emily gazed down at her friend. "I wish it was me instead," she said. "Alassa deserves so much better."

"I understand the feeling," Lady Barb said, squeezing Emily's shoulder. "Go to bed, Emily. You'll have more to do in the morning."

"I could stay and help," Emily protested. "I'm not drained…"

"You need your sleep," Lady Barb told her. "The Grandmaster is intent on keeping things as normal as possible, even with half the school in comas."

"Pointless," Emily muttered. "There's no way this is *normal*."

She shook her head, slowly. Shadye had attacked in her first year at Whitehall, the Mimic had prowled the corridors in the second…she hadn't been at Whitehall for most of her third year, but in her *fourth* year students had started falling into comas. No, she corrected herself; something had been very wrong before Alassa and Imaiqah collapsed. The staff had noticed that something was odd, but they just hadn't been able to deal with it before it was too late.

"Maybe it's my fault," she said, softly.

"You can't go blaming yourself for everything," Lady Barb said, sharply. "Unless you cast the spell yourself, it probably isn't your fault."

Emily nodded - she didn't really want to believe the older woman - and moved to Imaiqah's bed. Her hands were wrapped in bandages; her mouth had been wiped clean, but blood-tainted drool stained her nightgown. She looked fragile, Emily saw, as if the three years since they'd met had never occurred. Beside her, the Gorgon looked inhuman, her face twisted softly as if she were having a nightmare. But the entire school seemed to be having a nightmare.

Maybe it attacks us through our dreams, Emily thought. *Or perhaps our uncertainties.*

"Explain," Lady Barb ordered, when Emily said that out loud. "What do you mean?"

Emily took a moment to gather her thoughts. "Imaiqah doubts herself," she said, "and so she showed a nervous tic. She was chewing her fingers. Alassa was admiring herself in the mirror - but, at the same time, she fears being defined by her appearance. Aloha has a crush on Master Grey. She may think I have a crush on him too."

Lady Barb barked a harsh laugh. "He'd be roasted alive, literally, if he touched her while she was his student," she said. "There are strict laws against having any kind of relationship with your apprentice."

"She could still have a crush on him," Emily pointed out. She'd known at least one girl on Earth who'd had a schoolgirl crush on a teacher they'd shared. She seemed to spend half of the lessons just staring at him with stars in her eyes. "He's just the sort of person she likes."

"I'll mention it to the Grandmaster," Lady Barb said. "Go get some sleep, Emily. You'll need it."

Emily sighed, but did as she was told. Frieda seemed to have moved into her bedroom, setting up a nest of blankets against the wall; Emily took a look at her sleeping form, shook her head tiredly and climbed into bed without bothering to do more than remove her shirt and trousers. It felt like she'd barely closed her eyes when her bed quivered, threatening to hurl her out onto the floor, but when she looked at her watch she discovered it was eight bells. She'd slept so deeply, she hadn't even dreamed.

That's a relief, she thought, remembering the nightmares that had tormented her after Shadye and the Mimic. *But I would have liked some rest too.*

She smiled at Frieda, who was still fast asleep, took a quick shower and dressed in her school robes. Lady Barb had told her she'd need the sleep, but Emily still felt tired. She drank some water and gently nudged Frieda, suddenly terrified that she too might have fallen into a coma. Frieda jerked awake, then smiled at her in surprise.

"I think that's cheating," Emily said, lightly. "You're not meant to sleep on the floor."

"I didn't want to risk sleeping in any of the beds," Frieda said, as she sat upright and stared down at the floor. "And you can't be kicked out of bed if you're not in it."

"I suppose," Emily said.

She waited for Frieda to shower, then they went down to breakfast together. It looked, at first glance, as though there hadn't been any more victims, but as she looked around she noticed a handful of missing faces. Maybe they were trying to catch up with their sleep, or helping with the patients...she shook her head, bitterly, as Frieda passed her a bowl of cereal. She couldn't be that lucky. The missing faces were in comas.

This could catch us all, she thought, morbidly. A disease striking magic-users - she hadn't heard of any of the servants falling into comas - could be disastrous, if it spread out of Whitehall. *Shadye was too inhuman to catch a bug, but every other magician might die.*

She shuddered at the thought.

She gritted her teeth as Master Grey walked into the Dining Hall and strode over to her table. He couldn't have had more sleep than she did, Emily was sure, but he looked annoyingly fresh as he came to a halt and peered down at her. The robes he wore were carefully tailored to draw attention to his muscles, reminding her of one of his more interesting lessons. Putting on different styles of clothing had almost been fun. It *would* have been fun if they'd had a different tutor.

"Emily," Master Grey said. "You will report to my office after breakfast."

"Yes, sir," Emily said, fighting to keep her feelings from showing. She wanted to go back to bed, not do *anything* with Master Grey. Right now, she was too tired to handle him. "Should I wear anything special?"

"Just bring your wand," Master Grey ordered.

He turned and stamped off, ignoring a pair of boys who were pushing and shoving at each other at the far table. Emily sighed, then drank her Kava, hoping the bitter taste would jolt her awake. But it didn't seem to work.

She ate as much as she could, said goodbye to Frieda and headed for the Armory. A handful of younger students were talking in low voices as she walked past them, their gazes following her movement. She couldn't tell if they were admiring her, laughing at her or merely making sure she was out of earshot before they resumed their conversation.

"Emily," Master Grey said once she was there. He pointed to a chair, where he'd left a book. "You will stay here and read until I call you. Do *not* attempt to leave the room."

Emily blinked in surprise. "Sir?"

"You will stay here and read until I call you," Master Grey repeated, in a manner one might use to rebuke a child. "Do *not* attempt to leave the room."

Emily flushed, sat down and picked up the book. It was an older textbook, covering the different uses of dragon's blood in combat. Master Grey slipped out of the room while she opened the covers and started to read, carefully. Given just how expensive it was to buy even a pint of dragon's blood, she was mildly surprised there were so many uses. It would have been much simpler for alchemists to stick with one or two.

But it is the most powerfully-magical substance known to exist, she thought. *They might have been able to deduce other prospective uses before going to work.*

She was midway through the book when Master Grey returned. "Come with me," he ordered, curtly. "You have work to do."

Emily put the book on his table, making a mental note to ask to borrow it later, then followed him out of the room and down to the spellchamber. Master Grey removed a pair of locking hexes before motioning for her to enter the room. Inside, it was dark and cold; a shape lay on a table, set in the exact center of the chamber. It was surrounded by a privacy ward so strong Emily couldn't tell anything more about it, save for the fact it was there.

"Your objective is simple," Master Grey said. "The person there" - he pointed a hand at the table - "has been cursed. Your task is to remove the curse before it kills her. You may use your wand, if you feel you need it, but nothing else. There will be no help from me or anyone else."

Emily shivered. "I…"

Master Grey ignored her. "The curse in question is currently frozen," he said. "When I drop the ward, it will go active. You will have roughly seven minutes before the damage becomes irreversible. Do you understand me?"

"Yes, sir," Emily said, shocked. Had he actually cursed someone just to provide a learning experience for her? "Who…"

"Go," Master Grey said.

He snapped his fingers and the ward vanished. Emily stared in horror as Frieda appeared, lying on the table. Her skin was already mottled as the curse started to dig into her body, threatening to kill her. Emily stared, then forced herself forward, hastily casting spells to determine just which curse had been used. It rapidly became apparent that Master Grey had used something so complex that trying to bat it away from Frieda would only knock it into a more dangerous form. He'd deliberately set Frieda up to die if Emily couldn't save her.

"Six minutes, thirty seconds," Master Grey said.

Emily wanted to scream at him as blood started to trickle from Frieda's nose. Instead, she closed her eyes and forced her mind into the maelstrom of magic surrounding her friend, trying to parse out the exact shape of the curse. It hung around its victim, a complex mixture of spellwork that would have been almost beautiful if it wasn't ripping her apart, cell by cell. Emily forced down panic and picked out the vital pieces, then swallowed a curse as she realized the spell was actually designed to reconfigure itself even if she took out the most important sections and fall on its victim like a hawk falling on a mouse. She would need to push it *all* away at once, or take the risk of sucking it into *her* wards and hope she could deal with it.

"Six minutes," Master Grey said.

"Shut up," Emily snarled at him.

He said nothing as she kept scrutinizing the curse. Whoever had designed it had been good, very good. The important sections clung to its victim, surrounded by unimportant spell components that might turn lethal if they failed to distract the curse-breaker. Emily felt Frieda's heart start to beat faster as the curse took effect, trying to parse out the best way to remove the curse. Every time she thought she had a handle on it, it slipped out from under her gaze and escaped. It was almost as if it was alive and aware...

It isn't anything like as complex as a Mimic, she told herself, firmly. Everything she'd been told about magic suggested that genuine artificial intelligence was impossible, but she'd been sure the Mimic had showed a certain level of adaptive intelligence. *It's designed to make it harder for the curse-breaker to get a grip.*

She braced herself as she realized what she had to do. The only way to break the curse was to hold its separate components in place, gripping them all at once. But, in doing so, she might set off a reaction that would kill Frieda. Master Grey had to be out of his mind! Maybe he was allowed to make her train relentlessly, maybe he was allowed to give her impossible tasks; she was sure he wasn't allowed to harm another student. And yet, if she failed, she would have to watch her friend die.

Hatred and rage seared through her mind as she targeted the curse, then lashed out with her magic. Dozens of spell components froze in place; others, components out of her reach, kept moving. Frieda's body jerked under her hand as the fragmented curse started to slash at her soul.

"Three minutes," Master Grey said.

Emily ignored him, splitting her attention as best as she could. Lady Barb had once told her that women made the best curse-breakers and, now, she understood why. One part of her attention kept the frozen pieces of the curse still; another part, desperately, snatched at other parts of the curse and wiped them from existence before they could threaten Frieda's life. It wasn't easy to focus her mind enough to shatter the frozen pieces of the curse, but - eventually - it worked. The curse seemed to fragment...

...And then it pulled itself back together.

Shit, Emily thought, as Frieda gasped in pain. The curse was worse than she'd realized, lodged deep within Frieda's magic. It was actually forcing her magic to turn on her, as if Frieda were literally cursing herself. Emily had believed that to be impossible, but if she could cut her skin to provide blood, why not cast a curse on herself? It wasn't as if she hadn't turned herself into all kinds of things.

She swore mentally, then desperately grabbed the curse as it started to hack its way into Frieda's soul. There was no longer any time to experiment; she thrust her magic at the curse, tearing into it with savage intensity. Her wards started to flicker as the curse tried to jump into her - she thought she could destroy it, but the way it was spawning suggested that it wouldn't save Frieda if she took as much as she could into her own protections - yet she did her best to ignore it. The curse flickered and flared...

And then Frieda's body jerked one final time, then lay still.

Emily opened her eyes. Frieda was lying there, dead. For a long moment, she just stared, unable to quite believe her eyes. Master Grey couldn't have killed her friend, could he? He couldn't have...

She spun around, fists balled. "You *bastard*!"

Master Grey looked oddly amused. "And why are you insulting a teacher to his face?"

"You *killed* her," Emily shouted. "You..."

"You failed her," Master Grey said.

"You *cursed* her," Emily said. Magic crackled over her fingertips, demanding escape. It would be so easy to just throw a curse at him, even if she was expelled - or worse. "You..."

Master Grey pointed a finger at the body. Emily turned back, just in time to see Frieda's features melt into a homunculus. He would have taken some of her hair or blood, perhaps, to make the illusion terrifyingly realistic, but...she swallowed hard, feeling faint. He'd forced her into a position where she'd thought, where she'd *believed*, her friend was on the verge of death. It had been so realistic she hadn't even thought to *question* it.

"You will face worse, if you go on to be a Mediator," Master Grey said. His voice dripped fake sympathy, too exaggerated to fool her for an instant. "It's for your own good."

"You're a fucking sadist," Emily swore at him. "You can't just do that and expect me to be *happy*!"

"Of course not," Master Grey agreed. "I expect you to learn how to handle yourself."

Emily opened her mouth, but she was cut off by the door opening. Lady Barb stepped into the room, looking grim.

"Emily," she said. "The Grandmaster requests your presence and that of Master Grey, immediately. Come with me."

I swore at a tutor, Emily thought, feeling her rage draining away. *I swore at a tutor and...*

She gathered herself as best as she could. It wasn't real. It had never been real.

"I'm coming," she said. Her entire body was trembling, but somehow she managed to bring it under control. "Where are we going?"

"The infirmary," Lady Barb said. At least it wasn't his office. "The Grandmaster has had an idea."

Chapter Thirty

THEY'D MOVED ALASSA INTO A SIDEROOM, EMILY NOTED, AS SHE FOLLOWED LADY BARB into the infirmary. The Grandmaster was standing by her bed, leaning on a staff; he turned to face Emily and gave her a tight smile before waving her into a chair. It didn't look as though she was in trouble, Emily thought, but that would change. Master Grey would report she'd sworn at him, that she'd shouted at him, and do his level best to get her expelled.

Or simply refuse to teach me any longer, Emily thought, as she sat. *The man makes no sense.*

The Grandmaster cast a privacy ward in the air, and leaned forward. "Emily," he said. "I am given to understand that you touched Alassa's mind once before."

Emily hesitated. Blood magic wasn't exactly illegal, but it wasn't regarded as something anyone should do. Shadye had used blood magic to control her, years ago; she'd barely touched Alassa's mind, yet she knew her friend had had every reason to be angry about it.

"Yes, sir," she said, finally.

"I would like you to try touching her mind again," the Grandmaster said. "She seems to be one of the few students still fighting against...against whatever has gripped their minds."

Master Grey stepped forward. "Grandmaster," he said, "that would be incredibly dangerous."

As if you care, Emily thought. She was damned if she would forgive him for scaring her so badly. *You'd probably be happy if I lost myself in Alassa's mind.*

"Yes, it would be," the Grandmaster agreed. "However, I don't see any other options."

"We may have to seal the school again," Lady Barb said. "The White Council won't let the epidemic, whatever it is, spread."

Which would be a waste of time if someone has come up with a magical biological weapon, Emily thought. *Now that they know it worked, they can introduce it somewhere else.*

She pushed the thought aside and looked at the Grandmaster.

"I'll do it," she said. Alassa would be furious when she woke up, but at least she would be *alive.* "If I did it once before, I have a better chance of actually succeeding."

"Yes," the Grandmaster said. "But you might be infected yourself. Or you might be unable to break contact and escape. People have *died* because they were unable to drag themselves out of someone's mind."

Emily swallowed. It wasn't a pleasant thought. The books she'd read at Mountaintop had talked about blood magic...and possible ways to turn it into a weapon. One magician had planted a seed of his own mind in his victim, which had eventually flowered into a split personality; another, perhaps with darker intentions, had used it to bind his family to him as slaves. Magic was terrifyingly easy to abuse and, without a comprehensive knowledge of every branch of magic, even the most experienced magicians could be caught out.

"I know, sir," she said. Alassa was her friend. "I'll take the risk."

"You may go mad," Lady Barb warned. "Or you may die in there, leaving your body uninhabited."

Emily nodded, not trusting herself to speak. She feared mental harm far more than physical harm, if only because anything that didn't kill her outright could be cured through magic. But a mental problem? She'd be lucky if she were locked up in the Halfway House for study, rather than simply killed out of hand as a potential danger. Necromancers were mad, after all, and embracing necromancy might seem the sane option if she were already mad.

"Very well," the Grandmaster said. "We shall make the preparations."

Lady Barb cleared her throat. "Do you want to rest first? Or eat something?"

"No, thank you," Emily said. The longer she delayed, the harder it would be to take the plunge into Alassa's mind. "Can we just get on with it?"

Master Grey gave her an odd look, but said nothing. Emily couldn't help feeling heartened; he'd probably meant to make a cutting remark, then remembered where he was. The Grandmaster wouldn't have tolerated him snapping at Emily, not in front of him and Lady Barb. Oddly, it made Emily feel better. Master Grey might be intimidating, but he could be intimidated himself.

The Grandmaster produced a silver knife from his belt and carefully cut Alassa's hand. Blood welled up; Emily swallowed, unable to keep herself from feeling nervous. All of the horror stories she'd read, the ones intended to dissuade magicians from experimenting with blood magic, suddenly felt very real. Jumping into a person's mind could be dangerous; hell, one book had likened it to jumping off a cliff, without any real idea of what was below. The Grandmaster passed her the knife, then waited.

"You don't have to do this," Lady Barb said, as Emily stood and knelt beside Alassa. "Emily, there are other people who can touch minds."

Emily shook her head. She was, as far as she knew, the *only* person who had ever touched Alassa's mind. It wasn't *that* much experience, but it was better than anyone else. Hell, she'd managed to reach Alassa and bring her out, back into the real world. If she could do that again, Alassa would be alive...and then they could start rescuing the others, one by one.

"I do," she said. She slashed her own palm, then deliberately gripped Alassa's hand, allowing their blood to mingle. "Someone has to do it."

She muttered the incantation under her breath and waited. For a long moment, nothing happened; Alassa's body felt warm but empty. Emily didn't want to think about the possibilities, yet she knew they had to be faced. Could Alassa's soul have fled a long time ago?

And then *something* reached out for her.

Emily plummeted forward, into Alassa's mind. Everything went black...

...And then she was standing in a grey mist, looking around helplessly. She couldn't see anything but the mist; it floated around her like a physical thing, close enough to touch and yet completely out of reach. Emily lifted her hand and watched as the mist fell back, refusing to allow her to touch it. The air felt damp and cold.

This isn't right, she thought. Last time, she'd been bombarded with memories and sensations; now, there was just the grey mist. *Is she dead? Is this a dead mind?*

She refused to consider the thought. "Alassa," she called. Her voice faded into the nothingness surrounding her. "Alassa!"

There was no response. She looked down, wondering what she was standing on, but saw nothing. It was quite possible she was still plummeting, she thought; maybe she was still falling and had yet to reach bottom. But there was no sense of falling, no sensation at all apart from the cold. It seemed to reach through her skin and into her very soul.

She closed her eyes, then opened them again. Nothing changed.

"Alassa," she called, again. "Where *are* you?"

A chuckle, cruel and evil, echoed through the mist.

Emily jumped. *That* hadn't been Alassa. She'd heard her friend laugh, or giggle, or even snicker at someone's misfortune...and it hadn't sounded anything but feminine. She looked from side to side, bracing herself for an attack that could come from anywhere, yet there was nothing but the mist. And then she heard a second chuckle, so loud it seemed to be coming from all around her. She would have sworn it was masculine, except there was something about it that was inhuman. Utterly inhuman.

Something moved, above her. She looked up and froze. A giant face peered down at her, so utterly inhuman that it was hard to pick out any details. It leered, one hand reaching down towards her; Emily cringed back, reaching desperately for her magic, but it refused to work. The mist seemed to spin around her...

...And, when it cleared, she stood facing the creature. It held a puppet on strings dangling from one hand. Emily was somehow unsurprised to realize the puppet was Alassa, frozen in a moment of time.

She forced herself to look at the creature. It was humanoid, but clearly far less human than the Gorgon. It's arms and legs were long and gangly, bending in ways no human could match; it's face was angular and sharp, with long pointy ears that reached to the sky. And its eyes were bright, and sharp, and so very cruel.

"Well," it said. "Welcome."

"You're a demon," Emily said. It was hard to even *look* at the demon, but she forced herself to stand her ground. "Aren't you?"

"In a manner of speaking," it agreed.

Emily thought, fast. The one time she'd met a demon, she'd raised it herself, within a protective circle. It might have been able to pick its words to harm her, but it wouldn't have been able to hurt her physically. *This* demon, however, was loose within Alassa's mind; it might not be under any restraints at all. It might well be able to hurt both of them.

"Alassa didn't summon you," she said, flatly. "How are you even here?"

"Now *there's* an interesting story," the demon said. "And I will even tell it to you for free."

Emily's eyes narrowed. Demons *never* did anything for free. And they couldn't lie...

But was that true of a demon that *hadn't* been raised with the proper rites? Even the DemonMasters of old hadn't dared to tamper with the rites, not when losing control could easily lead to a horrible death. Maybe it *could* lie to her.

And even if it couldn't, she knew better than to take everything it said on faith. It might not be able to lie, but it certainly could bend the truth until it was completely unrecognizable.

"Once upon a time," the demon said, "there was a magician with more power than sense. He reached into the Darkness, demanding a warden for his fortress, and dragged me out into the light. I was bound to his fortress, bound so tightly that even his death didn't free me."

Its voice burned at Emily's mind, each word tearing into her thoughts. She wanted to cover her ears, but she knew it would be pointless. The demon wasn't speaking into her ears; it was speaking directly into her mind. And it was trying to make it hard for her to think clearly.

"Shadye," Emily said. "He summoned you as a guard dog?"

The demon's eyes flashed with brilliant malice. "None dared approach his fortress," it said, with a hint of pride. "Those who *did* became my prey. They were *mine* to play with as I willed. He wished me to keep his domain free of intruders and I did as I was bid."

As the terms of enslavement bound you, Emily thought. Some of the DemonMasters had done the same thing, according to the books, but it had almost always ended badly. The demons had broken free as soon as their master died. *And yet, Shadye managed to bind you so thoroughly you remained trapped even after he died.*

"And then his heir arrived," the demon added. "It was *such* a surprise to discover that the person who'd killed him was a young, innocent girl."

Emily winced. She had a nasty feeling she knew where this was going.

"You took the object that bound me out of the Dark Fortress and, *quite* by accident, granted me permission to enter Whitehall," it said. "Your Grandmaster, alack for him, is blind; we took his eyes."

Emily stared. "*You* took his eyes?"

"He raised a demon long ago," the demon said. It made a show of rubbing its clawed hands together in glee. "The experience blinded him to us. He could no more see demonic influence than the spots on your face. It was beyond him to realize that you had picked up my container, or that I rode you back to Whitehall."

It clicked its fingers. Emily recalled suddenly, with a clarity that startled her, picking up a ring from among Shadye's possessions. It hadn't struck her as anything special at the time; the Grandmaster had simply added it to the collection for later study. But if the demon had been bound to the ring...

"The Grandmaster gave you permission to enter when he took you through the wards," she said, slowly. "But they should have kept you out..."

"I'm not a Dark Wizard," the demon sneered. "The wards could not keep me out if I had permission to enter."

Its face twisted into a leer. "I reached into the dreams of your fellow students, Heir to Shadye," it said. "I whispered to them at night, touching and twisting their minds until they bowed to me. Many have secret shames they wish to hide; many more have secret desires, desires I brought out into the open. The more I gathered, the easier it became to touch others..."

"Until they started to collapse into comas," Emily said. How much power did the demon need to maintain itself? It clearly hadn't been drawing power from the wards, or the nexus point. That would have been noticeable. A thought struck her and she leaned forward. "You were the Nightmare Hex, weren't you?"

The demon shifted, becoming her stepfather. "It is so much fun to watch people drive themselves to death," it said. The voice was perfect, sending chills down her spine, but she stood firmly in place. Master Grey was far more terrifying than her stepfather. "Your worst nightmare would have eventually killed you."

Emily took a long breath. "You're not really here, are you? I mean, you're lodged in another dimension, bound to the ring. We can take it out of the school..."

"Too late," the demon said. It morphed back into its inhuman form. "I'm now lodged in the minds of your fellow students. The only way to banish me would be to kill everyone I touched."

It threw back its head and cackled. The hell of it, Emily realized, was that it was telling the exact truth. If it had moved from the ring, if it had grabbed hold of several hundred minds, destroying the ring would be pointless. It could keep reaching for more victims until everyone in Whitehall was in its thrall.

"We'll all die, eventually," Emily said. "You'll run out of souls."

The demon shrugged. "So what?"

She shuddered as it opened its mouth and bared its teeth at her, revealing sharp fangs stained with blood. It didn't care, she realized; it didn't have any long-term plans or ambitions of its own. There was no objective beyond twisting the screws as much as possible. It wanted them to suffer, it wanted them to bleed, to rend and tear at their own minds...

...And then it would just fall back into the Darkness, until the next time.

"I'll fight you," she swore. "Whatever it takes..."

The demon laughed at her. "You'll have to kill your own friends," it said. "Do you have the nerve to *kill?*"

It jangled the puppet at her. Now, it looked like Imaiqah; no, it looked like hundreds of faces, each one visible for a brief moment before vanishing again. It had them all on a string, she thought numbly. Maybe *she* had some immunity, because she'd killed Shadye...or maybe the demon had simply intended to ride her back to Whitehall all along. But no matter what she did, she couldn't touch the demon directly.

"I'll drop your ring into a volcano," she threatened.

"Go right ahead," the demon said. "What do you think that will do to *me?*"

Nothing, Emily thought.

"Nothing," the demon said.

It took her a moment to realize it had read the thought right out of her mind. She was in Alassa's mind, which was effectively the demon's territory; it could read her thoughts, if it wished. It snickered unpleasantly, the sound slashing through her very soul, and started to advance towards her. Her skin crawled as its eyes met hers, holding her firmly in place. It was too late to run.

"I can be anyone," the demon said. It morphed into Caleb, then into Lady Barb. "Or anything. This is *my* domain and I can hold you here indefinitely."

Emily wanted to run, but her body refused to move. The demon shifted back into its original form, then pressed its hand on her chest, between her breasts. Emily shivered, utterly repulsed by the touch. The demon was so inhuman that even *looking* at it felt as if she was looking at something *wrong*. It spread out its fingers, then pushed hard. Emily felt as though someone had stabbed her in the chest...

...And then she fell backwards, right into her body. Someone was screaming; it took her several seconds to realize that *she* was doing the screaming. Everything felt so *wrong*...

"Emily," Lady Barb said. She sounded as though she was panicking. "Can you *hear* me?"

It took Emily a moment to gather herself. Her chest hurt so badly she was *sure* she was bleeding, that the demon had reached into her flesh and crushed her heart, but when she looked down it became clear she was unharmed. Alassa, on the other hand, was shaking violently, her hands flailing at random. Lady Barb cast a pair of spells to hold her still, but neither seemed to work. In the distance, Emily heard the demon snicker.

I won't kill my friends, she thought.

"Emily," the Grandmaster said. His voice was so calm she knew he was trying hard to keep himself under control. "What did you see?"

"Tell me what you saw, you stupid girl," Master Grey added.

Emily flushed with anger. "I saw a demon," she said. It was hard to talk; her mouth felt sore, as if she'd been slapped. "There's a demon loose in Whitehall."

Chapter Thirty-One

THE GRANDMASTER STAGGERED AS IF HE'D BEEN HIT. LADY BARB STARED AT HER WITH OPEN horror; Master Grey eyed her with cool calculation.

"A demon," the Grandmaster said. "Are you *sure?*"

"I think so," Emily said. Had the demon actually *called* itself a demon? "It said Shadye dragged it out of the Darkness and bound it to his service."

The Grandmaster groaned, one hand rubbing his hidden eyes. Emily watched, concerned; the demon had claimed the Grandmaster was blind, particularly to demons. What had he done, in the past, that had blinded him? Aurelius hadn't been blind and *he'd* raised several demons before his untimely death.

"And we brought it back with us," he said, bitterly. "You wouldn't have known what you were seeing, and I *couldn't* see it."

"I didn't see anything," Emily said. She'd watched as he'd checked Shadye's small hoard of objects, one by one. "There was nothing to suggest we were carrying a demon with us."

"Of *course* there wasn't," Master Grey snapped. His face was paler than normal, but he seemed otherwise composed. "Just another case of you making a mistake that has disastrous consequences. Didn't you think you'd run out of luck eventually?"

Emily opened her mouth to retort, but the Grandmaster spoke first.

"Tell me what happened," he said. "I need to know in as much detail as possible."

"I'll do my best," Emily said. She gathered herself, then carefully went through the entire story, starting with the mist and ending with the demon shoving her out of Alassa's mind and back into her body. Her chest still hurt, although she knew there was no real injury. But it had felt so *real*! "It said it had woven its way into their thoughts."

"That's what demons do," the Grandmaster said. "It didn't make an overt deal with them, I suspect; it just touched their sleeping minds and laid their traps."

"Shadye would have bound it to the ring," Master Grey sneered. "It didn't *need* to make a deal to remain on this plane."

"It said as much," Emily said. She looked at the Grandmaster. "Can't you take the ring out and deny permission for the demon to enter? Or simply destroy the ring?"

"It's firmly lodged in their minds now," the Grandmaster said. He looked down at Alassa, clearly choosing his next words carefully. "They effectively gave it permission to remain anyway."

"But you rule Whitehall," Emily protested. "If you could accidentally allow the demon entry..."

"I don't rule the students," the Grandmaster said. "They would have to forsake the demon on their own, which will be hard while they're in comas. It laid its plans very well."

"You brought the demon here," Master Grey said, looking at Emily. "If it wasn't for you, it would never have gained access to the school."

Emily looked down at the floor. Cold logic told her he was wrong...but emotion told her something else. If she hadn't insisted on going to the Dark Fortress after defeating Shadye, the demon might have simply remained where it was, destroying the lives of anyone stupid enough to visit the fortress. Whatever Shadye had left there would be safe enough as long as the demon stood on guard. But she'd gone to the Dark Fortress...

The Grandmaster didn't escape the Nightmare Hex, she thought, numbly. *I broke free and that snapped him out too.*

"She didn't know what she - what *they* - were doing," Lady Barb said. "You can't blame her for ignorance."

"She *should* have known," Master Grey insisted. "Is ignorance a defense when hundreds of students are trapped in thrall to a *demon*? Is ignorance a defense when those innocent students will have to be killed to dislodge the demon from our world?"

"We're not killing anyone," Emily said. "There has to be a way to free them."

"There isn't," Master Grey said. "The only way to convince a demon to let go would be to find something it wanted and make a trade, but what would it want? Demons enjoy suffering! They like watching us scream!"

"We will go through the older books," the Grandmaster said, coolly. "It may be that there is a solution. Lord Whitehall was known for banishing demons in his time."

Lady Barb frowned. "Can you read the books?"

"You can," the Grandmaster said. "And there are other collections elsewhere."

Mountaintop, Emily thought.

"None of that changes the fact that the White Council will order us to do something drastic," Master Grey snapped. "We'll have to *kill* everyone touched by the demon!"

"We can keep the demon from spreading its wings further," the Grandmaster said. "Now that we know what we're dealing with, we can keep it in check."

Master Grey glowered at Emily. "How many students are on the verge of falling prey to its influence?"

"I don't know," Emily said.

She gritted her teeth. Her body hurt, a dull ache that seemed to pervade every last cell and even her soul. She wanted bed, desperately; she knew she didn't dare sleep, not with a demon spreading its influence through the school. And Master Grey just wouldn't shut up! She had to fight to keep her temper in check, after she'd been forced to watch Frieda die. He'd made it seem real...

"I don't know," Master Grey mocked. "I don't know! That could almost be your refrain!"

He glared at her, savagely. "Several hundred students are about to die at our hands," he snapped. "Several *hundred* students! And it's all your fault."

"Quiet," the Grandmaster ordered. "I was with her. The responsibility is mine."

"Everyone knows there are things you can't see," Master Grey said. He sneered at Emily. "But *she* should have been able to see them."

Emily forced herself to ignore him. "There's a library in Mountaintop," she said. "Zed said I could go there, if I wanted. There are books on demons there."

"You *wrecked* Mountaintop," Master Grey thundered. His voice turned accusing. "And now you've wrecked Whitehall! Do you think the school will remain open when we know there's a demon on the prowl?"

The Grandmaster sagged, resting on his staff. Lady Barb gave Emily a warning look, then hurried to his side. Emily felt another stab of bitter guilt. She liked the Grandmaster, she'd enjoyed the walk through the Blighted Lands...everything that had happened, since then, felt like her fault. And Master Grey's words, his harsh words, cut into her very soul. They made her want to throw caution to the winds.

"Mountaintop was killing its students to sustain the wards," Emily shouted, feeling her temper fray. It was hard, so hard, to believe he was wrong. If she hadn't gone to the Dark Fortress, the demon would never have come to Whitehall. Alassa, Imaiqah, the Gorgon, Aloha, and everyone else would be working on their coursework, not resting in demon-induced comas. "Did you *know* that, when you left? How many of your friends died to keep the school running?"

"Hard choices have to be made," Master Grey shouted back at her. "Do you think you can just pick matters up and then drop them again? Be committed, or don't commit yourself at all!"

He took a breath. "And don't waste my time babbling about things you don't understand, you ignorant child," he snapped. "Just shut up!"

Emily's temper snapped. "If you think you can shut me up," she shouted, caught between rage and exhaustion, "shut me up!"

Master Grey, just for a second, showed a flicker of triumph. "I accept your challenge," he said, in a voice so polite that it was shockingly clear he'd faked his earlier rage. "My second will discuss the details of the duel later today. To the death, of course."

"No, he won't," the Grandmaster growled. He pulled himself upright and fixed Master Grey with a stern look. "I do not permit dueling in my school."

Master Grey stared back at him evenly. "She issued the challenge," he said. It dawned on Emily that she might have made a horrific mistake. "It is my right to settle it as I see fit."

"Then you can wait until after the exams," the Grandmaster told him, flatly. "Or are you disputing *my* right to issue orders in *my* school?"

"Very well," Master Grey said. "The duel can wait."

He bowed politely to the Grandmaster, then strode out of the room, closing the door loudly behind him. The Grandmaster took a moment to center himself before he opened the door and followed Master Grey. Emily turned, wincing as Lady Barb caught her arm in a vice-like grip. A wave of her hand closed the door, then established a privacy ward.

"Sit," Lady Barb grated. "Do you have *any* idea how much trouble you're in?"

Emily hesitated, then shook her head. "No."

Christopher Nuttall

"You practically challenged him to a duel," Lady Barb said. "And he saw fit to *accept* your challenge. He's going to kill you."

She glared at Emily, then started to pace from side to side, her fists clenched. "You were manipulated," she added, tiredly. "We were *all* manipulated."

Emily didn't see it. "By the demon?"

"Perhaps," Lady Barb said. She swung around, her eyes flickering as if she were searching for an invisible enemy. "But no; I think Master Grey intended to goad you to a point where you issued something that could be taken as a challenge. Making you think you'd watched your little friend die...that you'd failed to save her...might have been intended to push you over the brink."

"I didn't mean to challenge him," Emily said, stunned. Master Grey had switched from asshole to teacher and then back to asshole, time and time again...had he been deliberately trying to keep her off balance? She could have endured constant disdain, but it had been hard to cope when she'd never known which of his two personalities would emerge to take the lesson. "I..."

"You told him to shut you up," Lady Barb said. "It might not be the formal slap, but it's certainly close enough. The White Council might rule in his favor if it came to court."

Emily closed her eyes and tried to recollect what she'd been taught about dueling. She'd never felt inclined to duel for fun, so the only real lessons she'd taken had been at Mountaintop and the rules were softer for students. A tutor couldn't challenge a student, she was sure, but a student could challenge a tutor. There were rules, she thought, yet she'd never bothered to look them up. It had never seemed important.

She opened her eyes, feeling a terrible numbness spreading through her chest. "What do we do?"

"*You* can't do anything," Lady Barb snapped. "I imagine the Grandmaster will try to bring pressure on him to refuse your challenge, perhaps with some face-saving formula about blaming everything on the demon. It might work; hellfire, it might even be true. If not..."

She sat on the bed, facing Emily. "You don't have many options," she said, tiredly. "You didn't accuse him of something unforgivable, so you can't discover his innocence and retract your challenge on those grounds. He'd have every right to make you eat crow if you issued a false accusation, even if you believed it to be true at the time. Or you could retract it anyway...?"

Emily frowned. "What's the catch?"

"He might claim compensation from you," Lady Barb said. "It isn't impossible for him to lay claim to Cockatrice itself. The White Council *might* back him up, if they heard the case; he could presumably argue that he'd won by default and was thus entitled to everything you own. King Randor wouldn't be pleased, but trial by combat has been laid down in his law. It might be hard for him to object.

"Or he might demand *you*. As a slave."

"No," Emily said.

"He could," Lady Barb said. "There is precedent for that, too."

She met Emily's eyes. "Everything he did, it seems, was done to create a situation where he can kill you, without fear of retaliation," she warned. "Or otherwise render you harmless. If you ran, and you *could* run, your property would be seized and your reputation destroyed. I don't think anyone would believe you actually killed two necromancers if you couldn't face a single combat sorcerer."

"I can't," Emily said.

"He has twenty years of experience," Lady Barb agreed. She tapped her palm as she spoke, underlining each word. "He's stronger than you, faster than you, tougher than you and nastier than you. You don't stand a chance."

I could blow him up, Emily thought, vindictively. She could reuse the nuke-spell, if they were somewhere isolated. Master Grey wouldn't be expecting a small nuclear blast. It would probably kill her too, but she wasn't inclined to care. *Or...*

She looked at Lady Barb. "Where will we be fighting?"

"Here, perhaps," Lady Barb said. "The seconds are normally charged with finding a suitable place."

Emily groaned. Using the nuke-spell in Whitehall would not only destroy the school, killing everyone inside, but also destabilize the nexus point. The resulting explosion would devastate the land for hundreds of miles around, slaughtering millions of innocent civilians and unleashing wild magic in its wake. She couldn't have that on her conscience, not if all she wanted to do was drag him down beside her. She'd have to fight without the greatest weapon in her arsenal.

I could use the battery, she thought. *But to do what?*

Lady Barb met Emily's eyes. "I suggest you write to Void," she added. "You might wind up owing him a *second* favor, but he might be able and willing to help. Although...if he kills Master Grey now, it's going to look very bad."

"As if I went running to daddy," Emily said.

"Quite," Lady Barb agreed. "It would make him look bad too, of course."

"Of course," Emily echoed. "If I fight, I die; if I retract the duel, I lose everything; if I run, I lose everything, *apart* from my freedom?"

"Correct," Lady Barb said, coldly. "You have enemies, Emily. I dare say that both the Ashworths and Ashfalls have good reason to want to hammer you. Others...will recall what you did last summer and decide it might be better to have you rendered harmless. Some of the Mountaintop alumni will certainly blame you for what you did to their school. It wouldn't look good for you, if the matter did come to court."

She sucked in her breath. "Run."

Emily blinked. "What?"

"Take some money and your books and run," Lady Barb repeated. She leaned forward, her blue eyes suddenly intent. "You can't best him and you don't want to wind up a slave. Go!"

"I can't," Emily said. She looked at Alassa, lying still and silent on the bed. "I can't leave them like this."

Lady Barb shook her head. "What can you do to help?"

"I don't know," Emily said. She thought hard, but no ideas came to her. What could she offer a demon that it might want? "But I can't do nothing. I can go to Mountaintop..."

"Zed might take you in," Lady Barb said. "Master Grey wouldn't be able to force him to throw you to the wolves, if he gave you his protection. But you'd still lose everything else."

"And be trapped there," Emily said. Mountaintop had been stuffy and claustrophobic even before she'd discovered the school's darkest secret. "I wouldn't want to stay there..."

"You will die," Lady Barb said. "Don't you understand me? You will die!"

She reached forward suddenly, magic crackling around her fingertips. Emily, already tired and drained, could barely resist as Lady Barb shattered her remaining wards, yanked Emily to her feet and bent her backwards over her knee, hooking her leg over Emily's legs to keep them trapped. Emily was utterly trapped, unable to move.

"I did that, easily," Lady Barb said. "I could break your neck in this position and you wouldn't be able to stop me. Do you think he'll be any slower than me? Or weaker?"

"No," Emily gasped.

Lady Barb pushed her to her feet, and sighed. "I'd beat you black and blue if I thought it would help," she said. "*He* should have sent you for a thrashing, not chosen to take it as a challenge. If I'd realized in time...he must have had this planned for months, just gauging what buttons to press to make you angry..."

She shook her head. "Go back to your room and get some rest," she ordered. "Make sure you set up a warding circle first or..."

"The demon might not be able to touch you," she added. "You are, after all, Shadye's Heir. It practically admitted as much."

"I'll set up the circle anyway," Emily said. She didn't want to take the word of a demon, not when she was too tired and depressed to think clearly. "What about Frieda?"

"I'll speak to her," Lady Barb said. "She can share a room with one of the other Fourth Years, if necessary. I can take you to Mountaintop tomorrow morning, if you wish; let me know so I can contact the MageMaster ahead of time."

Emily yawned. "Maybe in the afternoon," she said. She took one last look at Alassa, her face inhumanly still. "He did say I can visit whenever I wanted."

"Better not to presume too much on that," Lady Barb warned. "And Emily?"

"Yes?"

"Think," Lady Barb said. "Think as hard as you can. Because if you don't find a way out, you will die."

I can't beat him in a fight, Emily thought, numbly. She knew that was true. A man who'd been the undisputed champion on the dueling circle was unlikely to be beaten by a simple trick. *And if I run, I lose everything.*

Chapter Thirty-Two

IT WASN'T AN EASY NIGHT.

Emily slept poorly, despite the warding circle and the potion she had taken as a last resort to help her sleep. Nightmares of the demon, and Master Grey, haunted her dreams, blurring together into a single malevolent entity. By the time she finally gave up on sleep and forced herself to get out of bed, she felt as though she hadn't slept at all. She stumbled into the shower and washed herself in cold water, then dressed in her robes. Her body felt so tired and drained she just wanted to lie back down and sleep. But there was no time for sleep.

She picked up a handful of books from her bedside table and frowned as she saw the parchment, glowing faintly to alert her to unread messages. Jade had sent several messages, frantically asking what was going on. Where *was* everyone? Emily stared at it blearily for a long moment before recalling that everyone with a copy of the parchment, save for herself and Jade, was under the demon's thrall. She reached for a pen, but stopped herself. What could she tell Jade? How could she tell him that his fiancée was held by a demon and his former master intended to kill Emily in a duel? And yet, she knew she had to tell him *something*. He would probably have heard all sorts of rumors, if he'd checked with the other magicians in Zangaria...

And he might even be on his way here by now, Emily thought. It would have been nice to talk to him, but she knew he'd be more worried about Alassa than herself. And he should be, she was sure. They were in love. *And what will he think about the duel?*

Thinking about it made her feel sick, but she had no choice. She wrote a quick message on the parchment, outlining everything that had happened, concluding by telling him that she was going to the library. Lady Aliya had banned all chat parchments from the library, even though they would probably be helpful; she wouldn't make an exception for Emily, even though Emily knew Jade would have questions and demands as soon as he read her message and realized the true horror that had been unleashed in Whitehall. Leaving the parchment on the desk, Emily strode from the room and down the corridor. The school felt different, almost unwelcoming. Now that she knew it was there, she could practically *feel* the demon nesting within the school's wards.

They must have warned the remaining students to protect themselves. Emily thought, as she stepped through the door and out into the main corridor. There was no one in sight, not even a tutor on patrol. *They might even have started sending them home.*

She pushed the thought aside as she walked through a twisting maze of corridors and upstairs to the library. It was closed, but Lady Aliya had never bothered to remove Emily from the list of student assistants who were granted access at all times. She stepped through the door, cast a light globe into the air and walked over to the small section of books on honor and etiquette. There would be something on the *Code Duello* there, she was sure. It wasn't uncommon, she'd learned from her history books, for people in the Allied Lands to settle issues by combat, rather than a formal trial. The gods, it was believed, granted the victory to the true innocent party.

Which is fucking silly, she thought, bitterly. *The victor would be the one who was better trained and more experienced, not the one who just happened to be innocent.*

She found a couple of thin books, took them both and settled down at the nearest desk to skim-read. Unusually for books on etiquette, the first one merely concentrated on the facts; the second one discussed a series of incidents that had been recorded over the ages, ranging from deliberate challenges to ones that had been issued in response to intolerable insults or threats. It was quite possible, Emily read with growing horror, for a challenge to be issued by accident...or for someone to use a challenge as a trick to bury their guilt. An accusation of madness, or necromancy, could be forgotten if the accused killed the accuser.

And she *had* issued a challenge, if Master Grey chose to take it that way. And he had.

She swallowed, feeling a cold lump of despair in her stomach, and read through the fine print, searching for loopholes. There weren't many. A challenge could be retracted if new evidence surfaced - if the accused swore an oath, perhaps - but that hardly applied to her. A handful of case studies showed the former challenged issuing a challenge of his own, once his innocence had actually been proven. Why not? He'd just been accused of something that would overshadow the rest of his life, despite being innocent. Emily could hardly blame him for wanting a little revenge.

There didn't seem to be any other ways to escape the duel - or the stigma of having issued a challenge, then fleeing the consequences. If she fled for her life, Master Grey could claim everything she owned; Cockatrice, Markus's bank...maybe King Randor would object to him claiming the Barony, but it would no longer be *hers*. And no one would ever take her seriously again. She would be outcast, isolated from the entire world; hell, she could be killed on sight and her killer would suffer no punishment. It was brutal, it was barbaric...and it was pointed right at her. Master Grey might even be *praying* for her to flee. He would inherit everything she owned and destroy her reputation without suffering any backlash from killing a student.

But I killed two necromancers, Emily thought, sourly. *They might see him as the brave one, the one who could have evaded the challenge with ease. Not me.*

She blinked tears away, angrily. Master Grey should have ignored what she'd said, or set the terms so he could teach her a lesson, not kill her outright. But in hindsight it was clear that Lady Barb was right. He'd never liked her, he'd never *trusted* her... and he'd certainly deduced that her reputation was vastly overblown. He'd set out to create a situation where he could kill her without repercussion and he'd succeeded, magnificently. And the hell of it was that he might have a point. Emily had killed two necromancers, figured out the true nature of the Mimics, shattered Mountaintop, rebuked two powerful families and turned the Allied Lands upside down, all in less than four years. To him, she had to seem more like a child of chaos than destiny.

And she honestly didn't know what to do.

She glared down at the slim tome lying open in front of her. Fight the duel...and lose, unless she found a way to win. Or run, leaving a shattered reputation behind. Or...

There won't be much room for tricks, she thought. *He won't give me any room to play games.*

She gritted her teeth. The rules for a duel to the death were quite simple. Each of the challengers would enter the arena, carrying only a wand or a staff - she recalled from her first duel that they were allowed to wear clothes, although the book wasn't specific - and nothing else. Hell, Master Grey could set the rules to exclude both wands and staffs if he felt like it. She couldn't take a battery into the arena and, even if she did, she wasn't sure what she could do with it. It would be simple enough to repeat her trick of casting super-powered anti-magic wards, only Master Grey wouldn't be impressed. He was bigger, stronger and faster than her; she knew that all too well. He'd just march over to her and beat her to death.

And he has over two decades more experience than me, she thought, in despair. *I can't match him in tossing spells around the room...*

She looked up, sharply, as she heard someone open the door and enter the library. It didn't sound like Lady Aliya...she peered into the gloom beyond the light globe, letting out a sigh of relief as she recognized Caleb. His face was very pale, but looked relieved the moment he saw Emily. She felt oddly pleased to see him, combined with a primal urge to just duck under the table and hide. Caleb...was a reminder of better times she'd thrown away.

"Emily," Caleb said. There was a low urgency to his voice that worried her. "Is it true?"

Of course the whole school knows, Emily thought, sourly. *It was meant to be a secret, after all, so naturally everyone knows.*

"Yeah," she said, too tired to come up with any clever responses. Not that Caleb would be fooled by anything she might say, after all. The books open in front of her wouldn't be necessary for anything else. "It's probably true."

Caleb sat down facing her and reached out to take one of her hands. "Emily...he'll kill you."

"Probably," Emily said. She looked back down at the books, refusing to meet his eyes. "I suppose he told everyone?"

"The rumor went flying around the school last night," Caleb said. "I don't know how it started."

"Master Grey probably bragged about it," Emily said, sourly.

She puzzled over it for a long moment. It wouldn't make him look good, if he had, but he might well believe he wasn't going to come out looking good no matter who won. Maybe he'd had a private chat with Sergeant Miles, after making sure they could be overheard. Or maybe he hadn't meant to share the news and it had slipped out by accident. He'd need to ask *someone* to serve as his second. Sergeant Miles? She hoped he'd refused, if he'd been asked. It would have strained his relationship with Lady Barb...

Brilliant, Emily thought. She couldn't help feeling guilty. *They were happy together.*

"He'll kill you," Caleb repeated. "Unless you have a way to beat him..."

Emily shook her head slowly. Everything she had was either incredibly destructive - there was no way she could convince Master Grey to let her define the arena circle as anything large enough to contain a nuclear blast - or useless. She knew a handful of killing spells, thanks to Martial Magic, but Master Grey would not only know them too, he would have used them in combat. Unless...she thought through her list of concepts, the list she hadn't dared use in Whitehall or Mountaintop. There were some that might catch Master Grey by surprise...

Assuming I have the time to use them, she thought. She'd seen Master Grey duel, back before they'd gone to the Cairngorms. He'd beaten his opponent quickly and ruthlessly, ending the match with a kill. *He won't give me time to be clever.*

"Then run," Caleb urged. "I'll come with you."

Emily looked up at him, seeing naked horror and despair all over his face. "What will your parents think of that?"

"I don't care," Caleb said. "I just want you to live."

"You'll be disowned," Emily said. Anyone who helped an outcast became outcast themselves, she knew. It was written in the books in front of her. An outcast had no friends, no family, if only for fear it might rub off. "Your parents will say you're no longer their son."

"It isn't like I ever fit in anyway," Caleb said, softly. "Croce will take my place as the second son and he'll do my father proud, damn him."

Emily squeezed his hand, gently. "I can't let you do that," she said. "You'll be alone..."

"I'll be with you," Caleb said. He blushed, suddenly. "I..."

Emily blushed too. Did Caleb really understand what he was offering? She'd had to fend for herself from a very early age, while Caleb...had had decent parents, even if he had never quite fit in with them. Being alone, being outcast, might destroy him. But then, he *was* a skilled magician. It was possible he'd find somewhere reasonably comfortable to live even as an outcast. Emily...wouldn't have so many options.

Caleb swallowed. "I have something to confess," he said. "It's...it's important."

"Oh," Emily said, feeling her blood run cold. Had he changed his mind? Or had he kept something hidden from her? Her imagination provided too many possibilities, each worse than the last. "What?"

"Last summer, I fell in love with you," Caleb said, hesitantly. He had to be afraid she would run again. "I...I asked my parents for permission to start a Courtship."

Emily blinked in surprise. Imaiqah had made her look up the rules in Second Year, after Jade had proposed to her, and a Courtship was *serious*. Asking a girl out on a date was one thing - students at Whitehall could spend their free time together, if they wished - but a Courtship, which involved the families, was a clear statement of intent. Caleb had told his parents he wanted to *marry* Emily.

"That must have been an...an *interesting* discussion," she said.

"It was," Caleb said. His blush deepened. "They were insistent I aim for a long Courtship, if that was my choice."

Emily forced herself to think. Courtship required the happy couple to spend time together, to learn if they were compatible, but it also involved both families. At some point, she suspected, the couple would be pressured into marrying, even if they had discovered they weren't truly compatible. The families would have invested too much time and pride into the Courtship. And, in this case, Caleb's father would have faced the prospect of opening negotiations with a Lone Power. She was mildly surprised he hadn't shot the idea down, right from the start.

And then she looked up at Caleb as it hit her. "You wanted to *court* me?"

"I chickened out," Caleb confessed. "I should have written to you, formally, or approached you as soon as we were in school. Instead...I was terrified of taking that first step."

Emily found it hard to blame him. Boys were...*odd*...about approaching girls; Jade had said nothing to her until the very last day of term, even though he must have decided to propose to her months before. Imaiqah had dozens of stories; she'd even advised Emily that the simplest way to get a man was to run, but not run very fast. *Make them work to catch you*, she'd advised. Emily hadn't been too impressed at the time.

And Caleb? If he'd chickened out completely, his father would have been less than amused about the whole thing.

"You made it," she said, finally. Suddenly, the sketches she'd seen of her in his notebook made a great deal of sense. "You did manage to ask me out."

"I wanted it to be more," Caleb said, hesitatingly. "You were...*impressive*, right from the start."

And then I ran, Emily thought. Caleb must have been *very* confused. *He must have panicked.*

She pushed her embarrassment aside and tried to think. It was hard not to feel flattered and worried at the same time. A Courtship...it would have implications for her future, even if it failed. And at some point Caleb's father would have to approach Void, who would say...*what?* Emily had asked him to ignore all the letters he'd received asking for her hand in marriage. What would he say if Emily asked him to open negotiations instead?

He may not be my father, she thought, *but he is my Guardian of record...*

It was an odd thought. She'd never had a father looking out for her interests...and, indeed, she found it somewhat insulting. She was *nineteen*! It wasn't as if she'd grown up in a world where she required her father's permission to marry, or knew her parents would arrange her marriage for her and push her into it, even if she objected. God knew she wasn't a child of the Nameless World...

...But, at the same time, the thought of someone looking out for her was welcome.

She cleared her throat. "I am not wholly familiar with the rules of Courtship," she said, truthfully. "How long do we have before our...before our fathers have to talk?"

Caleb looked relieved. "Normally, two years after...after we start talking," he said. "I think it would be starting from today, when I told you I was courting you."

After you checked your parents weren't adamantly opposed to the match, Emily thought, ruefully. Given her reputation, she couldn't help wondering how tempted his parents had been to forbid him to even *think* about courting her. *What would you have done if they'd said no?*

"I don't know what will happen," she admitted. "My life might be about to come to an end."

"Kill him now," Caleb urged. "Poison the bastard."

Emily stared at him - she had forgotten that Caleb had spent two years at Stronghold, where he'd been taught there was nothing more important than winning - then shook her head.

"He'll be watching for tricks," she said. Master Grey had reminded her, several times, to always check her food and drink before taking even the tiniest bite. He'd even sprinkled a handful of potions on her food to make sure she kept it in mind. "And if he did die ahead of time, everyone would point the finger at me anyway."

"Come with me, then," Caleb said. "Emily..."

"Not yet," Emily said. "I have until the end of the school year, after all. *Something* may happen. The horse may learn to sing."

Caleb blinked. "Pardon?"

"Old story," Emily said. She recited as much of it as she could from memory, and smiled tiredly. "Something might happen."

"I see," Caleb said. He hesitated, before he leaned across the table to kiss her. "Emily..."

Emily kissed him back, feeling conflicted. She liked Caleb, but a Courtship? It could trap her as easily as it could trap him. And...

She jumped and spun around as someone cleared their throat, loudly. Lady Barb was standing behind her.

"I need to talk to you," Lady Barb said, curtly. She glanced at Caleb. "You; out."

"I'll see you later," Caleb said. "Be safe."

"Out," Lady Barb ordered. "Now."

Chapter Thirty-Three

H E'S TRYING TO COURT ME," EMILY SAID, AS SOON AS CALEB LEFT THE LIBRARY. "HE EVEN asked his parents."

"And that might have come to a crashing halt," Lady Barb said, sharply. She glanced past Emily and looked at the books on the table. "Have you found any loopholes?"

"None," Emily admitted. If Lady Barb hadn't been able to suggest any, she knew it was unlikely she'd be able to find a loophole for herself. "He seems to have me in check."

"He does," Lady Barb confirmed. "The Grandmaster may find something, but I'm not hopeful."

She scowled at Emily, then shrugged. "Be that as it may, I have spoken to Mountaintop's authorities," she added. "They have agreed to allow you to visit to check their books."

Emily rose, smoothing down her robes. "Thank you," she said. Maybe she'd find something useful in the ancient tomes. "When do we leave?"

"Now," Lady Barb said. "Get changed into something that doesn't remind everyone of Whitehall, then meet me in the Entrance Hall in thirty minutes. And don't tell anyone where you're going, if anyone asks."

Emily nodded, hurried back to her room and changed rapidly into her walking trousers and shirt, throwing a cloak over her shoulders. Mountaintop could be bitterly cold and it was better to wear something warm, rather than waste magic warming herself. She picked up a notebook, checked the chat parchment - Jade had apparently decided to head directly to Whitehall, rather than stay away - and walked back down to the Entrance Hall. Lady Barb was already there, wearing a long fur coat over her shirt and trousers. She didn't look pleased when Emily arrived, even though she was sure she hadn't taken more than twenty minutes to change her clothes.

"Come," she ordered.

Emily followed her, feeling the wards slowly fading away as they walked over the grass, away from the school. There was no portal linking Whitehall and Mountaintop together; they'd have to teleport, once they were safely away from the wards. Lady Barb kept walking until they were well clear of the wards, then grabbed Emily's arm. Emily winced, but hastily prepared herself for the jump. Teleporting wasn't *quite* as bad as stepping through a portal, not for her, but it was quite bad enough.

"Master Grey has offered to continue your training sessions," she said, glowering down at Emily. "The Grandmaster told him to shut up. Your remaining sessions will be spent with me, preparing for a fight you cannot win. You would be well advised to run before completing your final exam."

"I understand," Emily said.

"Good," Lady Barb said, tartly. "Emily..."

She shook her head, unable to finish the sentence, and triggered the spell. The world flared white for a long moment, then faded, revealing the barren grounds over Mountaintop. It didn't look to have changed much, Emily noted, as she staggered slightly against Lady Barb, but she could *feel* the presence of hidden wards pulsing below the earth. Maybe Zed *had* managed to find another way to power the school, she told herself. She had no idea how the negotiations for Red Rose or another nexus point were going.

"Lady Emily," a voice said. It was cool and dispassionate. "Welcome back."

Emily let go of Lady Barb and turned to see Mistress Mauve, standing in front of an entrance that hadn't been there a moment ago. She was tall, with cold grey eyes and an utterly merciless demeanor, a harder version of Professor Lombardi. But then, they'd both seen hundreds of students making mistakes through carelessness that could have easily killed someone. Charms tutors were *always* strict. They couldn't afford to be anything else.

"Lady Barb waits here," Mistress Mauve added, firmly. "Lady Emily comes with me."

Lady Barb looked at Emily, and shrugged. "I'll be here," she said, sitting down on a flat rock and producing a book from her bag. "Good luck."

Emily swallowed, cast a night vision spell - unlike her previous visit, the spell worked perfectly - and followed Mistress Mauve down the long dark tunnel into Mountaintop. The wards scrutinized her as she passed through, both more complex and less powerful than she recalled; they didn't seem very welcoming, but Zed must have keyed her into the wards when he'd become MageMaster. Or, perhaps, she'd held the Key long enough to earn an honorary position within the school. The tunnel broadened as she reached the end, revealing a handful of glowing crystals casting an eerie light from high overhead. Zed, it seemed, had decided that keeping the school shrouded in darkness was silly.

"Do not speak to anyone you encounter in the corridors," Mistress Mauve ordered, as they made their way through the underground labyrinth. "The MageMaster does not wish your presence known to anyone."

"Of course," Emily agreed. Zed had to be in two minds about allowing her anywhere near Mountaintop. The last time she'd visited, abducted by his predecessor, she'd discovered the dread secret of Mountaintop and shattered the wards. "I won't speak to anyone, save you."

Mistress Mauve gave her a sharp look and kept walking. A handful of students ran past, heading in the other direction, but none of them seemed to notice Emily. She smiled at them anyway, but frowned as Mistress Mauve stopped outside Aurelius's office. It looked to have been sealed, rather than passed to his successor. Emily wondered briefly why they hadn't cleared the rooms, then dismissed the thought. Zed would probably have wanted to seal them rather than move someone else into the rooms at some point, someone who might have ideas of his or her own. Mistress Mauve opened the door and beckoned Emily to follow her inside. It felt as if nothing had changed, as if all she had to do was look up to see Aurelius sitting behind his desk. A shiver ran down her spine as Mistress Mauve pointed at the door to Aurelius's private library. Could Aurelius still be alive?

Probably not, she thought. *But how do I really know that?*

"You will be locked into this section," Mistress Mauve said, curtly. "You can find Kava in the pot, if you wish; milk is stored in the jug beside it. Ring the bell--" she pointed to a silver bell, placed on the desk "--when you are ready to leave."

She nodded once, turned, and left the room.

Emily shook her head as she felt the wards shift, locking her into the compartment, then turned and walked through the door into the private library. It looked just like she remembered, a collection of ancient books - some so rare there were only one or two copies outside Mountaintop - and the notebooks of countless magicians, including the former MageMaster himself. She sucked in her breath, fighting down the temptation to just pick a book at random, and reached for the first book on demonology. There had to be something she could use.

The books, even the ones she hadn't glanced at before, weren't as useful as she'd hoped. Aurelius had told her that most of the DemonMasters had been careful to hide their secrets, burying nuggets of useful information in mountains of maniacal ravings, yet there were kernels of truth in everything they wrote. Demons could be summoned, if someone was prepared to pay the price; demons could be used as guard dogs, if the proper rites and rituals were performed. And yet, there were odd limits. A bound demon could affect everyone who stumbled into its area of influence - Shadye's demon had posed as a Nightmare Hex - but it couldn't chase them outside its territory. Only a complete idiot, the books agreed, would risk summoning a demon without some form of binding.

I may not have any influence over the demon at all, Emily thought, sourly. The chains binding the demon in place should have broken after Shadye's death, dislodging the creature from the human realm. That it had stayed where it had been bound was odd, to say the least; it should have been freed. Unless Shadye had done something to keep it in place...it made no sense to her. *And that means we might not be able to get rid of it at all.*

Four books later, she thought she had the answer. Shadye had granted the demon power over everyone who entered his territory without invitation; later, the Grandmaster and Emily had inadvertently allowed it access to Whitehall. It hadn't been compelled to give everyone in Whitehall the treatment it had handed out to trespassers...no, in a sense, it hadn't been *able* to give them that treatment. Instead, it had needed to slowly dig its way into the minds of its victims and eventually send them into comas. She recalled Imaiqah chewing her fingernails and shuddered. It had been the first sign of demonic possession. And yet...

We need to find a way to trade, she thought. *But what can we offer the demon in exchange for letting go and leaving the wards?*

She skimmed through the next couple of books, thinking hard. Demons didn't need wealth or power, magical or mundane. They hated humans, hated everyone who summoned them into the human realm; they wanted nothing more than revenge, to cruelly torment the humans who had summoned them. And Shadye was dead. There was no way she could throw the necromancer into the demon's arms...

A thought crossed her mind. Perhaps there *was* something she could offer, after all.

Or I could try to throw Master Grey at the demon, she thought, feeling an odd flicker of amusement. *Solve two problems with one stone.*

She shook her head. It wouldn't be enough.

The last two books only confirmed her earlier readings. Even the most powerful DemonMasters had hesitated to bind a demon permanently, knowing that they or their families would be the first to die if the demon broke free. They always ensured that the demon would be banished when they died, despite the risks. Shadye... seemed to have skipped a few lessons while preparing his defenses. Or maybe he'd been mad enough not to care. If it had broken free earlier, Shadye would have been the first to die.

Pity, she thought, morbidly. *It would have solved a great many problems.*

The earlier thought returned to her head. This time, it refused to leave.

There's no choice, she thought. She shuddered as she remembered the demon's cruel, sadistic eyes. In the mindscape, it had presented itself as it was. *We don't have anything else to offer the creature.*

She looked up as she felt the wards shift, already knowing who was entering the compartment. Moments later, the door to the library opened, revealing Zed. The Alchemist wore the long white robes of the MageMaster, walking slowly as if he were burdened under some great weight. Emily felt a stab of sympathy, mixed with a strange combination of fear, respect and even liking. Zed had far better reasons than Master Grey to dislike her, but he hadn't taken it out on her.

But if he had, Aurelius would have killed him, she thought. The former Administrator had gone to great lengths to seduce her to his side. *Zed chose to play mind games instead.*

"Emily," Zed said. He closed the door behind him, and sat in one of the comfortable armchairs on the other side of the library. "Have you found anything useful?"

"I may have," Emily said, slowly. She didn't want to talk about it, not even to Lady Barb. Zed was definitely not her first choice of confidante. "It will have to be tried before I know if I have something workable."

"Good, good," Zed said. He looked up at the books. "Quite an interesting collection here, I must say. Aurelius must have spent a large fortune on collecting them."

Emily nodded, fingering the bracelet at her wrist. "Some of these tomes are literally priceless," she agreed. One of the older books was worth more than the entire Barony of Cockatrice. "And others should be destroyed, on general principles."

"There would be a riot if the last copies were to be burned," Zed pointed out. He looked back at her, sharply. "I understand you have challenged a tutor to a duel."

"Something like that," Emily said. She wasn't in the mood for semantics. "Does that matter, at the moment?"

Zed met her eyes. "You would be welcome to come here, if you wished," he said. "There will always be a place for you here."

Emily blinked in surprise, feeling an odd surge of warmth. "And what would happen to you if you were hosting an outcast?"

"I wouldn't tell anyone," Zed said. "It isn't as if there aren't plenty of tunnels here we could use to hide you."

Emily nodded slowly. Mountaintop was huge, yet it covered only a tiny percentage of the tunnels and catacombs below the earth. She'd gone exploring with Frieda, back when she'd been an unwilling student; there had been chambers filled with sleeping monsters, chambers where underground rivers ran through the earth and even a handful of chambers where Mountaintop's staff had carried out their secretive experiments. Zed was right. There was no shortage of space for her, if she chose to hide at Mountaintop. And it was the last place anyone would expect her to go.

But he'd want me to work for him, she thought, numbly. It wasn't something that had occurred to her earlier, but it should have done. Caleb wasn't the only person who had something to trade. *Share my ideas with him in exchange for sanctuary.*

"I'll think about it," she promised, instead. Maybe it would serve as a last resort. "Did you manage to come to an agreement with Red Rose?"

Zed showed no surprise at the change in subject. "King Rupert was reluctant, but finally agreed we could gain the nexus point in exchange for a few major concessions," he said. "Princess Mariah shows traces of magic, even though it hasn't blossomed yet; her father wishes us to train her, without allowing her to enter the general curriculum. It will not be difficult for us to find her a private tutor."

Emily nodded. Princess Mariah had been somewhere around twelve when Emily had met the younger girl; she'd be thirteen or fourteen now and would probably come into her magic within a year or two. It was a shame she'd miss out on studying with other students, but she could see certain advantages to the plan. The Princess's true powers would never be public knowledge, without any need to contrive an excuse to expel her. King Randor might have preferred Alassa to receive private tutoring, but she'd needed the chance to meet other students as equals.

"I'm sure she would be happy," Emily said. She'd barely met Princess Mariah. All she could remember was that the younger girl hadn't found her father very amusing, back when he'd been cracking absurd jokes. *Emily* hadn't found him very funny either. "And with a nexus point, Mountaintop can bloom."

"Yes, it can," Zed said. He looked down at the table, then picked up one of the books. "I have not dared to read some of these tomes."

Emily blinked in surprise. "You haven't?"

"They are a temptation on the mind," Zed said. "Once someone gains a piece of forbidden knowledge, there is always the impulse to try it. And, sometimes, that ends in disaster - or it ends in a quest to gain *more* forbidden knowledge, to push the limits until they finally break and someone dies. Demons are *never* safe to mess with, Emily. Did *he* teach you nothing?"

"You're an Alchemist," Emily said. Professor Thande had told her, right at the start, that some alchemists were encouraged to live somewhere well away from the rest of the world, just so they could carry out their experiments with no one else at risk. "Don't you always push the limits?"

"That's *Alchemy*," Zed said. He held the book out in front of her so she could see the cover, the sketch of a demonic face. It would have been almost angelic if it hadn't been baring its teeth at the viewer. "*This* is Demonology. It is not *safe*. The forces the DemonMasters played with are living entities with wills of their own and boundless malevolence. You can do everything right and *still* wind up dead. Or worse."

"I know," Emily said, quietly.

"I hope so," Zed said. He rose to his feet. "The offer was sincere, Lady Emily. You would be welcome to come here, if you need a place to hide."

"I'll think about it," Emily promised. She glanced at some of the books again before she started to return them to the shelves. "But right now I have to return to Whitehall."

"I will speak to Master Grey," Zed said. "But I doubt I have much influence over him. I wasn't a tutor here while he was a lad."

He sighed. "I'll have you escorted back to the surface," he added. He started to turn, but stopped himself. "Unless...unless you want to meet anyone here?"

Emily shook her head. The only person at Mountaintop she'd been close to had been Frieda, who'd come with her when she'd left the underground school. None of the others had been more than acquaintances, not when she had never dared let down her guard. And Nanette...

She looked up as a thought struck her. "What happened to Nanette?"

"She vanished," Zed said. "I believe she fled the school shortly after the wards failed. I assume she must have sought medical treatment for her hand, perhaps paid to have a Healer regrow the lost limb. After that...I don't know where she went, or even if she's still alive."

"It doesn't matter," Emily said. She finished shelving the books, then took one final look around the library. Zed was right; it *was* an interesting collection. She could have happily spent several months reading and rereading the books, if she'd had the time. "And thank you."

Zed eyed her bleakly. "For what?"

Chapter Thirty-Four

Y OU WEREN'T AS LONG AS I HAD FEARED," LADY BARB SAID, AS EMILY EMERGED FROM THE tunnels into a different sort of darkness. Night was already beginning to fall over the land. "Did you find anything?"

"I may have," Emily said. "But I need to talk to the Grandmaster."

Lady Barb gave her a sharp look. "What are you thinking?"

"Pablo doesn't have to be confined to the Halfway House," Emily said. It was something she'd considered earlier, something that might distract the older woman. "Give him a secretary and a chat parchment, perhaps more than one. He could serve as an adviser even if he can't actually serve as a Mediator."

She had to force herself not to flinch back from Lady Barb's glare. "Emily, your friends are likely to be killed by a demon and you yourself will be killed by a far stronger magician, if you don't find a way out of the trap," Lady Barb snapped. "This isn't the time to talk about anything else!"

Emily met the older woman's eyes...and saw fear and grief hidden behind the anger. It struck her like a knife in the gut. Lady Barb *cared* for her, maybe even considered her a daughter of sorts...and now Lady Barb had to watch her die. She'd wracked her brains searching for a loophole and found nothing. Master Grey would kill Emily and there was nothing Lady Barb could do to prevent it, not even by challenging Master Grey first. *He* could refuse a challenge, if one were offered. And sticking a knife in his back would destroy the older woman's reputation as surely as running from a duel would shatter Emily's.

"I'm sorry," Emily said, tiredly. "But the Grandmaster is the only one I can speak to."

"Very well," Lady Barb said. She took Emily's arm. "Brace yourself."

Emily closed her eyes as the spell built up around them. When she opened them, they were standing just outside Whitehall's wards. The school no longer felt welcoming; she could have sworn, as she stepped through the first set of defenses, that she heard a faint titter in her mind from the demon. No doubt it was reaching out for new victims, now that it held over a hundred students in its thrall. It would whisper doubts and fears into unprotected minds until they surrendered and bared themselves for the slaughter. And even if the other students were protected now, it could still taunt them from afar, enjoying their helpless rage and fear.

"It's still here," she muttered, quietly.

"Yes, it is," Lady Barb answered. "And it won't let go of anyone. Why should it?"

Emily said nothing as they walked through empty corridors and up to the Grandmaster's office. A handful of students walked past them, escorted by Master Grey and Professor Lombardi; Emily forced herself to meet Master Grey's eyes as they passed over her, then walked onwards. The students stared, clearly unsure of what would happen if - when - the duel actually took place. Master Grey was an experienced sorcerer, but Emily had cowed *dozens* of experienced sorcerers at Cockatrice.

And would that have worked, she asked herself, *if so many of them hadn't wanted to fight?*

"By tradition, you're not supposed to speak with him, except through seconds," Lady Barb said, tartly. "I don't know *what* he was thinking, offering to continue to teach you."

"Maybe he was trying to make a point," Emily said. It was a mystery to her too. "Perhaps he thought people would believe that he was preparing me for the duel."

Lady Barb snorted. "If he offers you any special training, you would be well advised to refuse," she warned. "I wouldn't trust him not to cripple you in some way."

"I don't think he would need to bother," Emily said. Two decades of experience would be hard to beat. "Old age and treachery beats youth and enthusiasm any time."

"Don't underestimate him," Lady Barb said. "Rigging the arena may be impossible, but finding ways to hamper your opponent is an old and dishonorable tradition."

She sighed as they stopped outside the Grandmaster's office. "I'll speak to you about training later," she said. "Until this state of emergency ends, we may as well make good use of the time."

"Yes," Emily said. She surprised herself by giving the older woman a hug. "And thank you."

Lady Barb hugged her briefly, and headed off down the corridor. Emily sighed, turned to the door and knocked once. It clicked open, allowing her to step inside. The Grandmaster was seated in front of his desk, poring over a book. His blindfold was lying on the table, exposing his eyes. Emily recoiled in shock as he looked up at her, revealing that both of his eyeballs were missing. Two empty sockets looked back at her.

"Not many people have seen that," the Grandmaster observed. He reached for his blindfold and pulled it back over his eyes. "I suggest you keep it to yourself, please."

"I will," Emily promised. It was an order, however phrased, and she'd be wise to treat it as such. "How do you read books?"

"Magic," the Grandmaster said, dryly. "There is no shortage of spells for overcoming physical disabilities, if you have enough magic."

He cleared his throat and pointed at the chair on the other side of his desk. "Sit," he ordered. "Did you find anything?"

"I may have," Emily said. She glanced at the book he'd been reading, but it was upside down and she couldn't make out the title. "Did you?"

"Not much," the Grandmaster said. "I spent several hours divining the nature of the demon and the spells binding it in place. Shadye was really quite lucky the demon didn't break free and devour him years ago."

Emily nodded impatiently. She'd already figured that out.

"Shadye could probably tell the demon to leave and it would have to go," he added, after a moment. "But *we* couldn't banish it ourselves."

"Maybe we can," Emily said. "It called me Shadye's Heir."

The Grandmaster frowned. "You *might* be able to tell it to leave," he said. "But it may choose to refuse to accept you as holding any authority. Demons can always be relied upon to interpret the rules in their favor and...well, you're *not* Shadye's blood relative. It could assert that it was I, not you, who brought it into Whitehall. Or it could simply claim that the normal rules of inheritance don't apply to bound demons."

He looked up. "Do you want to try?"

"We don't have a choice," Emily said. And if it didn't work, there was always her other idea. "I can go back into Alassa and..."

The Grandmaster seemed to peer at her. "And what?"

"Tell it to leave," Emily said. "It *might* work."

"And what else?" The Grandmaster asked. His voice was deceptively mild. "I can tell when someone is holding back the truth."

Emily swallowed. The Grandmaster had looked into her mind once, when Shadye had used her as his puppet to break through the defenses. It had left her feeling naked and vulnerable...she thought, now, she was protected, that Void's spell could keep her mind inviolate. But she didn't want to find out if she was wrong.

"There's another option," she said. "I can offer *myself* to the demon."

"Yourself," the Grandmaster said. His voice went flat. "And what makes you think the demon will *want* you?"

"I'm Shadye's Heir," Emily said. "I also *killed* Shadye, depriving the demon of its chance to exact revenge. And I'd be offering myself freely, in exchange for the release of its victims and the demon returning home."

"Taking you with it," the Grandmaster said, flatly. "Emily, you'd spend the rest of eternity in its clutches."

"There are too many students caught in its clutches," Emily pointed out. "If it will take me in exchange for them..."

"It should, according to the laws," the Grandmaster said. "And yes, it could accept you as Shadye's Heir..."

His face twisted into a grimace. "But you would, at the very least, wind up dead."

"I know," Emily said. "But Master Grey is going to kill me anyway, isn't he? If the demon kills me instead, my property will be distributed in line with my will, not transferred to him."

"That's arguable," the Grandmaster said. "But it would probably stand up in court, if Master Grey felt inclined to challenge it. I don't think he will."

Emily nodded slowly. Alassa and Imaiqah would receive money; Frieda would receive the Barony, if King Randor saw fit to accept her as Emily's heir. Lady Barb would inherit the notebooks Emily had stored in her trunk, along with the books and the snake-bracelet. She would have to see if Frieda could take Aurelius as a familiar, or destroy the snake if the younger girl couldn't bond with him. The Death Viper was just too dangerous to be left alone if he couldn't find another partner. She smirked at the thought of Master Grey picking up the bracelet from her dead body, then getting a horrific surprise as Aurelius reverted back to his natural form. It might well prove fatal.

"I can do something to make sure of it," the Grandmaster added. "Under the circumstances, it would be the least I could do."

Maybe I should leave the bracelet to Master Grey, Emily thought. *Alter the spells, keeping the snake in that form for several hours without me...*

She pushed the thought aside and looked at the Grandmaster. "I am willing," she said, feeling oddly free. If she couldn't win, and it seemed to be a choice between Master Grey and the demon, she could at least pick the time and place of her death. "Can we start now?"

"Soon," the Grandmaster said. "Do you not wish to speak to anyone...?"

"No," Emily said. She didn't want to speak to anyone, not with the knowledge of her impending death hanging over her like a shroud. Lady Barb and Frieda - and Caleb - would be horrified, while her other friends were in comas. "I'll write letters for them, if you don't mind."

"I will see they are delivered," the Grandmaster said. He tilted his head to one side, almost like an owl. "You do realize that you will be leaving many people who love you behind?"

"I know," Emily said. "But I will be leaving them now or leaving them when Master Grey kills me."

Or when I go on the run, she added, silently. She couldn't accept Caleb's offer, not when it meant separating him from his family permanently. *I couldn't take anyone with me either.*

"Welcome to power," the Grandmaster said.

Emily frowned. "What do you mean?"

"Making the choice about who lives and who dies," the Grandmaster said. "*That* is true power. Everything else is just window-dressing."

"I see," Emily said. She took her courage in both hands and asked the question that had been nagging at her, ever since the first meeting with the demon. "What happened to make you blind?"

The Grandmaster looked at her. "And if I told you that merely *asking* that question would get you in a great deal of trouble, young lady, would you still ask it?"

Emily had to smile. "Can I get in worse trouble?"

He smiled back. "My father was an odd man," he said, softly. "He believed there were ways to gain power through twins, even though magical twins simply don't exist. His solution to this problem was to marry four wives and impregnate them all at the same time. He calculated that the babies - all sons - would be born within days of each other, all half-brothers."

He paused. "It worked better than he had hoped," he said. "We were all born on the same *day.*"

Emily blinked. "Did he plan it that way?"

"Maybe," the Grandmaster said. He shrugged. "Our father always kept pushing the limits, Emily. He managed to kill himself when we were nine years old, after yet another demented experiment went badly wrong. None of us really missed him. He wasn't abusive, but he kept forcing us to try different spells in the hopes of bringing out our magic early. He had this theory that the four of us would balance each other, making it easier for us to handle magic as children. Nothing worked, thankfully. We wouldn't have survived puberty."

"I'm sorry," Emily said.

"It wasn't your fault," the Grandmaster said. "Our mothers weren't regarded as welcome by the rest of our father's family. His family took most of what our father had left behind, leaving us with a pittance. You won't believe just how resentful we were at how we were treated, at how easy it had been for our uncles to take everything. If our father hadn't paid the fees for Whitehall in advance, we would have been left without any hope of training.

"It left us with a hunger for power. By the time we were in Sixth Year, as the oddest family in Whitehall, we wanted more. Brilliant careers, brilliant apprenticeships, loomed. But it wasn't enough for us. We'd explored the forbidden sections of the library and...*recovered*...our father's old books. One of them told us how to summon a demon. It promised great power to anyone who raised a demon with the proper ceremonies. We wouldn't need to spend years developing our powers, we thought. All we needed to do was raise a demon and make a deal."

"But if it was so easy," Emily said, "why doesn't everyone do it?"

"A question we would have been wise to ask," the Grandmaster said. "I - we - spent the last few months at Whitehall looking for problems, but we found nothing. It seemed safe, so after we graduated we found a secluded place up in the mountains and performed the ritual. It went badly wrong. Two of my brothers died; I was blinded. The fourth was left with scars on his soul. No one ever knew what we'd done. When I was asked, later, why I was blind, I told them I'd traded my sight for knowledge. Everyone assumed I'd performed a Know Thyself ritual and accepted it without question. I studied under a master, completed an apprenticeship and went into teaching. Eventually, I became Grandmaster."

"The demon said you were blind to demons," Emily recalled.

"It never occurred to me that Shadye would have successfully raised and bound a demon," the Grandmaster said. His voice darkened for a long moment. "If it had, I would have brought someone else along, someone who might have sensed the demon's presence before I took it back to Whitehall."

Emily frowned. "That doesn't answer the question."

The Grandmaster sighed, heavily. "Everything comes with a price, Emily," he said. "I can see magic, still, but not demonic energy. It nearly killed me twice before I realized what I'd lost, when my eyeballs burst in my head. To a demon, destroying my eyes would have been more than a mere sadistic joke. Symbolically, it removed my ability to see or sense demonic presences."

"A loophole," Emily said, slowly. Her blood ran cold as something fell into place. "Demons see the future, or glimpses of it. Could Shadye have summoned the same demon as you and your brothers? Could it have blinded you then to allow itself access to Whitehall *now?*"

"It's a possibility," the Grandmaster said. He looked down at the table. "Emily, my brothers and I held the top spots at Whitehall. The only student currently at school who may match us, one day, is Aloha. Even *you* don't have the same level of genius."

"Thank you," Emily said, sourly.

"Shadye was a lukewarm student at best," the Grandmaster added, ignoring her remark. "The thought of him not only being able to summon the demon, but bind it successfully where we failed, is galling. He had raw power and nothing else. On the other hand, the demon might have played along. It was certainly willing to torment me while it had me in its grasp."

Emily shook her head. "We may never know," she said. She cleared her throat. "What happened to your other brother?"

"We rarely talk," the Grandmaster said. He rose and started to pace the room. "Our uncles died shortly afterwards. I always assumed it was his work, but I never asked. It wasn't something I wanted to know for sure, not really. After our mothers died...I cut my remaining ties with the family for good and shed my name. I don't even know if they know I was promoted to Grandmaster."

He sighed. "That isn't something I ever told anyone else," he added. "Emily..."

"I won't tell anyone," Emily promised. "There won't be time, will there?"

"It probably doesn't matter," the Grandmaster said. He sat down, resting his hands on the table. "My family probably prefers to forget that the four of us ever existed. We were just another crazy experiment that went wrong."

Emily nodded. She had a feeling her mother - and her stepfather - felt the same way. If her mother could forget having a daughter when they were sharing a home, she'd probably not even noticed when Emily had vanished one day. Maybe someone at school had noticed she was missing and called the police. It was even possible her stepfather had been arrested for murder...

Or that they think I just ran away, she thought. She understood, all too well, why the Grandmaster and his brothers would want a little revenge. Whatever their father had been, treating his children as pariahs because of it was unforgivable. *If I could go back, with magic, I'd want revenge too.*

"Go write your letters," the Grandmaster ordered. "And update your will, if you wish. I'll meet you in the infirmary in a couple of hours. I have some preparations to make."

"Yes, sir," Emily said.

Chapter Thirty-Five

A LASSA HADN'T MOVED.

Emily felt another chill run down her spine as she entered the private room and sat down facing her friend. Alassa's body looked completely still, as if she were a waxwork rather than a living human; Emily honestly wasn't sure if she was breathing. She touched her friend's hand lightly and recoiled at the clammy feel of it, as if Alassa was no longer human. The demon was slowly laying claim to her body as well as her soul.

"I'm sorry," she said, very quietly. "I wish I had the chance to talk to you one last time, but I don't and I won't. I'm sorry."

Alassa showed no reaction.

Emily shook her head, bitterly. Friend or foe, Alassa had always been *alive*; now, she might as well be dead. She had no idea what weaknesses and insecurities the demon had used to worm its way into her mind, but it had succeeded magnificently. Alassa couldn't hope to free herself, not now. All she could do, if she was aware at all, was pray that someone else managed to free her.

Of course she will be aware, Emily thought. *The demon will want her to understand just how badly she's screwed.*

She closed her eyes for a long moment, opening them and looking up as the door opened and the Grandmaster stepped into the room. He had discarded his normal robes; instead, he wore a long dark cloak that wrapped around his body, concealing everything. Emily raised an eyebrow, but he merely shrugged and sat down on the other side of the bed. It looked as though he'd pulled his blindfold so tight that it was clear he no longer possessed eyeballs, although that could merely be her imagination filling in the blanks. She *knew* his eyeballs had been taken long ago.

Everyone makes mistakes, she thought.

She sighed, bitterly. It seemed to be true of all magicians, herself included. If the young Grandmaster could summon a demon and pay for it, her own mistakes seemed small and tragic in comparison. But she'd meant well...*of course she had*, she told herself, and so had the Grandmaster. Demons might have little real power in the human realm, at least without being summoned by humans, but they were skilled at luring people into temptation and using that temptation to overcome their reservations. Someone could be tricked into surrender long before they realized they'd gone too far down the slippery slope. Who knew *what* had happened to the Grandmaster's surviving brother?

"Emily," the Grandmaster said. "Are you sure you wish to proceed?"

"Yes," Emily said, flatly. There was no choice. She surrendered to the demon, freeing her friends in the process, or she waited for Master Grey to kill her. Or she could run, knowing she was abandoning everything she cared about. "I am ready."

The Grandmaster passed her a small knife. "I believe you know the procedure," he said, calmly. His voice was very flat. "Unless you wish to say goodbye to anyone else...?"

"I wrote letters," Emily said. She'd written to everyone: Frieda, Jade, Lady Barb, Caleb, and everyone trapped within the demon's grasp. "I don't really want to face anyone right now."

"I understand," the Grandmaster said. "But you do have friends, Emily. More, I think, than you realize."

Emily shrugged. It had been hard for her to get used to the idea of having friends; harder still, perhaps, to understand what friendship *meant*. Part of her had always envied the people who'd made friends easily, who could walk into a gathering and make themselves heard; part of her had always known it came with a price. And Caleb? It struck her, suddenly, that she might have been granted an unexpected advantage. The books seemed to agree that demons prized the souls of virgin girls and she *was* virgin. But then, Imaiqah was *not* and the demon had swallowed her too.

"They'll understand," she said, finally. "Can we get on with it?"

The Grandmaster gave her a long look, then nodded. "If we must," he said, "we must."

Emily took the knife and cut into her skin before taking Alassa's palm and pressing her bloodstained hand against the scar she'd made earlier. Nothing happened; grimly, she pressed the knife against Alassa's flesh and cut her gently, allowing their blood to mingle. There were places, her mind noted, where sharing blood was considered a marriage rite...the thought made her smile, just before she felt her mind being tugged forward into the demon's spell. She didn't try to resist as she plummeted through the mists to where the demon waited, lounging on a stone throne.

"I thought I'd redecorate," the demon said, in a breathy voice. The throne looked far too large for its body, but its malevolent presence more than made up for it. "Do you not recognize the throne?"

"King Randor's," Emily said, flatly. The mists were pressing in around her, strange voices echoing through her mind. "You took that image from her mind."

"Among other things," the demon said. "Would you like to know her most private secrets? I could tell you."

"No," Emily said.

"But you're tempted," the demon said. It wasn't a question. "You would *like* to know everything."

"Everyone has secrets and little shames," Emily said, thinking of the Grandmaster. She hadn't known he had brothers, let alone that two of them were dead, until he'd told her, even though she'd looked him up in the scrolls. He'd buried his past very well. "I don't want to know hers."

"I could tell you that she used to be in love with you," the demon said. "I could tell you that there was a time when she seriously considered marrying you."

Emily felt her mouth drop open. Alassa had said, more than once, that if Emily had been born a man King Randor would have insisted that she - he - marry Alassa. It had never occurred to her that Alassa might be interested in her personally, no matter how close they'd become since they'd been forced to work together. *No one* had questioned Alassa's duty to marry a man and bear children to succeed the throne. They'd never wondered if Alassa was interested in women, rather than men.

Because if she had been, it wouldn't have mattered, Emily thought. *She would still have had to bear children, even if she'd had to do it with a stranger...*

She scowled as the penny dropped. "You *could* tell me?"

The demon bared its bloodstained teeth. "You are wise in the ways of demons."

No, I'm not, Emily thought. The demon couldn't lie, but it had never actually *lied.* It had merely tried to mislead her and it had almost succeeded. *And if I start believing I can't be outsmarted, I will be outsmarted.*

She drew herself up to her full height and looked the demon in the eyes. It wasn't easy.

"You know why I'm here," she said.

The demon giggled. "Nothing may be known until it is spoken."

"I'm Shadye's Heir," Emily said. "I command you to leave."

The demon snickered. "Not *that* sort of heir, I'm afraid," it said. "Do you have something else you wish to say?"

Emily clenched her fists. It could read her thoughts, she was sure; she'd willingly plunged herself into its mind. But it was going to force her to spell everything out, just to humiliate her one step further...

"I offer you my life and soul, in exchange for the release of my...of everyone you hold in your thrall, including the school," she said. Her heartbeat raced as she realized how close she'd come to screwing up. She didn't count everyone trapped in the demon's clutches as a friend and it knew it as well as she did. "Take me, free them, and leave us for good."

The demon stroked its pointed goatee. "And why should I accept you when I already have so many?"

"Because I am offering myself willingly," Emily said, simply. "None of the others gave themselves to you of their own free will."

"Are you sure?" The demon asked. "I worked my way into their minds..."

"They were in no state to make a decision," Emily countered. "You twisted their thoughts to the point where they couldn't tell right from wrong, life from death, freedom from submission. You won their souls through trickery."

The demon giggled, again. This time, the sound cut right into her soul.

"There's always a trick," it said. "So *few* humans choose to come to us willingly."

It stood up, the throne vanishing in the mists, and walked towards her. Emily forced herself to stand her ground as it stopped in front of her, then reached forward and stroked her chin in a mocking parody of intimacy. Caleb had stroked her too, she recalled; the demon had seen it in her mind and turned it into a weapon. It was all she could do to ignore its touch and keep her mind focused. There was no way to avoid it using her own weaknesses against her. All she could do was remind herself that her friends - and countless others - depended on her keeping her cool.

"But I could offer you so much more," it added, darkly. "Would you like to wake up in a hospital bed, on Earth? Leave this world for good?"

It leaned forward until it was whispering into her ear. "And then she woke up and it was all a dream?"

Emily felt her blood run cold. "You wouldn't have *me*, if you did," she pointed out, somehow. It had *been* the Nightmare Hex, she recalled. "I wouldn't *know* I belonged to you."

The demon smirked, drawing back. "Are you *sure?*"

"...No," Emily admitted. There was no point in trying to lie. The demon could not only read her mind and know she was lying, it knew when she was *thinking* about lying. "But I believe you would want me personally."

"And, without you, the Allied Lands will be in deep trouble," the demon said. It reached forward again and touched her neck, one sharp fingernail scratching her skin. "You would sacrifice yourself to save a hundred students, but your absence *will* cost the lives of thousands - millions - of innocents. And *that* is the truth."

Emily paled. The demon couldn't lie. If she allowed herself to die, here and now, she would save everyone in its clutches, but she would no longer be able to help the Allied Lands. It was manipulating her, she knew, and it wasn't even *trying* to hide it. There was no *need* to keep her from recognizing the manipulation.

And if that is true, she thought, *there must be a way to escape Master Grey...*

She pushed the thought aside. "You see possibilities, not certainties," she said. "What you predict *might* come to pass..."

"It will," the demon said. "But in which reality?"

Cheat, Emily thought.

"Of course," the demon said, answering her thought. "We *always* cheat."

Emily took a breath. "And that means that I may not save the Allied Lands anyway," she snapped. It would be just like the demon to tempt her into abandoning her friends, after deciding that the good of the majority outweighed the good of the few, then manipulate events so that she lost anyway. She would betray her friends for nothing. "If I surrender myself to you, at least my friends and the other students will have a chance."

"How true," the demon agreed.

"Then I offer myself to you, in exchange for their freedom," Emily said. She braced herself, and dropped to her knees. The demon loomed over her, seemingly larger than before. But then, it wasn't human and it could present itself to her in any manner it chose. "Take me and leave this world."

The demon reached down and stroked her hair, as someone might pet a dog. "Are you *sure?*"

"Get on with it," Emily said. She knew she could expect nothing but endless torment. The demon would break her, body and soul. It wouldn't matter, not if her friends were freed. "I am sure."

"Very well," the demon said. Its voice became a sneer. "I will remove my taint from those I lured into my clutches, my sweet, but they will still have to bear the memories of what I did to them. It will haunt them for the rest of their lives."

"Take those memories," Emily said.

"You have nothing else to bargain with," the demon said. "You're mine."

"No," a quiet voice said.

Emily's head snapped up. The Grandmaster was standing there, looking younger than ever before. It took her a moment to realize that he wasn't wearing his blindfold and he had both eyeballs. She stared at him in shock, unsure just what he was doing in Alassa's mind. He couldn't be here, could he? Was the demon playing games? Or...

"Well," the demon said. "How *nice* to see you again."

It reached down and gripped Emily by the shoulder. "I'm afraid it's too late to save this young sweetheart from my clutches," it said. "One more failure to add to a very long list."

The Grandmaster kept his eyes fixed on the demon. "It is you, isn't it? The demon we tried to summon, decades ago."

"I could be," the demon said. It smiled, cruelly. "I assure you that you will never *know.*"

Emily looked up. "How could you see him *again* if you hadn't seen him for the first time?"

The demon pushed her forward until she was prostrating herself in front of it, then rested its foot on the back of her neck. "Silence," it ordered. Emily grunted in pain as it pushed down, threatening to break bones. "You're mine."

"Not yet," the Grandmaster said.

"I have released all I held in my thrall," the demon said. "She made the deal, understanding and accepting the consequences. I can do anything to her."

Emily screamed as it stamped down. Her neck broke...then snapped back together as the demon lifted its foot. Pain seared through her, burning every cell of her body, then faded away as she recoiled. It took her a long moment to realize that she was trapped in the demon's mentality, that it could hurt her any way it wanted without actually killing her...and that it was waiting.

But waiting for what?

"Another failure," the demon taunted, addressing the Grandmaster. "How many times have you failed?"

"Too many," the Grandmaster said. "I offer you myself in exchange for her."

"Oh," the demon said. "And what makes you think I *want* you?"

"I think you and I have unfinished business," the Grandmaster said. "And even if you're *not* the demon we summoned, you could certainly trade me to it."

"No," Emily said. She'd accepted her own death - and worse - but she didn't want to watch the Grandmaster die. Or have him surrender his own life for hers. "I..."

"She doesn't want you to die," the demon mocked. "Are you so willing to trade yourself for her?"

"Yes," the Grandmaster said.

"Your death will make life harder for her," the demon said. It clamped a hand over Emily's mouth before she could protest again. "She may not even survive the week."

"I know," the Grandmaster said. "But she doesn't deserve eternal torment."

"Matter of opinion," the demon said. "You people, blessed with the precious gift of free will, invariably become tainted. Emily was *never* an obedient child."

I had no choice, Emily thought. *What would I have become if I'd obeyed my stepfather?*

"I have yet to meet the person who was truly pure," the Grandmaster pointed out. "Free will may allow us to make mistakes, to become tainted, but it also allows us to work to overcome and survive our errors."

"It also allows you to make excuses," the demon sneered. It threw Emily a sharp look, reminding her that it knew what she was thinking. "To justify bad behavior to yourself. I assure you that very few humans truly believe themselves to be evil, whatever society thinks."

"Yes," the Grandmaster said. He gave the demon a long look, then dropped to his knees. "I offer myself in exchange for her freedom."

The demon tilted its head, then let go of Emily's mouth. "And what do *you* think of that?"

"Don't," Emily pleaded. "The Allied Lands need you."

"You *want* him to make the trade," the demon said. "Whatever you may say, a few moments as my possession was enough to make you regret bargaining with me."

Emily felt her cheeks burn. "That's true," she admitted. There was no point in trying to deny it. The demon could spend decades tormenting her for its own amusement. "But that doesn't mean I'm right to ask him to make the trade himself."

"Then you will have to live with the memory of him making the trade," the demon said. It turned back to the Grandmaster. "I accept your offer. I'm afraid there's no time to say goodbye."

"No," Emily said, desperately. "I..."

There was a flash of light. When it faded, she was back in her own body. Her hand felt wet, stained by the co-mingled blood, but she barely noticed. The Grandmaster had fallen off his chair and was lying on the floor, his face twisted in agony. She stumbled to her feet and knelt beside him, checking his heartbeat even though she knew it was already too late. The demon had accepted the Grandmaster's offer and then reached out to claim him.

Then you will have to live with the memory of him making the trade, it had said...

Alassa's body jerked; she coughed, loudly, as she started to make her way back to herself. Emily heard bells ringing in the distance as monitoring spells alerted the Healers that their charges were waking up. She wanted to rise to her feet, to assist her friend, but the darkness welled up in her mind and swallowed her.

By the time they burst into the room, she was unconscious on the floor.

Chapter Thirty-Six

Y OU'RE BEING AN IDIOT," LADY BARB SAID. EMILY BARELY HEARD HER THROUGH A HAZE OF pain that hung over her thoughts. "You're risking everything for an unintended insult!"

It dawned on Emily slowly, very slowly, that *she* wasn't the one who was being berated. Lady Barb was talking to someone else...and, even through the haze, she had a feeling she knew just who was being attacked. Who else could it be?

"You're risking the wrath of a Lone Power, and all her friends and allies, and even the very safety of the Allied Lands," Lady Barb thundered. "Why are you doing this?"

Emily coughed and opened her eyes. Her head hurt so badly she could barely think; her mouth was so dry she couldn't speak. Lady Barb was standing at the edge of her bed, facing Master Grey. The two Mediators looked as though they were going to start fighting at any moment. Magic crackled around them threateningly.

"Water," Emily croaked, as Lady Barb turned to face her. "Water, please."

Master Grey picked a glass of water off the bedside table and held it out to her, holding it in place so she could drink her fill. His eyes were bright, either with suppressed amusement or anticipation; Emily eyed him darkly, then remembered the demon. There were worse things than Master Grey out there. Oddly, she no longer felt scared of him.

"The Grandmaster is dead," Lady Barb said. "What happened?"

"He offered himself to the demon in exchange for me," Emily said. She cursed inwardly as Master Grey withdrew the glass and refilled it. The demon had hurt her - she wanted to rub her neck to make sure it wasn't broken - and she knew she was glad to escape, but she hadn't wanted the Grandmaster to die. He must have planned it from the moment she'd told him what she had in mind. "He offered himself and the demon accepted."

She coughed, again. "Have they awoken?"

"They're starting to wake up," Master Grey answered. "It will be some time before they recover completely, but they will return to the world."

"Thank you," Emily said, quietly.

Master Grey cleared his throat. "I'm afraid there is worse news," he said. "The absence of the Grandmaster means that his edicts are now powerless. You will face me in a duel two days from now."

Unless I choose to run, Emily thought, bitterly. Cold hatred ran through her heart as she stared up at him. *You'd beat me either way.*

Lady Barb swung around to face him. "You'd face a bedridden girl?"

"She will recover," Master Grey said, shortly. "And my reputation is not an issue here."

He turned and swept out of the room. Emily watched him go, cursing the Grandmaster under her breath. She'd calculated that offering herself to the demon would not only save her friends, but save most of what she'd built. Now...either she fought or ran...and if she lost, everything she'd built would be at risk. No doubt Master Grey wouldn't see value in the bank, either. Or understand what it meant for the long-term future of the Allied Lands.

"The Grandmaster was hoping to find a way to put pressure on him," Lady Barb said. Her voice was so cold that Emily felt chills running down her spine. "He could have found something, if there had been time. Instead...there won't be another Grandmaster until the end of the school year. The White Council will take that long to decide on a successor. By then..."

"The duel will have been fought," Emily said. She sat upright, rubbing her forehead. The water had helped dull the pain, but she still felt unwell. No doubt the demon had left a parting gift, even though it had removed its taint. She'd have to spend the rest of her life knowing that the Grandmaster had traded himself for her. "And everything will come to an end."

"Then run," Lady Barb said. "Go now and don't look back."

Emily looked down at her hands. "I've been running all my life," she said, bitterly. It was true. "I don't want to run anymore."

"You don't have a choice," Lady Barb said. "If you face him, you will die."

Maybe not, Emily thought. There were ideas, countless ideas, she'd dreamed up to use in a fight. She'd withheld them out of fear of what others could do with them, but now...she owed it to the Grandmaster to fight, to preserve what she'd built. He'd offered his life in exchange for hers. *If I surprised him...*

Lady Barb gripped her shoulder. "I understand how you're feeling," she said. "But... you cannot win."

"We'll see," Emily said. "Do we have time for some training? I need to know how a Mediator fights."

"You've already seen him fight," Lady Barb reminded her. She helped Emily to her feet, then threw open the cabinet to reveal a set of clean clothes. "But if you're insistent on seeing just how hard it will be, I'll do my best to help you."

Emily nodded, shucked off the gown - someone had changed her clothes while she was asleep - and pulled on the clean set of clothes. The snake-bracelet hadn't been removed from her wrist, thankfully; she stroked it gently, feeling the scaly pattern against her fingernails. Master Grey would be in for a very nasty surprise if he claimed it as part of his reward for beating her...

She pushed the thought aside. "How long was I out?"

"Nine hours," Lady Barb said. "The Grandmaster's body was removed to the crypt, where it will be held until burial. By tradition, it will be at least three weeks before he is cremated and placed in the ground."

So he can't rise again, Emily thought. Zombies were a very real threat in the Nameless World, even though she'd never seen one. Death Magics had been a thoroughly horrifying class. *And the demon will have his soul forever.*

It was a bitter thought. None of the books had suggested any way to recover a soul, once the body had died. Demons held their prey closely, refusing to let them go. Even if she summoned the demon herself and offered the trade, it was quite possible the demon would refuse. She'd already traded herself, after all. She cursed under her breath before following Lady Barb out of the room and past a long row of occupied beds. The demon's former victims were slowly fighting their way back to awareness.

They'll have to live with what the demon whispered into their minds, she thought, grimly. *It will overshadow the rest of their lives.*

It wasn't a pleasant thought. If their weaknesses had been enough to convince them to subconsciously lower their defenses and allow the demon into their souls, it had to be bad. Who knew what private dreams or petty guilt pervaded their minds? Or what insecurities weakened their defenses? There was no way to know. If the demon could play at being a Nightmare Hex, it could reach into their souls and drag out the very worst of their fears.

Lady Barb kept walking until they reached the Armory, and led the way into a large spellchamber. "The last duel at Whitehall was fought in the Great Hall," she said, as she closed and warded the door. "By tradition, senior students and tutors were allowed to witness the contests before the Grandmaster banned them from taking place. I imagine Master Grey will insist on having as many witnesses as possible."

Emily nodded, unsurprised.

"You and he will step into the dueling circle, carrying only a wand or a staff," Lady Barb continued. "His second will be required to search you, to verify that you are carrying nothing that could give you an unfair advantage; your second will do the same to him. Once the circle is sealed, only one of you will leave alive."

"I know," Emily said. She leaned forward. "Who's his second?"

"I don't know," Lady Barb said. "I believe he wanted Sergeant Miles, but Miles flatly refused when asked. He said there were plenty of ways to teach you to watch your mouth without a duel to the death."

"That's good," Emily said.

"Maybe," Lady Barb said. She looked Emily in the eye. "Given the nature of the duel, it's unlikely either second will have to do anything. There are few rules to actually break."

"True," Emily agreed. "Will you be my second?"

"If you like," Lady Barb said. She gave Emily a sharp look. "I can't fight the duel for you."

"I know," Emily said. "Is there anything else I should know?"

"Master Grey is experienced in both duels and bare-knuckle fighting," Lady Barb said, as she checked the spellchamber's wards. "Don't expect him to give you a fighting chance, or to waste time showing off instead of actually trying to kill you. I have no idea why he set out to contrive a duel, but I don't think he'll try to make it look even. He just wants you dead."

She stepped into the warded circle and held up her hand. "Watch," she said. She tossed a handful of fireballs at the wards, then followed up with a lightning bolt and a spell Emily didn't recognize. "You'll understand, I think, that each of those fireballs will snatch away one of your protective wards."

"I understand," Emily said. Lady Barb cast a dozen more fireballs with no apparent effort, and stopped. "How many fireballs can he produce?"

"Far more than you," Lady Barb said, tartly. "The fireball is a popular spell because it is simple to cast and very effective, even against a warded target. He can hammer your wards down faster than you can replenish them."

"It isn't imaginative," Emily pointed out.

Lady Barb tossed a fireball at her. It smashed against Emily's wards and vanished.

"It doesn't have to be," Lady Barb said, as the fireball faded away. There was hardly any heat. "The only thing that matters is winning. You won't get points for being imaginative."

Emily swallowed. Sergeant Miles had said much the same, back when he'd been asked about dueling lessons. A duel, particularly a non-lethal duel, was judged on fighting technique as much as who actually won. Someone who performed a particularly tricky spell might win on points, even though they lost the fight. But a lethal duel...she could perform a dozen fancy spells and still wind up dead.

"Mediators are trained to win," Lady Barb added. "That's why the training is so hard. We see it as better to expose weakness now, while someone is an apprentice, rather than when they're on the front lines."

She motioned Emily into the circle. "Time for you to show off what you've learned," she concluded. "I expect you not to hold back, not even once."

Emily blanched. "I could *kill* you!"

"Master Grey *will* kill you, unless you kill him first," Lady Barb pointed out. She waved a hand at Emily, who felt herself shoved back into the wards by an invisible force. "Go into the arena prepared to kill, or run now. You have no other choice."

Emily gritted her teeth and knuckled down to some hard fighting. It rapidly became clear that she was out of her depth, as long as she stuck to standard spells. Lady Barb was a tough opponent, even when she kept her distance; Emily could barely keep her wards in place as Lady Barb slammed spell after spell into her defenses. And then she unleashed other spells that nosed right *through* her wards...Emily felt the world shrink around her as she was turned into a tiny statue, utterly unable to move. By the time she broke the spell, Lady Barb could have killed her a dozen times over.

"You need to watch for tricks like that," Lady Barb said, as Emily stumbled back to her feet and lifted her hands in a defensive crouch. "One common trick is to throw several fireballs so closely together that the ward cannot dispel them in time. You'd be burned quite badly, at the very least."

I see, Emily thought. It suggested...possibilities. She'd have to borrow a spellchamber and practice. *But would he expect something based on Earthly science?*

She tossed a transfiguration spell at Lady Barb, trying to turn her into a toad. The spell struck the older woman's wards and vanished, the sheer complexity of the spell - even if it was intended for a prank - working against it. Lady Barb gave her a sharp look that promised pain, clearly believing that Emily wasn't taking it seriously. Emily ignored her and tossed three more spells at her, watching how and when they faded away. Lady Barb's wards seemed to ignore anything that didn't pass close enough to her to be effective.

Makes sense, Emily thought, coldly. *She wouldn't want to waste magic on protecting herself from something that isn't a threat.*

She ducked another spell, throwing herself to the side as Lady Barb launched a powerful force punch at her. If it had struck home, it would have slammed her into the wards and probably stunned her. Lady Barb lunged forward, throwing a set of ward-breaking spells directly at Emily before grabbing her by the arm and throwing her to the stone floor. Emily gasped in pain, recoiling as Lady Barb made a show of slamming her fist into Emily's neck. It would have killed her if Lady Barb hadn't pulled her punch.

"You can't stop him," Lady Barb said, as she stepped backwards and held out a hand to help Emily to her feet. She didn't even seem winded by throwing so many spells around. "You have to run."

Emily said nothing. Her entire body was aching, while her magic felt drained, as if she'd used too much too quickly. Older magicians could use more magic, she knew from bitter experience, and Lady Barb was at least a decade older than her, perhaps more. Master Grey could wait for her to exhaust herself, then move in for the kill. Or perhaps simply charge at her, overwhelm her wards with his own and then snap her neck.

"I tried to talk him out of it," Lady Barb added. "He's adamant."

"Maybe he just wants revenge for Mountaintop," Emily said. Zed had cautioned her that he had little influence over Master Grey...how hard had he tried? Perhaps he'd made the choice to do nothing, to leave Emily in the bed she'd made for herself. God knew he might still have some lingering dislike for her. "Or..."

She shook her head. Master Grey had clearly disliked her even before they'd met for the first time. Jade had told her that he'd been angry when he'd written to her... and that she'd withheld the truth about Shadye's death. But if she *had* told the truth, the entire world would have found out soon enough. The necromancers would know her reputation was largely based on a bluff. Without a nexus point, snapping a second necromancer out of existence was impossible.

"I don't think it matters," Lady Barb said. She sighed and dispelled the wards. "Take a horse from the stable, take supplies...and *go*."

"No," Emily said. "I'm *tired* of running."

"You're feeling guilty," Lady Barb said. "I understand. It's never easy to live when someone dies. But you won't bring the Grandmaster back by throwing away your life."

"Then everything I built goes to him," Emily said. She cursed herself for the oversight. It wouldn't have been hard to gift Frieda some money, if nothing else; she could have written the bank charter so she had only non-voting stock. "I can't let that happen."

"It will happen anyway, when he wins," Lady Barb said. "He could lay claim to everything you ever touched."

"I'd like to see him try to put the genie back in the bottle," Emily muttered. She'd introduced too many ideas for them to be easily suppressed, not now. Trying to stop people using English letters and numbers would be impossible. Printing presses? Steam engines? The basic concepts were hardly a secret, not any longer. Gunpowder was the only concept he might manage to suppress, if Imaiqah's father and King Randor didn't keep quiet. "I don't think he could succeed."

"He could try," Lady Barb said. "Emily..."

Emily shook her head. "We need to keep practicing," she said, shortly. "I'm learning a great deal from you."

"Then you can learn how easy it is for me to beat you," Lady Barb said. She restored the wards and stamped over to the far side of the chamber. "I wondered if this was some demented attempt to Claim you, but he was utterly adamant that nothing less than your death would suffice. Once you two enter the circle, like I said, only one of you will leave alive."

She held up her hand, clearly ready to cast a spell. "And if I have to beat you black and blue to make it clear that you don't have a chance, I will."

"I know," Emily said. "Are there any rules about *how* he wins?"

"No," Lady Barb said, shortly. "It's a duel to the death. All he has to do is kill you. It doesn't matter if he burns you to ash, or snaps your neck, or cracks your skull with his fist and tears your brain apart. The only real rule, once you're in the circle..."

"...Is that only one of us will come out," Emily finished. It was a very simple rule. "It doesn't matter if I use a new spell?"

"He knows spells you've never encountered," Lady Barb snapped. "I don't think anyone will care, as long as one of you dies."

Emily nodded, and braced herself. Lady Barb wouldn't go easy on her.

Chapter Thirty-Seven

THIS ISN'T A SAFE PLACE TO BE," MASTER GREY SAID.

Emily refused to give him the satisfaction of jumping at his voice. She'd been unable to sleep, so she'd wandered through the darkened halls and up to the battlements, where they'd held the ill-fated midnight feast. The moon hung high overhead, casting an eerie light over the school; she'd just sat on the battlements and stared out at the darkened lands beneath the castle.

"It isn't as if you care," she said, finally.

"I would prefer you didn't die in a stupid accident," Master Grey said. "There are no wards to catch you if you stumbled and fell off the battlements at midnight."

"Yes, I *know*," Emily said. She'd had to jump out of a window to escape the Mimic. "But there's no need to care."

Master Grey shrugged, then sat down a safe distance from her. Emily briefly entertained the idea of tossing the Death Viper at him, then realized it would probably be pointless. His stance told her that he was ready for a murderous attack. No doubt he thought he could escape anything she did and wait for her to show up for the duel.

She turned to look at him, bitterly. "Why are you doing this?"

"It has to be done," Master Grey said. There was no hatred or anger in his voice, merely calm acceptance. "You need to be removed."

Emily clenched her fists. "I killed two necromancers and *this* is my thanks?"

"You also came within a hair's breadth of triggering a war between two families," Master Grey said, curtly. "Thousands of people, including some of the most prominent magicians in the world, could have died. The changes you have wrought will reshape the world..."

"That isn't a bad thing," Emily snapped.

"...And cause chaos when we need to face the gathering storm on our borders," Master Grey continued, as though she hadn't spoken. "You make changes, you reshape the world, without ever considering the consequences. The damage you did to Mountaintop alone will weaken our ability to produce more combat sorcerers to defend our lands."

"Mountaintop was draining the life and magic from some of its pupils to feed the wards," Emily snarled.

Master Grey looked back at her evenly. "Would you prefer they were drained by advancing necromancers?"

He went on before she could formulate an answer. "Our one priority is to defeat the necromancers, nothing else," he said. "The balance between magicians, kingdoms and city-states is a reflection of our single overarching goal. We do not have time to quibble over the methods we use to fight, nor do we have time to scrabble over who rules the roost."

"Says the people in charge," Emily pointed out.

Master Grey shrugged. "You should know just how few people take the threat over there--" he pointed a finger towards the Blighted Lands "--seriously," he said.

"Too many kings and princes would prefer to forget the necromancers exist."

"*I* never forgot," Emily snapped.

"And yet you were prepared to cripple us," Master Grey said. "Your actions have proven far too dangerous, Emily. You introduce revolutionary new ideas to kingdoms, threatening the balance of power; you crippled Mountaintop, threatening our ability to fight; you insisted on returning to the Dark Fortress, bringing back a demon that attacked students and eventually claimed the Grandmaster's life. You're just too dangerous to be allowed to live."

Emily looked out over the land. Would it have been better if she'd done nothing? If she'd plunged herself into magical studies and chosen not to introduce any new ideas? But Shadye wouldn't have let her be, she knew, even if she hadn't befriended anyone at Whitehall. He would have gone after her anyway...

...And so would far too many others.

"I'm sorry you feel that way," she said, finally.

"So am I," Master Grey said. Oddly, she had the feeling he was being completely sincere. "But I don't have a choice."

Emily *looked* at him. "Who put you up to this?"

"I beg your pardon?"

"Your reputation will not survive beating a nineteen-year-old schoolgirl," Emily said, bitterly. "Even if you manage to survive the repercussions, no one will ever trust or hire you again. You're throwing away a career for...what? The pleasure of killing me with your bare hands? Who made it worth your while to sacrifice everything?"

"I have always placed the good of the Allied Lands ahead of my personal desires," Master Grey said, stiffly. "I didn't need someone to tell me you had to be killed."

"Your career will come to an end," Emily said. "Would you really surrender everything that means something to you because you want to kill me?"

"I owe someone a favor I cannot refuse," Master Grey admitted. "But I did not need to be talked into recognizing you as a possible threat."

"Fulvia," Emily guessed. Master Grey had ties to the Ashworths...ties that might not have snapped when he'd become a Mediator. "Who else could it be?"

"You *did* risk her life and that of her entire family," Master Grey pointed out. It wasn't a denial. "She has good reason to hate you."

"She was going to arrange for her eldest granddaughter to be married off against her will," Emily snapped. She'd known it happened, intellectually, but she still had some problems understanding how anyone could tolerate it. "How is that different from rape?"

"It isn't," Master Grey said. She blinked in surprise. "But we must all sacrifice our personal desires to protect the Allied Lands."

"Says the person who doesn't have to open his legs for a rapist," Emily snarled. Cold hatred flared through her voice. It would have been easier, perhaps, if he'd invented a justification for arranging and then forcing marriage. "You'd feel differently if it was *you* being given away as easily as a stud bull."

Master Grey showed no visible reaction. "I *am* sacrificing my career," he reminded her. "I don't have the freedom to deal with you without a price."

"Damn you," Emily swore.

"No doubt," Master Grey said. He rose to his feet. "We are due to meet one final time, Lady Emily, in nine hours. I would advise you to get some sleep, but..."

"You'd prefer to meet me when I'm half-asleep," Emily muttered. She thought about all the spells she'd invented, all the concepts she'd tested in the spellchambers, when Lady Barb wasn't beating her into the ground time and time again. How well would they work in a real duel? "Be seeing you."

Master Grey nodded curtly and stalked off.

Emily turned back to stare out over the darkened lands. It would be easy to walk down to the stable, steal a horse and run. The tutors were too busy dealing with the recovering students to patrol the corridors as thoroughly as they normally did...hell, unless Mistress Irene happened to be monitoring the wards closely, they wouldn't see her slip down the stairs and out into the gardens. A few hours hard riding would get her far enough from Whitehall that she could lose herself in the nearest city-state, changing her face and hair...

But she was tired of running.

She glanced up as she heard someone opening the heavy door and stepping out onto the battlements. Her heart sank as she saw Frieda, her face pale, wearing a long white nightgown that reflected the moonlight. The younger girl smiled wanly as she saw Emily, hurrying over to sit next to her. Emily let out a sigh, and wrapped her arm around Frieda's shivering body. She hadn't even thought to don a coat before sneaking up to the roof.

"You should be resting," she said, leaning into Emily's embrace. "Tomorrow..."

"I know," Emily said. "I have a duel to fight."

"You'll win," Frieda said. "Caleb is panicking, but you'll win. I'm sure of it."

"I wish I was," Emily muttered. At least Caleb hadn't shown up, something she wasn't sure was a mercy or a curse. It would be nice to kiss him one final time. "He might well kill me."

"He won't," Frieda said. "You killed two necromancers and a Mimic. I think you'll beat him."

"I had help with the Mimic," Emily said. It had been her idea, but she'd needed help to make it work. And she'd cheated with the necromancers. Master Grey... wouldn't allow her any room to cheat. "Frieda..."

"And you saved me from Mountaintop," Frieda continued, smoothly. "There isn't anything you can't do, if you put your mind to it."

Emily rested her head in her hand. "I won't have a chance to speak to the others," she said, softly. Jade was still sitting with Alassa - not that she blamed him for putting his fiancée first - and everyone else was still recovering. Imaiqah had opened her eyes briefly, she'd been told, but no one else had shown more than a few weak signs of life. "If I die..."

"You won't," Frieda said.

"If I die," Emily repeated, "tell them I'm sorry and...and that there are letters for them, held by Lady Barb."

She sighed. She'd given Lady Barb her notebooks, cautioning her to keep them to herself. It wasn't clear if Master Grey could claim anything she gave away before the duel, but there was no point in taking chances. Lady Barb could use the concepts she'd created, including the nuke-spell, if she felt like it. Or burn them, if she thought they were too dangerous to risk unleashing on the world. She'd been there, after all, when the nuke-spell had been used for the first time. She knew, on a very primal level, just what it could do.

"You can tell them yourself," Frieda said. "I have faith in you."

"Thank you," Emily said. She rose to her feet, helping the shivering Frieda to stand. "I had better get some rest."

Frieda wrapped her arms around Emily and hugged her, tightly. "You'll be fine," she said, firmly. "I expect you to win."

Emily smiled tiredly, and headed downstairs towards the dorms. Madame Beauregard was standing in front of the door, holding a strap in one hand, but she merely nodded and stood aside when Emily stepped past her. Clearly, she had more important things to worry about than punishing two girls for being out of bounds. Frieda followed Emily into her room and settled down on Alassa's bed, looking determined to resist any attempt to eject her. Emily shrugged, laid down and closed her eyes. It felt like bare minutes had passed before she heard a knock on the door and sat up. Lady Barb stepped into the room, wearing formal robes.

"You have to remain in this room until it's time to go down to the Great Hall," she said, shortly. "And I can't let you run any longer."

"I understand," Emily said, climbing out of bed. The cold pit in her stomach was growing worse. "Did you bring my clothes?"

Lady Barb nodded and held up a set of dueling robes. Emily eyed them warily before standing and heading to the shower. She washed herself thoroughly before returning to the bedroom and getting dressed. As soon as she finished, there was a knock at the door. Lady Barb opened it, accepted the plate of breakfast and placed it on the table in front of Emily. Emily felt her stomach twist in protest as she saw the huge sausages, eggs, bacon and fried potatoes, but forced herself to eat as much as she could. She'd need the energy to fight, when the time came.

"Leave the rest here; eat if you feel you can," Lady Barb ordered. She looked Emily up and down, and nodded critically. "Your staff is in the pocket, shrunk down. I suggest you use the next hour to prime it with the spells you intend to use."

She glanced at Frieda. "You'd better leave Emily alone now," she added. "She will need time to think and meditate."

"I'm staying with her," Frieda said, firmly. She crossed her arms under her breasts in stubborn determination. "*Someone* needs to stay here."

Lady Barb glowered at her, clearly reining in her temper. "You have a choice," she said, flatly. "You can leave now, or I can remove you from the room and send you to face the Warden. Custom dictates that the duelists remain alone until the time comes for them to face one another."

"Emily," Frieda began.

"Go," Emily said. The nervousness in her chest was growing worse. "I'll see you soon enough."

Frieda gave her a quick hug, jumped back and fled the room before Lady Barb could catch her. Emily half-hoped she wouldn't watch the duel - the thought of dying was bad enough, but the thought of dying in front of her friend was worse - yet she knew that it was hard, almost impossible, to deter Frieda once she'd set her heart on something. She *would* watch the duel.

The bitter sensation in her stomach grew stronger. Emily swallowed hard, as if she was on the verge of throwing up. All her thoughts, all her plans, might prove to be useless when she stepped into the dueling circle.

"That's a good friend you have," Lady Barb said. "Quite loyal, too."

"Please take care of her, afterwards," Emily said. Frieda had discovered her confidence at Mountaintop, but she wouldn't have an easy life. "Don't let her do anything stupid."

"My track record for keeping people from doing stupid things isn't very impressive," Lady Barb said, darkly. "You should have run."

"Not this time," Emily said, flatly.

"I hope you're right and you will survive," Lady Barb said. She reached out and stroked Emily's hair. "Good luck."

Emily swallowed. "Thank you."

Lady Barb nodded and withdrew, closing the door behind her. Emily felt a locking ward slide into place; not strong enough to keep her from leaving, but perfectly capable of alerting Lady Barb if Emily tried to leave. She was trapped. God alone knew what would happen if she was *caught* trying to escape, now that the duel was barely half an hour away, but she doubted it would be good. Gritting her teeth, she strode to the dressing table and sat down facing the mirror.

Her face looked back at her, pale and wan. Alassa had told her, more than once, that brushing her hair was relaxing - she made sure to brush her hair one hundred times before bed - but Emily had never seen the attraction. She'd never really seen the point of taking care of herself before Shadye had kidnapped her; if she looked good, she'd feared, it would just mark her out for attention. But now...she looked resolute, as if she'd finally grown into her looks. Her long brown hair fanned out around the dark leather shirt, loose enough to allow her to move freely...

I look like an adult, she thought, suddenly.

She pushed the thought aside and reached for the hairbrush, brushing her hair before tying it back into a long ponytail. It was relaxing, the monotony of the task helping to calm her thoughts, even though she couldn't escape the thought of the duel for long. Putting down the hairbrush - she couldn't be bothered to count the strokes - she reached for the staff, restored it to normal size and started inputting spells, one by one. Master Grey would expect her to use something offensive, she was sure; instead, she intended to use the staff to defend herself, as she'd done when he'd pitted her against the Third Years. It would keep him off balance.

She hoped.

The staff seemed to be humming with power when she had finished, dozens of spells ready to be triggered on command. Emily put the staff down and rose to her feet. There was nothing else to do but wait. She tried to force herself to choke down some more food, but her stomach rebelled, threatening to reject everything she'd eaten. Emily reached for a book, glanced at the first page, and shook her head. There was no way she could concentrate on anything but the impending duel.

She looked back at the mirror, wondering just what the Grandmaster would have thought if he'd seen her. Had he expected her to run? He had to have known that Master Grey would move at once, claiming the right to set the time and place of the duel as soon as the Grandmaster had died. Or had he thought that Master Grey would wait? Or that someone the Grandmaster had known would pressure Master Grey to abandon the duel? Or...

There was a knock on the door. "Come in!"

Lady Barb entered, holding a staff of her own in one hand. "It's time," she said. "Emily..."

"Don't worry," Emily said. She had to fight down the overwhelming urge to run. "I made my choice."

"Yes, you did," Lady Barb said. "Come with me."

Emily nodded. "Who's his second?"

"Lady Daniele," Lady Barb said. The name meant nothing to Emily. "She's a Mediator, one of his former apprentices. Not someone to be underestimated."

"I know," Emily said. "It wasn't your fault."

Lady Barb's lips thinned. "I told the Grandmaster I thought that I couldn't give you the harsh training you needed without snapping your mind," she said, flatly. He face was impassive, as if she were determined to show no sign of emotion. "You would not have responded well, I think, to me acting like him. If I'd said anything else..."

"It wasn't your fault," Emily repeated. She wanted the older woman to believe that, if nothing else. "And thank you. Thank you for everything."

Head held high, she walked out of the room, through the corridors and into the Great Hall.

Chapter Thirty-Eight

T HE GREAT HALL WAS BRIGHTLY LIT WHEN SHE STEPPED THROUGH THE DOOR, THE TABLES
and chairs cleared away and a large dueling circle drawn on the floor. Mistress
Irene stood beside a handful of the staff, while over forty students stood leaning
against the stone walls, watching and waiting as the two duelists entered the chamber. Master Grey waited on the other side of the dueling circle, his eyes meeting
Emily as soon as she appeared and never leaving her face. A dark-skinned woman
with long white hair - Lady Daniele, Emily assumed - stood next to him. There was
a tart expression on her face, as if she'd bitten into something unpleasant. If Sergeant
Miles had refused to serve as Master Grey's second, Emily wondered, what pressure
had he put on Lady Daniele to take the role?

She refused to show any sign of fear as she walked up to the edge of the circle,
feeling almost as if she were watching herself from outside. The wards gently pressed
against her magic; she tested them, satisfying herself that they only served as protective walls, rather than reflecting spells in all directions. At least she wouldn't have
to worry about Master Grey bouncing a spell off the wards and striking her in the
back. She'd had that happen to her once before and it had been embarrassing, to say
the least. Perhaps, part of her mind noted, she should have paid more attention in
dueling lessons. They had seemed immaterial to her, at Mountaintop, but now they
would have come in handy.

But he still has two decades on me, she thought bleakly, as Lady Barb stepped up
behind Emily. *And he was trained at Mountaintop.*

Mistress Irene cleared her throat. "The challenged may choose to refuse the duel,"
she said, her voice echoing in the chamber. She turned to look at Master Grey. "Are
you insistent on accepting the challenge?"

"I am," Master Grey said, simply.

A low rustle ran through the chamber. Emily understood; it wasn't common for
the referee to remind the challenged - Master Grey - that he could refuse the duel.
Mistress Irene was asking him, all but begging him, to withdraw his acceptance. But
Emily wasn't surprised at his refusal. He'd set out to kill her, after all. There was
literally nothing she could offer him that would compensate for turning down the
challenge. He couldn't repay Fulvia whatever he owed her if he let Emily go.

Bitch, Emily thought, coldly. Melissa had told her that Fulvia could be vindictive,
but she'd never expected anything like *this*. *She'd let the world burn just so she could
have her revenge.*

She gritted her teeth, fighting down the urge to wipe her sweaty palms against
her trousers. It hadn't been easy, forcing herself to use a memory charm to re-watch
the one duel she'd seen him fight, but she'd done it. He always let his opponent
strike first...Emily hoped - feared - that her first strike would be fatal, yet she had her
doubts. Master Grey was not only experienced, he was more flexible and adaptable
than she was. She felt her heartbeat start to pound in her chest - so loudly that she

thought everyone could hear it - as Mistress Irene started to speak for the second time.

"Then I must remind the contestants of the rules," Mistress Irene said, coldly. "You must enter the circle, which will then be sealed..."

Get on with it, Emily thought, as the Charms Mistress droned on. Was she stalling for time? Expecting Void to burst in or Emily to flee? Or, perhaps, to strike at Master Grey before they entered the circle? It was futile; even if she'd found a way to kill him before they fought, she would have been the prime suspect. Who *else* would have had a motive to kill him?

She raised her eyes to the gathered students and instantly regretted it. Frieda was standing with a couple of Second Years, her eyes shining as she watched; Melissa was standing alone, her arms crossed under her breasts. There was no sign of Caleb or Jade; Emily was almost relieved. They might be stuck helping the demon's victims, but at least they wouldn't have to watch the duel. She wanted to send Frieda away, but she knew it was too late. The younger girl would just have to watch.

"The contestants will now be searched," Mistress Irene said.

Emily gritted her teeth as Lady Daniele walked around the circle, stopped in front of Emily and patted her down without enthusiasm. One finger touched the snake-bracelet, clearly parsing out the spell, before motioning to Emily to remove it. Had Master Grey deduced the snake's existence from Nanette's injury, if he'd seen it? Or had someone told him? Emily pushed the thought aside - there was no way to know, beyond asking a very revealing question - removed the bracelet, and passed it to Lady Barb. She'd know to keep the snake under control if Emily died. Anyone else would get a very unwelcome surprise.

Lady Daniele cleared her throat - Emily was sure, just for a moment, that she was going to insist on taking the bracelet herself - before she thought better of it. Emily was almost relieved. It was clear that Lady Daniele wasn't a willing participant; she didn't deserve to find herself holding a lethal snake. She watched as Lady Barb searched Master Grey, finding nothing. Master Grey hadn't deigned to bring anything more than his staff and dueling robes.

He doesn't need to cheat, her own thoughts mocked her.

"You may now enter the circle," Mistress Irene said, finally.

Emily had to force herself to step forward. The circle's wards rose up around her, thrumming with power, fading as she passed through them. They'd block anyone from leaving now, she knew; they wouldn't fall until one of them was dead. She wondered, absurdly, if the wards *couldn't* be dismantled from outside? What would have happened if they'd come to a peaceful resolution at the very last minute?

Concentrate on the fight, she advised herself, sternly. *This is no time for your mind to wander.*

Master Grey leaned on his staff, his eyes following her every move. Emily declined the unspoken offer of a staring contest; instead, she braced herself and allowed her magic to flicker against her own staff. The spells responded to her touch, ready and raring to defend her against all threats. They'd buy her time to cast more aggressive spells of her own. It was unusual, according to the books, but workable. Besides, a conventional duel would give him all the advantages. She tested the floor - the wards pervaded it, holding the stone in place - and sighed inwardly. One of her concepts was doomed before the duel even began.

There are alternatives, she thought, darkly. *But they will have to be used under pressure.*

She pushed the thought aside as Mistress Irene walked to a point, just outside the circle, where she could see everything. Emily had no idea why she even bothered - it wasn't as if there was any way to actually *cheat* - but it hardly mattered. Maybe she just wanted a solid memory to show Void, later. He *was* Emily's Guardian of Record...

"You may begin," Mistress Irene said.

Emily braced herself, then relaxed and triggered the first defensive spells. Master Grey quirked an eyebrow - he'd clearly expected her to launch a devastating offensive as her first move - but did nothing, apart from watching her. Emily solidified her defenses and gathered herself.

Master Grey did nothing...nothing she could see.

She couldn't help wondering if he was mocking her, or if he had a plan of his own. Lady Barb had warned her, after all, that he *wouldn't* waste time. A duel to the death was no place to show off.

Or he just wants to stomp me into the ground, she thought. *I...*

Master Grey stepped forward. Emily braced herself, and aimed the first set of transfiguration spells at him. She saw his eyes go wide with astonishment, then anger, as the spells glinted and broke against his wards. He had to think she was mocking him. The prank spells would be devastating against a mundane opponent, but any magician worth his salt would be able to counter them with ease. Emily smiled, and launched the second set of spells. One of them was different, aimed at the air around him. Lady Barb had missed it, when she'd tested the concept, but would Master Grey...?

She smiled savagely as the air turned to pure oxygen, then threw the fireball. Poison gas - even something as simple as carbon monoxide - would have triggered his wards, but oxygen was safe. Master Grey jumped backwards as the air seemed to burst into flame, *mundane* flames. Wards designed to shatter spellware into nothingness weren't able to stop *fire*. It was a weakness Emily had noted years ago and kept to herself. Wards capable of stopping physical objects were much harder to build and far more draining to keep in place.

Master Grey snarled, and threw back a series of fireballs of his own. They struck the pure oxygen in the air and exploded just outside his wards. Emily saw him grimace in pain, and fire off a lethal combination of ward-killing spells. She cast a counterspell through her staff, allowing the spells to latch on before she killed the wards herself.

Master Grey threw a second set of fireballs, then a tongue of flame that lashed out towards her. Emily ducked back as fire crackled around her wards, and muttered a summoning spell. Water droplets manifested in front of her, quenching the flame, just as a wave of magic struck her and sent her flying back into the wards. Master Grey was resorting to brute force. She hastily altered her own wards, deflecting rather than absorbing the spellwork. She hadn't been sure it would work, but it seemed to; the magic crackled *around* her, rather than falling apart.

Gritting her teeth, she cast the next set of spells, aiming a makeshift laser at him. His wards flared, suddenly overloaded; clearly, he'd modified them after her trick with the fire. She followed up with blinding light, but it didn't seem to slow him down. Blinding someone through light was such an obvious trick, she realized, that *someone* had to have thought of it in the past.

She darted to one side as Master Grey fired off a set of spells she didn't recognize, and threw another set of transfiguration spells at him. This time, the air became gunpowder; the explosion threw Master Grey back, snapping one of his arms as he slammed into the wards with terrifying force. Emily hesitated, unsure if she'd won...

The moment of hesitation almost killed her. He slammed *something* into her wards. It was another ward-killing spell, but grossly overpowered; it flared from ward to ward, breaking them down before she could cancel them herself. She had no choice but to cancel all the spells and rebuild them, giving him time to heal himself and come after her.

Master Grey pulled himself back upright, his dark eyes glowering. He'd expected an easy win, Emily realized, feeling a flicker of pride. Even if he won, he'd know he'd been in a fight. He stared at her for a long moment before hurling yet another set of fireballs at her.

Emily tightened her wards before she pushed one at him. The fireballs splattered against it, vanishing into nothingness rather than burning through her defenses. She countered with fireballs of her own, and followed up with a pressure spell. Master Grey dodged it, countering the spell even though he couldn't have been sure of what it actually *was*.

She threw a disintegration spell at him, allowing it to trail along the floor. Unfortunately, the wards holding them within the circle refused to allow it to tear up the stone. He cancelled the spell before it could rip him into dust, and waved his hand at her. Jagged flashes of lightning flickered out of nowhere and tore into her wards, brilliant flickers of light tearing them apart, the feedback screaming into her mind.

Emily stumbled back, caught between two fires; if she cancelled the wards, the lightning would kill her, but if she *didn't* cancel the wards they would eventually shatter anyway.

She forced herself to hold on, thrust the staff forward, using a kinetic spell to hurl it towards him at blinding speed. His wards weren't prepared for something *thrown* at him; she'd seen enough stones stop in midair and fall to the ground to know that most kinetic spells didn't actually impart velocity, merely pushed the objects forward. Lightning flared around him as the staff slammed into his arm, ripping it off. The staff shattered. Emily caught the dust with another spell and threw it at him, following up with more fireballs of her own.

He grunted in pain, and threw something back at her. The world seemed to shimmer around her and her stepfather appeared...

Not again, she thought, dispelling the Nightmare Hex. Cold rage flared through her mind. How *dare* he throw *that* at her? *That won't work anymore.*

But it had won him time.

She had no idea how he managed to heal himself - she'd been warned never to try to heal herself unless she was completely out of options - but he managed to stop the bleeding and even start repairing his arm. And she was reaching her own limits...she had to stop to gather herself, no matter what he did.

She saw his eyes glimmer with suppressed amusement and triumph - it struck her, suddenly, that part of him was *enjoying* the challenge - and felt her temper snap. Magic flared around her and she threw it at him, not trying to shape it into a spell.

He held up his remaining hand, deflecting the magic into the wards, and cast something back at her. The air seemed to turn to ice, trapping her in place. She hastily cast a counterspell, to no avail. It took her a long moment to realize he'd effectively duplicated her trick. There was no magic in the ice to dispel.

He marched towards her, eyes dark and shadowed.

Emily felt panic snapping at her mind; she summoned fire, lashing out with it to melt the ice. Her clothes were suddenly drenched in warm water as she stumbled back and turned the water to steam. Master Grey strode through, his face showing no sign of pain, as he fixed his eyes on her face. He'd tightened his wards, but it wouldn't be enough.

She turned the puddles of water into acid, forced herself to move back. He grunted in pain, and cast a spell of his own, throwing the acid towards her. She barely managed to deflect it before the liquid scarred her face permanently.

Moments later, he slapped her across the face, sending her stumbling back against the wards. Pain flared through her head, again, but somehow she managed to cast another fireball. It smashed into his wards and vanished.

You can't fight him hand to hand, she told herself, urgently. If she'd had the snake-bracelet, she might have dared him into closing with her...she briefly considered trying to summon the snake anyway, before dismissing it as too dangerous. Lady Barb couldn't touch the snake without being poisoned. *Maybe if I...*

He slammed a wave of magic into her, hammering her body against the wards. Emily tried to counter the spell, but she couldn't focus her mind any longer. She was sure she felt a couple of bones break, yet she was too dazed to feel any real pain. Her body staggered and fell to the ground, half-leaning against the wards.

Master Grey advanced, looming over her, already drawing back his fists to beat her to death. Emily threw caution to the winds and reached out with one of the soul magic spells she'd learned at Mountaintop. Master Grey froze, his eyes going wide with shock. But she was too drained to press her advantage.

And then he shook it off and slapped her again. She'd made him mad.

She tasted blood in her mouth as he caught her by the shirt and hauled her to her feet. If she'd been mad at the Nightmare Hex, *he* was mad at her reaching into his soul and confronting him with his darkest fears about himself. It was worse, far worse, than a Nightmare Hex...he shook her, violently, and tossed her right across the circle.

She landed on her arm, which snapped under the force of the impact; she hastily cast a numbing spell, even though she knew it was pointless. There was no way she could heal herself before he beat her to death.

And then it struck her.

She gathered herself, feeling blood trickling down her shirt, as he reached for her, bringing their skin into contact. The forbidden spell glittered in her mind; the moment they touched, she cast it.

Master Grey's skin rapidly started to bruise, as if she'd beaten him to within an inch of his life. His eyes went wide with horror, but he couldn't hope to counter the spell in time. There was a very good reason why it was not only considered forbidden, at least to non-Healers, but buried. It was tearing him apart, cell by cell.

Burn the body, her thoughts yammered at her. *Destroy it before they find out what you did!*

She cursed softly as he stumbled backwards, falling to his knees, and summoned the last traces of her magic. Master Grey's body caught fire, the blaze roaring through decaying skin and wiping out the evidence; she pushed it forward, setting his very bones on fire. The smell of burning flesh made her retch...she wondered, dully, if his body was going to fall on her. It would be only just, after she'd killed him in such a horrifying manner...

And then the darkness rose up and she knew no more.

Chapter Thirty-Nine

P AIN.

It was all she could feel, endless sheets of pain cascading through her body. She floated in and out of awareness, crying for her friends, screaming as she saw the faces of her enemies peering down at her. Shadye's inhuman face, Mother Holly's desperate snarl, the Mimic switching from shape to shape as it loomed over her...she thought, dimly, that she might be in hell. Someone was laughing in the distance...

And then she opened her eyes.

She was lying in the infirmary, staring up at the white ceiling. Her body felt numb, as if someone had cast a painkilling spell on her or forced potion down her throat. She tried to raise her hand, only to discover that it was tied down. Was she a prisoner? Her head sparked with pain when she tried to look up, but she forced herself to move. If she was trapped, she had to escape.

"Lie still," a familiar voice said. "You are lucky to be alive."

Emily blinked. *Void?*

The Lone Power came into view, standing by the edge of the bed and peering down at her with sparkling dark eyes. His long black hair was tied into a pony tail, drawn back to reveal the shape of his cheekbones; the long dark robes he wore marked him as a sorcerer of consequence. She hadn't seen him since Mountaintop, over a year ago, but she couldn't help feeling relieved to see him now. He'd cared enough to come for her.

"*Don't* try to use magic," Void said, firmly. "You drained yourself almost completely. It will take time - weeks, perhaps - for your powers to regenerate. You may have to retake the entire school year."

"No," Emily croaked.

"You will have difficulty completing your exams without magic," Void pointed out. He reached for a bottle of water and held it to her lips. "And they will have to get a replacement for Master Grey."

His lips quirked. "They may have some problems," he added, as she sipped the water. "I don't know how many tutors would be eager to take on an apprentice who killed a master."

"Oh," Emily said. It was hard to talk. "You...you could teach me."

"I'm a lousy teacher, as I believe I told you," Void said. He pulled the bottle back, then capped it and placed it by the side of the bed. "You wouldn't learn the right lessons from me...and far too many of the wrong ones."

Emily groaned, forcing the matter out of her head. It was too hard to think clearly, as her head was starting to pound. She tried to move her hands, only to rediscover that they were tied to the bed. Void gave her a long, considering look before he reached down and undid the straps, one by one. Her hands, when she brought them into view, showed the telltale signs of having her skin regrown. They were almost inhumanly pale. Beside them, the snake-bracelet - Lady Barb must have returned it - looked odd. It would take time for her skin to return to its natural color.

"You were trying to gouge out your own eyes," Void said, dispassionately. "I have strict orders from the Healers to freeze you if you start trying to blind yourself again."

Emily flushed. "I wasn't..."

Void shrugged, then reached for a mirror and held it up in front of her. Emily started in shock; her pale face was covered with scratches and scars, some dug so deep into her skin that it was clear they might well become infected. The Healers had stopped the bleeding, but they hadn't repaired the surface damage. Given how badly she'd been hurt, they might not have had the time. They wouldn't have wanted her to carry the scars if she'd been so badly out of it she hadn't known what she'd been doing.

"Shit," she said, finally.

"You were pushed right to the limit," Void said. "Your life has hung in the balance for days."

"You said," Emily muttered. She tried to sit up, but couldn't. Her memories were all jumbled. How many of them were real and how many were nightmares? "The Grandmaster is dead, isn't he?"

"Yes," Void said. His voice was completely flat, betraying no trace of emotion. "And so is Master Grey. You were very nearly the third to die."

Emily nodded, trying to sort out her thoughts. "And the demon's victims? The people the demon touched?"

"Alive and well," Void said. "They've been trying to see you - or they were, until the Healers chased them out."

Emily felt an odd flicker of *déjà vu*. "How long was I out?"

"Two weeks," Void said. "The Healers had to work hard to save your life, Emily. There were times when they almost lost you, before they healed up most of the damage. And then they felt it would be better to leave you to rest, rather than allow you to wake up. This was the earliest moment they thought they could wake you."

Emily ran her hand through her hair. It felt greasy, as if she hadn't washed it for weeks...which was true enough, she supposed. Healers washed the bodies of those in their care, Lady Barb had taught her, but it was always very basic. They rarely had time to do more than wipe a patient with wet cloths before moving on to the next patient. She hoped she'd be allowed a shower soon, even if she wasn't permitted to leave the infirmary.

She sighed, suddenly. "Can I speak to them?"

"If you feel up to it," Void said. He winked at her. "Your young man was quite persistent, even with *me* in the room."

Emily blushed, furiously. "What did you say to him?"

"Told him to wait," Void said. His face twisted into a dark smile. "Oh, and a set of graphic threats of what would happen if he mistreated you."

"I hope you're joking," Emily said. "I..."

"Maybe a little," Void said. He cleared his throat. "All jokes aside, be careful what you do over the next few weeks. You are *not* in a good state."

"I know," Emily said.

"Trust me on this," Void added. He met her eyes, warningly. "Using magic now will hamper your recovery significantly. And any form of...*strenuous* physical exercise will do the same."

It took Emily a moment to realize what he meant. When she did, she blushed again.

"He said he was planning to Court me," she admitted. "Are you going to act as my Guardian?"

"If you wish," Void said. He rose to his feet. "You have no obligation to make up your mind quickly, Emily, although it would be...*unkind* to lead him on if you are set against it. Take your time, meet his family and decide if you want them as *your* family. And if you can't handle them, tell him so and leave."

He paused. "I believe Lady Daniele wishes to speak to you first," he said. "I'll inform her that you are awake and aware. After that...well, your friends can visit if they wish."

"Wait," Emily croaked. "Are you not going to stay?"

"I need to discuss your future with Mistress Irene," Void said. "For the moment, you and I have been assigned a suite of rooms on the upper levels. You will stay with me for some weeks, mainly to keep you safe. Master Grey...might have blackened his reputation a little, but he still had friends and allies who will not be pleased about his death. Luckily, the formal rules of a challenge prohibit anyone from trying to extract revenge."

"Great," Emily said, sourly. She had no doubt there would be people who wanted to extract illicit revenge. "And after that?"

"We will see," Void said.

He nodded to her, and stepped out of the room.

Emily leaned back, forcing herself to relax despite the growing pain in her head. Lady Daniele was the last person she wanted to see, but she had a feeling she had no choice. She'd been Master Grey's second, after all, no matter how little she'd wanted the role. And she'd once been his apprentice.

She braced herself and forced herself to sit up, despite the pain, as the door opened. Lady Daniele stepped into the room, wearing a long white dress that clung to her body, leaving very little to the imagination. If she hadn't carried a sword and a wand at her belt, Emily would have mistaken her for a noblewoman, someone just waiting for the arranged marriage that would cement her family's place in the local power structure. Instead, she was a powerful magician, a Mediator. And formidable...

"Lady Emily," Lady Daniele said. She bowed formally, and peered down at Emily. "As Master Grey's second, it is my duty to concede the duel to you. My congratulations on your victory."

Emily would have laughed, if her head hadn't been throbbing. Master Grey had died in front of her; no, she'd *killed* him. The duel had been won and lost the moment he'd died. She didn't need Lady Daniele to tell her it was over. Hell, it wasn't as if there were any rules for either of them to break, so the results could be dismissed on a technicality. She'd won and that was all that mattered.

"Thank you," she said, finally. It wasn't Lady Daniele's fault that Master Grey had been an ass.

"As the victor, you have a claim on everything he owned," Lady Daniele continued. "I have prepared a list of his possessions and will hand it over to you, once you have escaped this room. You will have a month, from that moment, to take possession of anything you want, after which the remainder will be distributed in line with his will. Certain items will need to be registered with the White Council, but we will go over that if you wish to take them."

"Thank you," Emily said, numbly. It hadn't occurred to her that she would inherit anything from Master Grey, but it should have. She didn't really want any of his possessions, yet...who knew? He might have some interesting or rare books. Or she could send Fulvia something she'd recognize, just to let her know that Emily knew...

She shook her head. "I'm not well," she said. "Can we discuss the details later?"

"We will," Lady Daniele said. Her voice softened. "On a personal note, Lady Emily, I wish to apologize for my role in the farce. Or what I *thought* was a farce. I would have declined, if I hadn't owed him a favor."

Emily shrugged. "It doesn't matter," she said. Fulvia had started everything, after all; she promised herself, quietly, that the ancient crone wouldn't get away with it. "I forgive you."

"I don't think you can," Lady Daniele said. She met Emily's eyes. "In compensation, if you wish, I would be happy to undertake the task of tutoring both you and your friend. And I would swear whatever oaths you wished to ensure you felt safe with me."

"I don't know," Emily said, after a moment. Aloha would probably be delighted; *she* wouldn't have any problems using magic, once she recovered from demonic possession. But then, maybe she'd be mad at Emily. She'd practically had a crush on Master Grey. "Let me recover first, then we will see."

"As you wish," Lady Daniele said. There was a flicker of definite respect in her eyes. "The offer stands - or, if you wish, you may ask for something else in recompense."

She bowed, then walked out the door.

Emily sighed, rubbing her aching forehead, and looked around for something to distract herself from the pain. But there was nothing; Void, or whoever else had been watching over her while she slept, hadn't left any books within reach. She doubted she could get out of bed and walk more than a couple of steps without collapsing. She'd have to ask someone to bring her a handful of books from the library.

The door opened. Caleb walked into the room, looking nervous.

"Emily," he said, hastily closing the door behind him and hurrying over to the bed. "I...I didn't dare watch."

"I don't blame you," Emily said. *She* wouldn't have liked to watch Caleb fight a duel to the death either. "I'm glad you weren't there."

"I should have been," Caleb said. She could hear bitter guilt in his voice. "I..."

He reached out and took her hand, gently. "I don't know what to say!"

"Then don't say anything," Emily advised, dryly. She wasn't sure she wanted to know the answer to the next question, but she had to ask. "What did...what did my father say?"

"Just to make sure I behaved myself," Caleb said. He shook his head, slowly. "I was expecting horrific threats, but I think he found the whole idea funny."

"I suppose he did," Emily said. She took a breath. "I may have screwed our joint project..."

Caleb shook his head. "The Grandmaster approved what we'd done before his death," he said, shortly. "Even if you can't use magic for a month or two, Emily, we can complete the project together. I think that would be counted in your favor if you had to retake Fourth Year."

"That would be a relief," Emily said. She yawned, suddenly. "Would you mind if I spoke with the others before I fall asleep again?"

"Not at all," Caleb assured her. He gave her a long look. "Are you all right?"

"No," Emily said, flatly. Master Grey had died at her hands. No matter what he'd done, no matter how he'd contrived to manipulate her into challenging him, she couldn't escape what she'd done. "But I will survive."

"My mother was impressed," Caleb said. He looked embarrassed. "I believe she wishes to meet you. She never liked Master Grey."

"When I'm feeling better," Emily promised. She wasn't sure she wanted to meet another Mediator, not now. "I..."

She swallowed, unsure of her own feelings. Caleb nodded, kissed her gently on the forehead and then hurried out of the room. Moments later, Alassa, Imaiqah, and Frieda entered, the first two looking haunted. The demon had mocked her, Emily recalled; it might have abandoned its grip on their minds, it might have faded back into the Darkness, but it had left its mark on their souls. Her friends would never be quite the same.

"You won," Frieda crowed. "I *told* you you'd win."

Alassa cuffed the back of her head. "Shut up," she snapped. "I don't think she wants to hear any of *that*!"

Imaiqah hurried over to the bed. "How are you feeling?"

"Headachy," Emily said. She yawned. "And tired."

"You saved us all, again," Alassa said. "What..."

"The Grandmaster saved you," Emily said. In hindsight, she realized, he'd known what they'd have to do right from the start. He would have offered himself sooner if there hadn't been a faint chance that *Emily* would be able to banish the demon. "God alone knows where he is now."

"Lost," Imaiqah said, flatly. "Or so your *father* said."

Frieda sat on the edge of the bed, looking up at Emily with bright eyes. "Your father said you weren't allowed to use magic," she said. "That any attempt to use magic would be its own punishment."

Emily nodded. She'd been aware of her own magic ever since Mistress Irene had taught her how to unlock it, but now there was a haze covering the part of her brain that channeled *mana* and cast spells. Trying to use magic before she had recovered would cause blinding headaches, she was sure, if she was lucky. Void was quite right. If she pushed the limits too far, she might hamper her own recovery...or die.

"I probably need to spend time doing something - anything - else," she said, softly. "They won't let me go back to classes for a while."

"Go walking in the mountains," Frieda advised. "I could come with you. Or go swimming? Or even boating? Talia said that boating was always fun."

"Take Caleb," Imaiqah added, mischievously. "Go for a walk through the Forest of Flowers."

Emily blushed. The Forest of Flowers was a popular place for couples to find some private time together. She hadn't thought their relationship had progressed far enough to go there - Caleb had certainly never invited her - but maybe...she pushed the thought aside, angrily. It would be weeks before she was able to do more than totter around like an elderly woman.

"Rest first," Alassa advised. She cleared her throat. "Jade...was too embarrassed to face you. He blames himself."

"He shouldn't," Emily said.

"Master Grey bombarded him with questions about you," Alassa said. She sounded quietly furious. Jade was her fiancé and he'd been manipulated, used to hurt one of her friends. "The bastard probably used what Jade told him to help lure you into a trap. And it *was* a trap."

"I know," Emily said.

Imaiqah snorted. "Tell Jade you won't kiss him for a month, if he really feels he deserves punishment," she advised. "*That* should change his mind."

"You have a filthy mind," Alassa countered. "And besides, who is that meant to punish?"

"It wasn't his fault," Emily said. She yawned, again. Jade couldn't have known what his former master intended to do. If he had, she knew he would have warned her. "Tell him I forgive him everything, just in case he really believes it."

"He does," Alassa said. She shook her head in mock disbelief. "You'd better sleep now, Emily. Maybe you'll feel better when you wake."

"I hope so," Emily said. She leaned back in the bed, feeling oddly comfortable. "I'll be out of here soon."

"Wait until you're actually feeling better," Imaiqah said, sternly. "I'll tie you to the bed if necessary."

"She would," Alassa said. She smiled at Imaiqah before she again looked at Emily. "Sleep tight. We'll be here until they toss us out."

Emily opened her mouth to say something, but yawned instead.

"Lady Barb said she'd talk to you later, once...once your father was gone," Imaiqah added, hastily. Emily barely heard her through the haze. "Something to do with an oath..."

She must have sworn not to face Void again, Emily thought. *I...*

"Good night," Frieda said, as sleep overcame Emily. "We'll see you soon."

Chapter Forty

THE GRANDMASTER'S BODY LAY ON THE FUNERAL PYRE, PRESERVED BY MAGIC AND WRAPPED in his finest robes. Emily stood next to Void and watched, from their vantage point, as countless magicians and noblemen gathered in the gardens, preparing to say farewell to a man who had ruled Whitehall for nearly thirty years. Most of the students had been refused permission to attend; Emily and a handful of Sixth Years were the only ones present. She couldn't help noticing just how many of the visitors, powerful magicians in their own right, stared at her as they passed. They knew she'd killed a magician twenty years her senior.

Maybe I should run to Mountaintop, she thought, numbly. It had been a week since she'd recovered, a week of slowly regaining her strength. *Somewhere I can just hide from the world.*

She shook her head, dismissing the thought. There was no way she *could* hide from the world. Perhaps, just perhaps, she might have been ignored, if she'd kept her knowledge and concepts to herself, but it was too late now. The entire world knew her now; she could either play a role in their games or learn to play the game for herself.

She gritted her teeth and held her head as high as she could. The Grandmaster had died to offer her a second chance at life. She was damned if she was wasting it.

"Grandmaster Hasdrubal was a remarkable man," Mistress Irene said. She spoke softly, but magic carried her words across the gardens. "He graduated from Whitehall with the highest scores on record, then entered a brilliant apprenticeship and quali-fied as a Charms Master in just under two years. His love for Whitehall was so strong that he returned to the school to serve as a tutor five years after his departure; he worked his way up the ranks until he was the only clear choice for Grandmaster. The White Council made no mistake when they offered him the role."

They knew nothing about the demon, Emily thought. *Or about how he lost his eyes.*

"He was a brave and brilliant man," Mistress Irene continued, "but he was always kind and understanding to the students. Those who struggled with their coursework found help; those who tried to cause trouble ran into firm but considerate discipline that reshaped their lives for the better. He was a part of the school for so long that his absence leaves a gaping hole in our hearts, an emptiness at the heart of Whitehall."

Emily shivered. The second demon she'd met, at Mountaintop, had shown her a vision; *there is a gaping emptiness at the heart of Whitehall*. Had it been predicting the Grandmaster's death? Or was it something else, something that had been deflected... or was yet to materialize? The same demon had also shown her kissing someone...but it hadn't been Caleb. Had she been likely to meet someone else? Or was that, too, something that had yet to come to pass? There was no way to know.

"He wanted me to say a few words from him, written when he knew he was going to die," Mistress Irene said. She produced a scrap of parchment from her robes and peered down at it. "I have been good and I have been evil; I have been human. My successes and mistakes are a matter of public record, my pride and my shame are mine alone to bear. If you would learn from my mistakes, I would consider my life well lived."

She paused, folding up the piece of parchment. Emily felt tears prickling at the corner of her eyes, even though many of the observers looked puzzled. The Grandmaster's mistakes, she suspected, were not really part of the public record, buried - deliberately or otherwise - by his public persona and friends in high places. She couldn't help wondering how long that would last, now that the Grandmaster was dead. History was written by the survivors, after all.

Mistress Irene cleared her throat. "We bid farewell to a great man," she said, simply. "And we count ourselves lucky that we knew him."

She snapped her fingers. The pyre caught fire, flames licking through the wood and rapidly consuming the Grandmaster's body. Emily forced herself to watch as the whole edifice slowly crumbled into ash, which would be scattered over the gardens when the fire was finally extinguished. The Grandmaster, in a very real sense, would be part of Whitehall for the rest of time.

"There will be a wake for him, afterwards," Void said, quietly. "Do you wish to attend?"

Emily shook her head, mutely. Too many older magicians were glancing at both of them, their gazes cold and calculating. Perhaps Void hadn't been the only one quietly covering her back; the Grandmaster's combination of magic and political power would have deterred many from trying to co-opt or simply kill her. But it hadn't been enough to stop Master Grey from contriving a challenge...

"A wise decision," Void said. "Mistress Irene has something for you, I believe."

They waited until the crowds had started to move around the front of the castle, then headed over to where Mistress Irene stood beside the ashes. The older woman looked tired, almost grief-stricken; Emily couldn't help wondering why she, rather than the Grandmaster's sole surviving brother, had been left to manage the funeral. Tradition, she thought, dictated that the oldest member of the family handled his affairs. But if the Grandmaster's brother was among the throng, she didn't recognize him.

"Emily," Mistress Irene said. She reached into her pouch, producing a role of parchment and an iron key. "He wished me to give these to you, if you won the duel."

"Thank you," Emily said. There was a charm on the wax seal covering the parchment and another on the key. "I..."

"We'll discuss your future education later," Mistress Irene said, cutting her off. She looked at Void. "There's a coach and a pair of horses in the courtyard."

"I thank you," Void said, gravely.

Emily blinked in surprise. "Are we going somewhere?"

"Yes. Yes, we are," Void said. "Come with me."

He strode off, not looking back. Emily hesitated, then followed him, tucking the parchment and the key into her robes. It reminded her of the Key to Mountaintop, only without the charms that had bound that key into the school's wards. And the Grandmaster had wanted her to have it? She honestly doubted it was the Key to

Whitehall. That, if there *was* such a thing, would be passed to his successor. She sighed inwardly as Void rounded the corner and strode into the courtyard. As promised, a coach and driver were already waiting for them. Lady Barb stood beside the coach, arms folded under her breasts.

"Take care of her," she said to Void. "Or we will see each other one final time."

"I will," Void said.

Emily looked from one to the other, unsure what to say or do. Lady Barb had spoken to her briefly, after she'd woken for the second time, but she'd been occupied with preparing the school for the Grandmaster's successor. She'd hoped to have a chance to speak to the older woman after the funeral, yet Void was taking her away.

"Get in," Void ordered, curtly.

Emily nodded and did as she was told. Inside, it felt surprisingly warm; the curtains were drawn, making it impossible for anyone to see in or out. Void scrambled in to join her, and tapped the wooden box. Moments later, the cart rattled to life and headed out of the courtyard. Void settled back next to her and sighed, loudly.

"You may as well read the letter," he said. "He wrote it for you. Mistress Irene would have held onto it, ready to burn his last words to ashes if Master Grey had won the duel."

"I know," Emily said.

She was surprisingly reluctant to open the parchment, no matter who it had come from. She wasn't sure she wanted to know what it said. But she pulled at the wax until it came free, the charm sparking over her fingertips to verify her identity before vanishing into nothingness. If it hadn't been meant for her, she knew, she would have been frozen or cursed or even killed on the spot. Or the parchment could simply have disintegrated. The Grandmaster could have attached any number of nasty spells to his personal seal.

> *Emily.*
>
> *Don't weep for me, or feel regret. In truth, I suspected that the demon was the same as the one who took my eyes from the very moment you told me what it was. It would have known that we would eventually cross paths once again and allowed Shadye to bind it, confident that a necromancer would eventually lose control or simply die. Someone would have to willingly hand themselves to the demon in order to banish it. I could not let you sacrifice your soul in my place. And it would have known that too.*
>
> *I was stunned when I realized the truth, too stunned to cut Master Grey off before it was too late. I had known he would push you hard, that he would have to play the stern unrelenting tutor to both you and your friend; I underestimated the degree of personal animosity he felt for you (or, perhaps, the pressure someone had brought to bear against him.) He played his role very well, maintaining deniability right up until the moment you challenged him. And, at that moment, it was too late. I could have killed him, and maybe I should have, but that*

would undermine your position too. All I could do was play for time and hope. But time ran out.

I told myself that you had a knack for surviving, that you would find a way to fight back and win. Or, at least, that you would not sacrifice yourself to a demon. Your soul would go onwards to the gods you worship, if you died, not plunge into the Darkness. I consoled myself with that thought because I failed you.

But if you are reading this letter, you won the duel.

I did not choose to hand anything over to you on the moment of my death. Master Grey would be able to claim it, if I had. I crafted a living will, with detailed instructions to only open it after the funeral. Most of my possessions have been left to the school, but I am leaving one very specific thing to you. Void will take you there and assist you in taking it for yourself.

Times will get harder for you, I suspect. My death will leave a power vacuum that will be filled, sooner rather than later, and my successor may not be so inclined to view you as a young girl, rather than a potential enemy or outright threat. I do not know who will take my place. Watch your back.

I doubt we will see each other again, in this world or the next, so I remain, faithfully yours;

Hasdrubal, Grandmaster of Whitehall.

"I never knew his name," Emily said, softly. She found herself fighting to hold back the tears. "Or that he cared..."

"He cared about everyone," Void said. The coach rattled to a halt. "That was his problem, really. He cared too much."

Emily gave him a sharp look, which he ignored as he opened the door and stepped outside. A wave of cold air struck her in the face as she followed, looking around with interest. The coach had stopped in front of a pair of gates; beyond the gates, she could see a large house surrounded by an unkempt garden. She glanced at the walls and realized that someone had crafted powerful wards to keep out uninvited guests. Void helped her down, then waved to the coachman. He cracked the whip and the coach headed off down the street.

"Pass me the key," he ordered.

"Here," Emily said, fishing it out of her pocket. "Where are we?"

"Dragon's Den," Void said, dryly. "Don't you recognize the smell?"

Emily flushed. They hadn't been in the coach long enough to go anywhere else; indeed, she was surprised Void hadn't teleported them both down to the city. Perhaps he'd feared what would happen to her if he did or...maybe he'd just wanted to give her a chance to read the letter in private. He'd definitely known it existed before Mistress Irene had given it to her.

"This is the part of town where the wealthy and powerful live," Void added, as he pressed the key against the gates. "It's also the safest. A couple of the sorcerers who live here cast spells to keep thieves and supernatural vermin out of the houses of their neighbors. Very few people would come here unless they were invited."

"I've never been up here," Emily said.

"You wouldn't have," Void agreed.

Emily shrugged, glanced at a handful of the other houses and frowned. Some of them looked fancy enough to pass for aristocratic mansions; hell, in some ways, they *were* aristocratic mansions. Dragon's Den was a Free City; its rulers were those who had earned money through business and trade, rather than blue blood and inheritance. A handful even had private guards manning their gates.

Void opened the gate, then beckoned her inside. Emily followed him as they walked up the garden path and stopped in front of the door, which clicked open when he pressed the key against a concealed wardstone. Inside, it was cool; she sensed countless preservation spells running through the house, protecting it against dust and decay. It felt abandoned...and yet, there was a sense that the original owner could come back at any moment.

She looked at Void as he closed the door behind them. "What is this place?"

"Yours," Void said.

"*What?*"

"The Grandmaster bought this house when he accepted a permanent position at Whitehall," Void said. He didn't seem surprised by her shock, merely amused. "He was the Charms Master at the time; he wouldn't have been permitted to entertain in the school without special permission. It served as his refuge when he wanted to escape his role for a few days, or carry out experiments of his own. I imagine he thought he would retire here, one day."

Emily looked down at the floor. "Why did he leave it to me?"

"I imagine he thought it would be sensible for you to have a house of your own, somewhere outside Cockatrice," Void said. "Come."

He led her down a flight of stairs into the basement, where a single hearthstone waited for them, glowing faintly in the darkened room. Void reached into his pocket, producing a vial of blood and a small knife, which he held out to her. Emily took them both numbly, realizing the Grandmaster must have left some of his blood behind for her. It would have been a gift beyond price, if he'd survived. Instead...

"I believe you know how to take control for yourself," Void said. "Touching the hearthstone with magic should be safe enough, but *don't* try anything else. Do you want me to leave you here?"

Emily shook her head, staring at the hearthstone. It was calling to her...no, calling to the blood in her hand. On some level, it knew its master was dead.

"I don't know if I should accept this," she said, bitterly. "He died..."

"He left it to you," Void said. "I can *assure* you that he only made the change in his will after realizing that he would have to sacrifice himself to the demon. He wanted you to have the house and everything inside."

Emily sighed. "Are there servants? Someone to maintain the property?"

"No," Void said. "He left the building sealed while he lived at the school. There are a great many preservation spells here, keeping the food safe to eat, but no servants. You will have to clean up your own messes, unless you hire someone."

"I'll see," Emily said. A thought struck her. "You've been here before, haven't you?"

"Once or twice," Void said. He nodded to the hearthstone. "I suggest you proceed before it decides we're really not meant to be here."

Emily nodded, opened the vial of blood and poured it onto the hearthstone. It started to bubble at once, the wards reaching out to grip her mind, as she cut her palm and allowed her blood to mingle with the Grandmaster's. There was a sense of raw power pulsing around her, an awareness of everything in the house...and then it faded away, leaving her with only a faint connection to the wards. Her head started to pound as her magic flared; she stumbled back, almost falling before Void caught her. It was so much easier than binding herself to Cockatrice...

...And yet, the mere effort had almost killed her.

"No more magic," Void reminded her. He cast a spell, levitating her into the air and manoeuvring her up the stairs. "I think you need a nap."

"No," Emily said. "I..."

She broke off as her head spun. Void eyed her for a long moment, before floating her up two flights of stairs and into a large bedroom dominated by a four-poster bed. The walls were lined with bookcases, packed to busting with tomes she didn't recognize.

"Sleep," Void said, placing her on the bed. "You need to recover."

It was the master bedroom, Emily realized bitterly, as Void withdrew from the room. The Grandmaster would have slept here, if he had chosen to stay in his house; his position as master of the house wouldn't have allowed anything else. Someone had changed the sheets, either the Grandmaster himself or a servant, but it was still his bed. And he was dead and now it was hers...

The tears came bubbling up again. This time, she let them fall.

End of Book Seven

Emily Will Return In

Wedding Hells

About the author

Christopher G. Nuttall was born in Edinburgh, studied in Manchester, married in Malaysia and currently living in Scotland, United Kingdom with his wife and baby son. He is the author of twenty novels from various publishers and thirty-nine self-published novels.

Current and forthcoming titles published by Twilight Times Books

Schooled in Magic YA fantasy series
Schooled in Magic -- book 1
Lessons in Etiquette -- book 2
A Study in Slaughter -- book 3
Work Experience -- book 4
The School of Hard Knocks -- book 5
Love's Labor's Won – book 6
Trial By Fire – book 7
Wedding Hells – book 8

The Decline and Fall of the Galactic Empire military SF series
Barbarians at the Gates -- book 1
The Shadow of Cincinnatus – book 2
The Barbarian Bride – book 3

Chris has also produced *The Empire's Corps* series, the *Outside Context Problem* series and many others. He is also responsible for two fan-made Posleen novels, both set in John Ringo's famous Posleen universe. They can both be downloaded from his site.
Website: http://www.chrishanger.net/
Blog: http://chrishanger.wordpress.com/
Facebook: https://www.facebook.com/ChristopherGNuttall

CPSIA information can be obtained
at www.ICGtesting.com
Printed in the USA
FFOW04n0119051016
28190FF